THE RECOVERY RUN

MELISSA DAVIES

ABOUT THE BOOK

He may be the guide, but she's the one taking them to the finish line in this *Brittany Runs a Marathon* meets *Wild Hearts Can't be Broken* contemporary romance.

Nearing thirty, Jensen Larsen still hasn't hit her stride. The visually impaired assistant disability coordinator never chases what she wants. Jobs. Friendships. Love. Faced with another romantic disappointment, she's ready to run toward what she wants, just like her brother. The year they turn thirty, men from her family run a marathon and find the love of their lives.

There are a few obstacles in her way; Jensen hates running, and her idea of a marathon is binging *Bridgerton*. Trust issues from past relationships continue to make it difficult for her, as a blind woman, to find a guide runner she trusts. Enter her brother's best friend, Dr. Garrett Marlowe.

For the last five years, Garrett has only worried about himself. Outside of being a reluctant cat dad, Garrett isn't looking for emotional attachments. Until the woman who both vexes him and makes him smile needs help.

It may not just be Jensen's stride that Garrett, the experienced marathon runner, is helping find. As Jensen deals with her trust issues, Garrett faces the pain of the tragic event that led him to seal off his heart. With each running session, Jensen and Garrett must learn to trust each other and themselves.

But marathon training, just like life, is a mental game, and the obstacles they face may trip them up before they even reach the starting line.

Copyright © 2024 by Melissa Whitney

All rights reserved.

This is a work of fiction. The characters are products of the author's imagination, and any resemblance to actual events or actual persons, living or dead, is entirely coincidental. Although it's fair to say that anyone enjoying a life so full of love is lucky indeed.

No part of this book may be reproduced in any form or by any electronic or mechanical means, including information storage and retrieval systems, without written permission from the author, except for the use of brief quotations in a book review.

The author expressly prohibits any entity from using any part of this publication, including text and graphics, for purposes of training artificial intelligence (AI) technologies to generate text or graphics, including without limitation technologies that are capable of generating works in the same style or genre as this publication.

The author reserves all rights to license uses of this work for generative AI training and development of machine learning language models.

ISBN:

To everyone who picked on me as a kid, hope you enjoy watching me run.

A NOTE FROM THE AUTHOR
CONTENT WARNING

Dear Reader,

I can't believe this is my eighth published novel. Whether this is your first Melissa Whitney novel or you've been with me for the entire ride, I am so deeply grateful for my readers. My stories wouldn't find their way into the world without you.

The Recovery Run has a special place in my heart. It's my second story with a legally blind FMC. This started with someone tagging me in a Thread where someone wanted a romance featuring a blind/guide runner pairing. I laughed, but the suggestion stuck with me. I'm not a marathon runner, but I have done 5/10Ks with my husband as my guide runner in the past. Then Jensen and Garrett started speaking to me, as do all my characters.

Before I knew it, I was down the research rabbit hole. I devoured stories and YouTube videos about blind/guide running. I joined an online blind/guide runners' group and interviewed blind and guide runner pairs. I pulled from my own experience as a legally blind woman who has run with her husband, and blind marathon runners to craft as realistic of an experience as possible.

This book is deeply personal. If you're a regular reader of mine, you know each of my books is woven with the personal. I sprinkle a little bit of my heart/self into each story. I pulled from my experience as a legally blind woman to tell this story.

That being said, it is still a work of fiction. Any resemblance to real places, events, or people is strictly a coincidence. As well literary license is taken with some things such as description of locations, events, or processes. If you're looking for a true how to guide on running a marathon or serving as a guide runner, this book isn't a resource. This is a fictionalized contemporary romance with a guaranteed happy ending.

While this is a romance with a happy ending, there are some things in this book that may be triggering for some readers. Please be aware that this book contains depictions of ableism, gaslighting (not between the MMC/FMC), discussion of toxic relationships (not between the MMC/FMC), consensual sex on page, use of curse words, depiction of casual alcohol use, discussion of death of a loved one, and depiction of therapy, exploration of grief/loss. Please do what you need to do to take care of yourself as you are reading.

Again, thank you for choosing to read one of my books. I am so grateful to each of my readers.

Thank you,
Melissa

1

MILE ONE
LITERARY FUCKBOY

"An espresso martini?" I guffaw, nestling against the chair's high back.

Early 2000s pop music melds with the chatter of patrons in the bar. It's just another happy hour at Harkey's Hideaway. I'm nursing a prosecco as I sit across from my brother at a high-top table, teasing him about whatever fancy cocktail he's drinking.

"Don't be judgy, Jensen. They're delicious." Anker takes a long swig of his drink before letting out a contented sigh.

"If you're a mother of two out for ladies' night," Garrett deadpans.

There is seldom a happy hour with my brother that his best friend isn't at. Though the jury is still out on whether he's the third wheel for a sibling outing, or if I'm the one tagging along to their post-work guys' nights. Considering my social calendar, I'm sure it's the latter, not the former.

"Ladies' night," Anker hums. "Where I always drink for free."

"Of course you do." I shake my head.

A year older, my brother is a steady current of self-confidence. He's unabashed in his enthusiasm for the things he likes—never second-guessing anything. His career. Relationships. Himself.

Whereas I'm in a constant state of self-doubt. Aside from the thick brown hair and hazel eyes we inherited from our mother, we're the antithesis of one another. Anker never worries about being liked, unlike me.

"You're aware the purpose of ladies' night is for *you* to buy *the ladies* drinks?" I smirk.

"I can't help it if the ladies love me," he says cheekily.

Of course. A crease dips my brow. "At least, one of us is getting drinks bought for them," I say, trying to keep the grumble out of my voice.

Unlike Anker, whose good looks are reinforced by most of my friends having crushes on him, I buy my own drinks. Not just because I'm an independent woman, but because nobody's offering—at least nobody I want.

"No worries. Garrett's treat." He slaps Garrett's back. "We Larsens are too pretty to buy our own drinks."

My eyeroll is both involuntary and necessary. *Garrett Marlowe.*

Since meeting five years ago, it's crystal clear that Garrett has little motivation to buy me a drink, unless it's to appease my brother. If I didn't have years of his judgmental comments or exasperated sighs, the memory of overhearing him refer to me as a "Yappy Yorkie" within an hour of meeting me has burned into my psyche how he feels about me. Garrett's mode with me has three settings—polite indifference, best friend's younger sister, and judgy tolerance.

"Didn't realize I was here just to provide you and Jensen external validation of your worth," Garrett mutters in his deep, silky bass.

Somehow, he's gathered up all the derision in his body to infuse it into the judgmental way he says my name. It's almost an auditory scowl... *Jensen.*

"Is someone just grumpy because nobody's offering to buy them drinks?" My mouth pulls into a mock pout.

I meet Garrett's not-so-subtle distaste for me with wry smiles and venom-laced teases. Most people like to avoid the bear, but I poke. At least, this bear. With everyone else, I worry about them liking me, but not with Garrett, since he seems to merely tolerate my existence.

It also helps me push back against the stupid, nagging little crush I have on him. Yeah, because that's healthy. I blame Jane Austen. Just had to read *Pride and Prejudice* as a teenager and form a lifelong crush on the Mr. Darcy types.

Ms. Austen aside, it's on-brand for me. I have a bad habit of liking men who don't seem to like me back.

He clears his throat. "Some of us don't require external validation."

"Not all of us enjoy being an antisocial dickwad." My coo is acidic.

"Corners, you two," Anker laughingly groans.

"Perhaps we can find a dark corner for Garrett to sulk in because the bar doesn't have the blood of his enemies on tap." Smirking, I toss my long hair over my shoulder.

"Or maybe there's a corner with a doctoral student that fancies himself the next Jack Kerouac for *you* to buy drinks for all night," he drawls.

Asshole. Of course, he goes there. It's the easiest bullseye to hit. My chronic singlehood is well-known. My relationship history is littered with unrequited crushes, an ill-fated situationship, and a *maybe something* with a man who is not a student.

"Miles is a doctor," I say, my brow puckering.

"Of English," Garrett scoffs.

The medical doctor snobbery aside, Garrett tends to be standoffish with most people. Besides Anker, I may be the only other human he interacts with outside of the hospital, and most of the time, I annoy him.

Miles, however, seems to enjoy everyone. I just wish he liked me in the way I want to be liked. Since meeting ten months ago at the university where I work as an assistant disability services coordinator, our relationship has teetered between friends and something more. Beyond the occasional dinner before one of his evening classes and a few steamy make-out sessions worthy of a soapy drama, he hasn't asked me out.

Of course, I haven't asked him out either. I've just been waiting. It seems like waiting is my not-so-cool superpower, or kryptonite, depending on your perspective. My patience is endless, but all this waiting leaves me always wanting.

"I'll be sure to call the literary fuckboy if I have a misplaced semicolon emergency," Garrett snarks.

"Prick," I mumble under my breath.

Anker lets out a long groan. "I hope you two aren't going to be like this tomorrow and ruin my churro waffle with your bickering."

Before we fly to New York City tomorrow for Anker to run the marathon, we're brunching with some friends. It's the first time he's running it. In the last four years, he's ran the Los Angeles, San Francisco, and Long Beach marathons with Garrett, but in New York City, he'll run solo.

It's a Larsen male rite of passage. My father and his brothers not only ran a marathon the year they turned thirty, but found love because of it. Uncle Pedro was in Uncle Christian's marathon training running group. Aunt Margot was a volunteer at Uncle Hans's race. Our mom worked at the coffee shop in the hotel where our dad stayed when he ran his.

"*I* can behave." Hand on my chest, I bat my eyes. "It's Garrett the Grumbly that I worry about. Is he even allowed out in the daytime? I wouldn't want him to burst into flames."

"I'll wear sunscreen," Garrett deadpans.

Snorting, I almost spit out my drink but swallow it back and choke a bit.

"On that note…" He chuckles. "I'll grab us another round. I have your egos to feed, after all." The chair screeches as he stands up. "Same drinks?"

"Make mine the apple martini this round," Anker says, no doubt waggling his brows at me.

Shaking my head, I laugh. "I'm good with just the one drink. I'd like to keep a clear head for the bus home."

"I can drive you, Jensen," Garrett offers.

"I like the bus."

"It's dark out."

"In fairness, with my eyesight, it's always dark out," I quip.

There are few advantages of my legal blindness since my Stargardts diagnosis at the age of ten, outside of getting through airport security quicker, but this is one. I do enjoy a perfectly timed blind joke. Even if my limited vision doesn't let me see the smile tugging at the edges of Garrett's mouth, his quiet chuckle telegraphs it.

"Such an asshole." Laughter underscoring his retort, Garrett shakes his head.

"You are the expert." An unbridled grin kicks across my face.

Poking this bear is extra delicious when I make him smile. I'm not a complete masochist with this crush. It's not like I thrive around men who are mean to me.

"How about a soda, then?" Garrett says, the quirk of his mouth betrayed in the lightness of his timbre.

"Sure." I beam with all the bluster of a wrestler hoisting up a championship belt. *He's totally smiling, and he hates it.*

"Diet, right?"

"Yeah… Thanks."

"I'll be back," he says, pushing away from the table.

"I can't decide if you two sometimes dislike each other or if this is a really long game of verbal foreplay," Anker teases.

"Eww." I wrinkle my nose.

A loud chortle belts out of him. "Imagine the *hate* sex, you'd have."

No! I will not imagine that with my brother sitting a foot away from me. Also, that will never happen. Not to mention, my brother may tease, but I know he'd never be cool with the idea of his younger sister being dicked-down by his best friend, who is also his boss at the hospital where they are physicians.

"No more martinis for you. You're clearly drunk," I say, slipping my blazer off and draping it over the back of my chair with my purse.

"Says the woman who's disrobing." He leans across the table and flicks my nose. "Is someone hot and bothered?"

I swat at him but miss entirely.

"God, I love having a blind sister." His laugh is hearty.

"Uncool." Laughing, I kick his shin underneath the table.

"*Oof...* And you wore pointy shoes."

"Serves you right." I preen just a bit. "Also, you tease, but shall I remind you of how you freaked when you caught me making out with Everett Haney in high school?"

He makes a disgusted noise. "Fair point."

Everett Haney is just another notch in my dismal romantic history belt. My brother discovering us beneath the bleachers —Everett's hand up my blouse—wasn't the most embarrassing part. It was later, when I learned that I was just a bet Everett made to prove he could get the school's blind girl to go all the way.

To this day, Anker doesn't know about the bet. It was humiliating enough without him learning the truth and going full vengeful older brother.

Anker, however, dated at least three of my girlfriends from high school. My brother's typical rotating door of relationships is nonexistent at the moment. Except for texter girl, AKA Sonora Jefferies.

"Will you meet up with Sonora in New York? You know, go full *You've Got Mail*—minus bankrupting her bookstore?" Elbows on the table's edge, I rest my chin on my hands and flash a cheeky expression.

"Maybe." He draws out the word with a playful lilt.

Over the last six months, Anker struck up a flirtation with a woman from a social media guide/blind runner's group. Running with a white cane or a dog guide isn't ideal or safe, so visually impaired runners run with human guides to navigate the course safely. My brother, an avid runner, has served as a guide for several visually impaired runners over the last few years.

Outside of the twenty-minute jog/walk I do on the elliptical in my apartment building's gym three times a week, I don't enjoy the sport like my former track star brother. While running's appeal is akin to a root canal for me, Anker did talk me into doing one 5K charity run with him. It was less running and more arguing until I skinned my knee and was carried off the course. *So embarrassing.*

It's difficult to turn off my brain and let someone else take control. The entire time we'd run, anxiety pulsed through me. It's not that I don't trust Anker. I don't trust me. What if I make a mistake and he gets hurt? What if I can't keep up with him and he gets frustrated? It was all too overwhelming.

"I'm surprised you're not serving as her guide runner for the race. Isn't marathon running peak romance to you people?" I tease.

He tilts his head. "You people?"

"Masochists," I sass. "Seriously, what if Sonora is the future love of your life? Serving as her guide for the marathon, combined with the Larsen male love prophecy, is Hallmark-level romance."

"First, you don't just guide-run a marathon at the first

meeting. You know better than anyone that it takes time to build that trust. Hell, I've been your brother for twenty-nine years, and we didn't make it to the one-mile marker."

I roll my eyes. "Second?"

"Maybe you should test the theory that it's just the Larsen male line that finds love at a marathon the year they turn thirty."

"That sounds as appealing as a body scrub performed by a porcupine."

Not only would running a marathon be my own personal version of hell, but I am not a devout believer in this little family myth. It's swoony to daydream about, but even my romance novel-loving brain doesn't put much stock in it.

"Come on. You don't turn thirty until next year. That's more than enough time to train," he says.

"You have to, like, qualify for the New York City marathon. It's at least a two-year commitment—"

"It doesn't have to be New York. You can run any marathon. The Seal Beach one next October doesn't require any pre-reqs. You can just register. Not to mention, even if it was the hospital is one of the sponsors, so I can pull strings."

"Sure." I draw out the word with an eyeroll. "And are you going to be my guide and train with me?"

"Pass... Garrett can do it."

"Hard pass!" I grimace. "The only marathon I plan to do is binge-watching *Bridgerton.*" I tip my head back and let out a squeal. "You've not lived until you've listened to the descriptive video of that carriage scene from season three."

"Really?" He leans forward, his tone conspiratorial. "Is there descriptive porn?"

Of course Garrett picks that moment to return to the table with our drinks. "Seriously, the conversations you two have," he groans. The glasses make a hollow *clunk* as he sets them down. "Jensen, your soda is at three o'clock."

"Thanks." Palm flat on the table, I slide my right hand to

where three would be if the space were a clock and wrap my fingers around the cool glass.

Stop it, butterflies! And this is why I like Garrett. He always tells me the course's landscape so I can navigate easily. Items on tables. A room layout. This week's ice cream flavors at Marie's Scoops. He somehow does it without being asked or making me feel like an imposition.

It's adorable. It's also infuriating. No matter how much he annoys me, he does something like this, and my heart does that stupid pitter-patter thing.

"So, how does this audio porn work, anyhow?" Anker sounds bemused.

"It's called erotic audio." I shake my head. "It's just a voice actor that walks you through a scenario."

"Like deep-voiced men who talk you through *sexy times* and call someone a 'good girl?'"

Heat flushes my cheeks. "Sometimes."

"Fascinating…"

"And this is like a *thing*?" Garrett's question oozes with dismissiveness.

"It's huge, Garrett… Though that's something a woman has probably never said to you."

A loud laugh belts out of Anker.

I can almost picture Garrett's scowl. Well, what I imagine it looks like. Thanks to the few times we've done human guide, I know he's tall with broad shoulders and a muscular build. His always-present five o'clock shadow, green eyes, and short chestnut-colored hair are what I've put together between my limited vision and others' descriptions.

"Smartass." His mouth's upward curl is audible in Garrett's humor-laced mutter.

Grinning, I go on, "Erotic audio is a big deal. It appeals to those of us who tend to be more imaginatively or auditorily stimulated." I lift my glass to my lips and take a self-congratulatory sip. The cool drink fizzes in my throat.

"Who knew an entire world of verbal porn existed?" Anker puffs a breath.

"*Your* sister apparently knew."

"Ugh, don't want to think about that." He clicks his tongue. "You know, Garrett, if doctoring doesn't turn out for us, we may have backup careers as erotic vocal actors."

"Don't you dare!" I cover my face with my hands.

The idea of my brother as an erotic vocal performer makes me consider canceling my *Pillow Talk* subscription. As frustrating as Garrett is, I'll admit his timbre is similar to some of my favorite male voice actors. His "hot guy" voice was what first attracted me. Its deepness almost rumbles through me when he speaks.

Garrett's judgy remarks and dismissiveness about—well everything related to me—should snuff out my attraction to him. He's all Mr. Darcy before Lizzie visits Pemberly, with no sign of transitioning from prejudicial grump. Yet, I'm still attracted to him. *Seriously, what is wrong with me?*

Garrett clears his throat. "And *you* listen to this?"

That way he says "you" reeks of his trademark "Jensen Judgment." The question is reminiscent of a head pat accompanying an "Oh, you poor, sad, lonely woman with your dirty audios."

Screw that! My audios may be dirty, but I'm not sad. It's healthy. It's empowering.

"Don't answer that!" Anker's interruption is half-groan, half-laugh. "The existence of audio porn is one thing, but knowing my sister's phone is full of it may be too much."

A throat clears. "Audio porn, Jenny?"

That familiar smooth English accent sends a jolt of embarrassment up my spine.

"Miles… Hi," I breathe. *Oh god, did he just hear that?*

"Hey, gorgeous," he greets me with a chaste peck on my cheek.

"Hey… Hi," I repeat with a wince. Brushing my hair

behind my ears, I shift in my seat. "I thought the English Department had its midterm mixer tonight."

Seriously! I bite the inside of my cheek in mortification. It sounds like I'm keeping tabs on him. In my defense, I only knew this because my best friend Catherine is a fellow adjunct professor in the department.

"Those things are dreadful. I bounced." Miles leans close, his hot breath scented by alcohol. "And I'm glad I did because I'd much rather hear about this audio porn."

Kill me now!

"It's erotic audio." Garrett's interjection is curt.

"Erotic? Scandalous… And from our sweet Jenny. Tell me everything," Miles purrs with all the swagger of a rogue from an Austen novel.

While Garrett is all Mr. Darcy, Miles is Willoughby territory. He's charming, carefree, and always makes me smile. With him, I never doubt that he likes me. It's just unclear in what way he likes me—friend or the something more that I so desperately want from him.

Anker coughs. "Jenny?"

"Miles calls me Jenny." I nibble on my lower lip.

"Why?"

Miles drapes his arm over my shoulders. "Because our sweet Jensen here has Jenny Wren vibes."

"Jenny Wren? From Dickens?" A pinched brow is audible in Garrett's question.

"Yeah." I shift in my seat.

Besides my annual *A Muppet's Christmas Carol* watch with Anker, I'm not much of a Charles Dickens fan. Give me the swoon of Jane Austen or the angst of Elizabeth Gaskell. The only thing I know about Jenny Wren is that she's a character from Dickens' *Our Mutual Friend*. I could just Google it, but part of me is scared to know what those vibes are. They may keep my relationship strictly platonic—minus the mini make-out sessions—with Miles, and I don't want to lose the last flicker of hope for more with him.

Shifting in my seat, I change the subject. "So, you bailed on the department happy hour?"

"Naturally. A bunch of out-of-touch scholars droning on about the death of literature. A few of us skipped out."

"Is Catherine with you?"

He scoffs dismissively. "No. Presently, she's playing up to our department head."

After four years as an adjunct, Catherine is vying for an associate professor gig. For my bestie, who adjuncts at two other universities, this will offer her higher pay and a tenure track.

"And you didn't want to kiss up to Professor Bay-Cheng?"

"I prefer the freedom that an adjunct position affords me. Nothing tethering me. I can just pick up next semester and teach somewhere else or backpack around the US writing about my experiences, if I want."

"Just like Kerouac," Garrett drawls.

"Exactly!" Miles pounds his fist on the table, seeming not to catch the thinly veiled ridicule in Garrett's comment.

But I do and purse my lips. Most people may be blind to Garrett's mockery-filled undercurrent, but with him, I have perfect vision. Since their first meeting over the summer, it's clear that Garrett doesn't just dislike Miles, but he has zero respect for him.

"Are you a fan?" Miles shifts beside me, his body leaning onto the table. For whatever reason, Miles doesn't seem to notice. Though I'd imagine for a man like him the idea of somebody not liking him is like an undiscovered planet.

"Not really *my* thing."

"Garrett's thing is more reading the obituaries of the people he's bored to death," I shoot back.

"Ha!" A bark of laughter belts out of Miles.

Suck on that Garrett the Judgy. With a smirk, I move my hand and come into contact with a glass on the table's edge. Before I can react, it slides off the table. Cool liquid splashes onto my lap, and the sound of glass breaking fills my ears.

"Shit!" I hiss, my pulse ticking up.

"Jensen, are you okay? Did you get any glass on you?" Garrett moves to my side and places his hand on my arm.

I shake my head. "No."

"Here, napkins," Garrett takes my hand and places a small stack of cocktail napkins in it. "Are you sure you're okay?" His thumb skates along my wrist.

"Yeah." I yank my hand from his. The heat of humiliation blazes up my neck. No doubt, my face is pink with embarrassment.

"If you wanted to buy me a drink, you didn't need to go to these lengths, Jenny." Miles's tut is lighthearted.

"I didn't mean... I'm sorry," I whisper, wiping at my wet skirt.

"These things happen," Anker says. "Hell, I spilled an entire cup of coffee on my lap the other day. Thank God, it was iced coffee, or else making our parents' grandparents would be solely on you." His chair screeches as he rises. "Let me go grab staff to help with the cleanup. Be right back."

"Yeah. These things happen," Miles seconds.

"Especially when you just set your drink there without telling her where it is." Garrett's voice has a hard edge. It's not his typical dismissiveness, but angry.

I school my features into a forced smile. "It's totally fine... It's on me. *Literally*." Waving at my lap, I offer a halfhearted laugh. "I should have anchored with the table instead of just moving my hand without thinking. I'm sorry—"

"It's not your fault. It's his," Garrett jumps in.

"It was an accident, bloke," Miles says, his posture going rigid beside me.

"I..." Shaking my head, I swallow thickly to ease the

mortification clustering in my throat. "I'm going to run to the restroom to properly address this." Pushing back the prick of threatening tears, I unfold my white cane and head to the restroom without another word.

In the bathroom, I lean against the door, steadying my breath. For most people, this isn't a big deal. Glasses fall. They break. It happens, but when you're visually impaired, it feels different. There's this added layer that weighs you down in these moments. At least for me. If not for my vision loss, this wouldn't have happened. I'd have seen the glass. Staff wouldn't need to clean anything up. Anker wouldn't be comforting me. Garrett would just find another reason to be his grumpy self instead of doing unnecessary battle on my behalf. Miles wouldn't have been about to apologize until I interrupted him to spare both our feelings.

This incident likely reminds him why I'm *just* the friend he's kissed a few times. A relationship with me comes with rules, of sorts. As independent as I am, there are things I need from the people in my life to support that. Like letting me know when they've set something down in front of me and where it is.

No wonder he doesn't want me. That ever-present knot in my stomach in social situations pulls just a little tighter.

"Don't do that. You're *not* that teenage girl that boys only kissed as a bet, or that coed that someone… Nope, we're not going there." I wrap my arms around my torso in a soothing self-hug.

It's almost too cliché. Here I am, in the women's restroom on the brink of tears, like it's the eleventh-grade homecoming dance after I found out Everett only kissed me for a bet.

Choosing not to give in to self-pity, I push away from the wall. Grateful that I wore the black pencil skirt, instead of the pink one I'd thought about this morning, I dab it with a wet paper towel and do my best to pat it dry. A spritz of the perfume from my purse will help cover up the smoky aroma of scotch.

"No more being the sad, embarrassed girl," I say, patting my face dry after splashing cold water on it. "You're going to go out there. You're going to flirt with Miles, and tonight will be the night he'll realize that you're more than a friend."

Grabbing my cane, I open the door and head out.

"Jensen…"

"Crap…" My hand goes to my chest.

"Sorry. It's Garrett. I shouldn't have snuck up on you like that."

"I know who you are." I stand straighter. While I appreciate him announcing himself, my annoyance overrides his good blind person etiquette.

"Here." He reaches out and pushes something into my hand, it's fabric soft and warm. "To wear. You can wrap it around your waist."

I unfold the garment. "A hoodie?"

"Yeah."

"I'm fine. Thank you, though." I hold it out to him.

"Just take it."

"I don't need it."

"You do…" He puffs a breath. "There is a noticeable wet spot on your skirt."

Trailing my hand down, I swipe my fingers across the still-damp fabric. "Fine," I say as the corners of my mouth drag down.

It's not his goal. At least I tell myself that, but this hoodie digs at that self-pity I'm trying to stuff back down. Despite my best attempt to be the secure-in-herself blind woman, moments like this drag up old insecurities. Like, how if I were sighted, I'd know the wet spot on my skirt is noticeable.

"I can hold this, so you can put it on," he murmurs, curling his fingers over mine on the handle of my cane.

"Please, stop." I fight the shake in my voice.

"Stop what?" He moves closer, his body's warmth almost cradling me.

"Trying to take care of me. I can take care of myself." I know he means well, but it's just too much right now. It yanks free emotions that I am trying so hard to push down.

He makes a throaty growl noise. "Why do you have to be like this?"

"Like what?" My brow scrunches.

"Like Jensen."

"What does that mean?" I press my lips into a firm line.

"A stubborn pain-in-the-ass."

I glower. "You're the ass expert, since you're being one to Miles."

"The literary fuckboy?" He lets out an incredulous laugh. "I don't get your fascination with him."

"It's easy with Miles. He's fun," I say through clenched teeth.

He huffs a dismissive snort.

"There's nothing wrong with fun."

"He's a clown in his sports jackets with vintage T-shirts, spouting about being untethered. It's textbook *Peter Pan* bullshit. It's pathetic. You're wasting your time on him."

Pathetic? The word surges through me like hot lava, drowning any lingering self-pity. In its wake is only anger.

"I'm not pathetic."

"Jensen, I—"

"No. You don't get to call me pathetic and have me listen to you." I toss the sweatshirt at him and spin on my heels. Only to spin back. "You know what, I may be wasting my time with Miles, but at least he doesn't judge me. He doesn't treat me like an injured stray kitten he's obligated to take care of."

"I... You're being ridiculous. You're not—"

"You insult me, and *I'm* the ridiculous one." An unhinged laugh falls out of me.

"Jensen—"

"Nope—" I hold up my hand "—I don't have the energy to argue with you. To listen to a lecture. I'm done." Head high, I turn and move back to the table.

"You okay?" Anker asks once I reach the table.

"Perfect," I say through a tight smile, sliding into my seat and folding my cane.

"That's our Jenny Wren. No sense crying over spilled scotch." Miles bumps my shoulder with his.

I just nod and smile.

"*Yeah*... Speaking of drinks, I'm just about done with mine, so we should head out to Marie's and then home. We have an early start tomorrow, after all," Anker says.

It's the typical agenda for our happy hours. Two drinks each, followed by ice cream at Marie's Scoops down the street. Right now, I have no desire to spend additional time with Garrett. Breakfast tomorrow followed by the drive to LAX is enough prolonged proximity to him for me.

"Ready for ice cream?" Anker says, indicating Garrett's return to the table.

"Sure," Garrett grunts.

"Boo!" Miles's protest is playful. "And here I thought you were going to buy me a replacement drink, Jenny luv."

I bite back the smile blooming from his endearment. My belly battles between a swoop and a queasy sensation. No doubt Garrett wears a smug expression at my reaction to Miles's flirtation.

Fuck him! I replace the tamped-down smile with a sultry expression. "Only if you promise to buy me a drink after."

Miles leans close and purrs, "Gladly."

"What about ice cream?" Anker asks.

I wave him off with a flick of my wrist. "You can go without me."

"Are you sure? We could stay."

"No worries, gents. I've got her," Miles drawls.

"See. I'm good. I'll see you in the morning." I lean back in my chair.

"Okay…" Anker shrugs. "Text me when you get home."

"Yeah… Goodnight." I twist towards Miles. "Walk me to the bar, so I can buy the first round?"

"My lady," he coos, offering me his arm.

"Goodnight, Jensen," Garrett says as I walk away without a word.

2

MILE TWO
WHAT ARE YOU DOING HERE?

Harkey's subdued happy hour crowd becomes more boisterous as I sit beside Miles. After we grabbed fresh drinks at the bar, we joined some of his fellow professors who escaped the English department's mixer. Some I've met through Catherine or interactions through students of theirs.

As an assistant disability services coordinator for Pemberly, part of my job is assisting disabled students with needed accommodations. At times, this requires me to advocate, alongside the student, directly with the professor. Some professors are easier to work with than others. Edward, who blathers on about how the social media app, BookChat, is responsible for the downfall of literature, is one of my least favorite professors to deal with.

Miles's hot breath caresses the shell of my ear as he leans close and whispers, "Not sure why his drawers are in such a twist, I rather enjoy some of those BookChat books."

"Me too," I breathe.

"I bet you do, gorgeous." He tucks a loose strand of my hair behind my ear. "Especially the spicy ones."

The charge of his gaze fixed on me zings through every nerve ending. Even though my limited vision and the bar's dim lighting don't allow me to see his face, I know his eyes are on me. The crackle in the inches between us confirms it. It hums in my ears like a siren song pulling me deeper into crush-drunk waters.

This is it! The way Miles leans close and how he keeps touching me telegraphs he's feeling this as much as I am. Tonight I will transition from that "friend" he sometimes kisses to the woman who will, perhaps, invite him home with her. It's been a while since I've had sex, but thanks to my erotic audios and the spicier books I read, I know more than just the general mechanics.

"We've not yet discussed your audio porn fetish. It's almost too much to know someone as sweet as you may be a depraved little vixen." He runs his fingertip up my bare arm.

Yep, this is happening. Fuck Garrett and his sanctimonious judgment that I'm pathetic. Men like Miles Calloway, with an entire *Reddit* thread on the university about him being the hottest professor on campus, don't flirt with *pathetic* women.

"I'm not *that* sweet," I say, lifting my glass to my lips and taking a long, slow drink in an impression of someone cool and aloof.

It's all bluster. Internally, I am freaking out. In practice, I am as sweet as he teases, but in theory, I am depraved in the ways I'd let this man ruin me. Need prickles beneath my skin in anticipation of my daydreams becoming real. Since I took his arm, leaving behind Anker and Garrett before they headed out, Miles's flirtation has amped up.

"Perhaps you should educate me then?" His fingers draw slow circles against my bicep.

"I..." The breath whooshes out of me.

As much as I'm channeling this temptress persona, I'm out of my depth. Even the preamble to our two tipsy make-out sessions didn't ooze with this sexual chemistry. Not to mention, Miles is clear-headed. The scotch he nurses is technically his second and a half, since most of his second one currently lives on my nearly dry skirt.

"Calloway says you're off to New York tomorrow," Edward says, the ice of his drink clinking as he gestures with his glass. "I love the city in the fall. Are you going for business or pleasure?"

"Pleasure. I'll be in town for the marathon," I say, picking up my soda glass.

"*You're* running the marathon?" He releases an incredulous laugh.

"Is that so unbelievable?" I tilt my head towards where he sits beside me.

"It's not. It's just... You're... Umm..." he coughs and shifts in his seat, "...How does a blind person... Uh... Do you do it with a cane?"

Despite the annoyance now festering beneath my skin, I know he's not trying to be rude. It's clear he just doesn't know. Most people don't, unless they're in community with disabled people, or every four years when the Paralympics are held. Then it seems like everyone is suddenly an expert on adaptive sports.

"Jenny's brother is running the race, not her." Miles loops his arm around my shoulder. "Our Jenny is more the Broadway show kind of athlete."

"Oh. That makes more sense," Edward says. "Wait... How do *you* do Broadway?"

Okay, maybe he is being rude. I narrow my gaze at him. No wonder Catherine complains about this guy and his insistence that good literature hasn't been published since the seventeenth century.

"Here's where the riffraff jetted off to," a woman says, pulling the table's attention towards her. Her posh English accent is shaded with playfulness. "You cads deserted me at a pageant for the dullest professor masquerading as a department mixer."

"It's every professor for themselves at those things," Miles says, turning away from me and toward the voice.

Situations like this are always awkward. Non-visually impaired folks can follow who's talking and recognize familiar faces. If I've not been around someone enough to imprint their voice into my auditory memory, I tend to be at a loss. Right now, I have no idea whose talking and what's happening. Smiling, I sip my soda as the ping-pong conversation of familiar and unknown voices bounces around me.

"Where are my manners? Apologies. We've not met. Kayla O'Leary."

The beat of silence at the table is interrupted by Miles clearing his throat. "This is Jenny… Jensen Larsen."

"Sorry." I cringe. "I didn't realize you were addressing me."

"Sorry… She's blind," Miles says.

Heat crawls up my neck. I'm not sure if he's apologizing to Kayla, to me, or about me. Most of the time when we've hung out in a group setting Catherine, Anker, or Garrett are present, and can clue me in on the people landscape. This is the first time he's witnessed this fun blind girl party trick.

I let out a nervous laugh. "I'm blind…. Technically, legally blind. It's like permanent beer goggles… Minus the beer."

"Ha! Funny…" She chuckles. "I was worried I'd failed you or something."

"Jensen isn't a student. She works for the disability office on campus," Miles explains.

"She does look young enough to be a coed. Look at that baby face. You'll have to share your secret with me."

Baby face… Great! My mouth tightens. My round face, dimples, and button nose may have been adorable as a kid, but it doesn't help with the seductress vibe I'm going for.

"And here I thought Calloway over there was living up to his roguish reputation and robbing the coed cradle with you. You're quite pretty, Jensen," she says.

"Uh…thanks…" I shift in my seat.

Like any woman, I'm ripe for self-doubt about my looks. My physique is definitely on the plump side. I use a lot of product to smooth down my thick brown hair which frizzes at the mere mention of humidity. The only thing I'm ever confident about is my shoes and, ironically, my hazel eyes. They may not work well, but they are the only part of my body prone to compliments.

"Jenny doesn't look *that* young." Miles chuckles. "We're also just friends."

Gut-punch. While I am very much aware of that fact, it still stings. In those two words—*just friends*—all the hope spurred by the sexual tension between us tonight evaporates. How quickly the delusional tumble back to reality.

"Which of you turncoats will buy me a drink for deserting me at the mixer?" Kayla asks.

"I got it. Take my seat." Miles slips out of the chair beside me.

And just like *that*, the last flicker of hope is extinguished. Kayla replaces Miles beside me, shifting the last flirty hour to a few minutes of get-to-know-you chattering. The Austen scholar is a visiting professor from Oxford. Unlike Miles who moved here with his American mother and English father at sixteen, Kayla grew up outside of London.

After a brief exchange about how she's finding California versus the UK, I settle back into polite smiles and nods as they volley between various literary debates and complaints about colleagues. It's not at all how I saw the night going. I should be home, drifting asleep to an audiobook. Instead, I ditched my brother and Garrett for a chance to flirt with Miles, only to just sit here while he chats with someone else.

Stupid Garrett. This is *his* fault. If he'd not been himself, I'd be home now.

Would I? I nibble on my lower lip. How many times have I

lingered behind at happy hours with Catherine for the chance to talk to Miles? *God, he's right. I am pathetic.*

"I'm going to go to the restroom," I say, sliding off the seat and unfolding my white cane.

"Shall I join you and we gossip about this gaggle of literary miscreants who think Henry James is superior to Charlotte Brontë?" Kayla coos.

I bat the air. "I'm good. Thanks, though." With a nod, I head toward the restroom.

It's sweet for her to offer. Kayla seems nice and is the only one who's at least attempted to include me in their English department crossfire conversation. Right now, I just need a little respite from it. Peopling while blind can be a lot at times.

The louder the bar gets, the more difficult interactions are for me. It's hard to follow the conversations and know when to jump in and when not. Twice I've answered questions that weren't meant for me, or remained silent until someone said my name after a question came with a long pause because I didn't know they were addressing me.

It's easier when I'm with people who know to say my name when they're addressing me in large group settings. I should mention it, but besides Miles, I don't really know these people. Explaining blind person etiquette with each interaction is daunting. Not to mention it sometimes leads to people just not engaging at all.

They don't know what they don't know. I can hear my father's warm voice in my head. So much of my life is spent in situations where I either teach people how to interact with me or miss out. For the last hour, I've played spectator to my life versus participant. I have two choices: I can leave or go back out there—*really* go back out there. Jump into the fray of their conversations and tell them, "Hey, can you say my name when you're addressing me, so I can follow the conversation?"

Not to mention, I had intentions for tonight. Miles may be

distracted by his other colleagues—mostly Kayla—but I can get us back on our flirty path. *I hope...* It makes sense. She's charming, witty, and radiates a confidence I could only dream of.

"Stop dreaming, start living." I stare at my fuzzy image in the bathroom mirror. "You can do this. You're not pathetic. You're whatever the opposite of pathetic is." I wiggle my hips just a bit to pump myself up.

Grabbing my cane, I head back to the table. Determination builds with each step.

"Hey," I say, returning to the now quiet table.

"Hey. I was just about to head out, but wanted to make sure you knew," Edward says.

"O—kay." I lift one brow.

"Since Kayla and Miles headed out while you were in the restroom to make a ten o'clock start time for that darts tourney at the pub down the street, he asked me to let you know and see you home."

"They left? Together?" My heart sinks.

"Yeah…"

My entire body audibly sighs at that. No doubt my posture resembles a deflated balloon. So much for his "I've got her" that he promised Garrett and Anker earlier. Not that I need an escort home. I take the bus all the time. It's just… I'm just disappointed.

Edward shuffles and coughs. "Should I pull my car around or…"

"Thanks, but I'm going to take the bus."

As a woman—especially one with a disability—I am extra cautious about my safety. Too many people try to capitalize on the opportunity, and with my limited vision, I'm often at a disadvantage. Even with the self-defense workshop Catherine and I took last year, I have a policy not to get in a car with a man I don't really know. That includes rideshares and random English professors from the university.

"Alright… I'm going to settle my tab at the bar. Goodnight."

I offer a polite nod before scooping up my blazer and purse. Leaving the bar, a shiver runs up my spine from the sharp difference between the balmy inside and the cool November night air. The bar's muffled music quiets as I walk toward the bus stop down the street.

Locating the bench, I take a seat. Besides the distant laughter, it appears I'm the only one at the stop. Slipping my phone out of my purse, I pull up the bus schedule. My screen reader's robotic voice reads out the schedule, letting me know the next bus comes in thirty minutes.

"Awesome." Annoyance sighs through me.

This night just keeps getting better. While I'm grateful to live in a city with public transportation, it does mean I'm at the whim of its schedule. I should be curled up in bed all warm and cozy with an audiobook. Not sitting on a bench. Cold and alone.

Brow furrowed, I dig into my purse. "Damn it, where are my earbuds?" My mutter comes out whiny.

This night just goes from bad to worse. I spilled a drink on myself. Argued with Garrett. Ditched him and Anker to flirt with Miles, who left me at the bar for another woman. Serves me right to not be able to distract myself with an audiobook. Instead, I get to stew about my poor decisions.

"What are you doing here?"

Blinking, I look up. "What are *you* doing here?"

Fuck my life! Tonight just got worse…

3
─────

MILE THREE
COME WITH ME

*G*arrett *Fucking Marlowe.* The dim light of the streetlamp bathes him in a yellow glow. His tall, broad body is outlined in the velvet night like one of those shadow daddies from a steamy romantasy. He is darkness in the light, or light in the darkness. Either way, right now, I'm a fizzed-up soda can of emotions in his presence. Both relief and annoyance collide inside me at his unexpected appearance.

Of course he shows up ten minutes after Miles ditches me. My humiliation wouldn't be complete without an audience, especially one that called this possible outcome.

Sighing, I flick my wrist toward him. "Why are you here? Are you stalking me now?"

"Nice to see you too, Jensen." A smirk is audible in his deep timbre. "I left my phone at the creamery. As I was leaving Marie's, I noticed you here. Why are you at the bus stop?"

"How else does one get home when one doesn't drive?" I roll my eyes.

He steps closer to the bench. "Where's literary fuckboy?"

"Not here." I cross my arms in front of my chest.

"So much for having you," he says gruffly.

"So much." Mouth tight, I twist away from Garrett, letting my vision fix on the lit neon sign across the street.

The distance doesn't allow me to make out the fuzzy letters, but it's better than looking at Garrett. Even if I can't see his face, I can picture the I told you so scowl he's likely wearing.

"What happened? Did he do something?"

Despite the agitation wafting from Garrett, I don't turn to look at him. It's bad enough knowing the mix of smugness and pity that will likely twist his features once he learns how very right he was about Miles. Aching embarrassment already threatens to make me cry, and that's the last thing I want to do right now—especially in front of him.

"Nothing happened." I rub my temples. "He didn't *do* anything."

Isn't that the issue? Miles didn't do anything, and I waited too long to make my move.

Did I, though? I wasn't exactly subtle about my intentions. Even if I never said, "How about we move to the lovers' portion of our friends to lovers story," Miles isn't obtuse. Even my boss Andrew clocked my crush after Miles's first pop into our office.

It's obvious what I want—wanted—from Miles. Hell, Garrett had mocked me earlier tonight about my unrequited crush. His barb had hit the mark then, and its after-effect sloshes shame inside me. I followed Miles around like a puppy starved for any affection, only for him to walk away the moment someone better came along.

I wish I was more like Anker. Even if my brother has this steadfast belief in the Larsen lore, he's not waiting. He's running towards what he wants. He's not just standing by and letting life happen around him.

"Miles didn't do anything you didn't try to warn me about," I admit.

What a fool I've been about Miles. It's just Chase Rollins

all over again. In nine years, you'd think I would have learned not to make the same mistakes.

"What happened?" he says, taking the empty spot on the bench beside me.

The warmth of his body folds around me like a blanket. Right now, Garrett is the last person I want to talk about this with, but there's something in the tender inflection in his voice that uncurls my words.

"He ditched me for another woman."

"Jensen, I'm—"

"You warned me about him." I shake my head. "I was just too stupid to listen."

"You're not stupid."

"Sure." I scoff. "I followed him around like a devoted lovesick teenager, blind to the fact that he didn't want me. Not really. You think I'd learned something after Chase, but *no*, I go and fall for another charmer with their pretty words. God, I am pathetic."

"You're not pathetic."

"You said it yourself."

"I never said you're pathetic," he says, his voice rough.

I twist to face him. "You said it tonight. Outside the bathroom, or is your memory going in your advanced age?"

"I am only seven years older than you." He shakes his head. "Also, I never said *you're* pathetic. He's pathetic. Not you. Never you." He shifts to face me.

His green eyes bore into mine. Their intensity radiates through me, crackling awake every nerve ending. I may not be able to see Garrett's eyes, but I always feel them. I can sense when he looks at me. It's not a magic blind girl trick; it's just this sensation pulsing along my skin each time he meets my eyes, and he always does. Even when he tells me things I don't want to hear. He also never lies to me, even if it means my feelings get hurt.

"Guys like that know what they're doing. They know how

to manipulate and charm people into getting what they want out of them."

I huff a derisive laugh. "Well, clearly Miles doesn't want anything from me."

"Oh, he wants something."

"What does he want?" A crease dips my brow.

"Your attention to boost his ego or to keep you on the hook until he's ready to settle," he says.

"Settle?" I flinch. "Fuck you." I stand up and unfold my cane.

"Excuse me?" He rises beside me.

"I'm not the woman someone settles for." I turn to walk away, but spin back to face him. "I'm not anyone's backup plan. I'm their first choice. Even if they don't know it." I swallow the emotional tangle in my throat.

You're not girlfriend material. Chase's parting shot, minutes after he ended our situationship, echoes inside me. Only to me, I thought we'd been in an actual relationship, or at least becoming one.

"I know that." He steps close. The streetlamp offers enough illumination for me to make out the downward curve of his mouth.

"But you said—"

"Fuuuck." He scrubs his palms down his face. "I never say the right thing with you."

"You said settle."

"I meant settle down. You're the type of woman men settle down with, not the type they just have fun with."

"Ouch." I purse my lips.

Settle down with? That may be even worse than the woman someone settles for. I want to be the woman someone can't live without. My father once said falling in love with my mother was like emerging from the deep end, the air filling his lungs and causing him to wonder if he ever knew how to breathe before that moment.

I want to be the air someone breathes.

"Damn it!" Head tipped back, he lets out a loud groan. "I don't mean it like that. Stop making what I say negative."

"Stop saying negative things." I arch one eyebrow.

Raking his fingers into his hair, he releases a hard breath. "What I'm trying to say is he doesn't deserve you. You're better than this. Better than him."

I toss up a hand. "Well, maybe if you had said that instead of making fun of Miles, I may have listened to you about him."

"Like you'd ever listen to me."

"I listen to you. Sometimes." A small smile twitches at the corners of my lips. "I'm now taking vitamin D daily."

Not all of Garrett's critique is vexing. A lot of it is thoughtfulness wrapped up in his prickliness. Like how he lectures me to add more leafy greens to my diet, but still always brings my beloved garlic knots—along with salad that he will guilt me into eating—when we do movie nights at Anker's.

"Good. Wouldn't want you to die of scurvy." A hint of a smirk plays in his timbre.

"That's vitamin C." A soft chuckle falls out of me. "You're like the worst doctor ever."

"You say that now, but who do you call when you're sick? Not your brother who refuses to write prescriptions for family and friends, even if it's just antibiotics."

"What's even the point of having a doctor brother if you can't get drugs?" I mock pout. "Although, said antibiotics from you do come with a lecture about healthy eating and daily vitamin intake maintenance."

His chuckle reminds me of a rainstorm on a summery day. It's both refreshing and warm. It's moments like this that make the memory of our first meeting and his grumpy, sometimes judgy ways, extra fuzzy. It's almost as if he's two people at times. There's broody Garrett, and then there's my Garrett.

Though he's not mine. He's just my brother's best friend. Even if, at times, it feels like he's also my friend.

"Who's Chase, by the way?" he says, rubbing at his nape.

"Chase?" Head tilted, I wrinkle my brow.

"You mentioned earlier that this is just like with Chase."

"Of course I did," I mutter to myself.

No one knows about Chase Rollins outside of Catherine, my therapist, Dr. Nor, and Anker. Though Anker only knows the CliffsNotes version that I had been seeing someone and then I wasn't. If he knew the full truth, he would have got himself kicked off the university track team thanks to whatever retribution he took on Chase.

"He's my Miles from undergrad. Only worse." Shame blazes up my spine, and I pray that in the streetlamp's pale lighting, Garrett can't see the red I know flames my complexion. "I'm not the girl boys lined up for." I swallow thickly. "Not the woman either."

"Jensen—"

I hold up my palm. "Please keep whatever platitudes you're about to say to yourself. They won't make me feel better. I know the truth."

"What truth is that?"

"I'm not the girl men want to have fun with." Using his own words, I tip my gaze back to him. The ache of certainty twinges in my throat, making my words come out scratchy. "And despite what you say about me being the woman men *settle down* with, I'm not the type of girlfriend most men want."

"What does that mean?" I can almost hear the pinch of his brow in his question.

"You know what it means. Don't be deliberately obtuse," I say, incredulous.

"Enlighten me." He steps impossibly closer. The annoyance radiating from him takes up all the space in the scant inches between us.

"In my experience, most men don't want a girlfriend they need to let know where the drink is on the table, so that she doesn't accidentally knock it over. A girlfriend who can follow the crossfire conversation or knows when someone is addressing them without verbal cuing."

"That's bullshit," he growls.

"It is bullshit…" I shrug. "It's my life, though. My first kiss was with a boy who only did it on a bet. Boys used to dare each other to ask me to school dances, but then never showed. Hell, even my friends in high school used to ditch me or neglect to invite me places because they thought I'd be too much work."

"Those aren't friends."

"I'm aware, but they were all I had. Besides Anker." I sniffle, trying to push back the threatening tears.

After my diagnosis, so many of my relationships shifted to treating me like a problem to solve. It took a bit for my parents and Anker, even if he's still a little extra protective, to not worry so much about me. With my failing vision, friends in high school didn't always know what to do. They just wanted to be carefree kids, so they often did not invite me. They'd grumble how annoying it was if I asked for help, so I stopped asking. What they didn't realize was I just wanted to be a carefree kid, too. Instead, on top of my failing eyesight, I worried about both being too much and, somehow, not enough to belong.

"I was really lonely, and when I went to undergrad, I hoped it would be different. I met some girls early on who befriended me. They were upperclassmen and in a sorority. They invited me to pledge. I couldn't believe it. I had friends and would have sisters. Only, I found out that particular sorority had a bad reputation and thought a blind member would help revamp their image. When I declined to join, they dropped me."

"Assholes."

"That they were." I sigh. "Meeting people is always hard, but when you have a disability, there's an extra layer, so when Chase came along... I was starved for connection. It started off so innocent. We worked together at the student union. Everyone had a crush on him."

"Including you?"

"Yep." I blow out a long breath.

Those first few weeks with Chase were reminiscent of a sappy Hallmark movie. Random run-ins on campus turning into long walks, talking about books and music. Those walks turned into trying the different sugary lattes at the campus coffee shop. Then sitting crossed-legged in beanbags, an open pizza box between us, laughing at some stand-up comedy special on TV. To sweet kisses as he told me I was cute. Before I knew it, those sweet kisses morphed into his hand up my shirt, murmuring, "Let me be your first."

"I thought we were together. Like, that he was my boyfriend. He was the first man I had sex with." I clear my throat before I say the only man I've had sex with.

I'm doing enough emotional oversharing tonight. Garrett doesn't need to know that at twenty-nine, I have only kissed three men and had sex with one man just a handful of times. Though I imagine in the five years of me being single since we've met, it's not a secret that I'm unpracticed. As much as I've fantasized about other men, including the one who stands patient and quiet in front of me, I've been gun-shy about sex. Miles is the first man I seriously considered having sex with since Chase.

"I really liked Chase, and I thought I was special to him. But I was so wrong." I shift foot-to-foot. "Right before winter break, I found out he had a girlfriend back home. I was just someone he thought he could..." I swallow the emotions clogging my throat, their truth stinging the entire way down. "Guess I am just the girl you have fun with for some guys after all."

"Fuck them," he snaps. "Fuck them for making you think that… Just fuck them. It's total bullshit."

"I know." I slide my fingers beneath my glasses and wipe at the tears that have started to crest.

"Do you?" He tilts his head. "Because I don't think you do."

"I don't need a lecture, Garrett," I say, my brow puckering.

"I think you do." He tilts his head almost like a gunslinger in a campy western.

"Not from you." I reach out and poke his chest, ignoring how firm it is. *Vagina, we are mad at him right now, do not clench.*

"There she is," he says, his tone pleased.

"Excuse me?" I arch one eyebrow.

"Why can't you be this Jensen with everyone else?"

"What Jensen is that?" I say, pursing my lips.

"The pain-in-the-ass, takes no shit Jensen you are with me. No matter how I push or challenge, you never back down. You never worry about saying how you feel with me, and sometimes I wish you would."

"I don't know, maybe you're special." I narrow my eyes at him.

Because I really don't know. With most people, I'm tied up in knots about not asking too much or somehow being too much. With Garrett, I just exist. I never worry about saying the wrong things, because as much as we can bicker and poke at each other, he never leaves. And for some reason, neither do I.

"Lucky me," he says, humor shading his words. "Come with me."

"Where?"

"To someplace we can work on this."

"Work on what?" I gape.

4

MILE FOUR
LET'S GET YOU OUT OF THESE CLOTHES

Garrett pulls into a driveway—specifically *his* driveway. This isn't my first time at his place. Over the last five years, I've been here for random dinners, game nights, or his annual Super Bowl party. It's less party and more he and Anker glued to the TV, while I play with Ditka, Garrett's cat, between eating my weight in garlic knots.

This is the first time I've been here without Anker. In fact, this may be the most prolonged period I've spent alone with Garrett. I honestly don't know why I agreed to this, but here I am. The only clue Mr. Cryptic has given me thus far is that we're going to tap into *Feisty Jensen,* as he calls my sassier side, which seems to only come out with him.

"I've not rearranged since you were here last, if you want to go caneless," he says, unlocking his front door and ushering me in.

It's sweet how nonchalantly he says that. Anker does the same thing anytime I come over. They both always let me know if they've changed furniture at their places. Garrett organically took to some of the things Anker does around me like giving me heads up on room layouts and where things are on tables. With most people, there's a "training period" as they adjust to interacting with me. It's not that the visually impaired require a lot of adjustment, but just a few little tweaks here and there. Just like my best friend Catherine, Garrett took to it in a way that never makes me feel like I'm a chore.

"Thanks," I say, placing my cane in the corner near the front door before slipping my shoes off. "Is that my friend?" Smiling, I spin towards the sound of a bell jingling towards me. "Hey, baby boy." I scoop Ditka up.

"He's not a baby. He's a fearsome attack cat," Garrett grumbles.

"So fearsome," I coo at the pudgy tuxedo cat that lies flat on his back like a rag doll, allowing me to stroke the soft fur of his belly. His purr hums in my ears. "Who's daddy's pudgy little attack cat?"

"He's not pudgy. Also, I'm not his daddy. I'm his… human."

His human? My mouth tugs up. That might be even cuter than the idea of Garrett as a cat daddy. Though his feline parental origin story isn't exactly voluntary. Two years ago, the kitten fairy visited him in the form of Ditka being delivered to Garrett's front door with a note from his mom that read *This is my grandson, you best take care of him*.

"Just his human?" I flash a knowing expression. "Says the man who has cat beds in just about every room of his place and an app he watches his cat on while at work like a feline stalker."

"The app is just to make sure he doesn't destroy the place. Don't let the face fool you, he's a furry little terrorist," he mutters but still reaches over to offer ear scratches to Ditka, who leans into his daddy's touch.

"Don't let him fool you, Ditka, your daddy is just a big ole softy."

"You say that now. Just wait until you see what I have planned for you." The devilish curl of his mouth is audible.

No, no vagina. Ignoring that flutter low in my belly, I clear my throat. "What do you have planned?"

"Leave the cat, come with me."

"Okay, but after whatever you have planned, I get more Ditka cuddles. And snacks," I say, pressing a kiss to Ditka's head before depositing him on the floor.

"But first we need to get you out of those clothes."

"Excuse…me?" I choke out.

"Calm down, this isn't one of your dirty audios."

"Erotic," I say with all the indignation of a snooty noblewoman from a Regency novel. "What exactly do you have in mind for me?"

"Follow me to find out," he says, striding towards the hallway that snakes down to where the bedrooms and bathroom are.

I could just ignore his request and play with Ditka, but I hear his collar's bell jangle behind Garrett. "Traitor," I mutter.

"I'm in the guest room. Second door on the right," Garrett calls.

Stupid curiosity. It won't be the cat that dies, it will likely be me. Shaking my head, I trail along the wall, allowing it to guide me down the hallway. Even with how well-lit Garrett's house is and my familiarity with it, I still like to use things to anchor me, so I move around safely.

Garrett's house is similar to my brother's. It's a midcentury house at the end of a cul-de-sac in a neighborhood near the hospital and university. It's quiet and residential compared to my building near downtown, with its rows of shops, cafes, and restaurants easily accessible for me to walk or take the bus.

In the guest room, Garrett presents a pair of shorts that his sister Lara left on one of her recent trips and one of his T-shirts to change into. "You have to tell me what we're doing," I whine.

"We're channeling Feisty Jensen." His closeness and the room's light offer enough brightness for me to make out his lopsided grin.

"And what does athletic wear have to do with Feisty Jensen?" I hold up the clothes.

"Get changed and you'll find out." He turns and heads towards the door. "I'm going to change. Meet you in the hall in five."

"You suck!" I shout as he strides out of the room.

Still, I'm doing this. I trust Garrett, even when he annoys me, I know he wants what's best for me. Also, I don't want to go home and sit in my apartment—alone and stewing over tonight.

"See, it's already working." He laughs, shutting the door behind him.

Hands on my hips, I stand in front of the door leading into Garrett's garage. Like most houses in Southern California, the garage isn't for storing cars. As adorable as this house is with its blue shutters, open concept layout, and plush evergreen carpet that makes my bare feet feel as if they are in cozy slippers with each step, there's limited space. Anker's house is similar, but he uses his garage as a hangout space and storage. Garrett uses his for torture.

"You monster. You're going to make me exercise, aren't you?" I poke his chest.

His very firm chest, which is part of his chiseled-out-of-marble physique. All of which he gets from his healthy diet and commitment to exercise. I may do yoga with Catherine and hit the elliptical in my building three times a week, but I'm not at the "has a home gym" fitness dedication level the way Garrett is.

"It will be fun," he says.

"Fun? This may be why your only friend is technically your employee." I shake my head.

"I have friends."

I make a dismissive noise.

"Ditka. You. My family."

"I stand corrected." A smirk twists my features.

"Come on… I'll make you snacks after." He opens the door and clicks on the light.

"If you make me eat broccoli after this, I'm going to get Ditka a sibling."

Offering me his arm, Garrett guides me to a boxing bag near the center of the room. A few mats lay beneath it, making me grateful for their cushy warmth compared to the garage's cool cement floor. I've only been here once, so he describes the space's layout to me. A treadmill, weight bench, and shelf with various dumbbells are tucked up against the far-right wall. The left wall is made up of shelves full of boxes for storage. It's neat and clean. A light aroma fills the room from the dried eucalyptus leaves in a tall wooden vase in the corner, which combats the garage's stuffiness.

"Put your hands flat in front of you. Palm down and thumb out," he commands.

"What are you doing?" A crease forms at my brow's center as he starts to unravel a thin strap of fabric that reminds me of an Ace bandage.

"Wrapping your hands to protect them in the gloves."

"Are we boxing?" I gape.

"*We* are not, but you are."

"How? Are you just going to stand there and let me punch you?" My mouth ticks up. "That actually sounds fun."

"Not me. The bag, Jensen." He huffs a laugh.

"Oh. That makes more sense." I tip my gaze towards the large bag dangling from the ceiling. "How is this helpful?"

"Just trust me."

"I thought we established I trust the wrong men," I say, my tone teeters between snarky and self-deprecating.

"I'll endeavor to prove you wrong."

"Wrong for trusting you, or wrong about trusting the wrong men?" I nibble on the corner of my mouth.

I'm being sassy, but I do wonder. Do I trust all the wrong people? Will Garrett prove to be just like so many others in my life? Friends who ditch me. People who use me. Men who manipulate me. I am the common denominator in every single one of my heartbreaks. Whether I'm too much or not enough, I'm the one picking these people.

"These are as tight as I can make them. Are they okay?" he asks, tapping the boxing gloves he put on me.

"Yeah." I wrinkle my brow. "My glasses. Can you take them off? I don't want to accidentally break them."

"Yeah," he murmurs. "Let me..."

His fingers comb into my hair, brushing it behind my ears. For the briefest of seconds, his thumbs rasp against my cheeks before he takes hold of my glasses. I bite the inside of my cheek in hope the twinge will stamp out the impulse to melt into his touch.

"I'll put these on the weight bench."

"Yep," I breathe.

This is not why I am here. I'm not here to indulge in my crush. This isn't a sappy romance where he kisses me and declares it's always been you, or whatever foolish story my internal self is writing. I'm not here to get under Garrett. *Not that he'd want that.* I'm here to get over Miles, and the string of other poor choices I've made for my heart.

He guides me into a fighting stance. My left leg forward, and right leg back about half a foot.

"Let me show you." He moves behind me, his body's heat awakening my nerves as his strong hands land on my hips.

I sink my top teeth into my bottom lip to fight the little moan that wants to come out. It's not like Garrett has never touched me. Playful bumps of my shoulder with his. The warmth of his palm at the small of my back in crowds. The brush of his fingers as he hands me something. This is different, though. The way my entire body zings to life with the firm grip of his hands on my hips is a little alarming.

"You always want to face your opponent. It keeps your center of gravity where it needs to be, so you can move when needed or withstand a punch."

I twist to look at him over my shoulder. His mouth inches from my temple and hot breath kisses along my hairline.

"Should I worry about the bag knocking me on my butt?" My mouth lifts.

"Smartass." His chuckle is silent, but every quiet beat thrums within me. "Let me take you through the punches."

With a firm but gentle grip, his fingers press into my flesh, and I try to ignore the charge along my nerves with his touch. He guides me into the different positions. The hook. The jab. The uppercut. The cross. The heat from his body licks along my skin as he guides me through each formation, repeating it several times until he's satisfied, and I'm left wanting more the moment he releases me. My entire body hums for his touch.

"Ready to hit the bag?"

"Yep," I say, trying to stamp out the breathy quality of my voice.

If this is supposed to have me channel Feisty Jensen, all it's doing is coaxing awake Horny Jensen. The one who listens to the deep bass voice actors in my erotic audios, imagining it's Garrett acting out the scenes painted by their filthy words.

No good will come from getting lost in those daydreams.

Shaking away those thoughts with a wiggle of my shoulders, I step back into my fighting stance. With a slap of the bag, he starts to call out the punches.

It takes a bit before I get into a rhythm. The smack of my gloved fists hitting the bag and the melody of his deep bass meld into an almost musical beat. Jab. *Thwack.* Uppercut. *Thwack.* Cross. *Thwack.* Hook. *Thwack.*

Every muscle in my body burns awake. Despite the gentle ache radiating, this strange sense of joy surges inside me with each strike on the bag. It's similar, but different, to when I do yoga with Catherine. With that, a Zen sensation envelops me. Right now, I am the opposite of Zen. It's primal and fierce, as if I'm a fae warrior queen from one of my romantasy novels.

"If Miles were here, what would you say to him?" Garrett asks.

"What?" I blink, stopping my arm mid-swing.

"I didn't say to stop. Keep going." He slaps the bag twice.

"Bossy much." My retort is breathless.

"What would you say to literary fuckboy if he were here?" He slaps the bag again. "Tell the bag."

"I know what you're trying to do. This is textbook homespun therapy straight out of a paperback self-help book." I roll my eyes.

"Maybe Ms. MSW"—he shrugs— "but it works."

I bark out a disbelieving laugh.

"Prove me wrong then... Tell the bag."

"Fine." I move back into my fighting stance and do a quick jab to the bag's center. "This is stupid. You're stupid."

"And literary fuckboy?"

"Is also stupid," I grit out, my glove thwacking against the side of the bag with a right hook.

"Why?"

"Because he doesn't see me. Not how I should be seen. He doesn't want me how I should be wanted." I slam my fists against the bag.

"And how should you be wanted?"

"Like the air someone breathes," I hiss, punching my fist into the bag in a hard uppercut.

The fire once crackling quietly inside me roars awake every emotion that's laid unspoken and ignored within me about Miles. Frustration that he doesn't want me. Anger with myself for falling for yet another man who doesn't deserve me. Sadness that this is just a pathetic waltz I'll repeat the steps to again with whatever inappropriate man I fall for in the future.

"Fuck you, Miles, and your shitty taste in books. You don't deserve me!" Rotating my hips, I put as much of that fireball of emotions into each punch. "Fuck you, Everett, for making me think the only reason someone would kiss me is on a bet. Fuck you, Chase, for making me feel like I'm just a backup plan… And fuck me for choosing these men," I shout with one last cross.

Chest heaving, muscles aching, and sweat dotting my forehead, I step back and drop my arms to my sides. A strange sense of calm folds around me. Nothing is fixed. I'm still hurt, but I don't hurt. It's hard to explain, but the emotions roaring inside me are quiet.

"How do you feel?" Garrett releases the bag and steps closer to me.

"Annoyed that you were right," I pant out.

"Sounds about right."

"Garrett, who is Jenny Wren?" I tip my head up, meeting his stare that I know, in the way my body pulses, is tethered to mine.

I could look this up myself, but right now I want him to tell me. Not just because Garrett will never lie to me, even if it means my feelings will be hurt, but out of a need to know that there is one man outside of my family whom I can trust. Even if the dull ache in my heart warns that Garrett is yet another man who will never want me the way I want to be wanted, I know he'll never hurt me. Not in the way other men have hurt me.

"She's a disabled woman known for being an inspirational character from Dickens," he says, his tone matter-of-fact.

"Just as I thought." I take a deep breath. "Hold the bag, Garrett," I say, settling into my fighting stance.

5

MILE FIVE
MY WIFE

The burner's *click, click* causes me to tilt my head towards the kitchen. "Wait, I thought you were making me a PB and J?"

"I am," Garrett says. The soft clunk of a pan hitting the burner accompanies his response.

"Since when do you use the stove for PB and J's?" I yank on the hoodie he's lent me and then shuffle towards the counter island separating the kitchen and living room spaces.

The heat that coursed within me during our impromptu boxing session is dissipating, leaving me cold. I'm a California girl to my core and tend to complain anytime the temps drop below seventy.

"You do when it's a grilled PB and J."

"I didn't know you could grill them." I lean against the counter. A large grin kicks across my face.

"You can grill just about anything." He flips the sandwich.

"Ice cream. Soup. Pudding..." I sass, tapping on each finger.

"Just about anything, smartass."

I finger-comb my hair up into a messy bun. "Is this like the Dr. Marlowe medicine for getting over being ditched by literary fuckboys? First, rage against the boxing bag and then comfort PB and J's?"

He shrugs. "Sort of... Mom always made these for us when we had bad days as kids."

"And you still make them for yourself when you have a bad day?"

"Yeah."

I nibble on my lower lip, stopping the audible *Aw* that wants to come out. It's adorable to think of Garrett coming home after a long shift at the hospital to make himself comfort PB and Js. As much as I know about Garrett, there're closed drawers about this man I've never ruffled through.

"Did your mom have you *tell the bag* before you got your comfort sammy when you were a kid?" I slide onto the island stool.

"Sammy?" He huffs an incredulous snort. "We're not calling it that." He clicks off the burner and places the sandwich on a plate. After cutting the sandwich, he places the plate in front of me.

I pick up one of the triangles and take a bite. The salty sweetness explodes on my taste buds; the creamy peanut butter and the tart raspberry jam.

"Oh god." Eyes closed, I release a breathy moan. "This is next level."

"Thanks."

"No. You don't get it." I gesture with the sandwich. "Where has this been my entire life? I've been doing PB and Js totally wrong this entire time." I take another bite, licking excess jam from my lips.

"Glad you enjoy it," he says, amusement radiating from him.

"Have some." I push the plate toward where he stands on the other side of the counter. "Technically, you didn't *tell the bag*, but you earned a treat with this yumminess."

"Thanks." He picks up the other half.

"Where did telling the bag come from anyway?"

"Bryce recommended it to me a few years ago."

I've met Garrett's family a few times. His parents have been out here twice in the last five years. Both his older brother, Bryce, and younger sister, Lara, have also visited. Outside of those trips, Garrett doesn't seem to get back to Chicago to visit them that often. Which is weird because in the few interactions I've had with them, they seem close. Garrett even does virtual Sunday dinners with them each week, where they all cook the same thing and eat together via video chat.

It's odd. Anker and I drive up to Solvang to see our parents each month. Not to mention, we spend every holiday with them. Garrett spends most holidays here, unless we drag him along with us. Unlike my brother who uses all his leave to travel for races or to visit our parents, Garrett claims it's hard to take time off as the hospital's inpatient service chief. From what Anker explains, between he and a few other seasoned attendings, there are people who can cover, yet Garrett rarely takes time off.

"Bryce thought it would help me with my anger and emotions," he says before taking another bite.

"Anker says that about running for him. I think even if the Larsen lore wasn't a thing, he'd still be as voracious about running."

Our dad, a runner like my brother, got Anker into sports as a kid to manage his social anxiety. It's hard to think of my now-social-butterfly brother being awkward and shy, but he was. Athletics, especially running, gave him direction. Whenever emotions get too much, he goes for a run. I, on the other hand, turn to pastries or cry.

After tonight, I see the value in exercise as a coping strategy. Even if boxing didn't fix anything, I do feel better.

"Is boxing for general mental health maintenance or to

deal with specific emotions?" I take another bite of my sandwich.

"General now, but specific then." He clears his throat. "Probably still specific."

I meet his gaze in a silent conversation. Does he want me to ask more? I know I want to know. Let's face it, it's only a matter of seconds before I prod him. While I may hold back with most men, I'm incapable of doing that with Garrett. From our first meeting, just about every thought or question spinning inside me about him has come out. *Just about...*

"My wife," he says, as if that offers any explanation.

"You have a wife!" I say, mouth slack. "How? When? Where is she?"

This explains his almost monk-like existence, but what the actual fuck? In five years, you'd think he'd have mentioned that. In the whiplash-inducing relationship I have with Garrett, where one moment it's like we're friends and the next moment it's as if my existence is barely tolerable, this tips the scales in favor of me being nothing more than an inconvenience he has to deal with.

Don't friends tell each other things like this?

"*Had* a wife." He swallows thickly.

"Had?" A crease dips my brow.

"She died."

"Died?" I breathe.

I place my hands on the counter, trying to regain emotional equilibrium. Garrett had a wife who died. He had an entire life before moving here that I had no idea about. How long were they married? How did she die? Does my brother know?

"Almost six years ago," he says.

"Almost six years ago... Right before you moved here?"

"Yeah," he breathes.

"Is that why you moved here?"

"Yeah."

"Does Anker know?"

"Yeah."

"But you never told me, and I'm assuming you asked him not to tell me." A twinge in my throat makes my words come out gruff.

"I don't like to talk about it." He lets out a long breath. "And you like to talk about things."

He's not wrong, but it doesn't soothe the ache in my chest that, after all this time, he hasn't shared this with me. Even if he's telling me now, it doesn't mean we're friends. In the hot and cold relationship Garrett and I have had for the last five years, it may only be a few minutes before he closes himself off to me again. Just like the first night we met. One minute I'm asking him about the Palmer House in Chicago, and the next moment I'm overhearing him call me a yappy yorkie.

"Anker is the only one outside of my family and people back in Chicago who know about Val," he says. "It wasn't about keeping it from you... Well, only you. I don't like to talk about Val with anyone."

"Her name was Val?"

The curiosity to know more pulses inside me. *What was she like? How did you meet? What happened to take her away from you? Do you still love her?* They're all rude, and none of my business. Still, each question swirls inside me like confetti waiting to burst out.

"Yeah, her name was Val." He heaves a heavy breath. "We met in medical school, fell in love, and then she died."

It's succinct and unemotional, as if he's recalling what happened on a random Thursday. Though the way the air goes stale between us, I doubt it was a random day for him. I can't imagine having met your person, only to lose them.

Tonight, he has listened to me complain about the situationships that *broke* my heart, while he's experienced the real deal. Shame scalds me, flushing my cheeks at the idea of comparing what I've gone through with men to Garrett's heartbreak. That's true heartbreak.

"I'm such an indulgent twat." I rub at my temples. "God, here I am blathering on about men that I choose not liking me and calling it heartbreak, when you've lost a wife."

"Pain is pain," he says. "However we're cut, we feel it. We still hurt."

"And you still hurt?" I cringe. "Of course, you hurt. That was stupid to say."

"Yeah, I still hurt," he murmurs.

"Is it the same hurt as when it first happened?"

"No… I don't know. It's different. When she first died, everything was so hard. Breathing. Moving. Thinking. Not thinking. I just wanted to stop hurting."

Tilting my head, I take him in. The overhead lighting fixtures illuminate his features. His mouth is a firm line, posture rigid, and his hands are curled tight around the counter's edge.

"In Chicago, I'm Val's widower. With colleagues at the hospital where we worked. Our friends. Even with my family." He turns his head, breaking our tethered gaze.

"Is that why you left?"

"Yes."

"And why you rarely go back?"

"Yes," he rasps.

"Because there you are just Val's husband?"

The question is reminiscent of tentative steps onto a frozen pond. One misstep and I could slip. The present tense he uses telegraphs that to so many this is who he is. He's not Garrett —the often-grumpy man who begrudgingly dotes on his cat and makes comfort grilled PB and Js on bad days. He's Val's husband.

God, I understand what that's like. To only be seen as something that happened to you, instead of the many pieces that comprise you. For so many people, I'm just the blind woman.

"I'll always be Val's husband," he says sharply.

"I know... I didn't mean it like that." I look down at the sandwich and then back at him. "It just must be hard to be there without her, but with the constant reminder of her."

"It is," he says. His voice is hoarse and quiet.

"How did you meet?"

"Only you." Head shaking, he puffs out a soft laugh.

"Only me what?" I scrunch my nose.

"Would ask that. Most people would ask how she died. You want to know about our love story."

"Well, I do love a romance." My mouth curves up into a small smile.

"That you do." He taps his fingers against the counter. "Val and I met in medical school. It was the clichéd meeting in one of those books you gobble up where she literally ran into me at the campus coffee shop and spilled her iced mocha all over me. Six months later, I asked her to marry me, and two months later, my brother Bryce got ordained online and married us in my parents' backyard."

Eight months? It's hard to imagine the man who takes fifteen minutes to decide which ice cream flavor he wants at Marie's each week met, fell in love, and married someone so quickly. To my knowledge—from what Anker has shared—Garrett hasn't been in any relationships outside a woman from the hospital with whom he had a brief *colleagues with benefits* thing with before she moved to Atlanta.

"How long were you married?"

"Five years."

His speech is quiet and hesitant, as if trying not to wake a sleeping bear. Only I'm not sure if I'm the sleeping bear, or if it's him. The way the air buzzes around us reminds me of those moments when the sky rolls with dark clouds, but the sun still pokes out, making you uncertain if rain will come.

I'm not entirely sure what the rainstorm would look like with Garrett. Will he close down? Will he open up? I proceed, nonetheless.

"You were married in your parents' backyard?" I rake my teeth along my bottom lip to bite back the rest of that thought.

No wonder he rarely goes home. It must be sheer torture to be at his parents' house, surrounded by the memory of the day he and Val committed to a forever that would never be.

"My mom's favorite book is *Alice in Wonderland*, so my dad made this Mad Hatter meets an English garden vibe back there."

"It sounds lovely." Elbows on the counter, I lean my chin on my palms, imagining what that must look like.

The rainbow of yellow, pink, red, and white roses poking from vibrant green bushes. The assortment of mismatched patio tables and chairs that somehow go together perfectly. The decadent floral scent colliding with the hummingbird's song, creating this visceral experience.

"It was… It is," he says, his voice scratchy.

Shifting, I lean against the stool's hard back. "No wonder it's hard to go home."

"Yeah."

"How did it happen?"

"Car accident."

"Were you with her?"

"No. I wasn't," he says, his tone harsh.

"I'm sorry if I—"

"I don't want to talk about this anymore." He pushes away from the counter.

"Yeah… I get it." I fiddle with the hoodie's strings, twining it around my finger and pulling it tight.

Too far. Those words flash inside me. I took it too far. I seem to have a bad habit of that with Garrett. It's like I'm blind to the track's boundaries and always try to tug him off course with the things I ask or talk about. He's been clear this isn't his favorite topic, and I just keep asking anyway. *Why do I do this with him?*

"I'm sorry, Garrett... I—"

"It's fine." He picks up the now-empty plate and places it in the sink. "It's late, so I should get you home. I'm picking you and Anker up by seven for breakfast before the airport after all."

I shouldn't be surprised that he's slammed that door shut as quickly as he opened it. This is Garrett. Every moment that I think he's opening up; he shuts me out.

"I know you don't want to talk about this with me, but besides *telling the bag*, do you talk about it with anyone?"

"Jensen," he groans.

I hop off the stool and motion toward him. "Anker? Your family? A therapist?"

"Jensen."

"I know it hurts, but it's not healthy to keep these things bottled up. Clearly, you're still very much struggling with—"

"Damn it, Jensen," he mutters. "Why do you have to be such a pain-in-the-ass all the time?"

I toss my hands up. "Why do you have to be such a stubborn self-righteous prick?"

"And Feisty Jensen is back," he huffs, rounding the counter.

"Yes, she is." Brows linked, I tip my head up. "And she's calling you out on your bullshit."

"My bullshit?" he spits out.

"Yeah. You dragged me here to exercise my emotions about Miles while you clearly refuse to deal with your own shit. I'm sorry your wife died, and I hate that you're in pain, but you know better than anyone that wounds left untreated fester and infect. Telling the bag is just a bandage on..."

I search for the word. None seem appropriate. I can only imagine that losing the person you thought you'd have the rest of your life with is akin to losing a limb. It's painful. It's life-altering, but not ending. You adapt. You figure it out.

The grief journey I navigate with the loss of my vision teaches me this. So much of my life focused on what I lost until the work I am doing with Dr. Nor helped me to mourn that loss while not losing sight of what I have.

"I know how hard it is—"

"You don't know a thing about it," he grits. "I lost the woman I love, and the life I thought I was going to have. All in the thirty minutes from the time I told her to text me when she got home to when I got a call that she was dead. This isn't some fuckboy not returning my affections or using me."

"I wasn't talking about Miles…" I glare at him. "So much for pain being pain."

He steps back. "What were you talking about?"

"It doesn't matter. You're right. I don't." Emotion thickens in my throat from the freight-train force of his words slamming into me.

It's foolish to think I understand what he's lost. Garrett had, and lost, a great love. Fear riots within me that I'll never know his pain, because I'll never know the joy.

"Jensen… Fuck." Heaving a hard breath, he closes his eyes. "I'm—"

"It's late. I think it's time for me to go home."

"I shouldn't have said that."

"And I shouldn't have pushed, but that's what we do with each other."

Push. Pull. Hot. Cold. One moment, I imagine rising to my tiptoes and wrapping my arms around his neck to press myself against him and lean into how much I suspect we could fit together. Then, there are moments like this where I know deep in my bones that Garrett and I aren't even friends —not really. That my crush on him is just another symptom of my fucked up head about men. That I have my own bullshit that I need to deal with.

"Let me take you home," he says.

6

MILE SIX
YOU RUN A MARATHON?

Groaning, I toss my hair up into a messy bun. It's barely six thirty in the morning, and after a night of too little sleep, I'm exhausted. Besides a grunted "Good Night," Garrett drove me home in complete silence last night. A chainsaw may not have been able to cut through the tension during the five-minute drive from his place to mine.

After everything last night, I am a shaken-up soda can of emotions. It doesn't help that I checked my messages after Garrett dropped me off, and found a text from Miles saying, *Hope you got home safely, Jenny luv*. Twelve hours ago, when I was pre-ditched, my stomach would have impersonated a gymnast. Instead, my belly was tied up in knots—still is—between Miles deserting me at the bar, and the strange night with Garrett.

Garrett revealed so much about himself last night, yet he remains a puzzle, missing just enough pieces to leave you guessing what the image may be. The one thing clear about everything is that my romantic picker is broken. It may not have ever worked considering my checkered relationship past.

"*Relationships*... That's a bold statement," I mumble to

myself, tossing the hairbrush onto the counter before shuffling out of the bathroom.

Every man I have liked has been a mistake. This includes Garrett. Everything that happened last night reinforces that. This isn't *Pride and Prejudice*. He's not my Mr. Darcy, and I am certainly not his Miss Bennett. In fact, I may need to put myself on a moratorium on my annual rewatch of both the Colin Firth and Keira Knightley versions that I do each holiday season.

"Miss Austen, what have you done to me?" I whine, flopping onto the couch to scoop up my phone and text Catherine.

My bestie is meeting us for breakfast at Bread before Garrett takes Anker and me to the airport. It takes away the tiny pebble of guilt about texting barely past sunrise. With her first class at ten a.m., Catherine doesn't have to arrive on campus before nine on most days.

Me: Men suck!

Catherine: Duh. I do not envy you heterosexual girlypops. Is this a general suck or a specific one?

Despite my phone's robotic voiceover program reading out the message, I can almost hear Catherine's lyrical voice. On top of being one of my favorite humans, she has this vocal profile that reminds me of the smooth timbre of a cello.

Me: Specific.

It all spills out of me with the chaotic fury of a waterfall. The argument with Garrett at the bar. Me thinking last night I'd move Miles and my situationship to the next level. Perfect Kayla. Getting ditched. Val. Then my second spat with Garrett. And all of it within a four-hour period. It all vomits out of me until I deflate into my sofa's cushions.

Catherine: This is a lot to process at 6:38 a.m.

Me: I know! The ride home last night was awkward enough. Now I have to sit through breakfast with him and then LAX traffic.

Catherine: Should I call in a favor from that parking enforcement officer I went on a date with last week, and have her put a boot on Garrett's SUV, so he can't drive you?

Laughter tugs my lips into a broad smile. After years of my only real friend being my brother or parents, Catherine is almost too good to be true. Lucky for me, she is both one hundred percent real and mine. Four years ago, we became each other's people after bonding over our shared love of seasonal lattes at the campus coffee shop. What started off as just random chats in line each morning turned into sporadic lunch dates and morphed into a real friendship. Clearly one where she's not above calling in favors from her recent hookup.

As unlucky in love as I am, my bestie has the pick. Only she doesn't want anything serious at the moment, and is leaning into her easy, breezy single woman era.

Me: No favor needed. I'll survive.

Catherine: Should I plot Miles's downfall? Remember, I'm a Brontë scholar. Those gothic romances have all kinds of twisty forms of vengeance.

Me: As tempting as that is, let's hold off on locking him in the attic of your manor house for now.

Catherine: I'm ready at the stead to plot vengeance against him or any other future asshole.

My mouth drags down. Catherine's comment isn't a dig. I know that, but I can't help to worry that if I keep running this course, I'm going to end up with another Miles.

Me: I think I'm going to go on a romantic sabbatical.

Catherine: Like no dating? At all?

Me: Not until I can figure out why I keep falling for the same type of man.

In the wreckage that is my failed love life, I'm the thread weaving each heartbreak together. No more of this. It's time to reclaim my heart and stop wanting to give it to men who will break it. Everett, Chase, Miles, and even Garrett. Granted,

Garrett isn't like the others, but he's still all wrong for me. Yet, I still *like* him.

I look up at a knock on my door. Anker and Garrett are supposed to pick me up by seven. Of course, their type A personalities show up twenty minutes early. I type out a quick goodbye to Catherine and then shuffle to the door.

"Hey," Garrett says as I swing the door open. His massive frame takes up most of my entryway and blocks the yellowish light from the sconces along the hallway outside my studio.

This isn't one of the newer buildings in Seal Beach. It's a two-story brick building with mostly studio and one-bedroom apartments. Its closeness to downtown, the bus stop for me to get to the university, and being owned by friends of my parents—who I am pretty sure are giving me a significant cut on rent—makes it ideal for me. Not to mention, its nod to the art deco architecture style from the 1920s gives it this whimsical fancy I adore. My only complaint is the lack of closet space for my shoes.

"Hey." I shift foot-to-foot. "Where's Anker?"

"I haven't picked him up yet. I came here first."

"How'd you get into my building?"

"I held the door for an older woman with an unruly pug, and then followed her in."

"You broke in?" I tilt my head.

"Yeah… What were you talking about last night?" His low base is husky as if he's been up all night.

"What?"

"You said you weren't talking about Miles. What were you talking about?"

"It's not important." I wave my hand.

"It is important."

I want to double down on my lie and say it's nothing, but I can't. The intensity of his stare crawls inside me, causing an electric charge to pulse in my veins like that moment before you jump into the deep end.

"My vision loss." I jut my chin towards him.

"I knew it… I'm an asshole." He rakes his left hand into his chestnut hair.

"You didn't know." I tuck a loose strand of hair from my messy bun behind my ear.

"Because I didn't listen. I just reacted and cut you off. You were just trying to help, and I—"

"Don't want my help." I fiddle with the hem of my sweater. "You're more the helper than the being helped type."

"Doctors make terrible patients, after all," he mutters.

"That they do." My mouth lifts in a small smile.

"We share that trait. We both prefer being the helper versus the helpee."

"Is that even a word?" I laugh. "But you're right. Neither of us are comfortable in the being taken care of role. Though, I may have overstepped."

"As I do all the time with you." He sighs. "I mean, I did drag you back to my house at ten o'clock at night for some textbook self-help bullshit, as you called it."

"I don't think I called it bullshit exactly." I arch one eyebrow. "But, yes, you did… In turn, I needled you to talk about Val."

"We do like to get into each other's shit, don't we?" A soft chuckle resonates in his chest.

"It appears so." My rigid stance softens with each gentle beat of his chuckle.

And just like that, here we are again. Only, it's less we and more me. I'm pretty sure for Garrett, this is just the ebb and flow of our relationship. But I don't want that relationship anymore, and I don't want to keep having feelings for inappropriate men.

"Except I'm going to do something about my shit." I point to myself. "I'm going on a romantic sabbatical until I figure out why I keep falling for men who don't want me. At least in the way I deserve to be wanted."

Dr. Nor may be able to redecorate her office after I pay for the serious self-work we're going to do together. It's clear I have layers upon layers to unpeel to figure out why I keep picking the wrong men.

He clears his throat. "No more literary fuckboy, then?"

"Among other types of men." I lock my fuzzy vision on him. Determination causes me to make my spine tall.

This includes him. From here on out, I will no longer let myself be swept up in my Austen-induced fantasies of this modern-day Darcy, as I've dubbed him. If I have to wear a rubber band and flick it against my skin each time I think of him until the sting's memory wards off this stupid crush, I'll do that. He's not an appropriate crush. He's just my brother's friend.

"I don't want to sound patronizing, but I'm proud of you. It takes a strong person to deal with their shit," he says, his tone both gentle and sad.

"Thanks." Mouth closed, I swipe my tongue over my teeth in an internal debate before I decide to just say it. "If you ever decide to go beyond just telling the bag and deal with your own shit, I have an excellent therapist who can make recommendations."

"God, you are like a dog with a bone at times."

"How very *yorkie* of me." Crossing my arms over my chest, I toss him a sassy expression.

"What?" He tilts his head.

"Nothing." I shrug. "We should head out to get Anker." I turn to scoop up my purse and grab my luggage.

"Jensen, I...fuck..."

I turn. "What?"

"Sorry. The hospital is calling." He holds up his phone. "Dr. Marlowe... When was he brought in?"

I stiffen at the undercurrent of worry in Garrett's typically steady tone.

"Is he conscious?"

"What's happening?" I say, anxiety pulsing along my nerves.

"We'll be right there." His gaze pins me in place. "Anker was hurt. He's in the ED."

The scent of disinfectant fills my nostrils as Garrett guides me through the maze of gurneys, carts, and staff shuffling between different emergency department bays. Despite the early morning hour, the emergency department is a flurry of beeping sounds, phones ringing, and staff conversations.

From what the charge nurse who called Garrett had said, Anker had been brought in via ambulance just after six a.m. Outside of the fact that he'd fallen on a pre-dawn jog this morning and is busted up enough to warrant an ambulance, we're not sure what happened.

"Are you okay?" I rasp, wrapping my arms around Anker, who sits propped up in a gurney.

"Ouch," he groans. "Easy, She-Hulk, I have broken ribs."

"Broken ribs!" I gasp, stepping back and tilting my head to take him in with my still intact-*ish* peripheral vision.

Thanks to the hospital's fluorescent lighting and my closeness, I'm able to get a visual picture of his state. He's in a pair of black mesh shorts and a tattered gray T-shirt. Knowing my always put-together brother, that shirt's rip is related to his fall. His thick hair—the same as mine—is disheveled. A beige colored bandage along his hairline stands out against the contrast of his dark brown hair. Another bandage, this one dark blue, is wrapped around the knee of his right leg that rests on top of a large pillow on the gurney.

"This looks bad. How bad are you hurt? Are you in a lot of pain?" I motion towards him.

"It looks far worse than it is," someone says, pulling my attention to the other side of the gurney where a tall, lean man in a white lab coat stands. His warm smile is bright against his neat dark beard.

"Sorry…" My cheeks heat. "I didn't see you there."

"I'm Dr. Raymond Deridder. Ray," he says, his smooth baritone almost winks as if it's a private joke between us. "You must be Jensen, Anker's sister. He's mentioned you a few times."

"Nice to meet you." I brush a loose tendril of my hair behind my ear.

"Glad to meet you, too."

I clear my throat. "So, he's not hurt too bad."

"*Sure…* not *too* bad. Just bad enough to fuck up this weekend." Anker huffs a harsh breath.

"Sorry, Larsen. You'll be off your feet for a bit," Ray says.

"What's wrong with him?"

"We don't have time to figure that out," Garrett says dryly.

"Ha. Ha," Anker harrumphs.

The little exchange causes the tension inside me to unspool. If Anker was truly hurt, Garrett wouldn't tease him. At least the kind of hurt where there is something to worry about.

"Fractured ankle. Two broken ribs. Lacerations at the hairline and right knee. Possible concussion," Garrett says, his tone steady.

"That sounds bad." I twist to face Garrett, who stands behind me holding a tablet.

"He'll survive."

"Your bedside manner is top-notch, Marlowe," Anker snarks.

He ignores my brother. "Like Deridder says, it sounds worse than it is. He'll be okay." A hint of a tender smile plays in the gentle timbre of his voice.

"Thank you," I murmur.

Technically, he didn't do anything, but his reassurance calms the anxiety that has rippled inside me since the charge nurse called him. The thought of something happening to Anker terrifies me. He's not just a brother. Until Catherine, he was my only real friend—even if I don't always tell him everything. A dull ache radiates in my chest at the idea of anything happening to him.

"Garrett, are you using your hospital credentials to read my chart?" Anker says, aghast. "It's bad enough being brought into the hospital where I work and having my colleagues patch me up. I'd prefer my best friend not poke around in my medical records."

"Don't worry, I ignored the note about that foot fungus you needed antibiotics for a few months back."

I snort.

"Hilarious," Anker grumbles.

"Just doing my due diligence as inpatient chief to see if you'll require admission." Garrett looks up from the tablet.

The audible smirk in his snark causes my mouth to curl upward.

"Total abuse of power," Anker grumbles.

"I don't think his ankle needs surgery." He clicks his tongue twice.

"*Seriously.* I'm right here!"

Ignoring my brother, he continues, "Still, let's get an ortho consult just to be on the safe side."

"Agree." Ray taps something into his tablet.

"Don't agree with him. He's not my doctor. He doesn't even work in the ED," Anker mumbles with the fervor of an unruly child.

"File a complaint with HR."

He tosses his hands into the air. "HR, the shitty cherry on top of the turd sundae that is today."

"On that note, let me go see if the charge nurse can work his magic to get ortho down here sooner." Ray moves towards the room's entrance.

I pivot. "Thank you, Ray."

He stops, turning to look over his shoulder. "Of course. It was lovely meeting you."

"You, too." I wave as he slips out of the room.

"*Great.* My injury facilitates a meet-cute between my sister and the new head of emergency medicine."

"Hardly. He's just being polite."

"Your sister isn't available," Garrett says briskly.

"*Unavailable?* Please, tell me you're not with Mr. Semi-colon," Anker groans. "It's been a shitty enough morning."

"No. I'm not with Miles." Eyes narrow, I aim the full force of my glower on Garrett.

Clearly *Mr. We Get into Each Other's Shit* is sharing mine with my brother. I'll tell Anker about my romantic sabbatical —at least the CliffsNotes version—but while he's sitting busted up in the ED doesn't seem the right place to get into it.

"I'm taking a break from dating, but we have more important things to discuss at the moment." I look over my shoulder towards Garrett. "Hey, Dr. No Boundaries, how long will he be down for?"

"Again, I'm right here," Anker mutters.

"I have boundaries."

Garrett's tone paints the image of an indignant pout puckering his face. If I weren't a little annoyed with him for mentioning my break from dating, speeding up a conversation with my brother about it, I'd think it was adorable.

"The ribs will take a few weeks, but the ankle... Six months or so."

"Which means bye-bye New York." Anker sighs.

Mouth dragged down, I turn back to my brother. "I'm sorry about the race, Anker."

The journey to the New York City marathon has been almost two years in the making. Besides his general marathon training, he's had to run key races in the last year to qualify for a spot in the race. Unlike the Seal Beach marathon each October, you can't just fill out a registration form and pay a fee to run it.

"Me too." His entire essence resembles a crushed soda can.

"How did this happen anyway?"

"Fucking corgis." He crosses his arms over his chest.

Anker is more surly than normal, which is to be expected. He's likely both in physical pain and frustrated that this derails his intention to run the marathon on Sunday.

"What does that mean?" I scrunch my nose.

"It means Mr. Sloan's horde of stumpy-legged wannabe watchdogs got out of his backyard this morning and directly into the path of a guy on a bike who swerved to miss them and slammed into me as I rounded the corner on my morning jog."

"Are they okay?" I place my hand on my chest.

"The furry terrorists are fine. When I came to, after hitting my head in the fall, Mr. Sloan was there with his—now leashed—demon dogs and the bicyclist."

"I don't think the corgis were gunning for you," Garrett says.

"Their motivation aside, my ankle is broken, and the last sixteen months of work are flushed down the drain."

"I'm sorry, Anker." I squeeze his forearm. "I know how hard you've worked."

"Yeah… All for nothing." He shakes his head.

A sharp twinge radiates in my chest at this. It's not like my brother to be so forlorn. He's the endless sunny days of people. No matter the issue or misstep, he's the reassuring one. Each time I tripped or saw my vision slip further away, he'd reassure me.

"Six months." I look between Anker and Garrett. "The ankle will take six months to heal, and then he can train again. Right?"

"Six months or so." He looks at the tablet. "Even if ortho recommends surgery, which I doubt, it shouldn't be more than that with the shape your brother is in."

"You're not my doctor here." Anker wags his finger. "You're just my best friend and emergency contact."

"Wait, why is Garrett your emergency contact?"

"Because, unlike you, he answers his phone."

"He's not wrong there," Garrett says wryly.

"Whatever." I toss my hands up. "Anyways, if you'll be healed in six months, then you can still run New York. Just next November. Surely, they'll let you defer your entry a year due to this, so you don't have to qualify again."

"I'll be thirty-one by then."

"And?" I gesture at him.

"The point of running New York is to do it the year I turn thirty."

The Larsen lore. It's amazing to me that my scientist brother puts so much stock in this. Ever since we were kids, he'd light up each time my father or uncles talked about the year they turned thirty. Even I'll admit it did seem like a magical time. All three of them not only met their future people, but it seemed to be the time everything else clicked for them. Our father realized his passion for baking—part of which facilitated his meet-cute with our mom after he'd asked about the recipe for the scones at the coffee shop where she worked.

It's so easy to fall into the magic of their stories, but it's just the typical time in people's lives where they settle into careers and their futures. It's all just the natural flow of some people's lives masquerading as family legend. *And he thinks I read too many romance novels.*

"Okay, well you don't turn thirty-one until October fifteenth, so you'll have time to run a different marathon. It doesn't have to be New York."

"But it does need to be *the* year I turn thirty. That year ends in two months. It's not happening. It's over. Even before it started."

"It's not over. The race. Sonora. Your turning thirty bucket list. They're not gone. You just have to wait or find a new way." I sit on the edge of the gurney and take his hand.

My words almost mirror the ones he had given me on my sixteenth birthday. While classmates celebrated getting driver's licenses, allowing them greater freedom, I faced the realization that I wouldn't experience that milestone. I wasn't blind—pun intended—to the fact that I wasn't going to be able to drive. Still, turning sixteen made it real. It just reinforced the ways I wasn't like the rest of my classmates.

I would have been fine wallowing, but Anker didn't let me. Instead, he drove us three hours to spend my birthday at Knotts Berry Farm, specifically to do the bumper cars.

"Anytime you want to drive, I'll always ride shotgun," he'd said as we climbed out of one of the bumper cars. Laughter vibrated through us, and our legs wobbled after being crammed into those tiny cars.

"Thanks," I sniffled, wiping away grateful, happy tears from the edges of my eyes.

Not only does Anker always keep that promise, but most days he opted to walk to school with me, or take the bus, instead of driving us. Well, unless it was raining. The thick, sometimes frizzy, hair we inherited from our mother makes the rain our mortal enemy. Still, I know Anker did it so I didn't feel alone walking the path I'd been placed on.

"Next year is the year I turn thirty," I say, my eyes wide.

"What?" He says, his face likely pinched with confusion.

I squeeze his hand. "The Seal Beach marathon happens right after I turn thirty and exactly one week before you turn thirty-one. If we run it together, maybe whatever Larsen lore magic comes with running a marathon the year you turn thirty will transfer from me to you."

"How?"

"I don't know. I'm not the expert on mythical family folklore," I scoff.

"Yet you're suggesting this," Garrett drawls.

"You're not helping." I toss him an annoyed expression over my shoulder.

"You also don't believe in the Larsen lore," Anker says.

"That doesn't matter. What does is that you do." I look at him. "Plus, Mr. Scientific Method, wouldn't running the race together the year I turn thirty test your theory that it both exists and isn't exclusive to those with Y chromosomes in the Larsen gene pool?"

"That actually makes sense," Garrett adds, causing me to shift to face him.

"Did it hurt to say that out loud?"

"I may never recover." The upward tug of his lips is evident in his tenor.

"Good thing we're in a hospital." I smirk.

"You would run a marathon with me?" Anker says, disbelief punctuates his words.

"I would do anything for you." I meet his eyes, which are the same shade of hazel as mine.

In so many ways, my brother is the complete opposite of me. He's tall and lean compared to my shorter, plumper figure. He's the brightness that lights up every room, while I tend to stay tucked up against the wall. Still, we're both Larsens. We come from a family of helpers. It's why he's a doctor, and I got my master's in social work. Above all, he's one of my favorite people, and I would do anything to help him. Even run a marathon.

"Jensen, I love you, but you're not exactly the easiest person to guide run with. We didn't even make it a mile into that 5K." He points at me.

He's not wrong. Guide running involves a lot of trust. Something I tend to struggle with. Human guide isn't my favorite. There's always a charge along my nerve endings that I'll get hurt, left behind, or worse, that I'll hurt someone else. My cane gives me the control to ensure my own safety. Only running with a cane isn't safe or practical.

I heave a breath. "Well, I'll have six months or so to mentally prepare for that while you're recovering."

"Because that's realistic."

"Have faith."

"Says the woman whose idea of a marathon is binging *Masterpiece Theater* melodramas." He shifts on the gurney. "Jensen, you don't just wake up and run a marathon."

"I know." I purse my lips. "I'll look up some programs and hit the treadmill in my building."

"It's so much more than that. Diet. Conditioning. Simulating the race day experience. This isn't the twenty minutes you do on the elliptical a few times a week. Not to mention the work needed to get you comfortable with being guided for 26.2 miles."

26.2 miles? I'm aware that marathons are long, but this puts it in perspective. I don't even think Seal Beach is 26.2 miles in length. How the hell does it have a marathon?

"I appreciate you offering, but I don't… Unless…" He looks between Garrett and me. "You train her."

"Excuse me!" I choke out.

"You need to mentally and physically train for this. Garrett is perfect. Not only does he run marathons, but if you can trust him enough to be your guide runner, then there's hope that this race won't end with your knee skinned and us walking off the course like last time."

"I… We can't… This is a terrible idea." I gesture wildly.

All the reasons stack up. We'll argue. I'll keep crushing on him, even though he's inappropriate, because of my faulty heart.

"Plus, Garrett is busy and—"

"I'll do it," Garrett says.

7
─────────

MILE SEVEN
YOU HAVE A NICE BODY

Sunday mornings are my favorite. I spend most of the day curled up on the sofa, clad in sleep shorts and a hoodie, binging whatever my latest audiobook obsession is. That's what I should be doing now.

Instead, I stand in my building's basement gym, glaring at the treadmill. It's not my exercise equipment of choice. The elliptical offers far more safety with my feet in each paddle, so I don't have to worry about tripping. On the elliptical, unlike the treadmill, I don't have to fear pushing the wrong button and the belt turning up so fast that I go sailing off. A thing that *has* happened before.

The blind runners' group I joined recommends training on a treadmill. The group is the same online community for visually impaired runners and guides where Anker met Sonora. Once I got over the sticker shock from the posts about runners doing their second marathon in eight months and running a mile in six minutes, I settled into how helpful the group could be. Sprinkled between celebration posts and links to different race opportunities is a wealth of real-life advice on ways to train for a marathon.

One of which is supplementing the times you can't train

with your guide with the treadmill. They recommend it over the elliptical because it offers a more authentic running experience—*allegedly*. I think it's just a form of mental torture.

"Here we go," I groan my defeat as I step onto the belt. With a deep inhale, I run my fingers over the machine's flat screen panel.

Unlike the elliptical that sits quietly beside the treadmill, there are no tactile buttons. Even with the buttons, Anker spent extra time to orient me to the machine when I first moved into this building. The only button I can figure out is the large red one below the screen that I assume is the one you press to stop in case of emergency.

"Let's hope I don't need that." I sigh.

Sliding my phone from my pocket, I pull up the magnification feature. Most of the way I interact with the world is through auditory or tactile means, but sometimes in situations like this, I can tap into my remaining vision through magnifiers to figure things out.

Squinting, I try to make out the various power walk/running options on the screen. Between the glare and the screen's poor contrast, it's hard to read. After staring for a few minutes, I think I've figured it out and tap what I believe is a twenty-minute no incline option. My understanding is that most marathons tend to be flat, including Seal Beach.

Hands curled tight around the rails that run along the treadmill's sides, I start to walk with the robotic *three, two, one, start* that sounds from the machine. If they can have that verbal output, it would be nice if they had it for the rest of the treadmill's features. It starts off slow—my muscles fire awake and hips sway just a bit to the beat of the pop music playing in my earbuds.

Still, I hold on to the rails and concentrate on staying to the center of the belt. It's hard not to sway to the left or right. Without the cane, the rails are my only way to anchor me to where I'm supposed to be. The entire time, my heart thuds in my chest. Not because this is particularly taxing. It's barely a fast stroll. Fear thumps inside me, nonetheless.

I'll feel more comfortable once I'm better oriented to the machine to ensure I make the correct selection. *Note to self, get Catherine to help orientate me to the machine Tuesday after yoga.*

As the machine begins to speed up, tension spools tight in my muscles. My slow pace notches up to a power walk. It's not anything I can't handle, but I hit the stop button anyways. I don't want to risk a visit to the ED. One Larsen sibling busted up is enough for my parents, who fly back on Wednesday.

My brother insisted they remain in New York to do all the things we'd planned—minus cheering him on at the race. With the holidays being our parents' bakery's busiest time of the year, this is their last chance for respite until January's brief reprieve.

"How am I going to do this for 26.2 miles?" I whine as the machine comes to a complete stop. Head shaking, I climb off the machine and move to the elliptical. I may have failed on the treadmill, but at least I can get the twenty-minute power walk/jog in for now.

I hit two miles on the elliptical. I'll take that as a win. The thought of power walking—let alone running 24.2 more miles—radiates an ache in my calves. How can I do this? Why am I even doing this? Anker didn't even ask! He gave me a way out, but here I am.

I want to blame my ridiculous offer on the mix of emotions from everything that occurred in a twelve-hour period between Thursday night and Friday morning. A big part of me wants to back out, but Anker's gratefulness yesterday morning, after I stayed at his place just in case he needed anything, solidifies my resolve to do this. It's such a flip of the script for me to be the one looking after him. I don't want to fail him.

I also don't want to fail myself. Inside me, a tiny voice whispers, "What if the Larsen lore is real?" Not in the sense that fate will magically poof the love of my life into existence if I run a marathon next year, but that this is the step into charting a new course. Part of the work I'm going to do with Dr. Nor is to learn what causes me to make these same choices about men, friends, and so many other things. Past Jensen would never volunteer to run a marathon, but here I am, doing it. Maybe by doing something that breaks the mold of who I think I am, I can break other patterns.

Sighing, I grab the sweatshirt from the end of my bed and pull it over the tank top and leggings I changed into postshower. My wet hair is tied into two long braids.

I raise my head at a loud knock at my door. "Hello? Who is it?" I say, reaching the door.

"It's Garrett."

"Garrett?" Face scrunched, I unlock the deadbolt and open the door.

His large frame takes up the entire entryway. The brim of his black cap shadows his face, but the hint of a smile flashes. I drag my eyes down his form. The unzipped hoodie reveals a black T-shirt stretched over his broad chest. His muscular calves are on full display between the hem of his shorts and the tops of his sneakers.

"Jensen," he says, the heat of his stare rolling down my body, over my hoodie, to my bare feet, and back up my figure before he clears his throat. "Nice sweatshirt."

Crap! "Sorry. I should return this." I fiddle with the sleeves of the sweatshirt *he'd* leant me the other night. I don't know why I chose this one to wear today. In my defense, it's super comfy. Even if right now my cheeks flush from embarrassment.

"Keep it. It looks good on you."

And cue the stomach swoops. This is why I can't be around this man. One compliment and I'm sure there are hearts in my eyes like a cheesy cartoon character. No good will come from prolonged interaction with him.

"Thanks… It's cozy." I shift foot-to-foot. "How'd you break into my building this time?"

"Since *someone* didn't answer my text or call, I had to get creative." A teasing smirk plays in his words. "I held the door for a woman with a stroller and then slipped in behind her."

I lean against the doorjamb. "Playing the Good Samaritan again to break and enter. *Ruthless.* Perhaps I should tell the building's manager to be on the lookout for you."

"Perhaps *I* should have a chat with them. With how easily I got into this building, I do worry about its safety."

I shake my head. "Are you here to test the security of my apartment? Shall I lock the door and time how long it takes you to break in?" I sass.

"Cute."

"That I am." I bat my eyes.

"Can I come in?" he asks, his tone borders on playful exasperation.

"Asking permission to enter? Maybe you are a vampire after all." With a flick of my wrist, I step to the side. "You may enter."

"Vampires only need permission once, and you already gave it to me." He steps close, the warmth of his body licks my skin like flames from a bonfire that threatens to burn. "Or did you forget I was here two days ago?"

"I didn't forget," I breathe.

Our gazes tangle. Even without seeing his eyes, I know they are locked with mine. No doubt assessment swims in those green irises. That same assessment is likely reflected in my own pupils.

"Why are you here, Garrett?" I step back, putting distance between us.

"We have a marathon to train for." He shuts the door behind him.

"Yeah… About that…" I shuffle my bare feet against the hardwood floor.

"Are you not doing it anymore?"

"No…" I wrinkle my nose. "…I mean yes, I'm still doing it. Or rather, I'm going to try."

He points at me. "Then what's that face for?"

"What face?"

"That 'I have bad news, but I'm too chicken shit to say it' face."

"That's a rather specific and *rude* facial designation."

"Just say it, Jensen." His command is gruff.

My brow puckers. "Fine. I don't think you should be my guide."

"Why?"

"Because it's a lot." I motion between us, as if that fills in all the things I'm not saying.

"You know I've run marathons before, right? This isn't *my* first time." He places his hands on his hips. "I can handle this."

"I'm aware." I shrug.

"Then what's the problem?"

"It's my first time, and I'm afraid that I'm too much," I murmur, my eyes dropping to my pink-painted toes.

He closes the space between us. "You're not too much," he says softly, placing his thumb below my chin and guiding my stare to meet his.

"You tell me I'm too much all the time. I talk too much. I ask too many questions."

"You do…" he huffs a chuckle. "…But I like your brand of too much. Plus, I'm looking forward to seeing if you're able to maintain your incessant questions for twenty-six miles."

"It's technically 26.2 miles," I correct, the corners of my mouth lifting.

"See, you're already learning." He swipes his thumb across my jawline.

The tender stroke telegraphs an almost reflexive action. Like touching me is as natural as breathing for him. The way I melt into his touch mirrors that instinct. My head knows I should pull away, but my body remains.

Blinking to clear the Garrett-induced trance I'm in, I step back. "I appreciate you doing Anker the favor by helping me train, but—"

"I'm not doing this just for Anker."

"Why are you doing this then?"

"Because you need help, and like you said, it's a role I'm comfortable with."

"I'm not a damsel for you to rescue." I cross my arms over my chest.

"I know."

"I can find someone from that blind runners' group where Anker met Sonora."

"No," he almost growls.

I tip my head up, meeting his hidden gaze with my steely one. "Why? We're not friends. Not really. Hell, sometimes I don't even think you like me. Training me would be torture for you."

"I like you."

"Sure." I puff out a breath that resembles helicopter blades cutting through the sky.

"What makes you think I don't like you?"

"Besides the five years of whiplash from your nice one moment total dick the next moment behavior, you called me a yappy yorkie."

It's official, Feisty Jensen is out to play. In the push and pull of whatever this is with Garrett, I've never called it out like this. I've certainly never shared with him the remarks I overheard him say after our first meeting.

"I never called you a yappy yorkie."

"Yes, you did." I poke his chest. "At Anker's birthday five years ago, just after I met you."

For weeks, Anker had gone on about the Attending Physician at the hospital, who'd spend his lunch breaks going over patients' charts. I was so excited to meet the man who was helping Anker navigate his residency program.

"Fuck... I did say that. I'm sorry." He grips the brim of his hat. "Yorkies are adorable, though."

"They have old man faces," I say, indignation burns in my belly. "Also, now isn't the time to be cute. That hurt my feelings, Garrett."

"I'm sorry, Jensen." He places his hands on my shoulders. "This isn't an excuse, I swear. What I said was wrong, and I didn't mean it. I was just..." He sighs. "That was the first night I socialized with anyone since moving here. Hell, since Val had died the previous November. Nobody knew about her, not even Anker at the time. I thought it had been long enough—"

"Oh god, did I accidentally say something that triggered you?" My hand goes to my mouth, replaying that night.

"No. You didn't do anything. You were perfect."

"What?" My breath hitches.

His fingers knead into me through the sweatshirt's thin fabric. "For the first time in a long time I wasn't thinking about how shitty I felt. I wasn't thinking about Val. The only thing I could think about is you."

"Me?" My pulse thuds.

"You just burst into the room all bubbly spewing random facts about Chicago including that the brownie was invented there. All I could think about is how—"

"Annoying I am." My mouth tugs up.

"Yeah." A soft chuckle falls from him. "And how much

you'd love the Palmer House's brownie sundae. Then, I felt guilty. Like I was somehow betraying Val."

"You didn't do anything wrong, though," I say, my brow scrunched.

"I'm here and she's not."

The ache in his voice guts me. I just want to wrap my arms around him and tell him it's alright. That he did nothing wrong. But my arms have no ability to heal his pain, and holding him close is like placing my hand on the hot stove. At some point, I'll get burned.

"I'm sorry I've been a shit friend to you," he rasps.

"Are we friends?" I say softly.

"I want to be… I want to be your friend, Jensen." Releasing me, he straightens. "I don't deserve it, but I want a second chance with you. To be what you deserve."

The wise thing is to say no. To send him on his way and find a different guide to train with until my brother recovers. Isn't that what Feisty Jensen would do? The Feisty Jensen that he gets glimpses of. If I were that Jensen, I would have said these things to him a long time ago. I would have done a lot of things a long time ago.

I swallow down every protest whispering inside me. "I've researched some training plans."

I'm not Feisty Jensen. At least, not yet. I want to be, but right now, the desire to see what real friendship with Garrett looks like is too strong. My head and heart are at war. For the first time, I'm going to listen to my heart, because in the past I always heeded my head's warning to not take risks. A friendship with Garrett may be a bigger risk than finding someone unknown to train with.

"I've been doing research too." He flips his hat backwards, revealing a lopsided grin that I find far too adorable. "Shall we compare notes and make a plan?"

"You're sure about this?"

"Yes," he says without a hint of hesitation.

I bite my lower lip. "Does guide runner services come with grilled PB&Js?"

"Perhaps…"

For the next hour, we build a training plan. The little charge that zinged between us dissipates as we fall into comfortable companionship. He teases me about my collection of novelty mugs, and I tell him I don't take style advice from a man dressed like sporty Wednesday Adams in all black athletic wear. Pressed up against him—thanks to my not-Garrett-sized sofa—a smile curls my lips watching him drink from a penguin shaped mug while I drink from a polar bear cup I got at the aquarium.

We compare our notes. Mine are on my laptop and his on his phone. It appears we found a lot of the same plans. We choose a program broken into three phases.

The first three to four months will focus on base building, helping me gradually develop my ability to run longer distances. Phase two is training for a half-marathon. The last four months will focus on the big show—an actual marathon. Each phase comes with me running races to help me get comfortable with the racing environment. All our training will culminate next October, just under twelve months from now.

Depending on the phase, I'll be training three to five times a week. Garrett and my schedule won't allow us to always train together. We settle on Wednesdays after work and Sunday afternoons, allowing me to keep my lazy Sunday mornings and him to attend dinner with his family. The rest of the week, I'll train solo on the treadmill in my building's gym.

"I'm creating a shared calendar for our training, which I'll e-mail you," Garrett says, tapping on his phone.

"*Ooh*, a shared calendar. Can I put other things in it for you to do?"

"No," he grunts.

"Boo!" I pout but decide I'll do it anyway.

Perhaps I'll set up a daily reminder for him to smile more. There will certainly be a reminder for him to eat lunch, because Anker has shared that most days, Garrett skips it to work with residents. The possibilities are endless.

"I've also emailed some links to articles, guides, and videos on stretching and conditioning activities, and other things that may help you in your training."

"Other things?" Head tilted, I lift one eyebrow.

"Meal plans—"

"Ugh…" I groan, tipping my head back. "Is marathon running just your elaborate plot to get me to eat more vegetables?"

"You found me out. I orchestrated Anker's injury to Svengali this entire situation to get you to eat broccoli," he deadpans.

"Dastardly." I poke his side and then pull up his e-mail on my laptop.

"The meal plans will help give you the right energy and nutrition needed to do this. Don't worry, you can still have your lattes."

Opening the attached document labeled *Suggested Meals* in my email, my screen reader begins to read the document. It's similar to what I know Anker does while training.

"One a day!" I whine, at the little note about limiting me to one latte a day. "You made that one up." I elbow Garrett.

"You consume far too much sugar."

"It keeps me sweet." I kick his shin.

"Nearly diabetic," he mutters.

A furrow dips my brow. "Guess I shouldn't complain. All

this running and forced starvation will help me lose my snack pouch."

"This meal plan is hardly starvation—"

"Let me be melodramatic for a minute, you're taking away my lattes."

He shakes his head. "What is a snack pouch?"

"My belly." Sighing, I pat my stomach. "At least, this will help me get a nice bod."

"You already have a nice body."

What? I don't look at him. I don't even know how to look at him right now. He thinks I have a nice body? It's not as if he hasn't seen parts of me. We've been to the beach together. Though I'm more the full coverage tankini with a coverup type than the sexy swimsuit clad girls who seem to appear just to flirt with Garrett or Anker.

"I…" he coughs and shifts on the sofa beside me. "My suggestions aren't about me wanting you to change how you look, it's about keeping you healthy… Keeping you around for a long time."

I really don't know how to look at him, so I keep my gaze forward. Somehow this feels more meaningful than just him liking my body.

Don't be stupid. I shake off that thought. Of course, he worries about my health. For a man who's had a big loss, it's understandable that he's extra sensitive about doing what he can to keep the people in his life safe. That includes making them eat their veggies, and browbeating them into an only one-a-day latte habit.

Twisting toward him, I meet his gaze. "Can I have two lattes on special occasion days?"

"You can have whatever you want. These are just suggestions. I'm not in charge." He gestures at himself.

"But you are my guide."

"That doesn't mean I'm in charge. This is a team. A partnership." He pats my arm.

For the first time, this doesn't seem like he's doing me a favor, or being a good friend to Anker. We're in this together. Each of us is running this for our own reasons. I know mine, but what are his?

"Why are you being my guide?" I fiddle with my sleeve.

"Because that's what friends do."

"This goes beyond just wanting to be a better friend. Why? What do you get out of this?"

"Real friends do," he murmurs.

Besides Catherine, I've not had a real friend. One that doesn't have an angle. One that won't just leave me behind. I, especially, haven't had a male friend that fits that bill. If I'm going to do this—not just train with Garrett but have a second chance at a real friendship—I need to be open to the possibility that he may be a real friend.

"You're right." I nod. "Here's to real friends." I raise my mug in a toasting gesture.

Grinning, he taps his mug against mine. "Friends."

8

MILE EIGHT
LET ME TAKE YOU TO DINNER

Sweet relief. Arms stretched over my head, I arch my back and let out a contented sigh. The action eases the tense muscles in my back. It's not just the stiffness from sitting in front of my computer for the last two hours, but the quiet groans of my body thanks to two mornings in a row of pre-dawn runs on the treadmill.

Before Garrett left on Sunday, he oriented me to the treadmill. He even figured out that it's a newer model that offers audible instruction and showed me how to access that. I'm grateful, but right now the ache in my calves hates him for it. Although, my body may be even more angry after our first training session this evening.

Sighing, I tap on my keyboard. It's just after eleven, and my morning has been consumed by drafting this grant application. If it's approved, it will allow me to establish an access technology center on campus. The project has been a dream since I attended Pemberly University for undergrad. Technology is a game-changer for so many disabled people. It opens up entire experiences once denied to us.

This costs money, though. As a private university, there are limited resources for disability services. At least that's what the administration claims each year when my boss submits our department's budget. In my experience, the needs of disabled people are often an afterthought in most spaces. This grant will supplement our small budget to build a center beyond the two computers in our department's waiting area and the lone volunteer who does workshops every few months.

"Hey, my diva," Catherine announces in her sing-song lilt.

"Hey, my queen!" Grinning, I pull out the earbud I use to listen to my computer's screen reader while working.

"I've got treats!" She shakes something in front of her.

The *clank clank* of items hitting a tin container is a welcome song in my ears. "Is that what I think it is?"

"Maple candy courtesy of Grandma Flores." She plops down in the lone chair in front of my desk.

Clapping my hands together, I do a wiggly dance in my chair. One of my favorite things about my bestie is our insatiable sweet tooths. Between my bakery-owning parents who send pastries on the regular and her grandparents' candy shop—now run by her older brother—we hook each other up with all the treats.

"So good." Head tipped back, I moan with the first bite.

"Thought you'd enjoy a 'Holy Shit I'm Running a Marathon' treat."

"I don't think that name would fit on a label." Laughter curls my lips.

"This is why I write novels—at least, attempt to. Leave the quippy candy names to my brother. Hector is way better at that." She bites into one of the sweets.

I frown. "No luck pushing through the writer's block?"

Like many English professors, Catherine has literary ambitions. Half the department is either published or working on books. However, most of them are academic in nature. Studies of the Brontës impact on modern feminism, literary analysis of translated works from the antiquities and several essay collections make up her colleague's publications. Catherine's work is less academic, but more important—in my opinion.

"The tension! It's three chapters in, and they already want to smash." Head tipped back, she lets out a dramatic whine.

Laughter vibrates in my chest. Besides a deep love of sweets, Catherine and I are voracious romance readers. So much so that Catherine is writing a modern-day sapphic Jane Eyre retelling that explores the intersection of race, class, gender, and mental health. Knowing Catherine, it will also serve the most delicious spicy scenes. Give me all the layered exploration of deeper themes but toss in someone bent over a desk or pressed up against a wall. *Yes, and thank you.*

"Nothing wrong with a little chapter three visit to O-town." I waggle my brows.

"Absolutely not!" She waves her finger. "What would Charlotte Brontë say? It *cannot* happen that quickly. As sexy as the Brontës are, Jane and Edwina Rochester can't bang it out that early. It needs angst. I need the readers to scream at the page. Delayed gratification is very Brontë. Not to mention it's oh-so-sweet."

"Says the woman"—I shake the open candy tin sitting between us on my desk— "whom I'm eighty-five percent positive snuck a few pieces before bringing this to me."

"Jensen Antoinette Larsen—" she gasps. "I would *never*… admit to that."

"Worst middle name ever!" I scrunch my nose and let out a chuckling groan.

She pushes her glasses atop her short black bob. "Also, it's my moral obligation to ensure you don't overindulge on the sweet treats before your training session with Medical Mr. Darcy. Wouldn't want you to puke your guts out in front of one of the men you've sworn off but somehow got yourself more entangled with by running a marathon with him."

"First, I am only training with Garrett. He's just a substitute until Anker recovers." I point to my right wrist. "Second, I have a plan. Each time I have inappropriate feelings for Garrett, I'm going to snap this rubber band."

"Are you trying to Pavlov's dog your crush away?" She guffaws.

"Sort of... I want to rewire my brain about the men I choose, and while I'm working on that with Dr Nor, this will help me check those impulses."

"And this is something Dr. Nor recommends?"

I pick up another piece of candy and lean back in my chair. "Not exactly. Since I was supposed to be in New York for Anker's race this week, our regular appointment isn't until next week. So, I'm improvising."

She reaches across the desk and threads our fingers. "Take this with a grain of salt from a woman who maintains a borderline inappropriate emotional affair via texting with her high school crush; if at any point training with Garrett isn't good for you, walk away. I like Garrett. The *sometimes* broody male main character energy aside, he's a good guy. Anker and your birthday party reinforced that for me."

With just a few weeks between my birthday and my brother's, we've held joint parties for most of our lives. It was easier for my parents, but I also think it was a little to make me not feel so bad about my parties not being well-attended the few years we held separate ones. That holds true even today. My brother hosts at his place, and outside of Catherine, my boss Andrew and his husband, and one or two random people, the party is full of my brother's friends and colleagues.

"What did Garrett do at the party?" I ask.

"Miles brought pineapple champagne that I am positive he'd snagged from the English department's back-to-school Hawaiian-themed mixer they'd had a few weeks prior."

"But I drank the champagne he'd brought me for my birthday." My face twists in confusion.

Garrett offered to open it and brought me a glass. There's no way it was pineapple. I have a rare allergy to pineapple, kiwi, and papaya that causes mouth irritation and skin rashes. None of which happened after the two glasses I had consumed.

"Except you didn't. I saw Garrett dump it down the drain before he poured you a glass from a different bottle. You know…the kind that wouldn't result in you going to urgent care on your birthday." She shakes her head. "Miles really is the worst."

"I technically met him because of you." I smirk.

"True, but I never endorsed him. The Wickham and Willoughby types may be fun for a bit, but they are no good for your heart."

"Or overall health, apparently." I blow out a long breath. "I didn't know Garrett did that."

She shrugs. "I don't think he realized I'd spotted him doing it, but I'm not surprised. He always has your back, which is why I am both unworried about him being your running guide and also terrified. While I know Garrett would never hurt you, it doesn't mean you may not still get hurt by him."

Deep in my bones, I know she's right. Garrett would never intentionally hurt me. At least, not in the way other men have. It doesn't mean I can't still have my heart broken. Not by him, but due to this crush. It's why it's called a crush, because unrequited feelings have the power to break us into a million pieces like a boot coming down on a glass. I know this better than anyone.

"Just take care of yourself," she murmurs.

"I will. I promise." My mouth ticks up. "You're a good friend, Catherine. I'm lucky to have you in my life."

She clicks her tongue. "Could you mention that to the hiring panel before my interview next week?"

"Hiring panel?" My eyes go wide. "Did you get an interview?"

"Yep." She stands and shimmies.

"What!" I jump up, rounding the desk to hug her. "Look at you, Ms. Future Associate Professor!"

Since getting her doctorate three years ago, Catherine has been an adjunct at Pemberly and at two nearby community colleges. Academia is notorious for its difficulty to land adjunct positions, let alone full-time gigs like the associate professor one my bestie is up for.

"I have to get the job first."

"Details." I swat the air. "Do you want to do a mock interview this weekend? I do a mean stuffy male English professor impression"—I pitch my voice low— "Dr. Flores-O'Brien, how will your literary badassery translate to the classroom?"

She snorts. "God, you sound like Dr. Reynolds. *Never* do that again!"

"*What?* You don't find it sexy?" Batting my eyes, I prolong her torture with my terrible impression.

"I need a new best friend," she groans.

After finalizing plans for the weekend with Catherine, I get back to the flow of my day. One analysis of campus ramps, two hours of data mining for the grant application, and three student evaluations later, I start to pack up for the day. The day's busyness keeps my brain from wandering to anxious places—like my first training session with Garrett.

With each tick of the clock closer to four-thirty, the knot in my stomach pulls tighter. It's the first time since I agreed to a second chance on this friendship that I am seeing him. Between that and the worry about tripping him or falling on my face tonight, my nerves tingle with worry.

"Jenny, luv, heading out?"

I halt upon hearing Miles's silky English accent slinking into my office alcove. "Yep," I say briskly, plucking up the bag with my workout clothes and sneakers for me to change into.

"Pity. It's been days since I've seen you."

Six to be exact, but who's counting? There's been nothing from him since his lone text, hoping I got home safe after he ditched me for Kayla. No calls or texts to check in with me about Anker. Something—thanks to Catherine—I know he's aware of. Adding to the reasons why a crush on him was a huge mistake. One I don't want to repeat.

"Perhaps you'd like to keep me company instead. We can grab a quick bite before my evening class."

Mouth drawn into a firm line, I tug my bag onto my shoulder before unfolding my cane. "I'm headed out. Maybe *Kayla* can keep you company."

"Kayla..." he makes a dismissive noise. "She's at some Women in Academia function." He leans on the front of my desk.

"And you're not going with her?" I round my desk.

"Those things are dreadful. Not to mention it's only for women in academia, which I am not." Head tilted, he huffs a breathy laugh. "Are *you* jealous?"

"No."

It's a half-truth. As aware as I am that Miles Calloway isn't the man for me, the dregs of my dying crush twinges in my chest. For the last ten months, this man has occupied so many of my romantic daydreams. He doesn't deserve my attention, but still, he has it. I'm a work in progress, after all.

"Someone is a terrible liar… Jealous looks good on you." He reaches over and brushes a lock of my hair behind my ear. "Kayla and I are just friends."

"I'm well aware of your version of friendship." Scoffing, I step back, putting distance between us.

"Jenny," he coos.

"It's Jensen. Not Jenny," I say, my jaw tight.

"Wait"—he tilts his head—"Are you truly angry with me?"

"Yes... No... Ugh..." I cringe.

"Which is it?"

Eyes closed, I slosh a breath. "Both."

My insides are a boondoggle of emotions. I'm angry and disappointed. At him, sure, but mostly at me. I'm disappointed that I fell for him. I'm angry that despite everything that I still care that he hasn't reached out to me in the last six days.

"I think I'm more mad at me than you..." My shoulders slump with the hard sigh that rolls through me. "Though I don't appreciate the comparison to Jenny Wren. I'm not your —or anyone else's—inspirational porn."

"The comparison is meant to be complimentary," he says, affronted.

"It's not. It's patronizing."

"I thought you liked the nickname."

"I don't." Indignation roils inside me.

This is a played-out song that I've heard time and time again. *You inspire me. You're amazing. Blah, blah, blah...* It's tiresome to serve as inspiration porn for others. Especially from a man I wanted to see me as something else entirely.

"You never... If I had known..." he says softly.

I rub my temples. "I know. I didn't say anything."

"Why?"

I motion between us. "Because I liked when you called me Jenny... Until I knew who Jenny Wren was. Part of me thought..." I shake my head.

"Thought what?"

"That I was special." My admission is quiet.

"You are. Jen... Jensen, please forgive me." He steps close, placing his hand on my upper arm. "I care about you."

"Did you care about her when you ditched her at the bar?" A deep bass booms into the room.

"Excuse me?" Miles spins.

Blinking, I turn my head toward the voice. "Garrett? What are you doing here? You're twenty minutes early."

"I had a meeting at the medical school today," he says as if that explains everything.

"Bloke, what was that ditched her comment about?" Miles says.

"I think you know," Garrett grits, his words pointed like spears aimed and ready for attack.

"Enlighten me."

Garrett stalks closer, anger radiating off him. "You got her to stay with you at the bar and then deserted her... Does that enlighten you?"

"Garrett." His name is a warning from my lips.

"What are you talking about?"

"Am I not speaking plainly enough for you? Should I speak slower?" he seethes. "You left her at the bar."

"I left her with Edward." Miles bats at the air like it's nothing.

Like *I'm* nothing. While I don't want to be doted on or fussed over, I would like the people in my life to show more care about my safety.

"Pathetic." Garrett's grunted response is reminiscent of a guard dog's low growl. "You tell her brother you had her and then leave her with someone she doesn't know without a single word or asking her if she's okay."

"What's your problem, bloke?"

"You. I don't like the way you've treated Jensen."

"How very cliché alpha male of you." Smugness radiates from Miles. "The last time I checked, Jensen is an adult woman who doesn't need someone with a hero complex to swoop in."

"No but she needs, deserves, to be respected enough by

the people in her life to give a shit about her feelings and not just leave her behind without a care for how it may make her feel." He moves closer, towering over Miles. "Did you even check in on her? Wonder why she's here and not still in New York?"

"I texted that night, but didn't hear from her. When Catherine said her brother was hurt, I just assumed she was busy with that."

"The *she* you are speaking of is right here and can speak for herself." I hiss, glaring at both men.

"Sorry," Garrett mumbles.

"See, as I said, she's an adult woman able to make her own decisions. Perhaps you should learn to respect that." Miles juts his chin toward Garrett.

"Yes, I am." I stand just a little straighter. "But men who ditch me at the bar and, despite knowing about my brother getting hurt, that haven't reached out in six days to check in on me, don't get to lecture people on respect."

Garrett may be overstepping, but it comes from a good place. He's a natural protector. Just like with the pineapple champagne that I now know about, he sees danger and swoops in. I wonder how much is imprinted into the DNA of who he is versus the response to losing Val. Either way, I don't appreciate Miles—of all people—chiding Garrett about respecting me. It's not his place, and his behavior telegraphs a lack of respect for me.

"I…uhh…" He tugs at his blond hair. "Shit. That was a dick move," he says, turning to face me. "Jen…Jensen, I am sorry. For that, and for everything." Miles releases a hard breath and steps close. "I understand that I acted carelessly and hurt you, but that was never my intention, and I am truly sorry. I do care for you, please let me show you. May I take you to dinner? Please?" A soft coaxing nature punctuates his plea.

A tug-of-war rages inside me between what I know I

should do and those old wants. The intensity of Miles's focus twines around me, its warmth tugging me towards saying yes to his invitation. An invitation lathered in everything but what it should be. It's not desire for me. It's guilt.

"I accept your apology from earlier, but not your dinner invitation," I say, my spine straight.

"Alright…" He steps back. "Good night, Jensen." Turning, he leaves.

Tense silence takes up all the space between where I stand in front of my desk and where Garrett looms near the entryway. My limited vision tethered to his figure. Posture stiff, his stare is locked on me. He reminds me of a wild animal trying to assess if I'm friend or foe.

My sigh teeters between annoyance and relenting. "We may be friends, but you're an asshole."

"I know…" Garrett clears his throat. "At least I didn't punch him."

Laughter bubbles out of me. The earnestness in his ridiculous statement sends me into a fit of giggles.

"True." I shake my head.

"But I overstepped." He blows out a long breath. "I always do with you. I just don't want to see you get hurt."

"Neither do I, but it's in *my* job description to take care of myself, not yours."

"Friends take care of each other." He moves toward me.

"True." I tip my head up to him. "But in the future, *friend*, let me handle Miles or other men unless I request backup, okay?"

"Okay." He scrubs his hands down his face. "Sorry again."

"I know you are." I sigh. "I know it comes from a good place. It's just who you are. You're protective of…your friends." I wave my hand at him. "Have you always been this way, or…" I close my mouth.

"Or is this because of Val?"

"Yeah…" I rake my teeth along my lower lip. In the same

breath that I call him out for overstepping my boundaries, I do the same to him. *Classic Jensen.*

"I don't want to see the people I care about get hurt. If I have the ability to stop it, I will."

"And you care about me," I whisper and flick the rubber band twice against my wrist. Its sting settling the threatening belly swoop.

"Of course. We're friends." He rakes his fingers through his chestnut strands. "That doesn't change the fact that I crossed a line. Tell me your boundaries, and I'll try my best to follow."

"You'll *try* your best?"

"I never want to break a promise to you." The upward tug of his mouth is evident in his gentle timbre.

I flick the rubber band again. "Turnip."

"What?" He cocks his head.

"Anytime we cross that invisible line with each other, we say 'turnip' and that lets us know to stop. Boundaries are good, but I also know there are some that we may never realize we have, or times when it's not easy to talk about certain things. This way we have a safe word to reel both of us back, because let's face it, it's only a matter of time before one of us crosses another line."

"Turnip it is."

"Great. Now let me go change, so we can get this disaster movie that will be our first training session going." I grab my bag. "And after, you're buying me a latte. It's a special occasion after all, so today I get two."

9

MILE NINE
ROPE PLAY

The lamp posts lining the path leading towards the campus's visitors' parking lot hum awake as sunset approaches. Garrett and I stop by his SUV to drop off my purse and bag of clothes before we head to the track around the soccer field for our first training session. The entire way, I prattle on about my excitement that the campus coffee shop rolled out their holiday drinks earlier than normal this year.

"Do you have any idea the self-restraint it took for me not to go back for a second sugar cookie latte today?" I preen, just a bit, as we arrive at his vehicle.

"Your glucose levels will erect monuments to your self-control," he says wryly, digging something out of his backseat.

"Be nice or I won't invite you to the ribbon-cutting ceremony," I toss my bag into the passenger's side and pivot to face him.

"I have something for you." He hoists up a shopping bag.

"Is it a sugar cookie latte?" I coo.

"No," he grunts and hands me the bag.

"Boo!" Smirking, I take it. "What..." Brow creased, I dig into the bag and feel around and pull out a thick elastic exercise band and several different types of rope. "What is this?" I scrunch my nose. "Are you going to tie me up if I'm a naughty girl?"

"The thought has crossed my mind," he says, his rumbly tenor vibrating through my entire body.

"You have?" I breathe, trying to fight the mental image of Garrett's strong hands wrapping rope around my wrists and securing me to the headboard.

My body served up for his leisurely exploration. His hands trailing over every inch of my bare skin—down my throat to my collarbone, over the swell of my breasts, past my belly, and gripping my thighs before dipping his head between my legs and drinking me up like I'm the sugar cookie latte.

Oh god... I flick the rubber band on my wrist to combat the little coil cranking tight in my core with the idea of being at Garrett's mercy.

He coughs. "It's for tethering us together while running."

"Yeah... Ha. Ha..." With an awkward laugh falling out of me, I snap—for good measure—at the rubber band again. "I know. I'm just messing with you. Don't be pervy."

We will just ignore that I'm the one being pervy. Garrett brings rope for guide running purposes, and I want to live out some dormant, low-stakes bondage play that I had no idea lived inside me.

"I thought we could try different types out to see what works best for us. The band"—he pulls it from the bag—"keeps us snug together, but the rope will give you the ability to fluctuate how much slack or closeness you want. We can experiment."

"This is sweet." I grin, running my fingers along the braided rope.

"It's not a big deal. Anker mentioned it. He said you just did human guide for the 5K, but this might be a better idea for a marathon."

It's standard for most blind/guide pairs to use some sort of tether to maintain contact during races. Human guide is great for walking but proves challenging for running. The height differential aside, exercise means a lot of sweat. That can make it difficult to hold onto someone, especially for 26.2 miles. A tether allows a runner to remain connected to their guide but have the freedom to move.

"Let's test this one out." Selecting the thinner rope, I hold it up.

"Okay." He nods. "Do you want to leave your cane in the car, or do you want me to hold it? I thought we could just power walk tonight. It might be a good idea for our first few sessions to just focus on getting comfortable with each other."

I curl my hand tighter around my cane's handle. This is part of it. I know this. Running with my cane isn't possible. The cane poses a safety risk if holding it, and slows you down if strapped to you. It's best to have someone else hold it until you cross the finish line.

The idea of leaving it behind tightens the knot in my stomach just a little tighter. With the cane, I am safe. It not only helps me navigate spaces and find any obstacles that could trip me up, but also ensures I have the key to my own rescue in my hand. The cane is like a fail-safe guarantee that I'll never be left behind... *Not again.*

"Hey..." He places his palms on my shoulders, their heaviness soothing the worry sloshing inside me. "I can hold your cane."

"But it will slow us down." A furrow dips my brow.

"We're just starting, so no need to worry about timing. This is about getting comfortable with this. With each other. I'll hold onto your cane, so you know it's right there. That way you can practice without it, and if you need a mental break all you need to do is say 'turnip,' we'll stop, and I'll give you your cane."

My mouth pulls up with his use of our safe word. It's

supposed to be for our emotional boundaries, which I guess this is one. It's probably the biggest one that I have. As Anker says, I have trust issues. I don't trust that people won't hurt me. That they won't leave me behind. It's so cliché, but it's my truth.

Friends take care of each other. Garrett's words from my office echo inside me. He's right. Real friends have each other's backs. Just like they pour pineapple champagne down the drain, so their allergic friend doesn't drink it. They say nothing about it, so that same friend just smiles and thinks the man she likes brought her a delicious bottle of bubbly to celebrate her birthday.

I fold my cane and hand it to him. "Okay."

The sun hangs low over the quiet soccer field. We're the only people on the track. Despite that, I offer no slack. For the first lap around the track, I remain snug to Garrett. With each step, my muscles coil tight, seeming to brace for any possible misstep. The rope tethers us to one another, wrapped around each of our hands. Heart racing, we move around the track at a brisk pace.

"Bend," Garrett says, as we round the track.

I smile. Throughout our lap, he's called out changes in the path, including straightaways, bends, and ruts. I take a mental note to say something to the athletic department about the need to fill in some of these ruts that could lead to injuries.

Despite Garrett's communication, I remain locked to him. His large form is a step in front of me. I know I should loosen my grip, but anxiety pulses through me.

"How are you doing?"

"Awesome," Teeth gritted, I tug at the rope.

"Sure about that? Any closer and I'd be giving you a piggyback ride," he teases, as we start the second lap.

"Is that an option?"

"No," he laughs.

"Worst guide ever!" I pout.

"You hate this."

"So much!" I whine with the conviction of a toddler being told they have to eat their vegetables, which I kind of am.

"But you're still doing it." The upward drag of his mouth is audible in his encouraging tone. "You've not turniped me once."

"That's not a word." I bite my lower lip, tamping down the wide grin threatening to belt across my face.

"It should be. It's a fantastic word," he says, laughter punctuates his tone. "Seems like a real missed opportunity for one of your deep-voiced audiobook narrators to growl *turniped*"—his voice somehow gets impossibly lower— "or whatever nonsense they get up to in your dirty audios."

"Erotic audios." My correction is breathy, which we can pretend it's from our power walk's pace and not from the way his deep bass pulses through me. I also won't pretend that Garrett's voice isn't in my auditory spank bank.

"Pardon...erotic." He huffs a chuckle. "Straightaway."

My head tilts. We're halfway through the second lap without me realizing it. And, somehow, I've loosened the death-like grip on the rope, just a bit. It's now *almost* death-like. *If that's a thing?*

"Thank you," I say softly.

I feel him shrug his shoulders before he follows with a mumbled, "Just making small talk."

Soup. This man is soup. He nourishes. He's hot. He comes in a can that you need to pry open. Soup can also scald and burn if you try to eat it too soon. That's something I need to remind myself.

"Rut on the left, moving to the right," he calls out and moves us closer to the fence that hugs the field.

Anxiety may cascade within me, but it doesn't stop me. Even if I haven't loosened the reins completely, I still proceed. That is such a huge victory in itself. As we move down the first straight-away of our second lap, I offer just a little bit of slack. Not much. I still remain close enough to Garrett for his body heat to caress me like soothing kisses against my forehead, a promise that everything will be okay.

"Bend," he calls out again as we round the track and start our third lap.

The pattern of our path imprints itself into me. Each turn. Each little dip. Each avoided rut. My fingers twitch against the rope before I loosen the slack a little more. Garrett offers two quick tugs of the rope as I increase our distance. It's so quick, but those two tugs almost paint his pleased smile that I'm pushing past my own boundaries.

I must trust that Garrett will keep me safe. Just as he has to trust that I'll do the same thing. So often, people assume the human guides are the ones with all the responsibility. That's such a short-sighted way of looking at it. The visually impaired person is just as responsible for their pair's safety. This is a relationship where we both need each other in order to make it to the finish line safely.

The more familiar I get with this track, the less holding tight to Garrett I do. By the time we round for the fourth, and final lap, I've allowed myself to slacken the rope enough that I no longer feel his body's heat lapping against me.

"Crossing the finish line, but let's gradually slow to a walk before we stop," he calls out.

"Yup," I say, panting just a little bit. I try not to fixate on how his words are even-paced as if this is nothing, despite my shallow breath.

"Stopping," he says, as our now gentle walk slows to a halt. "You did it." He turns to face me.

Inhaling deeply, I look around the track. We're just where we started, but we're not. I did it. I power walked an entire mile without stopping. Without tripping him or myself. I trusted him, and more importantly, myself.

"We did it." I let out a breathless laugh.

He pulls on the rope, tugging me a little closer before unwrapping the binding from my hand. "I'm just the service human," he says, a smirk playing in his tone.

"Nope." I take his hand, threading it in mine. "We're a team, remember? I can't do this without you, so this is half yours."

"You can do this without me."

"Should I find a new service human?" I flash a sassy grin.

"Absolutely not."

That blasted pitter-patter ramps up in my chest with the swiftness of his response. Protectiveness of me. Loyalty to Anker. Dare I even daydream, jealousy? Whatever his reason, delight ripples within me at how exasperated he gets at the idea of me doing this with anyone else.

It isn't good for me to get caught up in those feelings. Clearing my throat, I drop his hand.

"That was a good first session." Nibbling on my lower lip, I pluck the rubber band at my wrist. The sting does its job, and I step back.

"Yeah." He rolls the rope around his hand. "One mile down."

"Only 25.2 more to go."

"Piece of cake."

Thanks to the darkening sky, I can't see his smile, but warmth radiates from him. I can almost picture the lopsidedness of his lips. It's as though his mouth isn't sure if it wants to smile or remain in a firm line.

"Piece of cake." My grin meets his. "Now, I want cake."

"Maybe they'll have a cake pop at the coffee shop. Here's your cane." He hands me my cane.

"Cake and a latte? Someone's breaking his own rules." I wink.

"Those aren't rules. They were suggestions." He shakes his head. His warm grin is evident with the lightness that underscores his words. "You can have anything you want."

Not anything.

"But first, let's stretch. There's a patch of grass about ten feet forward we can use."

"Do we need to stretch? I mean, we only power walked. It wasn't exactly high-intensity." I wrinkle my brow.

"True, but we should get into the habit. It's part of conditioning your body and helps aid in muscle recovery. That way, you're not stiff or experiencing muscle ache. Have you been doing the stretches I recommended after your morning runs?"

"You said those were suggestions." I point at him and hope the dim light from the lamp posts situated around the track hides the guilt flushing my cheeks.

"*Highly recommended* suggestions to avoid injury and muscle stiffness." He steps closer. "Have you been extra achy the last few days?"

"Is *achy* the medical term?" I make air quotes with my hands.

"Yeah. Achy." A defiant smirk plays in his joking exasperation.

Only Garrett can somehow be both annoyed and impish at the same time. It's the strangest combo, but somehow he wears it perfectly, like it's a jacket made just for him. It seems like as much as I may drive him batty, he enjoys it.

"Well… Maybe just a little achy," I say, ignoring the twinge in my calves.

"Come on then, doctor's orders."

I snap the rubber band twice against my wrist after experiencing the little clench low in my belly with the pitch of his low bass. Who knew this training session would reveal an unknown bondage kink and desire to be told what to do that I apparently have. Next week's session with Dr. Nor is going to be wild.

We claim the small patch of grass near the track's outside ring. The lone oak tree at the edge serves as a perfect barrier for us to do calve stretches. My calves almost sing with relief from the stretch.

"Oh god," I hum as I yank up my leg for a quad stretch. My palm flat against the tree to steady myself.

"See."

"I told you so's aren't cute." I roll my eyes.

"I'm always cute."

Laughter barks out of me.

"See." He bumps me with his shoulder, causing me to lose my balance. "Whoa…" His hands come to my hips, steadying my swaying body.

I release my leg, which falls to join the other on the ground, and my hands come to the tree's trunk.

"I got you," he rasps, pulling me against him.

A breathy laugh escapes, but stops at the realization that my back is pressed against his front. For a moment, I sink into the strange, cozy sensation of his firm chest. The mix of his body's heat, the scent of sweat, and his spicy cologne envelops me. It's reminiscent of being tucked in at night—snug, safe, and warm.

"We should get on the ground." His hot breath whispers along my skin.

"What?" I breathe into the electric charge that zings from where his fingers press into my soft flesh. Even through my yoga pants' thin layer, his touch brands me.

"Hamstring stretches." He steps back, but his hands remain on my hips.

I look over my shoulder and nod. "Okay."

"Okay." He releases me. "Sit on your butt with your legs in front of you."

"Okay." I flick the rubber band a few times before crouching to the grass.

I sit, stretching out my legs. The grass is cool against my backside, making me miss the temporary cozy spot I had pressed up against him.

"Bend one leg, keeping the other one straight, and then reach across your body toward the opposite side."

Nodding, I do just that. My muscles groan happily with the stretch.

"It's important to incorporate stretching into your training," he says, stretching his long legs in front of him. He sits near me, mirroring my positions, except facing me.

"For someone who says I'm in charge, you're awfully bossy."

"For someone who does yoga once a week, you're weirdly anti-stretching," he quips back.

"I'm not anti-stretching." I switch legs. "I'm pro-sleep."

"What?" He chuckles.

"I train in the mornings. Ten minutes of stretching is ten fewer minutes to sleep in. It's already bad enough I have to get up so early to train and get to work on time."

"Hip flexor stretch. Lie flat, keep one leg out, bend the other, and pull it toward your chest."

"Okay." I follow his instructions.

"You could always exercise at night. Then you have all the time. That's what I do."

"Just go home and *tell that bag* after a day dealing with patients and unruly residents?" My mouth twitches into a smile.

"Something like that. It helps me sleep."

I sit up. "Do you have trouble sleeping?"

"Sometimes." He sits up. "And before you ask... Yes, since Val died."

Bending my knees, I wrap my arms around them and look

over at him. "Do you have nightmares or intrusive thoughts that keep you awake?"

"Intrusive thoughts."

"Like what?"

My brain is screaming for me to shut up. To change the subject or just remain quiet, but the need to know more pulses within me. It's not just the natural curiosity I have, but Garrett is like a puzzle I want to put together. The image of this man is still fuzzy. Just as I think I know him, he reveals a little more. Each piece confirms the things I know to be true about him, but opens up whole other chapters about his story.

"All the ways I failed her," he whispers.

The pain underscoring his words surges an ache in my chest. It's raw and unabashed in self-blame. All I know is it was an accident, and he wasn't there. He'd said in the thirty minutes from the time he had told her to text him when she got home to when he was called about the accident, he'd lost her.

"What makes you think *you* failed her?"

"Because she's not here," he says, his voice small.

"Garrett," I breathe, rubbing my hand against the ache in my chest.

"Turnip," he rasps.

I want to ask more. Not to poke and prod at that wound, but to help dig out the pain that infects him. If the last few years of therapy with Dr. Nor has taught me anything, it's that the loud crack of broken hearts are not mended in silence. This is another piece of that story he's spoken out loud to me. Just like with marathon training, he needs to walk before he runs. And this seems like a big first step for Garrett. As much as I want to push, I want to honor.

"Turnip." I smile.

Nodding, he stands up. "Wanna get that latte?" He reaches down and offers me his hand.

"Yeah, I do." I take his hand, allowing him to pull me up.

"You really should stretch after your morning workouts," he says, bending to scoop up my folded cane which is resting at the base of the tree trunk.

"And *I'm* the yappy yorkie." I laugh. "You're like a dog with a bone sometimes."

"Just don't want to see you injured." He hands me the cane.

That comment blends with the brief brush of our hands. It's charge crisscrosses within me. It feels like this is about more than just achy, stiff muscles. It's about keeping me safe. Not just in the big ways like with the pineapple champagne, but in the tiny ways. Teasing me about eating my greens. The annoyance with Miles. He doesn't always do it in the right way, but I'm seeing that his sole mission in life may be to take care of the people he cares about, and he cares about me. We're friends, after all, and I'm starting to realize that to him we've always been.

"I could always add it to our shared training calendar. It actually has value compared to someone's twice-a-day reminder for me to *turn my frown upside down.*" He bumps me with his shoulder as we move towards the sidewalk that loops through campus.

Head tipped back, I groan. "Fine. I'll get up earlier and make sure I stretch, but I get to rage text you grumpy messages complaining about it."

"Counteroffer… if you want to work out at night I can drive you home. That way you can have more time at night to work out. I'd imagine the bus eats up a lot of time." He stops and turns to face me. "Or if you want to keep your morning routine, I can drive you to work. The hospital is right next to the university, and you live five minutes from me."

"This is sweet, but not necessary."

"It's selfish, not sweet. This way I can avoid grumpy texts." An earnest grin radiates within his cheeky timbre.

"Yeah, but you are at the hospital before seven a.m. most days. Not to mention you're there until after five." I motion to him.

"Didn't realize you were keeping tabs on me."

"I'm not." I bite back the flirty smile that flexes at the corners of my lips. "Anker has just mentioned it a few times."

"Anker has also said I need more work/life balance, so you'd be doing me a favor if you let me drive you home."

"You really are a dog with a bone." Laughter vibrates through me. "It would be nice. I'm so mentally wiped after peopling most days that not having to deal with the bus would be a relief."

Don't get me wrong, I'm grateful for the public transportation available. Nonetheless, it's still taxing. Buses run late, or the schedules change. If I miss one, it can be up to thirty minutes until the next one comes. The PA system announcing the stops often breaks, or the driver sometimes forgets to call out the stops. Not to mention the other humans can sometimes be a lot to deal with. I'm on guard the entire time, from when I arrive at the point to pick me up until I get home.

"Is dealing with people a lot for you?" he asks as he ushers me down the path.

"It can be, but it's less about the people. I spend most days hypervigilant about my surroundings, which can be mentally exhausting."

Situations like at the bar the other night is a prime example. Tension coils in every muscle as I track who's talking and the flow of conversation. It's tiring to be on constant alert in my environment. The moment I relax is when things happen —like glasses being accidentally knocked off the table.

"Going out is fine, especially when it's some place I'm familiar with or with people who get it."

"Is that why we tend to do Harkey's followed by the

creamery most Fridays?" he asks. The jangle of keys tells me that we're getting close to his vehicle.

"I guess. Anker sets up our happy hour outings." A crease wrinkles my brow. "Though, I imagine he'd not be up for it this week."

"Likely not… We're at my SUV." A little chirp accompanies his announcement. "Let me get the door for you. We should bring happy hour to him." He opens the door.

"Like we learn to make his frilly cocktails and have them at his place?"

"I was thinking more on the lines of bringing pizza and a bottle of wine."

"Plus garlic knots?" I bat my eyes.

"And a salad," he counters with a cheekiness.

"Monster!"

10

MILE TEN
STALKER DARCY

My heels click against the cement walkway that loops through the center of campus. The bustle of a late afternoon twines around me. Students huddle at outdoor tables outside the campus coffee shop. Conversations float in the cool Santa Ana breeze. In the distance, someone strums a guitar.

It's a typical autumn day at Pemberly. I pull tighter on my jacket. The crisp, late afternoon air causes my loose strands to brush against my face. Southern California isn't as cold as some places, but I'm a wimp anytime the temps drop below seventy. Thank goodness I agreed to Garrett driving me home after work. The siren song of his SUV's butt-warmer calls to me. Even if it's only a short ten-minute drive from campus to my place, the heated seats are an extra delicious bonus.

"Jensen!"

I stop and tilt my head toward the direction of the velvet-smooth female English accent. The only Englishwoman I know—besides feisty historical romance female main characters—is Kayla.

"Sorry, that was rude. You may not recognize my voice

yet." She clears her throat. "It's Kayla O'Leary. We met at Harkey's Hideaway the other night."

"Hi, Kayla... Yeah, I remember." I shift foot-to-foot. "How are you?"

"Excellent. You?"

"Awesome," I say through a tight smile.

I don't have *ill* feelings toward Kayla. She was pleasant at the bar, but she was the woman Miles left me for. Even though I know we weren't a couple, I still feel awkward around her.

"I am glad I ran into you. Miles mentioned you were supposed to be in New York this week, but that trip was interrupted by your brother being injured. I was sorry to hear that. How is he?"

A sweet, delicate aroma, like a rose garden in bloom, wafts off her. It's probably expensive. Like everything else about Kayla. According to Catherine, Kayla is tall and lean with long, bronzy blonde hair and Arctic blue eyes. She's always polished and glossy with the perfect shade of red lipstick that gives off "don't fuck with me" energy. It's unlikely she's ever been ditched at a bar before.

"He's on the mend. Thank you for asking." I offer a smile.

"Wonderful. It's terrifying when someone we love is unwell or hurt. My sister lives in London with her husband and my nieces. If something happened to her, I would be a wreck."

"Yeah... Especially when you're so far away from them." I scrunch my face. "Though I wouldn't know. I've never really been that far away from my family."

I'm pathetic. The corners of my lips tick down. At twenty-nine, I've never lived more than a ten-minute drive from a family member. It may have been one of the reasons I chose Pemberly for undergrad. Because Anker was a student here and then attended their medical school. Whereas Kayla resides an entire ocean away from her family.

"Besides Oxford, this is the furthest I've been away from my family," she says.

"Really?"

"Yeah. As much as I am enjoying my time here, it does get a little lonely to be so far away from them." Her admission is soft.

My heart twinges with her vulnerability. I can almost picture the downward curve of her mouth. It's hard to imagine the confident woman who commanded all the attention at the bar the other night showing this soft side.

Loneliness is something I understand. Relationships—even friendships—have been a struggle for me. I don't have other friends. I never have, despite how much I just wanted to belong. So much of my life was spent with my nose pressed up against the window, hoping to be let in and scared about what might happen if I was.

"What do you miss?" I shift foot-to-foot. "I mean, what things from home do you miss doing the most?"

"Brunch." Her sigh is laced with wistfulness. "My friends back home and I would go religiously. There's a pub near my flat that serves a modern take on an English breakfast. It had all the traditional items but with a twist; champagne, pastries, eggs, beans, and vegan blood sausage."

I guffaw. "Vegan blood sausage sounds atrocious."

"Vegan *anything* is a dreadful waste of food in my opinion, but do not repeat that. Half the department leans vegan, so I may be flayed."

"Would vegans flay a human?"

"Excellent point." Head tipped back, she lets out a musical laugh.

"Your secret is safe with me... Although I should warn you that I do like almond milk," I say with a cheeky expression.

"I shall endeavor to like you nonetheless." A smile is audible in her jest. "I also wanted to apologize to you."

"For what?"

"I didn't know that Miles and you had something going on when I left with him the other night. I feel terrible. I would never interfere with someone's relationship like that."

"No need to apologize." I bat at the air. "We didn't have anything going on. Not really. At least, nothing you should feel bad about, especially if you didn't know."

"That does make me feel better. Though, for the record, nothing happened with Miles. When I learned the truth, I gave him quite the tongue-lashing." She shakes her head. "Stupid boys masquerading as men."

"I don't disagree." I laugh. "Who told you?"

"Miles, of course."

"What?" I choke out. "*He* told you."

"He did. He's devastated." She tilts her head and clicks her tongue. "Well, I suppose as devastated as a modern-day Frank Churchill-type could be."

"He's devastated?" My slow, deliberate speech is akin to pinching yourself awake.

The idea of Miles Calloway being devastated over me is surreal. This is the man who devastates women, not the other way around. Despite my misguided crush, I'm quite aware of his reputation. He's been linked to several members of the female faculty and staff, along with a few rumors about smitten grad students.

"I'm not a Miles apologist. He's a bit of a cad, but one with a heart. Calloway is your classic late bloomer. He didn't come into his good looks and charm until graduate school, resulting in his current *Peter Pan* fuckboy era.".

"Miles?" I blink.

"Yes. Apparently, he had braces until he was twenty-five and spent most weekends writing Shakespeare fan fiction retellings." She shrugs. "Though I actually think that last one makes him more interesting."

"What does this have to do with me?" I gesture at her.

"He likes you. He really likes you, but he was caught up in his fuckboy ways. I think he thought…"

"That I'd just wait for him." I shake my head, because I may have done just that for him.

If Garrett hadn't shown up and used his Mr. Darcy Jedi mind tricks to get me to come home with him and *tell the bag*, I may still be waiting for Miles. Revulsion, not for Miles, but for me, sloshes in my belly with the thought.

"He's been a fool, and I think he's just now realizing that. Listen, I am not telling you what to do. Miles is a twat."

I snort. "Yes, he is."

"But he is a sorry twat. Whether you want to forgive him or not is up to you. I just wanted to let you know that I'm not interested in Miles. Never have been. Never will be. He's nice. Just not my type. I only went with him because he's the only friend I've made since moving here."

Brow wrinkled, I tilt my head. "But you seemed chummy with everyone at the bar."

"Those are colleagues, not friends. Not to mention, they're all men. Not to sound sexist, but I want female friends, especially those around my age. Another reason why I was upset with Miles. Our chat at the bar was brief, but I thought you were lovely and wanted to connect. When I asked Miles if he had your number, he shared everything."

Kayla may be intimidating, but she's also warm. Even at our introduction, though brief, I saw that.

"You call him Peter Pan fuckboy?" I smirk.

"To his face." Pride radiates from her.

"I have a friend who calls him literary fuckboy."

She claps her hands together. "Delicious."

"Catherine and I are going to brunch tomorrow," I blurt. "Do you want to join? I realize it's short notice…"

It's like someone else took over my mouth. It's not just men that I wait for to make the first move. Even with Catherine, she was the one who initiated our friendship. If I'm going to take risks and run a marathon, shouldn't I chart other courses? Not just with romantic relationships, but with friendships? Also, it's just brunch, so if it's a failure, there isn't a great loss. Not to mention she's a visiting professor, so there's a built-in expiration date if I'm wrong.

"I wouldn't want to intrude—"

I flick my wrist dismissively. "No, you'd be a perfect addition. In fact..." A crease notches my brow as if a lightbulb clicks on above me. "Are you on the interview panel for the associate professor position?"

"No. Why?"

"Catherine is interviewing for it, and I was going to do a mock interview pre-breakfast. You know, run her through her paces. Your input would be so valuable"—I swipe the windblown tendrils out of my face—"if you're open to that. No pressure about doing any interview tutoring. The invite isn't contingent. It could just be lady bonding."

"Both the *lady bonding* and the interview tutoring sound lovely. If it truly is not a bother."

"Not at all..." I let out a nervous laugh. "It's not a bother. It's a pleasure."

"Then I would absolutely love to join you two."

"There you are, Jensen," Garrett says, annoyance boosts his low bass.

I pivot towards his voice. "Yes... I am Jensen. Who is this?" I mock-simper.

Garrett's timbre's deep rumble is imprinted into my brain, allowing me to recognize him auditorily. We both know this, but the desire to mess with him is too strong. It's my favorite part about him taking me home each day. *That* and his heated car seats.

Reaching me, he lets out a beleaguered breath. "Smartass."

"My butt does have a genius-level IQ. It may even be in MENSA." I wiggle my backside just a bit.

"Seriously, Jensen." His groan offers a hint of a chuckle.

Yes! He's totally smiling. My wry grin is large, knowing that I got him. Joy cascades within me at Garrett betraying his grumpy nature. It's better than a brownie sundae, minus the cherry. The cherry on top of this dessert would be if I got him to laugh out loud, which I know I will. One day, this man will break and lose himself with me in belly-deep, full body-racking laughs.

"That was quite the greeting," Kayla muses.

"That's Jensen for you." No doubt a poker face expression covers Garrett's face.

"She certainly is," she chuckles. "Kayla O'Leary."

He reaches out his hand. "Garrett Marlowe."

"Nice to meet you."

"Sorry… I am terrible at intros. Garrett, Kayla. Kayla, Garrett"—I motion between us—"though you already know that."

"Stellar," he quips.

"What are you doing here?" My lips pucker into not quite a pout. "You're early, and this isn't even my office. Wait, how did you know I was even here? Are you stalking me? Seriously, we need to discuss putting your overprotective nature in airplane mode.".

"Stalking? Don't flatter yourself, Jensen. Since we're bringing dinner to Anker tonight, I left the hospital a little early. Nobody was at your office, and you didn't answer your phone, so I headed toward the coffee shop near the library because I assumed your sugary latte addiction led you there."

Mouth ticked up into a smirk, I place my free hand on my hip and pop it for emphasis. "Sounds pretty stalkery, would you agree, Kayla?"

"It does skirt the line."

"Seriously?" He laughingly scoffs. "If you picked up your phone once in a while, you'd know I was here."

"It is awfully dashing for your stalker to give you a warning," Kayla teases.

"It is, isn't it? Like something out of an Austen novel." I bat my eyes. "Stalker Darcy."

"You're hilarious," he mutters.

"I'm here all week." I curtsy.

"Speaking of Mr. Darcy, I have a talk at the Austen Literary Society, so I should dash. Garrett, it was nice meeting you."

"And you," he says.

"Jensen, let me air drop my contact information to you, so you can send me the details for brunch tomorrow," Kayla says.

"Good luck," Garrett snarks.

Taking advantage of my close proximity, I give his calf a gentle tap with my cane. "It's only your calls I ignore."

"Your banter with each other is infectious. Looks like Miles may not have a shot after all."

"Excuse…me?" I cough out.

"Blast. Sorry. I have a bad habit of saying the quiet parts out loud." She cringes. "This may be why I struggle finding friends. I can be a lot. Sorry."

A lot. Those two syllables thrum within me, waking up old memories of the many times someone called me that. I know far too well what it's like to be perceived as "too much" or "a lot" to deal with.

Despite mortification's heat creeping up my neck, I like Kayla. In fact, the comment strangely makes me like her more. She may appear poised, but she's as awkward as me. It validates that I'm making the right choice in inviting her to brunch.

"No worries. Garrett and I are just friends."

"Friends," he parrots.

Friends. He doesn't say, "I'm her brother's best friend," but that we're friends. Warmth envelops me with the way he claims it—claims me.

Whoa, stomach! You will not swoop at that thought. Friends, remember.

"Excellent. At least Miles still has a shot, then," she coos and then groans. "I did it again."

"Excuse me?" Garrett grunts.

"Well, I should dash before I say something else obnoxious that causes you to withdraw your brunch invitation. Jensen, I'll see you tomorrow. Garrett, I hope I see you again," she says sweetly.

"Sure." He nods as she turns and walks away. "She seems *nice*?"

"She is. I think I might have made a new friend today."

"I'm glad." His tone is soft.

"Me too."

He twists to face me. "What was that about Miles still having a chance?"

"Nothing." I shrug.

"Jensen, you're not seriously thinking about giving him another chance?" He steps close, his body eclipsing everything.

It should intimidate, but it doesn't. The furnace of his body ensconces me in cozy comfort. What once read as judgment about my life's choices now plays as concern. Garrett may not always say it in the right way, but he cares.

"Stand down, soldier." Smirking, I shake my head. "I'm still on my romantic hiatus."

Despite what Kayla thinks, Miles doesn't have a shot. I may be intrigued by him being devastated over losing me—*allegedly*—but Miles isn't for me. Better yet, I'm not for him, or anyone now.

"Good... He doesn't deserve you—never did," he rasps.

His intense gaze locks on me, pinning me in place. The truth of his words tingles along my nerves. Miles doesn't deserve me.

"What exactly is lady bonding?" Garrett tips his head towards me.

"Buy me a latte and I'll tell you all about it before we head to Anker's." With a bat of my lashes, I tap him with my cane.

"You're obnoxious."

"You're the one who put the idea in my head. I had no desire for a sugar cookie latte until you chastised me for my perfectly innocent addiction." I flash a sweet smile. "They have Diet Dr. Pepper in the cooler."

"Do they?"

"They do," I coo, taking in the almost nonexistent upward curve of his mouth.

"And how do you know that? You don't even drink the stuff?"

"I asked."

"Sounds very stalkery."

"Guess you're a bad influence on me." I bite back my smile.

11

MILE ELEVEN
LADY BONDING

Message from Miles, my phone's robotic voice announces. It's the fifth message since Monday. All of which I've not read.

Curiosity battles with indifference inside me. Though, indifference about Miles Calloway resembles an ill-fitting pair of shoes. It doesn't quite suit, because I'm not indifferent. I won't pretend otherwise. While I don't want him, after dinner with Garrett and Anker last night, I laid in my bed, thinking about Miles.

It wasn't in the typical way I think of him. I didn't daydream about Miles finding a way into my building to knock on my door to declare his feelings in a big romantic gesture from a cheesy rom-com. In fact, the only man who seems to break into my apartment building is Garrett, and neither time was romantic.

Part of me feels bad that Miles' feelings are hurt. Part of me wants to soothe that sting away. Even if I know it's not my doing. I was the one left behind. I was the one with the crush. The woman he thought would always be there.

This is just my curious nature at work. It's like how I often skip ahead to a book's last chapter to know there will be a happy ending. At least with romances, I don't have to do that because there is always one.

Kayla says Miles is devastated. I just want to make sure he's okay, but I worry that opening his messages may detour my course.

"Not going to happen." I turn my ringer off and slide my phone into my purse to head out for brunch with Catherine and Kayla.

Seal Beach's downtown hums with life. Chattering shoppers dip in and out of the boutiques, while others sit at metal bistro tables outside Main Street's many cafes. While my brother and Garrett live in more residential neighborhoods, my building is downtown, offering me walkable access to its businesses, the bus stop, and the beach at the end of the street. It's also a short five-minute walk to Bread, my favorite café/bakery.

"Hey Jensen!" Catherine greets me at the café's entrance. "Oh, look at this cozy sexy fall getup."

With the cool weather and Bread's seating being primarily outdoors, I've layered up. A long, chocolate-brown cardigan, knee-high black boots, a black dress, and a hunter green infinity scarf are paired with gold leaf-shaped dangle earrings that pop against my loose, wavy tendrils. It's cute, but warm.

"Cozy sexy?" I snort, leaning in to examine my friend. "Wait—" I trace up her arms, feeling the smooth fabric of her jacket "—is this a blazer? And are you…" I lean in and sniff. "…wearing perfume?"

She bats me away. "We're doing a mock-interview before we eat our weight in crepes, remember?"

I arch one eyebrow. "Since when do we do rehearsals in full dress?" I reach over, taking her wrist to feel for what I suspect she's wearing. "Oh my gosh, are we wearing Grandma O'Brien's lucky pearl set?"

In the tenure of our friendship, Catherine only pulls out the fancy pearl choker, bracelet, and earrings she'd inherited from her grandmother on special occasions, or when she needs the extra bit of luck.

"Just the bracelet and earrings. Not the necklace. That's showtime only," she tuts playfully.

"Naturally," I sass with a wiggle of my hips.

"Plus, Kayla O'Leary is going to be here."

"It's not a big deal. She's not on the interview panel, so no pressure." I bat at the air.

"Says you," she tuts. "She's the academic spank bank of accomplishments. Like I may want to be her when I grow up."

"You're the same age."

"Exactly!"

I place a hand on my hip. "Also, you're accomplished."

"Not like Kayla. She's tenured. She's published."

I wrinkle my brow. "You're published."

"I've had essays in a collection, co-authored a few papers, and am currently being bullied by my incomplete *Jane Eyre* retelling. It's hardly the *same* thing." She lets out a heavy sigh. "Kayla is a visiting professor from Oxford. She's one of academia's foremost Austen scholars. She's here to host graduate seminars exploring the intersections of gender, class, and sexuality in Ms. Austen's work, while I teach freshmen the proper placement of semicolons."

"Semicolons are very complicated." A scowl twists my face. "Also, my dad would call this some stinkin' thinkin'."

She groans.

I go on, "You're amazing. Look at everything you've accomplished. Be your own measuring stick."

"Ugh." She makes a disgusted noise. "I know. It's momentary imposter syndrome brought on by my nerves about this interview, the lack of progress in my writing, and the envy for hot professor Barbie."

"You are also a hot professor. Let us not forget the boys' baseball team getting in trouble for that top ten hottest professors ranking." I tilt my head and flash a cheeky expression.

"I was only number two." She makes a dismissive gesture.

"I demand a recount!" Kayla's smooth English accent pops our little bestie bubble.

"Kayla! Hi! Hey! You're here!" Spinning towards the sound of her voice, I grin awkwardly, hoping she didn't overhear Catherine calling her hot professor Barbie.

"Hello, ladies. For the record, you're number one in my book. Once we've concluded the mock interview, we'll use our lady bonding time to plan our vengeance for this injustice." Kayla motions to the hostess stand. "Shall we?"

Despite the crowds waiting for a table, Catherine uses her connections to sneak us in without a wait. The hostess, Jela, is one of Catherine's former students. She theorizes that since it's past tense, there are no ethical issues with Jela allowing us to cut the line forming in front of the restaurant.

Tucked into a table in the corner of the outdoor seating area, we place our order. We share a pot of English breakfast tea as Kayla and I put Catherine through her paces in our mock interview. Kayla reads from the questions I prepared but adds a few of her own.

Catherine's essence is reminiscent of a rainbow cutting through a gray sky. She is captivating with every response. Poised. Engaging. It's a sharp contrast from the self-doubting version of herself who appeared in front of the café.

"A proposed course exploring intersectional feminism and romance novels sounds intriguing. The department would be foolish not to scoop you up as an associate professor. Even more foolish to not add that course to the fall semester offerings… I've played with the idea of developing a course on the contemporary politics of the historical romance novel," Kayla muses before sipping her tea.

Catherine clears her throat. "You're a romance reader?"

"Devout. Any Austen scholar worth their weight in hardbacks is a romance reader."

I beam. "Catherine is a romance writer." I flinch at the pinch of my thigh from below the table.

"Oh, what subgenre? Is it published?" Kayla asks.

"It's not finished…" she says softly.

"It's a sapphic *Jane Eyre* retelling where Edwina Rochester is a grumpy ranch owner and Jane is the horse trainer," I add, ignoring the icy glare I'm sure Catherine is tossing my way.

My bestie is too modest at times. What snippets she's let me read are amazing. Perhaps some encouragement from Kayla will help smooth the imposter syndrome getting in Catherine's way from finishing this book.

"What!" Kayla squeals. "Brillant! A Brontë retelling with cowgirls, yes please."

"Agreed!" I hoot.

"Cowboys. Cowgirls. Werewolves. Dukes. Ghosts. I even got into Big Foot shifter romances last summer."

"Big Foot?" Catherine chokes on her drink.

"Don't mock it until you've tried it, *darling*," she coos with a flirty lilt.

"Please tell me there's an audiobook." I laugh.

"Read by Wesley Williamson."

"Yes!" I dance in my seat. "He's my favorite. I even bid on a chance to have a virtual meet and greet with him in a charity auction for Authors Against Book Bans, but lost."

"He's so talented. In fact, the deep voice he does reminds me of that man that you claim is *just a friend*, but gives off 'wants you to ride his face' energy," she says.

Now it's my turn to choke on my tea. "Excuse me?"

"Who's this?" Catherine asks, nudging her knee against mine.

"I believe his name is Garrett. *Apparently*, he's been driving Jensen home most days and was rather worried when he couldn't find her. It was very alpha male. I have an image of him cradling your face and saying"—she pitches her voice low—"'Who hurt you, baby?' before he burns down the world for you."

"He does have protector vibes." Catherine tips her head back and lets out a contented sigh.

"And sit on my face vibes." Kayla bobs her head.

"Agreed."

"He's just a friend." I shift in my chair.

"A friend you have a crush on." Catherine's sing-song taunt hits me like children singing, "Garrett and Jensen sitting in the tree k-i-s-s-i-n-g."

"Delicious! I must hear everything!" Kayla vibrates with excitement. "That man looks like he'd press you against a wall and do things to you that would crack the house's foundation, but then hold you tenderly after."

Something clenches low in my belly at that image. My legs wrapped around Garrett. His powerful body thrusting into me. His gruff voice a low rumble as he whispers dirty things into my ears.

"Someone's complexion is a little rosy right now," Catherine teases.

"It sure is." Kayla pours us each another cup of tea. "Please tell me we're transitioning to the lady bonding portion of brunch, because it's clear there's more to the 'just friends' moniker you're wearing with that man."

"There really isn't." I flick the rubber band at my wrist.

Catherine grabs my wrist and holds it up. "Says the woman trying to Pavlov dog her crush away."

"Lady bonding must commence. I need to know everything! How about we nix the tea and order mimosas?" Kayla claps her hands together.

By the second glass, and with our half-eaten meals in front

of us, I've let it all out. This includes that I do have a crush on Garrett. I may always have a bit of a crush on him. But liking someone doesn't make them right for you.

"I realize I only observed you two for five minutes, but you seem to have a real connection. There's a fondness there. It's playful and comfortable," Kayla says.

"You're not imagining their connection. There's definitely something there. Whether just a sexual tension, or more, I'm not sure, but there is something." Catherine sips her mimosa.

"Maybe just fuck and see what happens," Kayla suggests.

"I'm not built for that." I frown. "Also, it would be too messy. Not just with Anker, and the fact that Garrett wouldn't just disappear from my life if things got awkward. But he's still in the deep waters of grief about his wife."

Does one ever get over a loss like that? Our beagle died when I was twelve, and despite my love of dogs, I can't even think of getting another one. I can't imagine losing the love of my life.

"So—" Kayla places her hands below her chin and leans on her elbows "—we have one man who realizes he's fucked up and is trying to win you back, and one who isn't yet able to admit his own feelings. Classic love triangle."

"Or why choose?" Catherine snarks.

I scrunch my nose. "Garrett would murder Miles. He hates him."

"He's awfully protective," Kayla says smugly.

"Guess that nixes the why choose romance theory."

I roll my eyes. "I'm on a dating sabbatical. My romantic compass is broken. Until I get to the root of why I make poor choices, there will be nobody... And even if I wasn't, neither are appropriate. Miles is only interested because I no longer am, and Garrett is... Garrett.

There's a string of reasons why Garrett Marlowe is an inappropriate choice. He's my brother's best friend—not to mention his boss—which complicates everything. Even if the thought of him as "forbidden fruit" does pulse a tingle between my legs.

Then there's Val.

Kayla plucks the bottle out of the little ice bucket from the corner of the table and pours me more champagne. "I understand. I'm taking a break from dating, as well."

"Is it because you're here temporarily?" Catherine holds up her glass for a refill.

"Sort of. While I still think Garrett and you should smash, I'm a big believer in protecting your heart. Last year, I had what was supposed to be a casual thing with a doctor from a NGO. He was only in town for a few months before heading to his next assignment in Congo. I caught feelings, and he did not."

"Oh, Kayla." I trail my hand along the table to find her forearm and squeeze it.

"We had an understanding. I knew the rules. No feelings. No commitment. I went in with my eyes wide open and still got a broken heart." She sighs. "Whatever happens or doesn't happen with Garrett, protect your heart."

"I will," I whisper.

12

MILE TWELVE
SEE HER RUN

I shimmy into a pair of bright pink yoga pants in the stall in the bathroom down from my office. It's week three of my marathon training, which still blows my mind. Four days a week, I'm up by five-thirty to train before I get ready and head to work. Twice a week, Garrett and I hit the soccer field's track to continue the base-building phase of my training. Unlike the base-building he'd done the first time he'd trained for a marathon four years ago—thanks to my brother prodding him into it—we have to develop a language.

It's not just him or me on the track. It's us. Now, talking isn't as much of an issue since we haven't jogged yet. Our sessions have been power walking, and we're up to two miles. Once you toss in panted breath from running and the loudness the other runners describe at the race, our communication will need to be quick and, sometimes, done nonverbally through tugs of the rope that tethers us.

All of this on top of running 26.2 miles. On my solo treadmill sessions, I toggle between power walking and slow jogs, and I'm only up to 2 miles. Though it tips towards power walking most mornings.

Are you allowed to walk a marathon? *Oh god, how long will that take!*

Frowning, I tug on a hoodie and then scoop up my tote bag with my work clothes and head to my office. Garrett is meeting me there before we head to the track.

It's almost alarming how comfortable I'm getting with him showing up at the end of the workday. I should go back to taking the bus after work. After three weeks of getting up to work out *and stretching*—thanks to the little reminder he put in our shared calendar—I'm getting used to the ten fewer minutes of sleep.

I can pretend that the ride is about getting me home sooner, free use of his car's butt-warmers, and whatever story I'm telling myself to justify prolonged exposure to Garrett beyond our training. The truth is, I like the time we spend together each day. He grumbles about whatever little item I added to our joint calendar for the day. Today was a task to *Craft a poem about Ditka*. His *Seriously, Jensen?* text at 10:09 a.m. confirming his receipt, caused a happy thrill to zing through me.

An hour later, he texted that poem.

Roses are red,
Violets are blue,
I have a cat named Ditka,
Who has smelly poo.

The banshee-like laugh that chortled out of me startled my boss, Andrew. I like it when Garrett lets his goofy side out. It's not like I've never seen it before, but the more time we spend together, the more he's letting himself out to play.

Our daily walks from my office and ride to my apartment are sprinkled with teasing comments for each other. It's also full of just chatting about our day, our training, or random stuff. Like the recipe his mom sent for him and his siblings to cook this Sunday, or the reading that Kayla, Catherine, and I are going to at Heartbound Bookshop tomorrow night.

"Hello, Jensen... Or should I say Sporty Spice in that getup?"

I stop at a caramel-smooth English accent. The male version, not Kayla's lyrical tenor. She and Catherine pop into my office daily now, to whisk me away to grab a latte, ensuring that her voice is imprinted in my auditory catalog.

"Hello, Miles," I sigh, adjusting the bag on my shoulder and continuing my stride back to my office.

"I see you are still ignoring me, then?" He says, jogging up beside me.

"I just said hello, didn't I?"

"Because three weeks of my messages on unread screams dialogue." A sloshed breath washes away his snarky tone. "I suppose I deserve it."

"Yes, you do." My mouth forms a firm line.

"You're right... I do."

The sorrowful ache in his voice causes my mouth to droop. While I know Miles isn't appropriate for me, I don't want to hurt him, especially after Kayla said he was devastated. He's come up a few times when she's mentioned that he asks about me or that he's been extra mopey lately.

"I'm sorry," I say, my steps ceasing.

"No." He places a palm on my shoulder. "I'm the one who is sorry. The last few weeks have given me perspective on how I treated you. I was a bit of a bastard."

"You weren't a bastard *per se*. Just selfish."

"Ouch—" he presses a hand to his chest "—but accurate. The truth is, I enjoy our friendship, but I also rather enjoy kissing you. I didn't want to lose both. Your friendship or—"

"Kissing me." My brow puckers.

He rubs his nape. "Hence, me being a bastard."

"At least, you're an honest one."

I want to be angry at him. It seems like the appropriate thing to do here, but I can't muster it. Whether it's the remaining flicker of the torch I've carried for the last ten months, or just not wanting someone to be upset, I'm not sure. What I am sure of is that, whatever way you slice it, he never made me promises.

Sure, we kissed, flirted, and went out periodically, but neither of us broached the subject of being more. Because I just waited for him to declare his feelings like in one of my romance novels, rather than asking for what I want.

Not asking for what we want guarantees nobody ever says no. Dr. Nor's words from last night's session tap inside me like someone knocking at a car window to get your attention.

My shoulders slump. "Neither of us made promises to one another. I'm an adult and I made my own choices."

"As did I. I'm sorry if my actions toyed with your emotions in any way. Truly." He grips my upper arms, kneading his thumbs into me through my sweatshirt. "The last thing I ever intended was for you to feel hurt. I care about you, Jensen. Can we start again?"

"I don't want to be friends who kiss," I say, tipping my head up to meet his stare that I know implores me to say "yes."

"Neither do I." He steps closer, his timbre low and seductive.

My breath catches. "What are you asking?"

"I'd like to be more. To give us"—he raises his hand and caresses my cheek—"to give this a *real* shot."

My stomach twists. For months, I've daydreamed about Miles Calloway saying this to me. For me to not just be the girl pining, but to be *the* girl.

"I'm on sabbatical." I shake my head, breaking the momentary trance.

"What?" he says, bemused.

"I'm not dating anyone. Not right now. Not for…" I look down at my sneakers, which have gotten more use in the last three weeks than in the last six months. "Until October."

"October… As in next year?" he says, aghast.

I step back, breaking our physical connection. "Yeah. I'm focusing on me and the marathon."

"Kayla mentioned you were training." He cocks his head. "So, you're really doing that, then?"

"Yeah." I wave at myself. "Hence the Sporty Spice getup."

"And you're not dating until then?"

This romantic sabbatical is about making different choices. A month ago, I would have said yes to Miles. Just like I did with Chase. I'd happily scoop up the crumbs he offered, believing that's what I deserved.

Through this, my hope is to gain perspective on what I want, on what I deserve. Once I have that, I won't accept anything else. At least, that's what I hope.

"Correct."

"And that's it, then?" he says, his tone somber.

"We can be friends." I clear my throat. "Just friends. No kissing."

"Ever?" he murmurs.

"I don't know."

It's an honest answer. At the end of this, I may find that Miles is who I want. I may find out that he's not. It may be nobody at all. What I do know is that if I follow old patterns, I'll have the same results—a broken heart.

"I understand if that's not right for you, but it's what's good for me. I won't give you false hope, though. All I'm offering is friendship," I say, my shoulders squared.

He nods, seeming to take in my words, before he speaks, "Friendship then. I'm putting out my hand."

A small smile curls my lips at his verbal cue. It makes me think that there is a possibility of an actual friendship with Miles. His use of visually impaired person etiquette is a new development.

I accept Miles's hand. "No kissing."

"No kissing," he repeats with a cheekiness.

"I mean it."

"We'll see what happens by next October," he teases.

I roll my eyes.

"You know I'm a shameless flirt, even with my friends." He releases my hand. "But you've set your boundaries, and I'll comply. Though I won't pretend that I'm not on bated breath about what happens at the end of this sabbatical."

Me too.

With a goodbye to Miles, I head back to my office. The moment I open the door, Garrett's silky bass drifts from Andrew's office. Andrew, my boss, is the only one with an actual office. My space is an alcove off the small lobby.

"Are you sure? I wouldn't want it to be an imposition," Andrew says, his Midwest twang almost musical.

"It's not a problem," Garrett says.

"My daughter will appreciate your guidance. She's considering being pre-med."

So sweet, I mouth to myself. Waves of warmth fizz inside me like sparkling wine. *Is Garrett agreeing to be a mentor to Andrew's daughter?*

Andrew has met Garrett a few times since he's been picking me up after work. I'm not surprised by Andrew asking Garrett to mentor his daughter. He'd do anything for his children. As delighted as I am about this, I'm also not surprised by Garrett's agreement. It's just who he is. Giving. Self-sacrificing. Thoughtful.

"There you are." Pretending I wasn't just eavesdropping, I push into the open office and shoot a sassy look toward where Garrett sits in one of the chairs across from Andrew's desk.

"If you checked your messages, you'd know I was here." Garrett's tut is humor-laced

"Then whatever would you nag me about?" Chin raised, I flash a haughty expression

"I'm sure I could find something." He rises, amusement radiating from him.

Andrew huffs a laugh. "God, you two sound like me and my husband."

"If we were married, at least I would have gotten cake, instead of just Garrett's award-winning personality," I pretend to pout.

"I messaged my proposal, and you didn't read it, so you lost out on cake," he quips.

"Be still my ever-beating heart. Proposal via text message is peak romance." Hand on my forehead, I mock-swoon.

Andrew chortles.

"Come on, sassy mouth, we've got work to do." Garrett spins me and ushers me out of the office with a bump of his chest against my back.

"*So* bossy." A grin—that I know matches Garrett's from the laughter in his tone—kicks across my face. Making this man smile will never cease to be my favorite high.

By the time we make it to the soccer field, the sun has set. Soft light from the lamp posts circling the track cut through the velvet darkness settling onto campus. The soundtrack of crickets, the slap of sneakers from a few other runners on the track, and distant chattering twines around us.

"I thought we could ramp it up a bit today," Garrett says, unspooling the rope and handing me one end.

"Shall we do a piggyback for the two miles?"

"If you want, but I don't know if your back is strong enough."

"Ha!" I tip my head back and laugh. "Someone has all the jokes today."

"I'm in a good mood."

I can almost feel that lopsided grin flexing at the corners of his lips. More and more, I visualize every facial tick, twitch of the mouth, and lift of his eyebrows. Over the years, Garrett's vocal profile has become like music. Each note sings me a different song.

"Why are you in a good mood? Did you sacrifice a resident to the medical gods or something?" I tease.

"Just in a good mood, sassy girl." He tugs on his end of the rope. "I'm thinking tonight we jog."

"Now, I know you really have jokes." I give the rope one long tug, indicating my disagreement.

He gives it three quick tugs, which is our sign for keep going. "You got this. We'll go slow, and nobody expects you to jog the full two miles."

"What if I expect me to?" I run my fingers along the rope wrapped around my palm.

"Expectations can be dangerous. We can't control that what we want will happen," he says, his hard swallow is audible.

A furrow dips my brow. "Do you not have expectations for your life?"

"Just hope," he murmurs.

"What do you hope for?"

"For time with the people I care about." His words are scratchy like a rickety bridge that will break with just the wrong amount of pressure.

Time. The sadness underscoring that single word causes a dull twinge in my chest. I can't imagine what losing someone you love is like. Anker's accident is the first time anyone I love has ever been hurt. What must it be like to not just lose someone you love, but carry the burden of knowing it could happen again? Like Garrett says... Expectations are dangerous. You expect the people you love to always be there, and there's no guarantee of that. No matter what you do.

I tip my gaze up to him. "I'm going to do something, and if you need to say turnip, I'll understand."

Using the rope, I pull myself closer to him and wrap my

arms around his waist. For a moment, he stiffens but then folds his arms around me. Head pressed against his chest, we just remain like that. The rhythmic cadence of his heart hums in my ear. Each thump is a soothing lullaby.

Friends hug. That's what I keep telling myself as I burrow just a little deeper into him. Chin rested atop my head, he just holds me. This is for me as much as for him. I can't take away his fear of losing the people he cares about. All I can do is be there with him. I can't fix him, but I can offer comfort. I can just hold him, and somehow that knowledge lessens the ache of helplessness.

"You always take care of people." He breaks the silence cocooning us. "It's like you setting up a reminder for me to eat lunch every day, or you helping Catherine prep for her next round of interviews. Hell, even this marathon training. You're doing it to help your brother."

"It's just a hug," I whisper.

"Sure." He releases me. "Ready?"

Adjusting my glasses, I step back. "Yeah... Let's hope I don't fall on my face."

"I won't let you." He tugs three times on the rope.

The flutter in my chest is proof of that. It also confirms that even if I did fall, he'd catch me. Only falling on my face isn't what I'm worried about at this moment. It's that, no matter how many times I flick this rubber band on my wrist, this crush may never go away.

Tethered by the rope, we start our training. As always, we start slowly, eventually speeding up to a power walk. This pace allows our muscles to wake up, but also for Garrett to position us at the track's outer ring. It's something other runner/guide duos recommend. It tends to be less clustered and allows you to only deal with other runners on one side of you, versus both.

Eight laps equals two miles. That's just over one hundred and four laps to make up the 26.2 miles we'll do in the marathon. Technically not we, since Garrett is just the substitute guide runner for me to train with until Anker recovers. Somehow, I keep misplacing that nugget of information.

"Ready?" Garrett says, three tugs accompany his question.

"I'm not, but let's do this."

This is the first time I'm jogging with a guide. In the solo 5K I attempted and failed at with Anker, we never jogged. Garrett and I have only power walked. Somehow, jogging is more terrifying. It's like riding a bicycle downhill. There are brakes, but you still may hurt yourself or someone else.

"We'll go slow," he assures.

Nodding, I tug twice on the rope. We start slow. Though I wonder if Garrett is even actually jogging and not just walking fast. He's at least a foot taller than me, which means for every one step he takes, I take two. Not to mention my three weeks of more dedicated physical fitness don't compare to his years of athletic prowess. Just like Anker, Garrett was a college athlete, having played rugby, and has maintained his fitness levels after.

"Doing okay?" he asks as we round the third lap, having run the last two.

"Uh-huh," I say through panted breath.

It's only half a mile, but the sense of accomplishment battles with the doubt that I am going to be able to jog any further. My muscles groan, and sweat trickles down my spine, while athletic Mr. Darcy's breath remains steady. *So annoying.*

"Listen to your body," he says.

Right now, my body wants to kick him. How is he able to have a conversation?

"Slow when you need to. This is a marathon, after all."

I roll my eyes at his cheekiness. "Aren't I…supposed to push through? You know…find that runner's…high?" I pant.

"And you will. We're just base building. You have to learn your boundaries before you push past them."

"Is that more of your…self-help stuff like telling…the…bag?"

"Yeah." He chuckles.

"Fine." I give the rope a tug to indicate I need to slow down, and we do.

While I understand one needs to walk before they can run —*literally in this case*—frustration fires awake within me. It may be unreasonable to snap your fingers and just be able to run an entire marathon after three weeks of training…but call me Ms. Unreasonable. I want to be good at this. I don't want to fail Anker, Garrett, or myself.

"It was only half a mile," I mutter.

"Half a mile more than you jogged on Sunday."

"We only power walked on Sunday."

"Exactly." His unmuffled voice telegraphs that he's looking over his shoulder at me. "Remember, it's a marathon. Not a sprint."

"Are you just going to quote inspirational pillows now? Is that, like, your thing?"

"Live, laugh, love, my dear Jensen." An audible smile accompanies his dry snark.

"I'm too breathless to laugh!" I laugh nonetheless.

"Let's power walk half a mile and then jog another half mile to wrap."

I tug the rope in agreement. "Okay."

13

MILE THIRTEEN
DICKY MEN

The herby aroma of pizza fills Garrett's vehicle as we pull up to Anker's house. This may be my new favorite Friday night tradition. In lieu of happy hour at Harkey's, for the last three Fridays we've done pizza at Ankers.

Though, Garrett still hasn't agreed to learn to make fancy cocktails, but tonight he did agree to bring Ditka along. It's not uncommon for Ditka to come over to Anker's place when it's just us. Plus, my brother is Ditka's sitter on the rare occasions Garrett is out of town, so he has a litter box, treats, and a few toys for him at the ready. Tonight, Ditka will be my cuddle buddy, while his daddy and Anker watch hockey.

They're both diehard LA Bobcats fans, and with Anker still on crutches, they sold their tickets for tonight's game to watch at home. While a Friday night listening to them play wannabe hockey coach from the couch is unappealing, an evening cuddled with Garrett's furry squish-monster and eating garlic knots is top-tier.

"Thank god, I'm starving!" Anker's whiny bellow greets us as we walk through his front door.

"Why, hello, dear brother. Lovely to see you too," I tease, unleashing Ditka the moment I hear Garrett shut the door behind us. The feline trots down the small hall towards the kitchen, his bell jangling all the way.

"Hello. I'm starving!" he shouts from the living room.

"Are the chips and salsa you're eating not holding you over?" Garrett snarks.

"Man cannot live on snacks alone," he says between loud crunches.

With a head shake, I place my cane beside the door and slip off my heels. "Should we set up at the table?"

"No need for fancy. Just pop a squat here," Anker says through a mouth full of food.

Pop a squat? Face scrunched, I tilt my head toward the living room. This isn't like Anker. He lives for fancy. Pizza nights aren't merely a casual affair for him. He's the only human I know who pulls out actual plates and wine glasses for pizza, but this has been his state over the last month.

I shuffle fully into the living room. "Who are you and what have you done with my brother?"

Anker is propped up on the couch, his booted left foot resting on top of a stack of pillows on the coffee table. Mesh shorts and a hooded sweatshirt replace his typically put-together outfit. Even with my limited vision, I can tell that he hasn't shaved in several days, and his dark brown hair is messy.

"I see you're in your couch potato era," I quip with a wave of my hand.

"Says my blind sister." He bites into another chip.

"That's one." With an eyeroll, I wag my finger.

Few people joke with me about my vision. Anker is certainly one of them, but he only gets one teasing blind comment a day. It's an old rule my dad set for us as teens to ensure Anker never weaponized my disability. Though, he never would. Anker's teases aren't meant to be cruel.

"I'll set things up in the kitchen and we'll bring plates into the living room," Garrett says, coming beside me.

"I can help, since Count Cucumber is couch-ridden… Careful, big brother, if you sit too long, you may pickle," I sass.

"That's a lot of judgment from the woman who remains curled up on the couch all day on Christmas with an audiobook." Anker bites into another chip.

"Audiobook? More like one of her erotic audios," Garrett teases, his low timbre sending heat zipping up my spine and invading my cheeks.

"Eww, Jensen… On Christmas and in our parents' house," he groans.

"Gives a new meaning to the term stocking stuffer." Garrett bumps my shoulder, seeming to delight in torturing Anker.

"All I have to say is that I have a newfound appreciation for candy canes," I coo with a wiggle of my hips.

"Oh god!" Head tipped back, Anker lets out a dramatic groan.

"Candy canes?" Garrett clears his throat.

"Don't be judgy or I'll make you do the dishes." I poke his bicep. "Let's go set up."

He shakes his head. "Nah. You go change."

"Are you sure?"

"Yeah. Go get cozy." With a playful bump from his hip, Garrett turns towards the kitchen.

Stop it, stomach. I press a hand to the soft flesh of my belly, hoping the pressure will simmer down the butterflies that fluttered to life at the image of getting "cozy" with Garrett. His arm folded around me as I snuggle into his side, holding a purring Ditka as he watches the hockey game.

Bad girl. I snap the rubber band on my wrist.

The sting is a momentary reprieve from these intrusive crush thoughts, but it's clear my attempt to Pavlov's-dog-away this crush is failing. Yet, I remain in this man's presence six days a week. Part of me knows I should pull back. That my time with Garrett should be relegated to our training sessions. It's something Dr. Nor and I are discussing, but I don't want to.

"I'll go cozy-up then." With a bite of the inside of my cheek to tamp down my body's reaction to Garrett, I scoop up my tote bag from the entryway and head to the bathroom to change.

The bonus of Anker's recent love affair with his couch is that I get to rock comfy clothes all night. As fun as it is to dress cute, I love wearing leggings and a hoodie. I slip on some soft black leggings, a blue tank top, and tug on the hoodie I scooped up from the end of my bed this morning.

Pulling my hair up into a messy bun, I stride into the living room. Anker never moves furniture without prepping me and, despite his recent injury impacting his motivation to move around, he's kept things clear. His thoughtfulness allows me unrestricted movement through his house.

"Sausage, right?" Garrett calls from the kitchen.

"Yes, please," I shout. "Ooh…and—"

"Three garlic knots with two tablespoons of sauce," he laughs his reply.

"Thanks!" Grinning, I swipe my hand along the couch cushion to ensure there's nothing there and then plop down beside Anker. Within seconds, Ditka jumps up and snuggles onto my lap.

"Hey, buddy." Anker twists to offer Ditka ear scratches. "Jensen, why are you wearing Garrett's clothes?"

"Excuse me?" Brow creased, I look down at myself and then back at him, realization's heat creeps up my neck.

The sweatshirt I grabbed is the one Garrett had lent me when I went to his place after Miles ditched me at the bar. The hoodie I've been wearing far more than is appropriate for a woman trying to get over a crush, and for some unknown reason, I am wearing it now.

"I…" I gape, trying to find the words.

"I lent it to her," Garrett says, his tone matter-of-fact, as he enters the room with a plate in hand. "You know how cold our pampered princess gets."

"If it's not at least seventy degrees, she acts as if she's been left naked in the Arctic."

"That she does." Garrett chuckles. "Sorry, buddy, cuddles after food." He scoops up Ditka, who lets out a perturbed *meow*. "Plate. Pizza slice three o'clock, three garlic knots with your preferred sauce ratio at six o'clock, and some salad at nine o'clock," he murmurs, holding it in front of me.

"Salad?" I lift one eyebrow.

"The only greens in your diet can't be peanut M & M's." Garrett's scold is playful.

"Peanut M & M's are healthy. Everyone knows that. Peanuts are packed with protein." A wry expression kicks across my face.

"I'll be sure to share that with my patients," he drawls. "Fork, for the salad that you won't eat and *not* to stab me." He hands me a fork and a napkin.

"Now, there's an idea." Placing the plate on my lap, I hold up the fork and mimic how I imagine a swordswoman would threaten her enemies.

"Don't worry, her aim is shit," Anker teases. "She… Ouch!"

"What was that, dear brother?" I hum, tapping my free hand against where I just stabbed him—well, rather poked his upper arm forcefully—with my fork.

"Christ, Jensen," Anker grumbles.

"It's your own fault for breaking our no more than one blind joke a day rule." Smugness fills my features.

"Ruthless." Garrett's laugh is a low rumble that crackles awake every single one of my nerve endings.

His laugh. I bite back the giant grin lighting my face. It's not quite the unbridled belly-deep, body-racking laugh that's my goal, but the sound is still music to my ears.

"That better not leave a mark." Anker rubs at his upper arm.

I raise my hand and pat his cheek." Don't worry, you're still pretty. Single moms, divorcees, and married women looking to step out will still buy you espresso martinis during ladies' night once you emerge from couchland and return to the world of functional adult humans."

Swatting me away, he groans, "Shouldn't you be out of your bratty younger sister phase at twenty-nine?"

"I wouldn't have to act like a brat if you weren't acting like a buttheaded older brother," I coo in a saccharin-sweet voice.

"While you two reenact your childhood, let me grab my food and drinks." With a head shake, Garrett places Ditka on the large, cushy chair in the corner. "Soda? Wine? Beer?"

"Since you're driving me home, I'll take a glass of red."

"Two, please! There's a bottle in the fridge, just bring it." Anker shouts as Garrett strides away.

"You're on pain pills!"

"We wouldn't want you to end up in your own version of *Less Than Zero*," I quip.

"Haven't taken any in a week, so I can booze up... *Mom. Dad.*" A thin coat of annoyance laces Anker's retort.

"Jensen, I'm also getting you a new fork, so you have no excuse to *not* eat the salad you won't end up eating."

"Okay, *daddy*," I say saucily.

Anker makes a disgusted noise. "Oh god, never call Garrett that."

I wrinkle my nose. "Yeah... Agreed. I hear it." I dip a garlic knot in marinara, ignoring the clench low in my abdomen at the idea of me calling Garrett *daddy*. "Speaking of the land of the functional adult human, how are you feeling about returning to work on Monday?"

After a few weeks off, between the time he'd originally taken for New York and with his initial recovery, Anker is heading back to work on Monday. He's still in a boot and using crutches to get around, but the physical therapist issued him this scooter-like contraption he'll use to move about the hospital. Not only is this the longest period of time my brother has stayed homebound, but it is also the most inactive he's ever been. Even after he had COVID two years ago, he forced himself—way before it was appropriate—to at least walk on the treadmill in his guest room.

He shrugs. "It's fine."

"I bet the nurses you shamelessly flirt with will be happy to see you." I bump his side with mine, hoping to draw out a little more excitement than this.

Ever since we were kids, Anker's been the sun that everyone orbits around. As outgoing as I can be, I'm awkward in group settings. Give me one-on-one interactions. Those are the easiest to navigate. It's hard to imagine that at one time, Anker had been shy and awkward as a little boy.

"I'm sure they've survived." Anker forks up some salad.

"I don't know. They've only had Garrett for two weeks. They must be utterly starved for proper hot doctor interaction. You know one with the ability to not brood but have flirty banter." I toss a cheeky expression towards where I hear Garrett shuffle in from the kitchen.

"You do realize that Garrett and I aren't the only doctors who work at the hospital, right?" he snarks.

"Yes, but how many of them are hot?" My self-assured response is smug.

"Are you calling Garrett hot?"

"More importantly, did you just call your brother hot?" Garrett teases, placing the bottle of wine and some glasses on the coffee table in front of us.

"No…" Realization creases my brow. "Not…intentionally."

"Don't know if I like you sitting so close to me after calling me hot." Anker scoots away.

"Shut up." I tap my bare foot against his uninjured calf.

"So, you're not denying our mutual hotness," he purrs with what I imagine is a waggle of his eyebrows.

"Barf," I make a gagging noise. "It's not about looks. It's about your constant need to flirt with everyone. We know Garrett is more the sit broody in the corner type."

My gaze shifts to where Garrett now sits in a large leather chair in the corner. Though he's not exactly broody at this moment. The low lighting in the room paints him in shadows, but a lightness wafts off him.

"Don't let Garrett fool you. He's had his share of hospital liaisons," Anker says, filling each glass with wine and handing me one.

"Has he? Interesting." I clear my throat in a failed attempt to tamp down the high pitch in my voice.

I'm aware that Garrett isn't a monk. He has *relations* with women. As Anker describes it, they've all been short-term, low-stakes hookups, and none of them are current. It's clear that anything more is beyond his capability. Even more reason that the little spark of jealousy in my belly at the mere mention of him being with anyone else needs to die.

"It's not that interesting," Garrett mutters. "We all know your brother is more the resident flirt. Though his flirtation game is nonexistent these days."

"So, he's not the medical fuckboy anymore?" I smirk over the brim of my wine glass.

"Not for six months or so."

"Interesting." My smirk gets bigger.

Groaning, Anker tosses his head back. "Hush."

"How is Sonora doing?" I sip my wine.

It's clear Anker is disappointed about not getting to run the marathon, but I suspect his bigger regret is not meeting Sonora in person. In the seventeen years I've witnessed him date, I've never seen him talk about someone like he does Sonora.

"I'm not sure how she's doing," he says between bites.

Lips pursed, I tilt my head. "What do you mean, you're not sure? Don't you two text all the time?"

"We haven't talked since my accident."

"She hasn't messaged to check on you?" I say, indignation simmers in my bloodstream.

I know she's aware of his accident. I posted about it in the blind runners/guide group, which she's active in. She even commented about how sorry she was and hoped for a speedy recovery. Though, that seems a little cold and robotic considering they have been in almost daily communication over the last few months.

Maybe Sonora isn't the future "Mrs. Dr. Larsen" after all. Anyone who plans to be part of Anker's life will need to be as thoughtful about him as I know he is about everyone else. Hell, he sent flowers to her a few months ago after a bad sinus infection took her out for a week. The least she can do is check in on him after a concussion and a broken ankle and ribs take him out.

"She messages," he mumbles.

My head snaps toward him. "And *you*..." A scowl forms on my face.

"I'm focused on my recovery."

"And you can't take two minutes away from physical therapy appointments and wallowing on the couch to message her back?"

"Jensen..." He huffs a long sigh.

I aim my fork at him. "Dick move, big brother. It's clear Sonora cares for you, and you are gaga for her. The two of you engage in these epic-long text threads."

"We're just friends."

"Last time I checked, you don't send your friends flowers when they're sick." I tip my head toward Garrett in the corner. "You getting flowers from mopey-bear over here?"

"Nope." A smirk is audible in Garrett's response.

"Judas! I bring you yogurt," Anker counters.

"*Not* flowers."

"Plus, you told Mom about Sonora!" Placing my plate on the table, I sit up straighter.

We are a close family, but not *a tell Mom everything about our dating life* kind of family. She's obsessed with the cake she'll create for both of our weddings. Some moms imagine the dresses their daughter will wear, or what song they'll dance to with their son at the reception. But our mother daydreams about buttercream versus cream cheese frosting. Mentioning a significant other, or in this case, the possibility of one, isn't a casual thing with our mother.

"With Mom's internet stalking skills and Pinterest obsession, she likely has an entire wedding mood board for you two."

"It's not a big deal." He shrugs. "I've been busy."

"Busy! With what?"

"Recovery." He motions to his booted foot. "You seem to forget that I had all this to deal with."

"Sure, we'll go with that," I say, sarcasm lathers my tone. "Did you at least tell her that? Like, have you responded to let her know you're going to be disconnecting for a bit, or are you just ghosting her?"

Hot anger burns along my veins, thinking about poor Sonora, just waiting for a response. One minute she's in daily communication with Anker and then the next day, *poof* it's gone with no explanation. All because my brother's head has been up his ass since his accident.

"I expect better from you." Disappointment slithers into my voice, making it sound venomous.

"Leave the melodrama for your audiobooks. This isn't a big deal. Not to mention you're overstepping," he says with a dismissive head shake.

"It may not be a big deal to you, but I'd imagine to Sonora it is. It's clear from everything you've shared that she likes you, and you're just blowing her off. One minute you're making plans to meet at the marathon, and now you're ghosting her."

"Stop projecting," he says flippantly.

"What does that mean?" My brow pinches.

"It means that you're upset about whatever literary fuckboy did to push you into your romantic sabbatical or whatever the fuck you're calling it, and taking it out on me. I'm not Miles, and Sonora isn't you."

Blanching, I rear back. It's like foreign words are coming out of my brother's mouth.

"Watch it," Garrett snarls, causing both me and Anker to look at him. "Don't weaponize what happened with Miles against her."

"I am not... Fuck..." Anker heaves a loud breath. "I'm sorry, Jensen. I shouldn't have said that. I just... You just don't get it."

"I get you're being a jerk. All because you can't run a race." I toss my hands up. "I'm seeing the wrong side of six a.m. most mornings to make your Larsen lore fever dreams come true, the least you can do is pull your head out of your ass."

"Head out of my ass?" he grits. "You've spent a month training for something I've spent years training for. Not to mention, a lifetime working toward. I was supposed to go to New York, meet Sonora, and start my life. *You* wouldn't understand."

"Don't be an asshole," Garrett snaps. His body's rigid posture telegraphs the icy glare aimed at my brother.

"I have this, Garrett." I look between my friend and my brother. "But I do understand, Anker." I release a shaky breath. "I may not understand what you're going through right now, but I know what it's like to have expectations for how your life is supposed to unfold, but fate has different plans."

It might be why I lack the blind faith my brother has in the Larsen lore. Maybe it's because fate dealt each of us different cards from the deck. Anker has his lists and plans, but I have to adapt. With each degree of loss in my vision, I'm forced to figure out new ways of doing things. As well-adapted as I am, I am more the wait-and-see what happens type.

"Bad things happen all the time. Life doesn't turn out the way you want—hope for." My gaze drops on Garrett, who sits quietly in the chair across the room. "This sucks, but it's temporary. If you want to let it derail you from what you want, that's on you. But if you want to put your big boy panties on and adapt, I'm here."

He scrubs his hands down his face. "I am a dick."

"Yes, you are," Garrett says gruffly.

"I'm sorry, Jensen. I shouldn't have said those things."

"Thank you." I sit up straighter. "I am also sorry. I probably did project a bit, and I definitely overstepped. I just don't want to see you lose out on the things you want just because it doesn't happen the way you think it should happen."

This may be the first time my brother has faced life not happening the way he's planned. As charming and carefree as he is, he has plans for everything. His plans have plans. Hell, it's why he has emergency preparedness kits in his car and garage. Not to mention things for Ditka at his house, and both Garrett and my favorite snacks, just in case.

I'm used to life disappointing me, so I know how to adapt. Whether it's men I crush on not liking me back or restaurants without an accessible menu, I always figure it out.

"I'll get my head out of my ass and call Sonora tomorrow. It's after nine in New York, and I know she likes to go to bed early," he says.

"Good." My smile ticks up.

He shifts on the couch to face me. "I am really sorry for what I said, and if you want to pull out of the marathon, it's okay. I can do it on my own. Like you said, I just need to adapt and figure it out."

It would be so easy to take him up on his offer. I could revert to cheering him on from the sidelines, but I don't want to. I have no expectation that I will finish this race, but I have hope that I will and determination to try.

"And give up sisterly brownie points, never. You're stuck with me." I bump his shoulder.

He loops his arm around me and squeezes. "Thanks. For calling me a dick and running a marathon with me."

"Anytime."

14

MILE FOURTEEN
SKINNED KNEES

My fingers skate over the console until I swipe over the bump dot. With a happy sigh, I push it, turning on the heated seat. Garrett put the bump dot there a few weeks ago to make it easier for me to turn them on myself.

"Is your butt warm enough?" he drawls.

"My butt is perfect. *Thank you very much.*" I wiggle in my seat.

"Wouldn't want your bottom to freeze on this frigid sixty-two-degrees December evening." He backs out of the university's guest parking lot.

It's our typical Wednesday night training session. Except we won't be at the university's soccer field due to some holiday market they are having there tonight. All of which sounds way more fun than training. It's okay, though. Garrett will drop me at the market after, so I can meet Kayla and Catherine to wander through the vendor tents and drink hot chocolate.

Meanwhile, we're hitting a nearby park to train. We're up to three miles now. In just over six weeks, I've come so far, including jogging most of those three miles. I am kind of a running badass, or at least on my way to becoming one. More and more, I'm figuring out my limits, how to push past them, and when to listen to them.

At the moment, my limits are on high alert. This is the first time we're training somewhere that isn't the soccer field. As we start our power walk along the cement path that cuts through the park, anxiety crackles awake in each nerve ending. Unlike the soccer field's track, I don't know where all the ruts and dips are.

Not to mention, I don't know my way through this park. Not like with the university. At Pemberley, I am home. It's where I went to undergrad, grad, and where I now work. I have particular routes I take, and backups for the times I must alternate due to construction or any other factors that may detour me.

Here, I don't have any of that. It's just what I can hear, pick up through my limited vision, and Garrett. That knot may pull tight in my stomach, but I know this is as necessary as the post-run stretching. It's not like I get to train on the actual marathon course. Since it's made up of a series of streets and a coastal bike path, many of which are active thoroughfares, that wouldn't be an option. Not to mention they're cobbled together in a series of loops that add up to the 26.2-mile-long course.

In many ways, today is just as important as the endurance and conditioning training I do. So much of running is about mental endurance. It's something I'm coming to realize through discussions in the runner/guide group. Each runner and guide talks about how so much of this is a mental game. Today will be the first day I test that. My focus has thus far been on preparing my physical fitness and building the runner/guide bond with Garrett.

"And it's all flat?" I ask for the second time as we move down a straightaway.

Gripping my hand tight on the rope, I take in the park's soundtrack to paint an image of my surroundings. The distant barks of dogs. Muffled music from a small, lit building to our left. The screech of sneakers and slap of a ball against a court's surface.

"Flat. No steps. No drop-offs, except a small gap around some trees along the left, but we'll keep right to avoid them," he explains.

"Okay." I tug three times on the rope, signaling to him I'm ready to speed up.

We move into a gentle jog along the path. My heart thumps in time with the slap of my shoes against the pavement. Breath steady, I try to focus on my surroundings. Tension spools tight in my muscles as I detect the buzz of bicycles seeming to be getting closer.

"Bikes?" I pull back on the slack.

"Not near us."

"They sound close." I furrow my brow.

"They're not."

"But—"

"There's a bike path that runs parallel to our path, but is separated by a grass median."

I nod, but don't give any slack. I remain tucked in behind Garrett. Except for sporadic flashes of dim yellow lighting from random lamps along the path, it's dark. We're just a few days out from Winter Solstice, AKA the shortest day of the year, so it's to be expected it's this dark by five o'clock. Still, the darkness melds with the unfamiliar surroundings and causes worry to prickle my senses.

My interactions with so much of the world is non-visual, but I also use what limited vision I have to help supplement things. In a world not built for disabled people, we have to use everything we have to navigate it. So much of that is done with adaptive devices like my white cane, which currently sits in Garrett's SUV. I know I have Garrett, but right now my fingers twitch to wrap around my cane's handle.

"Walk?" Garrett calls out.

Shaking my head, I tug on the rope. "Nope."

Even if I don't know the path like the soccer field's track, certainty hums in my blood that we haven't gone half a mile yet. As uncomfortable as I am, I don't want to stop. I don't want to fail. I just remain tucked up close to Garrett. So close that his elbow nearly collides with me.

"Sorry," I pant, trying to position myself not on top of him, but close enough to… I don't know. I don't want to knock into him, but I don't want to be far away.

This isn't an issue when I have my cane. Even if I can't run with it, I'd feel more comfortable with it. At least with the cane I can trail along the path's edge to know where I'm going. With the cane, I'd be able to walk away if something happens to Garrett.

Heart racing, I curl my fingers even tighter on the rope. If I keep closing the gap between us, I'll be on his back. I loosen and then immediately grip the rope in debate, causing a tugging motion.

"Okay," Garrett says.

"Okay what…" I smack into him.

"Oof," he grunts, lurching forward.

Without thinking, I wrap my arms around him to both stop my own momentum and his. Only the force of my body makes it worse. Garrett falls to one knee in a lunge-like formation, while I remain pressed against his back, my legs on either side of him, and mortification blazing up my spine.

I cringe. "Are you okay?"

"Yeah." He groans just a bit.

"You don't sound okay. Did I hurt you?"

"Yes… I mean yes, I'm okay." His sigh vibrates in my chest from where I'm pressed against his back. "Just let go of me and stand straight, so I can get up without worrying about you," he says.

Worrying about me… Nice job, Jensen.

"Sure." Swallowing thickly, I do as he asks. Mortification not just inflames my cheeks but thickens my throat.

Garrett stands and turns to face me. "Are you okay?" He places his hands on my arms.

"Yeah… Are you?" I tip my head up to him.

"Yeah." He clears his throat. "Why didn't you stop?"

"Why did you stop?" I arch one eyebrow.

"You tugged on the rope to stop."

"No I didn't."

"Yes you did."

"I…" I rub at the center of my forehead. "Shit. That wasn't a tug. I was just trying to find the sweet spot for enough slack to give you space and enough closeness to make me feel comfortable… Sorry."

"It's okay."

"Are you sure you're not hurt?" I motion to him.

"Just a skinned knee."

"Ouch… I am so sorry." Guilt swirls in my belly.

None of this would have happened if I'd just been able to relax. If I had just trusted him like I've been doing, even if we're in an unfamiliar spot.

"It's fine. I'll survive."

"Are you sure?" I adjust my glasses, which got a little skewed in the collision with Garrett.

"Yeah." He rubs at his nape. "Why don't we call it a night. I'll take you to your place to change and then drop you back at the university to meet the girls."

"But we didn't finish…" I gnaw on the corner of my mouth.

"Yeah… It's fine. We can just call this one. I should clean my knee anyway."

"O-kay. Yeah… Makes sense." I look down at my feet and back up. "I'm really sorry."

"It's not a big deal."

The twist in my abdomen cautions that this is a big deal.

At least, it may become one. If I can't trust Garrett barely a mile into an unfamiliar path, how am I going to trust him for the 10K and half-marathon we'll need to run together before I transition to train with Anker? If I can't trust Garrett, can I trust Anker? For the first time, I worry that I can't do this. Not because of my physical fitness ability, because I'm learning my body is stronger than I thought.

It's my heart I worry about.

15

MILE FIFTEEN
TRUST

"Why can't I trust him?" I whine, falling back against the cushy couch in Dr. Nor's office.

It's our last session of the year. Tomorrow, I head to Solvang with Anker and Garrett for Christmas before I head off with Kayla and Catherine for a ladies' trip to the Bay Area. My sessions are on hiatus until after the new year.

"Why do you think you don't trust him?" she says in her always calm tone.

Pouting, I cross my arms over my chest. "Don't doctor me. Can you just tell me what the issue is?"

"Me telling you the answers isn't how this works."

"Can't we make an exception? It could be my Christmas gift from you?" I grab one of the pillows from the couch and hug it to my chest.

"Too late. I already gave you homemade fig thumbprint cookies," she quips. "You may think you want me to give you the answers, but you know that doesn't help you in the long run. Therapy is about you using the tools we work on to figure your own shit out. I'm just your guide."

Guide? I roll my lips together, taking in that word. I swirl it around inside me like newly-poured wine, debating on how it tastes.

She's right, of course. Damn me for having a smart, capable therapist. Dr. Nor is my guide to figure things out. Just as Garrett is my guide to run a marathon. A marathon that I'm using to… *Figure things out*, I release a hard breath.

"Garrett's my guide, too."

"Mmhmm…" she says, a smug smile evident in her cheekiness. "And do you trust Garrett?"

"Yes."

"Do you?"

"Yes," I repeat, sitting up straight. "There's no reason not to trust him. He's never done anything that warrants distrust."

"But yet your actions indicate that you don't… Not really. You trusted him when you were in a familiar place. A place where you knew you didn't truly need him. I'd imagine anywhere on campus, you could figure out how to keep yourself safe, correct?"

"Yes." I pull at the pillow's fringe.

"But the moment you were somewhere unfamiliar, somewhere you didn't have a plan B for, you stopped trusting him." She clicks her pen. "Or you stopped trusting yourself."

It's like a one-two punch to my heart. Trust. In Garrett. In myself. It knots inside me, making it difficult to pull apart. No matter how much I know I trust Garrett, it's clear that I am not able to.

"What's the first incident that comes to mind of the last time you were in an unfamiliar situation, and had to trust someone?" She tilts her head.

"Undergrad." I shift in my seat.

"The incident at the fraternity house?"

"Yeah…" I say, emotion thickens my throat.

"What feelings did you have that night?"

"Scared. Stupid. Worthless."

It aches to say those words. Memories of that night swirl around me. Music so loud that it vibrated through me. The air thick with the stench of alcohol and too many bodies pressed together dancing, or around tables playing beer pong. Back pressed tight against the wall, its coolness anchoring me, I stood alone, straining for any familiar voice. For anyone to rescue me.

"What other times did you have those feelings after having to trust someone?"

"Chase. Miles."

"And are those the same feelings you had with Garrett last night?"

"Sort of." A furrow dips my brow. "But it's not the same."

"Your body may not know that." She softens her posture, painting the impression of a tender gaze locked on me. "Trauma imprints itself, so that the body remembers and can keep itself safe. Even in situations that aren't unsafe. Your body doesn't know the difference."

"But how do I teach it to know the difference?" I question.

"You can't. We can't control how our body reacts. We can only recognize it and deal with it by learning what presents real danger versus perceived... Who are the real threats and who are not."

"And how do I do that?"

"Trust." Her wry expression is audible. "And before you give me a quippy response, I'll give you some homework to help. Step one is recognizing those feelings and the way your body reacts. Let's start there."

Later, as I sit at my desk finishing up the day, I mull over Dr. Nor's assignment. Garrett. Miles. Chace. Everett. High school and college friends. Interactions with each play like a grainy motion picture in my head.

A muffled ping pulls my attention from my thoughts. With a heaved breath, I pull open my desk drawer and grab my mobile. I still keep it tucked away so it doesn't distract me while working, but I now leave the sound on if I'm not in a meeting or with students. Opening the message app, my mouth ticks up at my phone's robotic voice reading out a message from Garrett that he's here.

"So, you *can* check your phone." Garrett's low bass steals into the room.

I tilt my head toward the entryway to my office space. "Did you *just* send that to test me?"

He says nothing.

"That's so creepy, even for you, Stalker Darcy."

"In truth"—he moves fully into the space—"I did it to mess with you. You looked all too serious for a woman about to go on a two-week vacation. Is everything okay?"

"Yeah... I'm fine." With a shrug, I start to gather my things.

He stops me, his hand resting on my upper arm. "You sure?"

"Just ready for a break." I force a smile. "Like you said, I'm a woman about to be on vacation for two weeks."

"Okay." His murmur sounds as unconvinced as I am.

"Let's head out." I sling my bag over my shoulder and grab my cane.

"Are you sure you're okay? I know last night didn't end like we thought." He places his hand on my shoulder, stopping my steps.

"Yeah... It's good, though. Just a long week." I offer a weak smile. "Nothing that butt-warmers and your off-key singing of Christmas carols can't fix. Remember, it's my turn to pick the music."

I'm fine, but I'm not. And I don't want to talk about it.

Wednesday night rattled me, and my session with Dr. Nor only brought more questions. I worry I'm wasting his time, and mine. It's only been six weeks, but we've already invested so much energy into this. What if I can't push past this?

"I have something for you," Garrett says, opening his passenger door.

"You do?" My brows knit.

He lifts a small gift bag from the passenger seat and hands it to me. "It's your Christmas present."

I take it, running my fingers along the thin tissue paper poking out of the bag. "Why not wait until Solvang to give this to me?" Face scrunched, I tip my head up to him.

He rubs his nape. "I'm not coming."

"But... You can't miss Christmas?" My words come out rushed and strangled.

For the last four years, he's joined us for the holidays. He'll hide in the corner while my uncles and Dad argue about who gets to carve the turkey each Thanksgiving. He doesn't fight my mom when she makes him help decorate cookies on Christmas Eve, even though he's worse than me at frosting them. And he sneaks out of the house with Anker and I during our family's Christmas Eve party to drink gingerbread hot chocolate from Mom's nutcracker-shaped thermos as we stroll along Solvang's main drag, taking in the Christmas lights.

It hurts to think about him not being there. To imagine him here, alone on Christmas. Unless….

"Did you decide to fly to Chicago to see your parents for Christmas?" My tone brightens at that idea.

"No… One of our doctors got the flu, so I'm staying back for coverage."

"But you'll miss Christmas."

"You know Christmas happens everywhere. Even in Seal Beach," he says wryly.

"Yeah, but you won't be with me..." I clear my throat. "...I mean you won't be with Anker and me. With us... We'll miss you."

"I'll miss you too... I'm sorry," he says softly.

"No..." I cringe. "I'm sorry. I'm being bratty. The hospital needs you, and knowing you, you're doing this so that none of the other doctors sacrifice time with their families."

He says nothing.

"Just as I thought." Humor underscores my tut.

"Still sorry that I won't be there," he says.

"Me too, but I understand." I offer a cheeky grin. "Hopefully, this gift makes up for it."

"Hopefully." His chuckle is warm. "Here. Let me take that so you can open it?" His hands swipe over mine, wrapped around my cane. His palm's warmth makes it so easy for me to let go and give him the cane.

If only I could have done that last night. Just lean into my body's normal reaction to Garrett, like a cozy sensation of sliding beneath blankets fresh out of the dryer. The warmth and fresh scent ensconcing you in safety.

"Thanks." I release the cane to him.

As he folds my cane and places it at the base of the passenger seat, I dig into the bag and find a small envelope. Opening it, a large smile takes over my entire face. It's a card, which is normally difficult for me since I can't read them without a video magnifier. This one, though, is braille. I run my fingertips across the *Merry Christmas* printed in raised dots above a tactile shape of a Christmas tree on the front of the card. Inside is a personalized message that causes me to snort.

"May the season be bright and your butt be warm?"

"It felt fitting." A boyish grin plays in his timbre. It's sweet and endearing coming from this man who oozes virile confidence.

"This is adorable."

"I found a woman online who makes tactile and braille items. She even has sweatshirts and tote bags. She worked with me to customize the card," he says, almost bashful.

"This is so sweet," I whisper, emotion thick in my throat.

I can't think of the last time someone got me a braille card. Anker used to do those recorded audio message cards when we were teenagers but stopped as we got older. Braille cards aren't readily available in the greeting card aisle, so it's not unexpected not to get them. Most people just don't give me cards, or if they do, they have to read it to me, or I take it home to look at it under my CCTV.

Slipping the card back into the bag, I pull out a pair of gloves. I run my fingers over their soft fabric.

"They're running gloves," he explains, taking my hand and running his finger along my palm. "From the now daily reminders to lotion my hands you've put on our shared calendar, I know how important hand maintenance is to you."

"Hand maintenance?" I guffaw.

"I'd imagine holding the rope, especially as we increase our distance, may rub and callous your hands. Thought these could protect them."

He traces slow patterns against my palms that are either the number eight or an infinity symbol. I'm not sure which, but what I am sure of is there is a bonfire of emotions within me. Each stroke against my skin stokes that fire just a little more.

"Garrett…" I sniffle, already losing the battle with my emotions. There's no prick of tears to push back… They just come.

"No… Please don't cry," He runs his hands up to my face, wiping away tears from my cheeks.

"God, I'm so obnoxious." I push my glasses up and wipe at my eyes. "I'm sorry. This happens when I get overwhelmed with emotions."

"I remember, but I still don't like it… I don't like making

you cry." Sighing, he presses his forehead against mine. "I'm so sorry."

"Please, don't apologize. You didn't..." My brow wrinkles. "Well, you did, but it's not bad. It's sweet. It's just... you're so sweet and thoughtful, and I'm already failing us."

"What?" He pulls back.

"These gloves." I motion between us with the gloves. "You're holding up your end of this partnership, and I'm not. I was a mess Wednesday night, because I couldn't trust you and this..." I hold the gloves up again. "You're so trustworthy, but..."

"But what?" His whispered question drips with worry.

"I don't trust myself." I cast my gaze downward. "I don't trust that I'm not making a mistake."

"With me?"

I look up at the pain in his voice. "Yes." My admission is so quiet.

"I can't promise you that I won't fail you—"

"No!" I shake my head.

I fold my arms around his torso, so he doesn't just hear what I'm about to say, but feels it. "Please understand me, this isn't about you not being amazing or me not trusting you. It's *me* I don't trust."

"It's okay if you don't—"

"But I do trust you." I tip my head up.

He lifts his hand and cradles the back of my head. "I believe you."

"Outside of my family, I don't have a lot of close people in my life besides Catherine and you. Kayla is becoming a good friend, but she's still new. We know I pick terrible men to have romantic feelings for, but I've also done that with friends... In high school and, again, in college. I told you about those sorority girls..."

Besides Dr. Nor, I've not really talked about this with anyone. Not my parents, Anker, or Catherine, but I want to tell him. Part of trusting someone is letting them see you at your most vulnerable. Each time I expose myself to this man, he remains in front of me. He doesn't run away. He doesn't leave me behind or tell me I'm "too much" to deal with.

I swallow down the acidic taste of the raw emotions of what I'm sharing, and push on, "I found out they only wanted me to rush to help with their reputation at a frat party they'd dragged me to. I'd never been there. I wasn't familiar with the house." I wipe at my eyes. "They convinced me to leave my cane, so I could just be *normal* for the night. Their words, not mine. They thought it might help me get a boyfriend, which they were teasing me about. After I found out that they were only using me and said I didn't want to rush, they ditched me there."

"Fuck... You didn't have your cane. How did you get home?"

I clear my throat. "Anker was gone that weekend for a track meet, so I didn't know what to do. He was the only other human I knew here. I stayed pressed up against the wall for what felt like forever, hoping someone would come along or they would come back. They didn't, but some drunk frat guy came along, and he got handsy and…"

"I'll fucking kill him," he snarls.

"He didn't get far. Chase came along. It was before he and I started our whatever that was. In fact, that's how it may have ramped up. Before that night, he was just the nice guy who worked at the student union with me. He rescued me that night."

"Only to break your heart another night." He sighs.

"Yeah." I wipe at the tears that wouldn't stop coming.

I don't want to be this woman. I don't want to be standing in front of a man, that deep in my marrow, I know will never hurt me, crying about those who did. A woman who is anchored down by her past, when she just wants to run free from it.

"I will kill him too," he growls, pressing me unimaginably closer to him.

It's almost as if he wants to tuck me inside his chest for safety. His thudding heart echoes in my ears. Like a siren's song, it coaxes me to continue to share these things with him. These things I don't like to talk about, but I do—with him.

"I need names. Addresses. Next of kin."

"It's fine. It was a long time ago." I let out a watery laugh.

"It's not fine."

"It's what I'm working on with Dr. Nor." I sigh. "So, I can tell the difference between real and perceived danger."

"And you perceive me as a danger?"

"No." I burrow into him. "Not you exactly. I know I'm safe with you. It's more that my body reacts, which then causes a tug between my heart and my body, and it confuses my brain."

He massages his fingers into my scalp. "Your heart versus your body? What does your heart say?"

I tilt my head up, meeting his stare. "That I trust you."

"You deserved…deserve…better. Fuck them. Fuck Chase. Fuck Miles. Fuck everyone who ever hurt you. Whoever made you question yourself. You didn't choose the wrong people; the wrong people took advantage of your kindness. You have such a big heart, and all you want to do is be loved. There's nothing wrong with that. You deserve that."

"I want to believe that so much…" My voice cracks.

Eyes closed, I press my head against his chest, his fingers soothe with each caress against my scalp. Without saying anything, he scoops me up like I weigh nothing. He slides into the passenger seat, facing the still-open door, and positions me on his lap, cradling me in his arms. He just holds me tight.

"It's the last thing I ever want to do, but I may fail you. I can't promise you that won't happen," he rasps as if it hurts to speak.

"I know you won't fail me." I nuzzle into him, not even letting myself question what's happening. All I want to do is lean into his warmth, his strength. "I know you have me."

It's not just all the evidence stacking up in support that Garrett Marlowe doesn't just have me, but will always have me; it's the certainty that fills me. For the first time, there's no whisper inside me that I'm making a mistake with Garrett. I can trust him. I can trust that I've made the right choice in who I'll run this race with.

"But I may…" He rests his chin atop my head. "I'm in a constant state of fear that I'll fail the people I care about. That I'll let them down, because I already did…"

"With Val?" I whisper.

"Yes." I feel his throat bob.

I want to push him to open up to me, but I know from the dull ache in my own chest that he's already revealed more to me tonight than he's used to. Garrett keeps so much behind his almost constant frown and, sometimes, gruff snark. Just sharing his fear is huge for him. As greedy as I am for more of this man, I need to be okay with walking before we run together.

"It happened at the holidays. It's why I don't go back this time of year," he says, his voice hoarse. "Bryce and Lara were in town. We were at this pub near my parents' place on the Southside. We'd been drinking."

I nod, thinking how Garrett never drinks. Soda. Coffee. The occasional fancy latte that I convince him to drink. Anker and I will indulge, but he never does.

"She had this junker car that was always having issues. We kept talking about getting her a new one but kept making excuses not to go to the dealership. Work. Family. Friends. It didn't seem like a big concern, because we worked at the same hospital and could carpool or take public transit. She was getting off shift, and the car wouldn't start. It was late and I'd been drinking, so she called a rideshare. I told her to text me when she got home. Thirty minutes later, I got the call about the accident. She was already gone."

I tilt my head up to take him in. The streetlamp replaces the dying light from the sunset. The yellow glow mixes with the shadows, only allowing me to make out the downward curve of his lips.

"If I hadn't been drinking. If I'd insisted on getting her a new car. If…"

"Ifs are as dangerous as expectations." Hand placed on his chest, I trail it up until I find his cheek. His stubble rasps against my palms as I bracket his face. "You didn't fail anyone."

"Turnip," he whispers.

I soothe my fingers against his cheeks. "Turnip."

"I'm sorry," he breathes.

"We don't have to explain turnip, remember?"

"I know… After tonight, I won't see you until January, and I don't want to spend the last night of the year that I have with you sad."

"Okay." Without thinking, I raise my hand and trace his frown. "Then let's turn this upside down." I feel the twitch of his lips.

"My silly girl," he murmurs.

Something flutters in my chest at that. "Will you go do something with me?" I bite my lower lip.

Garrett trusts me enough to share his story with me. It makes me want to be brave.

Thirty minutes later, we park on Second Street in Belmont Shore. The Long Beach neighborhood tucked against the Pacific Ocean is a busier version of downtown Seal Beach. It's also a short walk to Naples, where houses along the canal draped in Christmas lights brighten the night sky.

It's one of my favorite parts about Christmas. I have enough vision to enjoy the way the colorful decorations make the darkness sparkle.

We made a quick stop for me to change into jeans, a sweater, a scarf, and sneakers. Garrett laughed when I emerged in a sparkly pink Santa hat from my bathroom. I threatened him with the pair of reindeer antlers that now sit in his backseat.

As Garrett turns off the SUV, I look up at him. "Reindeer antlers?"

"Nope."

"Boo!" I give him a thumbs down. "Guess I'll be the lone festive fashionista in our duo."

"Come on, Mrs. Claus."

"I'm going to leave my cane here."

"Okay," he says slowly, seeming to take in my meaning.

From Second Street to Naples, through each side of the canal, and back will be approximately two to three miles. It will push me to be guided through a terrain that I'm not familiar with. Without my cane, I won't be able to anticipate ruts, drop-offs, bends, and other changes outside of what Garrett communicates as my guide.

"I hope it's okay that we just do regular human guide. I thought about the rope, but I didn't want to make this all about training. I wanted this to also be a little Christmas fun. Since you'll be working." I motion between us. "Though, I realize looking at Christmas lights is more my thing, so if you want to go steal all the presents from Whoville or whatever you like to do for the holidays, we can do that after."

He laughs.

I smile. "I know your mom loves to cook. Did she do a special meal for Christmas?"

"Pizza." A contented sigh escapes him. "Mom cooks all

the time, so the holidays are her days off. Christmas Eve, Dad orders pizza. Each of us get our favorite. We'd eat, play board games, and watch movies."

"An entire pizza for yourself?" My eyes widen. "Oh my god, I need to experience a Marlowe Christmas. It sounds perfect!" I grin.

He huffs a chuckle. "Hard pass. You and my mom would be dangerous."

"Moms love me," I say with mock indignation.

He laughs, opening his door. "That's what I'm scared of. You two would team up, and I'd never know peace again."

"Now this *has* to happen." I open my door. "We'll discuss travel plans after Christmas lights, during our pizza time. And sir…" I arch an eyebrow. "I will be ordering my own pizza *and* garlic knots."

He rounds the car. "I imagine you'll want a hot chocolate for our Christmas light stroll, too?"

"Naturally." I smirk. "And since hot chocolate isn't a latte, I'm made in the shade."

"Made in the shade?" A deep belly laugh belts out of him, causing a triumphant grin to pop across my face. "The things that come out of your mouth sometimes… You ready?" he offers me his arm.

"I'd be more ready if you put on the reindeer antlers."

"Not happening."

Biting my lip, I wrap my hand around his bicep and position myself just a step and slightly behind him. "Let's do this."

16

MILE SIXTEEN
THAT'S NOT ABOUT YOU

"My dear Jensen, it's Kayla and Catherine. We have come to kidnap you!" Kayla cheers, her heels clicking as she strides into my office.

Grinning, I yank the earbud from my ear and turn my head toward my friends. Since our ladies' trip a month ago, we've become extra tight. On top of our weekly brunch outing and daily lattes, we hit up Harkey's Hideaway each Friday with Anker and Garrett, now that my brother has forgone his couch and returned to the land of functional humans. Between training and time with my friends, I can't remember having such a full social schedule.

"I love that your kidnappers announce themselves." Andrew drawls from his office.

"Oh, hush, Andrew, or we won't bring you back a Danish," Catherine teases.

"They have blueberry today. Your favorite. You don't want to risk that, do you?" Hands on hips, Kayla coos.

"She-devils." Humor fills his grumble.

Standing, I grab my purse. "Leave Andrew alone. He just found out Elise got into school in Boston and wants to go there."

"Leave the purse. My treat." Catherine claps her hands together. "After all, we need to celebrate the salary bump I'm about to get as Pemberley's newest associate professor!"

"Shut up!" I squeal, rounding my desk.

"Yep!" She envelops me in a dancing hug. Her excitement vibrates her entire body. "Bay-Cheng made the offer on Friday, but I had to wait until HR sent the formal letter, which arrived this morning."

"And our queen here also finished her book's first draft last night." Kayla shimmies her hips.

"Way to go, Catherine!" Andrew hoots.

"This is amazing!" Jutting my butt, I join Kayla in a silly dance which causes Catherine to laugh. "Also, this will be our treat, so we can properly celebrate you."

"I've explained this to her, but you know Catherine…" Kayla says, her warm tone telegraphing the image of red painted lips tugged up into a broad grin.

"Hey, Grandma Flores would disown me for not sharing my good fortune with the people I care about." Catherine loops her arm in mine, and then Kayla's.

"Alright, details over lattes, but you have got to allow Kayla and me to properly celebrate you this weekend. Perhaps we can skip brunch and hit that steakhouse you love. We'll get gussied up for a Saturday night out! I'll even pull out my sexy push-up bra." I shimmy just a bit.

"TMI!" Andrew bellows from his office, but we ignore him.

"Yes, please. Little black dresses, steak, and red wine. This sounds very American. Count me in," Kayla hums.

"That does sound lovely, but I can't." Catherine sighs. "I have a date."

"A date?" Kayla clears her throat. "I thought you weren't doing the dating thing?"

"No, that's you two. I'm just not doing the *serious* dating thing. Just the casual dating thing," she explains.

While Kayla and I remain on sabbatical, Catherine is mingling. Though, this is the first mingling she's done since November. Much of her energy has been focused on the lengthy interview process with its multiple rounds and observed teaching sessions. Just watching her go through the process exhausts me, so I can't imagine having the bandwidth to date on top of that.

"Guess we have lots to celebrate then. New position, possible hookup, and soon-to-be bestselling book—"

"It's just a first draft," Catherine guffaws.

"A minor detail." Kayla flicks her wrist. "We should do dinner in lieu of drinks tonight."

"I can let Garrett and Anker know we won't meet them at Harkey's—"

"Invite them. I kind of enjoy this little fivesome we have going on," Catherine says.

My mouth twitches into a bigger smile. For so long I've wanted this—a group of friends to call my own. People who like me for me, and not what I can do for them.

Catherine bumps my hip with hers. "Plus, knowing those two big lugs, they'll pay for all of us."

"Big lugs?" I laugh.

"I said what I said."

I shake my head. "Also, how is having Garrett and Anker pay for dinner equate to *us* treating you?"

"Again, Grandma Flores would want me to share my good fortune with my friends," she says, a wink in her playful timbre.

"Does that good fortune include a blueberry Danish?" Andrew calls as we stroll out of the office.

"We'll get you two in honor of Elise's college acceptance and in consolation for your sadness!" Catherine shouts as we head out.

Garrett: Quinoa Protein Bowl

I lean back in my office chair, a pleased smile belts across my face, at Garrett's now-daily lunchtime text message. Despite my phone's robotic tone, I almost hear Garrett's deep timbre telling me what he's having for lunch.

For Christmas, I got him a subscription to a meal delivery service. Now, he has no excuse not to eat. It's delivered each Sunday to his house, and I set up a daily reminder for him to grab his meal and an additional nudge to eat said meal.

Me: Glad you're keeping up your strength. I, for one, am withering to nothing with this grilled chicken salad.

Garrett: I'm sure the red velvet cupcake latte you got earlier with Kayla and Catherine, plus the bag of chips you're probably eating with your salad, will hold you over.

Me: You're so creepy, Stalker Darcy.

I place my phone down and grab another chip to stifle my giggles and distract me from the little flutter in my chest at this playful exchange.

Crushing on men whom I won't ever have isn't new for me, but my self-control about this is. I'm not waiting for Garrett. I like him, but we're never going to happen. This isn't like Miles or Chase. It's better as I'm not twisted in knots, hoping he'll magically wake up one day ready to deal with his unresolved feelings about Val.

Past Jensen would have done just that. She'd be on bated breath and all the cliches. As I told Dr. Nor, I can recognize my feelings for Garrett without losing myself to them. I can be his friend without holding onto misguided hope that what we have will lead to more. Because I like being Garrett Marlowe's friend. New Jensen—or at least the one I'm becoming—is focused on our mission.

We're three months into our training. My ability to loosen

the rope is improving. Next week, we'll have our first test with Cupid Course, a Valentine's themed 10K benefiting the American Heart Association. Each leg of our training program comes with a race component to get us comfortable with a crowded race environment.

Both Anker and Garrett talk about the race being so different than training. The noise. The energy. The other runners. That gets ramped up for visually impaired runners. At least, that's what Sonora and others say in the online runners' group.

Tossing my empty food container into the trash, I use wet wipes to clean my hands before logging back into my computer. This week, the grant application to fund the access technology center is due. I want to do one last review of it before clicking the submit button. Just like the lengthy interview process Catherine just went through, I won't hear about the grant until spring. At least it doesn't involve several rounds of interviews.

"Jensen."

I look up from my work, happiness flutters in my chest. "Garrett."

"Good day?" He leans against the door jamb, a smirk evident in his question.

"Great day."

Once I submitted the grant application, I spent the rest of the day with students. It's one of my favorite parts of the job. Not just helping them figure out their path forward, but being a sounding board. Like me, a lot of them were the only disabled kid from their high school, or in their family. I hope they get as much out of working with me as I do with them.

With the application submitted, I now have a little additional time in my schedule to take on other projects. One of which I've been mulling over for a while.

"I think I'm going to start a disabled students' social club." I log out of my computer.

My department's focus is on disabled students' academic success, but education isn't just the classes we take. It's also the experiences we have. It's all the things that make us well-rounded individuals. This campus has clubs for just about everything. Many that aren't accessible—not really. If the last few months with my blossoming friendships have taught me anything, it's the importance of relationships.

I stand up and grab my purse. "I want to give students the community I am just now finding."

"That's great." He almost glows from the pride radiating off him. "You're amazing."

"Thanks…" My nerves sing with his praise. "Here I am babbling about my day. How was yours? I hope you had a good day."

"It is now."

Nope, we do not get stomach swoops at that. I flick that ineffective—but I nonetheless still wear it—rubber band. "What are you doing here?"

Brocato's, Catherine's favorite steakhouse, is only a block away from my building, so I planned to walk. In the group chat I set up to coordinate tonight's impromptu dinner celebration, I said I'd meet everyone there at six.

"I'm here to take you home."

"I said I'd meet everyone at Brocato's."

"Well, you didn't answer my text asking if that meant you didn't want a ride home, so I erred on the side of keeping your butt warm," he says, striding into the office.

"Sorry." I frown at my phone that remains quiet on my desk. With my afternoon meetings with students, I must have forgotten to turn the ringer back on.

"It's alright. This will give you more time to get dolled up like you all were prattling on about in the group chat."

"I tapped out before my afternoon meetings. Did Catherine and Anker decide on what tie he's going to wear?"

"They've moved on to shoes."

"I'm sure you found the dialogue riveting." I make jazz hands for some unknown reason, but go with it.

"Like paint drying," he deadpans. "What's SPUB, by the way?"

"SPUB?" I scrunch my nose.

"Catherine and Kayla said to not forget the SPUB you promised."

SPUB? What on earth are... My eyes widen. I will kill them both! Did they really put into a group chat with Garrett and my brother for me to wear the sexy push-up bra I joked about earlier?

"Nothing... Inside joke." Clearing my throat, I slip my phone into my bag. "You really don't need to drive me home tonight. I can take the bus, so you have time to get ready. I'm sure Anker has thoughts about your belt and shoe pairing."

"Nah... I'm good." He grabs my cane from the corner and hands it to me. "I'll drive you home, so you have plenty of time, and then we can head there together. Plus, if I go straight home, I'll have a crabby cat to contend with. Ditka enjoys his run of the house, but gets fussy if I dip in and out. He either wants me there or gone. There's no in-between with him."

"Oh, Ditka."

The logistics of getting dolled up in a studio apartment while Garrett sits on my sofa gives me pause as I stand in front of my closet. Grabbing the dress I plan to wear is fine, but how to stealthily gather up the sexy push-up bra and matching panties is something I didn't foresee when I said, "Come on up and hang out, while I get ready." Scooping everything into my arms, I shuffle into the bathroom.

Stripping off my work clothes, I toss them into the hamper. I tug on the black dress over my lacy red push-up bra and panties. The irony of changing into this behind a closed door, mere feet away from a man I both want to and am horrified at the idea of seeing me in, sends heat crawling up my neck. It's a simple, but sexy, scoop-neck black dress that hugs my breasts but flows out in an A-line skirt that stops at my knees. Its flowy bell sleeves offer a bit of whimsy like a princess from a fairytale. I leave my hair loose, fluff it a bit, and slip in a pair of gold chandelier earrings I bought on the ladies' trip.

I swipe red lip stain—also a purchase made on my trip based on Kayla's recommendation of how it popped against my fair skin—and stand in front of the mirror for just a moment. The bright bulbs offer enough light to take in my image. It's fuzzy, but pretty. At least, that's how I feel. Maybe it's just the pretty feeling inside me right now. Today feels like another mile marker on this journey I'm on. Tonight is about celebrating Catherine, but a little bit of me will be selfishly celebrating my own success. Even if I'm the only one who knows.

Sliding into the gold heels that match my earrings, I take a deep breath and step out of the bathroom. "Do you need to freshen up before we head out. Perhaps, a spritz of perfume, or I can lend you some lipstick. I think pink is your color," I sass.

"Funny," he grunts, rising and turning to face me. "Fuuuuck... Pretty..."

"Ah..." The breath wooshes out of me.

"I mean"—he rubs the back of his head—"you look pretty. I'm sure our fashion police friends will approve."

"Thank you," is all I can say through the erratic thump of my heart. All the warning bells are going off. I'm getting way too close to this fire, and it will consume me if I don't say something. If I don't say what I want. "Garrett..." Swallowing thickly, I cross the room to stand in front of him.

"Yeah." He steps closer.

The air crackles between us with possibility. The possibility of me closing the distance, smudging my lipstick with a claiming kiss. To know what his lips would feel like against mine. To feel his strong hands roam down my body as he pulls me flush against him. To be late for dinner because we're too busy feasting on one another. It's all there, but so is the blinking red sign warning of heartbreak.

"Sunset is at around 5:20 p.m.," I whisper.

"What?" His murmur is bemused.

"And I get off work around four thirty. I'm thinking that on non-training nights, I should start taking the bus again. It will be good for me to get back in the habit... You've been so kind, and I don't want to keep taking advantage."

"You're not..." he rasps. "You don't have to—"

"But I want to."

The only thing I want more than how I'm starting to *want* Garrett, is to not break my own heart. If the pain of Val stops him from even talking about what happened, he's not ready for what I want from him.

I'm sure Dr. Nor would challenge me on this. *"How do you know he's not ready, if you don't ask for what you want?"* The dangerous hope simmering inside me also whispers that. But I don't want to ask that out of fear of finding out that I'm not what he wants. As much as I want this man, I don't want to lose him. Even if all I have is just his friendship.

"I'm so grateful for you. For everything. Please know this isn't about me not appreciating you, or enjoying..." Nodding, I take a step back. "Plus, I know you sneak back to the hospital most nights. This way, you don't have to do that. You can just stay there to do what you need to do before you go home."

He looks down and then back at me. "Will you let me know when you get home on those nights?"

"Yes. I promise."

"Training. Dark. Raining," he says quickly.

"What?"

He lets out a breath. "Can I drive you home on training nights, when it's dark, and when it rains?"

"Okay," I murmur, trying to ignore that whispered hope that maybe the Southern California drought will end, and the rain will come. It's dangerous to hope for it, but I am, and that makes me fear that Past Jensen may still be lurking around.

17

MILE SEVENTEEN
IS HE...

Cupid Course is louder than I imagined. The whistles and hoots of spectators collide with the thump of rock music that vibrates in the early morning air. It's nothing like the 5K I attempted with Anker. There were only around a couple hundred runners and spectators at that race. There must be a thousand here.

I stand, my pulse thudding and fingers curled tight around my cane, soaking it all in. *How on earth will Garrett and I hear each other over this?*

"Never thought I'd be cheering you on at a race." Anker bumps my shoulder with his. "It's like we've done some *Freaky Friday* sibling swap."

I smirk. "Guess that means I'll kill my official time by stopping to flirt with the woman handing me a bottle of water on the track."

"*One* time... And *you* won't let me live it down. If you'd seen her, you would have got it." He loops his arm around my shoulders. "She had these big brown eyes."

"I don't think it was her *big brown eyes* that caught your attention." I bump his hip with mine.

"My dear sister, you may be so shallow to only check out a

woman's *bump dots* but I am an eyes man. They're the window into the soul, and the prettiest part of a lady."

"Is that why mom and dad put child blocker software on the computer when we were teens? Because of your fascination with eyes?" I poke him.

"Women who live in erotic audio houses shouldn't toss stones." His tut is laced with humor. "By the way, Sonora told me to wish you luck today."

My mouth lifts. Anker, indeed, got his head out of his ass and reached out to Sonora. From what I've observed in the runner/guide group since then, they appear to have fallen back into their playful exchanges.

"Tell her I said thanks." I twist to face him; my face flexed into a wry expression. "What color are Sonora's eyes, by the way?"

"Brown, and drop it." He points at me. "We're just friends."

"Stupid men." I roll my eyes. "Friends, but you want more."

Anker may have fucked up, but I don't think he's down and out. Not only are his and Sonora's interactions in the runner's group more frequent, but I know they are texting almost daily again. He was twenty minutes late for our celebratory dinner for Catherine last week because he was on the phone with Sonora.

"Her boyfriend wouldn't appreciate anything more than just friendly intentions," he says, a hint of a frown in his admission.

"Boyfriend? Since when?"

"She told me last week, after it became official. They met at the marathon."

My stomach drops at that. No doubt this is salt in Anker's wounds about the marathon. Not only did he not get to run it, but the woman I know he wants—even if he won't admit it—met someone else there.

"He's a reporter who interviewed her. Guess he reached out to do some follow-up, which led to a friendship, which led to…" He clears his throat. "She's happy, and that's all that matters."

"I'm so sorry." I reach out, squeezing his forearm.

He shrugs me off. "It's not a big deal. Just wasn't meant to be."

"It's not like they're married. Couples break up all the time. You never know what will happen."

He snorts a dismissive laugh. "I'd prefer not to hope for Sonora's heartbreak."

It's not exactly what I'm hoping for. *Though, isn't it?* For Anker to get a second chance at a first chance, someone's heart will need to break—Sonora's or her new boyfriend. While not all breakups equate to heartbreak, it still comes with a little sadness. I wouldn't want that for them, but I want my brother's happiness more.

"Plus, there are other big brown-eyed women out there," he says.

I see past his false bravado. Anker may wear the carefree cad mask, but I know what's underneath. With past failed relationships—or a prospect of one—Anker moved on. Despite the bevy of brown-eyed women out there, I suspect there's only one for my brother.

"You ready for this?" He motions around the race.

Cupid Course consists of a children's 1K and an adult 10K course looping through downtown Seal Beach. The course winds through neighborhoods, runs along the coast, and ends near the pier. Kayla and Catherine are at the ready with their phones to capture video at the finish line to send to my parents. Anker will join them there after Garrett arrives before our start time.

"Yup." I inhale deeply, allowing the kinetic energy of the race to wash over me.

I still can't believe I'm doing this. It's not like I wasn't aware that this would be today's environment. I've been at the finish lines for some of Anker's races, but it's so different when you're the one running it. Cupid Course is on a whole other level, with hundreds of participants broken into different running groups and start times throughout the day.

"This is just practice. It's just part of your training to prepare you for the big show with me in October." Anker squeezes my shoulder, pulling my attention to him. "Nobody expects you to set a course record."

Setting a record isn't the goal, but I do have expectations. Over the last few months, I've ramped up to a steady jog on the treadmill or with Garrett, hitting four to five miles without stopping to power walk. While I haven't yet run the 6.2 miles—without stopping—that make up a 10K, I'm determined to do that today. I know I'll have a second chance in March after I run my second of two planned 10Ks, but I want to knock this out of the park my first time at bat. I want to not just meet my own expectations, but have my friends have some for me beyond just finishing.

I pout. "Thanks for the vote of confidence."

"This isn't about doubting you. You've got this. You're *my* sister after all."

"Your modesty is boundless." I shake my head.

"It's probably one of my top ten features," he says cheekily. "But I know you have this. I just don't want you to put extra pressure on yourself. Whether you power walk or run it, finishing is the goal. You don't need to push yourself."

"The whole point of this is about pushing past my boundaries." I tip my head up to take in his face, my hat's brim further obscuring my vision, requiring me to scan a little more than usual.

"First, I thought the point of this was to help me prove the existence of the Larsen lore. Who knows, somewhere here may be the love of your life. It is the year you turn thirty, my dear sister."

"No thanks. I'm on hiatus." I roll my eyes.

Laughing, he loops his arm around my shoulder. "Also, the fact that you're even here is already far past the boundaries you once had. I just don't want you to put too much pressure on yourself. That's how mistakes happen."

That's how people get hurt is what he's not saying. It's the quiet warning beneath his words. Garrett. Me. Other runners. Any of us could get hurt if I make a mistake. Like weeds poking through sidewalk cracks, dread slinks through me.

"Don't get it twisted, sister"—he unzips his hoodie and points to his T-shirt—"I'm team Jensen all the way."

Squinting, I take in his shirt. "Is that…"

"Yup." He waves to himself. "It's your face below the words *See Her Run*."

"You are such a dork." I guffaw, wrapping my arms around him.

I know he says I just need to finish, but imagine his face if I run every mile of this race. If I place in the top fifty for my age/gender category. Better yet, if I match the times of some of the more experienced blind runners in the group. Though, given the fifty-two minute time Sonora ran in her New Year's Day race a month ago, it seems far-fetched for me to match or exceed that time.

"Speaking of shirts, I see your guide has his own *special* one on." Anker snorts.

"Oh god." I cringe, "Please tell me you did *not* make Garrett wear a shirt with my face on it."

Mortification blazes through me at the idea of my face on Garrett's body. Although, something else ignites at the image of my actual face pressed against his naked chest. The last week of only seeing each other for training hasn't cooled off my crush. On the contrary, it's gotten worse. I find myself making up the stupidest reasons to text him, and checking the weather report multiple times a day, hoping for rain and not as a means to end the drought.

Stupid sunny Southern California. Even more stupid me to set this boundary of limiting my time with Garrett. Even if I know it's for the best, I don't like it. This experience may be about pushing my boundaries, but it's also about adhering to the new ones I've set. The ones in place to avoid past mistakes.

"Hey," Garrett says, reaching us.

"Hey." I bite the inside of my cheek, hoping to slap down the flutter in my chest. The man says, "hey" and I may fucking swoon. *I am so pathetic.* "So, what shirt did he talk you into wearing?"

"May I?" He reaches out and takes my hand, and I comply.

He takes my fingers and brushes them across his chest. The swooning may commence at any minute, and not just by the rock-hard feel of his sculpted chest, but from the raised letters spelling out *Service Human*.

Laughter skips out of me. "Oh my god! How?"

"The woman I commissioned for your Christmas card made it."

It's standard practice for blind/guide duos to wear special shirts to let other runners know. It helps keep everyone safe on the course. I have a shirt that says *Watch Out: Blind Girl in Motion* that my parents gave me for Christmas. They can't be here today, but plan to come down for the marathon.

"Nice, and you got it in pink. Jensen's favorite color," Anker says with a loud *slap* against Garrett's back.

"This wasn't Anker's doing? You did this?" A gooeyness fills my chest at that.

"I also got you one," he says bashfully as he hands me a gift bag. "I know you have the shirt from your parents, but this won't be our last race."

The way "this won't be our last race" thrums within me drowns out the chaotic cacophony around us. Today is our first race. We have our second 10K in the spring and the half marathon in the summer before I transition to train with Anker. Something in the way he says it promises more than just those, or it may be the story I'm telling myself. I can't ignore the worry nipping inside me that I may be projecting meaning on something that is just a gift from a thoughtful man

Just enjoy the moment. I swallow those worries, choosing to deal with them during my next Dr. Nor session.

"This is so sweet. Thank you." I pull the shirt out of the bag and swipe my fingers over the tactile letters reading *Blind Queen*.

"Thought it was fitting, since I'm your service human," he says, a wry expression plays in his tease.

"Thank you, my dear subject. Your queen approves," I hum, channeling my best impression of Kayla's posh English accent.

"Excellent accent, Jensen," Miles drawls from nearby, causing me to turn towards his voice.

My head tilts. "Miles? What are you doing here?"

"Kayla mentioned you were racing today, so I thought I would come by to cheer you on. That's what friends do after all."

It is something friends do. I'm just shocked Miles is that type of friend. Besides a few chats at the coffee shop on campus and the one time he'd tagged along with Kayla for lunch with me and Catherine, our interactions have been minimal since we agreed to be just friends.

"Didn't realize friends bring other friends red roses," Garrett mutters.

"This friend does." Miles's retort is snide. "These are for you, luv." He leans in, pressing a peck to my cheek before handing me a bouquet.

"Thanks." I bring them up to my nose, inhaling deeply to capture their sweet perfume. "This is lovely."

"You really are the queen with men just coming to pay

tribute. I'm a little jealous." Anker tips his head toward Garrett. "In five years of friendship, you've never brought me flowers before a race."

"Flowers are impractical," Garrett grumbles.

"Excuse me?" Miles steps back, pivoting toward Garrett.

"She can't run with those."

"I'm aware." Hands on hips, Miles's tone is icy.

"Like two bucks." Anker's low mutter is barely audible.

If he weren't right next to me, I likely wouldn't have heard it. As much as I want to protest, this is exactly what this is like. Garrett and Miles are squared off like gunslingers. Each dig is a verbal bullet aimed at the other.

"Flowers are great, but typically a finish line thing." Anker's interjection is good-humored.

"Indeed." Miles chuckles, taking the bouquet back. "Just wanted to wish you luck. I'll hold on to these for you at the finish line."

"Thank you. It really was sweet," I say.

"On that note…" A nervous laugh falls out of Anker. "I'll take your cane and the tributes your adoring subjects have bestowed on you and go meet Kayla and Catherine at the finish line."

"You're going to smash this race, and then after we'll celebrate you like the proper queen you appear to be." Miles gives me a side hug before turning to leave with my brother.

"You're talking to literary fuckboy again?" Garrett says, his jaw clenched.

"We're just friends." I turn to face him, tipping my head up to take him in.

The brim of his hat shadows his face, but I know a firm line anchors his mouth. "Does he know that?"

"I've told him as much."

"He wants more." He gestures in the direction that I suspect Miles walked off to.

"Well, I don't… Not from him."

The man I want more from, I am too chicken shit to ask. Fear holds me back from just saying it to Garrett, because what if I'm wrong? What if he doesn't want me? What if he does, but won't let himself? Somehow, I'm here again with feelings for someone I shouldn't have feelings for. Someone who, if they do have feelings for me, isn't ready to admit them. Someone who, despite how much I don't want to be that woman anymore, I'd wait for. That I'd break my own heart for. I'll have lots to discuss during this week's session with Dr. Nor.

Cocking one eyebrow, I cross my arms over my chest. "I don't want to talk about Miles or your disapproval of my friendship with him. What I want to do is focus on the task at hand. We have a race to run. So, do you want to lecture me about Miles or run with me?"

"Jensen, I—"

"Turnip," I huff out.

He tips his head back, releases a hard breath, and then looks at me. "Fine… Let's run."

"Fine." I take his arm for him to lead me to the start line.

Now is not the time to deal with this. My head needs to be in this race, not thinking about either of these men. Not Miles with his definitely "more than friends" flowers, or Garrett, whose every action twists me into a knotted up ball of confusion about his feelings, and my own. One moment, I think we can just be friends. The next moment, the pull for more is so strong that I'm scared I'll break if I keep holding myself back from it—from him.

It's why I stopped having him drive me home. The line is getting blurred. I know that, but the thought of a Garrett-free existence guts me.

Ugh… I'm so fucked.

"I overstepped…" he says as we move through the crowd. "I am sorry. I just… I don't want to see you get hurt again."

"Me neither." I squeeze his bicep. "Running together is

about trust, and you've gotta trust me to make the right choices to keep myself safe. If you don't, this will never work."

He stops, twisting to face me. "I do trust you."

"And I trust you. Forget about Miles. Forget about everything else. There's just us and this race." I hit him with what I hope is a soft smile.

This is where my focus needs to be. Not on Miles. Not on my feelings for Garrett. Just on this moment. It may be my typical Jensen-self of waiting for things, but I can wait to deal with all this tomorrow. Today is my first—hopefully—victory lap on this journey. I just want to sink into that. The rest is for tomorrow's Jensen to deal with.

He nods. "Just us, and the race."

Positioned at the back of the cluster of readying runners, I unravel the rope, handing him one end, and begin to wrap the other end around my hand. Anxiety buzzes in my veins with each circle of the rope around my hand. This is happening. I'm doing this. It's not my first time running, but this one is important.

The time I ran with Anker was about making my brother happy. This time, it's about me. Even if I agreed to start this to help my brother, I want to prove that I can push past the things I thought I couldn't do, including the things I've always done.

"You ready?" Garrett's steady voice pulls my attention.

"Are you?" Brow furrowed, I tip my head up to him.

"It's okay to be nervous." He places his untethered hand on my upper arm.

"I'm not... I'm... I just don't want to..." I look down at the bright pink rope wrapped around my gloved hand and back up. "The last time I did this, it didn't mean anything. And I.... I just don't want to embarrass myself."

Every instance of embarrassment in my life whispers in the cool morning air. The time I tripped up the riser in high school and fell during a school concert. Crying in the girls' bathroom stall after Everett told me kissing me was just a bet. Knocking over Miles's drink at Harkey's. Any bit of confidence I had is deflating with each announcement over the PA system for runners to proceed to the starting line.

"I'm nervous, too."

My head tilts. "How? You've run other races. This is child's play for you."

"As you said, this time is different... *This* matters." He swallows thickly. "You're depending on me. I don't want to let you down." He soothes his fingers against my forearm.

Even through my shirt's thin fabric, I feel each sweet caress of his fingertips. It unspools the anxious knot inside me. It's both good and bad anxiety. The good that comes with excitement, and the bad that accompanies worry. A worry I know we share. He doesn't want to fail me, and I don't want to fail him. Just as I don't want to fail myself.

Knowing that we both are anxious strangely eases my worry. I'm not alone in this feeling, and neither is he.

For so long, Garrett has run solo. I forget what this might be like for him. For this man to open himself up to the possibility of letting someone down. The memory of his pained admission about failing Val aches in my chest.

"It's not just me. *We're* depending on each other." I tug on the rope that tethers us to one another. "You run, I run. You fall, I fall."

"Did you just quote *Titanic*?" The deep laugh that belts out of him hits me like I've drunk a glass of full-bodied red wine, leaving me warm and relaxed.

"How dare you! I would never!" I pop my hip. "I am paraphrasing at best."

The rich rumble vibrating from him soothes every frazzled nerve in me.

"I'm nervous too, but we've got this." I move my free

hand to touch his forearm, sliding it down to thread our untethered hands.

"We've got this."

"And if we don't, we'll just keep working until we do."

"Okay." He presses our joined hands to his chest.

A voice booms from the PA system. "Runners, take your mark."

With one last squeeze of our joined hands, we release and ready ourselves. Excitement ripples through the crowd like crashing waves. The chaotic soundtrack of noise makers, cowbells, and cheers drowns out the thud of my pulse. I can barely hear the bullhorn's siren as it signals the participants to start. I certainly can't hear Garrett's call out, but the three tugs he does on the rope tell me it's time to move.

My limited vision, combined with the dulling of my hearing due to the wall of noise surrounding me, causes my breath to come in rapid spurts. My grip tightens on the rope, keeping me close to Garrett as we start with a slow jog. Our group of runners remains clustered together as we move down the course, which is lined with cheering onlookers on each side.

"To the right," Garrett calls out and tugs the rope, guiding me to the course's far side.

It's our race strategy. We'll remain tucked up to the side to avoid groups of runners that tend to dominate the central paths. It also ensures that we only deal with runners on one side of us to keep everyone safe.

The quieting course—outside the slap of sneakers against pavement—allows me to settle into the run. The gentle burn of my muscles awakening, the steadying rhythm of my heartbeat, and the even cadence of my breath. It's the slow climb into the runner's high that I've just started experiencing over the last few weeks. The initial ache coursing through your body makes you think you can't do this, until euphoria washes it away with this weightless sensation. Each time I run, it envelops me around mile two, so with us just passing the first mile marker, I know I'm almost there.

"One down." Garrett's shout is muffled by the crash of cheers and noisemakers as we pass the first mile marker.

The hoots and whistles simmer from a roar to a hum the further along the course we go. Besides the periodic runners zipping past with call outs of "On your left," it's almost as if it's just us.

As my body relaxes into the pace of our run and the course's hummed soundtrack, I loosen the slack just a bit. I remain close to Garrett, but without the death grip hold on my rope. We fall into an easy pattern of me tightening and then loosening the slack each time we pass cheering crowds at the different markers, or an expected change in the terrain. For the most part, we run on paved streets with no curbs or drop-offs outside of random ruts that Garrett calls out and guides us around.

By the time we hit the fourth mile, my legs burn. This is the furthest I've run with Garrett without slowing to a power walk. Muscle memory seems to protest that I should slow down. Teeth gritted, I push just a little harder. It's a tug of war inside me. My heart wanting one thing, and my body another.

"Walk?" Garrett calls, his breath heavy.

"Nope," I pant out.

His only response is two gentle tugs on the rope.

We continue in silence. My breath is now unsteady, but my fingers are still gripping tight as we run beneath what I assume are trees that convert sunshine into shadow. With it comes a momentary sense of discombobulation. For runners, like Sonora, who are totally blind, this isn't as much of an issue. They're not as impacted by sudden light changes as those with some usable vision. The glare-to-shadow fluctuation disorients, but also hurts. My eyes sting and, if prolonged, it can cause migraines. My hat helps with the glare but intensifies the shadows when passing beneath trees or overhangs.

Despite the distraction by the change in lighting, my body is crying out to slow down. We're so close to the fifth mile marker. The increasing volume of the spectators as we move close makes me feel as if I could just reach out and take hold of the fifth mile marker. After that, it's only another 1.2. I'm so close.

"Walk?" Garrett booms over the roaring crowd.

"N—n—no," I stammer through my gasping breaths.

"Jensen." Somehow, my name comes out both a scold and a plea.

"Garrett." My brow puckers.

I know he's worried. The tether telegraphs so much between us. The slowing of my pace, followed by the forced pushes, are all told with each tug or tightened slack. It doesn't allow me to hide how I'm struggling.

"It's okay," he says.

"Mile six," is all I say.

"We'll still get there…" he pants, "…whether we run or walk a bit."

I know he's right. My body knows he's right. I just wanted to run this entire thing. I know I won't be able to run the entire marathon, but I wanted this. I wanted this victory lap.

"Three miles," he puffs out.

My face scrunches. "What?"

"I only jogged…three miles of my first…10K."

"Really?"

"Yeah." His reply is slightly strangled.

It's hard to imagine Garrett struggling with this. Like Anker, he's run for years. Just as nervousness about this surged in both of us, this is another thing we share. We've both started somewhere and had to be okay with that.

Nodding, I start to slow my pace. "Okay."

He tugs twice on the rope. "Okay."

We slow to a brisk walk. Relief sighs through my muscles. I loosen the tension on the rope but remain a step behind him.

"I wanted to run the whole thing," I say, emotion thick in my throat.

"I know."

"It's not failing, because I'm doing this, but…"

"You'd only fail if you stopped. You didn't stop. You're still doing this. Run. Walk. Piggyback. All that matters is you crossing the finish line, and you're doing that."

My lips curl. "Piggyback?"

"If you think your back is strong enough," he quips, looking back over his shoulder at me.

A breathless laugh sprints out of me. "You need a new joke."

"Still made you laugh." He twists his head forward.

"Thank you," I say, gratitude nestling deep in my chest.

He may worry. He may encourage. He never says to stop. Though, I imagine that's the hardest thing for my protective friend. Instead, he shared just another piece of himself and allowed me to come to my own decision.

"You're a good service human."

"Thank you," he says with a little tug of the rope that somehow feels as if he squeezes my hand in his. "Mile six we run, okay?"

"Okay."

With the increasing level of cheers, we increase our pace. From everything I know, the last leg of this race will be loud on top of loud. The entire course is flanked by spectators cheering on runners with an array of noisemakers. The heavy beat of rock music and booming voice of an announcer calling out end times for different runners, which are transmitted from the little tags we wear, greets us.

"Finish line!" Garrett yells.

"Congrats, Runner 1530, for finishing their first 10K race," the announcer says, eliciting loud hoots and cheers.

"That's me!" My shout is breathy as I realize I'm Runner 1530.

"Sure is!" Garrett laughs as he starts slowing our pace until we eventually walk.

I did it! Tears gather in my eyes, but I blink them away. This moment is too sweet for me to cry, which is why I'll probably cry at some point. Right now, I'm just going to let this high ride.

Chest heaving, mouth pulled up into a large grin, and heart feeling as if it will burst, we slow to a stop. "I did it!" My squeal is breathless.

Without thinking, I jump in the air and Garrett catches me. Lifting me into his arms, I circle his nape and my legs fold around his waist. Not one bit of me questions how natural this feels.

"You did it!" He leans away, allowing me to take in the shit-eating grin visible from below his cap's brim.

"*We* did it."

"That we did," he breathes, his mouth inches from mine.

This should be weird. I'm still tethered to him by the rope. Not to mention, he has a vise-like grip on my backside, and my legs are wrapped tight around him. The intensity of his gaze on me thrums within me. We're connected in so many ways, but one.

Reminiscent of wildfire threatening to consume everything in its path, desire burns inside me to claim him. The charge arcs between us like a dare. Just a few inches and my lips could meet his, sealing us together.

I trace my fingers along his jawline, delighting in the rasp of his stubble. His low groan and fingers' kneading into my ass urge me on. I trail my finger slowly to his mouth, tracing its outline.

"Jensen." He nuzzles his nose against mine. It's slow and gentle, as if testing the water's temperature before diving in.

"Garrett." I lick my lips.

"Jensen," he repeats my name like I am both the thing he wants, and the only one who can give it to him. His hot breath teases against my lips, sending a shudder up my spine.

"Garrett." I cradle his face to anchor myself to my target.

That fire within me destroys any resolve to stay away. I don't want to think about all the reasons this is a bad idea. I don't want to think about tomorrow. I just want this moment, and if that's all I have of him, I'll take it.

"Sorry to interrupt." A high-pitched female voice chuckles. "But we need to move folks along as we have more runners coming. There are far better places to stare longingly into each other's eyes than the finish line."

"Sorry," Garrett says, placing me on the ground.

"We weren't staring longingly," I mumble, even though that's exactly what we were doing.

Garrett's arms. A place I should not have been. No matter how good it felt pressed up against him, the heat of his body my own personal Garrett Snuggie. I blame the runner's high for the momentary breach in judgment.

"Sure," she sasses. "Here's your medals. Make sure to use hashtag Cupid Course on all social media posts." She places the medal around my neck and then around Garrett's before she scoots off.

I trace the medal and then look up at Garrett. "I didn't know we got medals."

"All the participants do for finishing."

We stand there awkwardly for a moment, just looking at each other.

We both start. Me with his name and he with "We…"

"Sorry." I wince and then gesture at him. "Go on."

"I…" He coughs and then shifts. "We should get moving. Like she said, other runners are coming in. Plus, everyone is waiting."

18

MILE EIGHTEEN
DO IT THEN

Did we almost kiss? Tension thickens the air between us as Garrett and I walk to meet our friends and my brother. It's not that delicious connection that buzzed between us at the finish line. This tension is full of regrets. Whether the emotions of finishing the race or the bond building between us over the last few months, it's clear we were both in it just now. We both were leaning in. It's also clear that neither of us is talking about it.

The brazen confidence I had moments after finishing the race is gone. I'm being a chicken shit again, waiting for him to broach the subject.

Ugh... I'm going to owe future Jensen a special treat for everything she'll need to deal with tomorrow.

"You did it!" Kayla squeals, slamming into my body for a hug.

"You're such a boss!" Catherine comes to my other side. She and Kayla sandwich me in a tight clench.

"So obnoxious. You're going to crush her," Anker teases.

"Says the man who knocked a drink out of someone's hand with his arm waving as he was cheering." Catherine's taunt is delivered with a side of playfulness.

"Guilty, but it's hard not to go full cheering soccer mom when your sister runs her first official 10K in under eighty minutes. She's a badass!"

"Thanks." Grinning, I look between my friends and Garrett, who remains quiet.

"You did great... Both of you." Anker taps Garrett's shoulder with his fist.

"Thanks," he grunts.

"We got it all on video." Catherine bumps my hip with hers.

Hopefully not everything. I offer a weak smile. The fact that Anker hasn't made a snarky comment about me wrapped around Garrett like a cat in heat makes me suspect he didn't witness our little moment. Not to mention, Kayla isn't subtle. If they knew, she'd have already blurted out a quippy comment about me trying to snog my Mr. Stalker Darcy.

But he's not mine. Even if we had a moment, Garrett isn't mine. I don't know what the thing that almost just happened means, but what I do know is he's not looking at me. A chill zips down my spine from the loss of his focus. I can always feel Garrett's attention, and right now I feel nothing except the pit growing in my stomach.

"We only got you crossing the finish line. Anker's fat head got in the way after that."

"My head is in perfect proportion with the rest of my body," he scoffs. "Want your cane, or should I keep it with your spoils, so Garrett and you can do a victory lap to Bread?" He chuckles.

"I'll take my cane," I say, knowing that if I'm close to Garrett, the temptation to bring up what just happened will be too great.

It's best if I avoid this until after our celebratory breakfast. He doesn't appear to be in a hurry to talk about it, and if I bring it up, part of me worries he'll call it a mistake or claim turnip rights. The mix of confusion and worry pulsing inside me makes it too hard to form the words needed to have this conversation. Right now, I choose a pretend smile while I sit across from him and enjoy what should be our celebratory breakfast with friends.

"Spoils?" I clear my throat.

"Garrett's gift, the race swag bag, and Wannabee Kerouac's flowers."

Miles. I forgot about him. It seems ages since the start line to here.

"Where is Miles?" I tilt my head.

"Not sure. He was with us at the finish line when you crossed and then suddenly said something came up, tossed Anker the flowers, and left," Kayla shrugs.

It appears *someone* may have seen what happened between Garrett and me. The tiniest bit of guilt nips at me. I'm on a romantic sabbatical. That's what I told Miles. Those are—were—my intentions. My confusion aside, it's clear Miles's goal today is romantic, and not just friendly, despite his claim. Even though I know Miles isn't who I want, I feel bad hurting him.

"That's a shame," Garrett says, his tone sarcastic and snide.

"It is. He offered to pay for everyone's breakfast," Kayla says with an audible pout.

"I'll pay."

"No, Garrett. You're not paying." I shake my head.

"Agreed. It's my treat. This breakfast is to celebrate both of you," Anker says.

"When you say 'my treat…'" Kayla coos.

"For a woman in Chanel, you never pick up a check," Catherine teases.

"How do you think I afford Chanel on a professor's salary?"

"Naturally, I'm buying for our champions and their

groupies." Anker laughs, unfolding my cane and handing it to me. "Your chariot."

"We prefer entourage," Kayla quips.

"Not to mention calling cheering women groupies is sexist." A cheeky grin plays in Catherine's tut.

"I'll atone for my casual sexism with bottomless mimosas."

"Mimosas will have to wait. Today is all about the lattes. It's a special occasion after all, so we're drinking Jensen's favorite to celebrate." Catherine bumps my hip with hers. "But only two. Doctor's orders… Right, Garrett?"

The sassiness in Catherine's lilt makes me wonder if my brother's head didn't obstruct as much of her view as she claims.

He clears his throat. "Jensen can have anything she wants."

Does anything I want include you? I bite back that question. It's not just the idea of doing this in front of everyone, so much as the fear of his answer holding me back. *I'm not ready for a girlfriend, especially you. I'm with someone else, but if I wasn't, it would never work. I want a girlfriend, not a project to take care of.*

Memories of the past times I asked for what I wanted from men hiss inside me.

"I'm sure she can have *anything* she wants." Catherine's retort is pointed.

Yup, she saw. Arching one eyebrow, I look between my friend and Garrett.

As we walk to the café, my mind wanders to this week's session with Dr. Nor, the memory drowning out the chatter around me. *Do you think the men you've picked may reinforce the narrative that you're not wanted?* Dr. Nor's words play on repeat inside me.

Is my crush on Garrett this? I'd asked that very question to

Dr. Nor. Her answer? *Maybe, or maybe it's more. Only you can determine if your feelings for Garrett are real or not.*

Stupid therapist and her cryptic answers. For the thirty-dollar copay, it sure would be nice if she just told me what to do instead of leaving it up to me to figure things out.

"Which latte do you want?" Anker taps my upper arm.

"What?" Blinking, I look up at him and then toward our server, who stands, tablet in hand, punching in our drink orders.

"They have a red velvet cupcake one for Valentine's," Garrett says, his low timbre quiet. "I know you like the special seasonal ones."

"Yeah..." I grin as a fizzy sensation sweeps through me. "I'll have that."

Warmth envelops me with the sensation of his eyes meeting mine from across the table. Every nerve ending sparks to life between our tethered gazes. It reassures me that we're still bonded, even with the weirdness of the last twenty minutes.

"Larsen! Marlowe!" A tall man with a rich baritone approaches our table.

"Good god, who is that?" Kayla leans in, her whisper breathy. "He's the most attractive man I've ever seen."

"Deridder," Anker says, rising and doing some complicated handshake, fist-bump, slapping-hug greeting.

"It's Ray Deridder from the hospital," Garrett says, providing verbal confirmation.

Deridder works at Sacred Heart with Anker and Garrett. I met him in the ED after Anker's accident. Kayla's reaction isn't unique. That day, the ED nurses teased that Dr. McSteamy was treating Dr. McDreamy as Ray took care of my brother. Thanks to the charge nurse, I learned they refer to Garrett as McBroody.

"Ray is, perhaps, the least attractive name for a man who may have just impregnated me with one look."

"He'll hear you," I mutter, elbowing her.

"God, I hope so." Kayla fans herself with her hand. "I may be rethinking my no hookups rule."

I snort.

"Deridder, you remember my sister Jensen, and this is Catherine and Kayla," Anker says.

"Nice to meet you." He juts his chin towards the table. "Jensen, it's lovely seeing you again."

"Nice to see you again, Ray." The corners of my lips tug up.

"Were you at the race?" Ray asks.

"Garrett and Jensen ran. We're celebrating. It's her first 10K, and she killed it." Anker fist pumps the air.

"Congrats! It was Liana's first race, so we're doing the same."

"Liana?" I tilt my head.

"My daughter. She's five and ran the kids' 1K fun run." He looks over and waves. "Liana, come here, sweetie."

"Daddy!" Liana squeals, running into his arms.

He hoists her up. "Liana, meet Daddy's friends."

He introduces each of us to her. Her bright smile is audible in each greeting. She reminds me so much of Anker as a child—sunshine in motion.

"This is Jensen." He motions to me.

"You're pretty," Liana says in a giggly lilt.

A nervous laugh falls out of me. "You're so sweet."

My current state isn't my cutest. I've nixed the cap, since we're under an umbrella, and my hair is swept up in a messy bun with wild tendrils falling out. We'd come straight here from the race, so I'm still in yoga pants, T-shirt, and a zip up hoodie to protect from the cool early morning air. If Liana thinks this is pretty, I need a daily dose of her to boost my self-confidence before I leave the house.

"Sorry." Liana buries her face into her dad's neck. "I forgot to not say my inside words out loud again."

"It's okay, sweetie."

"Inside words?" I tilt my head.

"Liana has a habit of saying everything she thinks, so we've been working on that." He chuckles.

"She'll fit in with this group," Catherine snarks. "Those three often say the quiet part out loud." She gestures to me, Kayla, and Anker.

"See, sweetie, it's all good."

Kayla releases a quiet sigh. "He just kissed the top of her head. He's an honest to god DILF," she whispers.

Stop, I mouth.

He goes on, "Remember saying inside words are okay when they are nice."

Liana raises her head, "And telling people they are pretty is nice."

"Especially when it's true." Ray looks from his daughter to me. "She is pretty… Very pretty."

"Thanks." Shifting in my seat, I blush.

"Look, Jensen, another subject to add to your court," Anker teases, causing the flames claiming my cheeks to turn fiery.

"Of course," Garrett mutters gruffly.

I'm not sure if the heat cascading within me is from the embarrassment from Ray's compliment, or from my complicated feelings at Garrett's clear jealousy. Apparently, it's not just Miles he doesn't appreciate… It's any man showing me attention. It's possessive. It's barbaric. *God, why is it turning me on?* I have issues.

"Sorry. Now I'm saying the inside words out loud." Ray clears his throat. "We should get back to my parents. I've gotta get this one to her moms' later." He plops Liana on the ground. "Enjoy your meal. Congrats on the race."

"Thank you."

"Bye!" Liana calls, skipping away.

"I hope to see you again, Jensen." With a quick nod, he turns to follow his daughter.

"Please, please tell me he's single, so Jensen can live out my single dad romance fever dreams with that Adonis." Kayla whines dramatically.

"He is. Liana's mom is his best friend. He donated the sperm, so she and her wife could have a baby. It's not your typical sperm donor situation. Deridder is really involved and shares custody," Anker explains.

"Yes! Yes! All this!" Kayla claps.

"I'm not sure how I feel about any of this," Anker grumbles.

"Especially because I don't think the single daddy trope is what Jensen is going for." Catherine's jest is wink-filled.

Perhaps her subtlety is waning a bit. Catherine is Team "Go for It" about me and Garrett. She and Kayla are up-to-date—minus what happened at the finish line. Kayla wavers back and forth. She cautions me to protect my heart, but also likes Garrett.

"What trope is she going for?"

Ignoring Anker, Catherine flicks her wrist and goes on, "Although, maybe hot single dad is a good option for Jensen. He seems respectful but not scared to make a move."

"I have to…" Garrett rises, his chair's screech loud. "Bathroom."

"Just as I thought." Catherine leans back in her chair, no doubt a triumphant expression covering her face.

I aim my narrowed gaze at my friend. It's clear she hit her mark. Guess my bestie plans to prod both of us to "go for it," and not just me.

Garrett moves away from our table so quickly that I barely register he's left until Anker snarks, "Small bladders the older you get." Garrett is mad. There's no question about it. But at whom? Miles? He's gone. Ray? He did nothing. At me?

Besides us not yet having the conversation we need to have, I've done nothing. Himself?

Fuck this! Garrett doesn't get to be a sullen child about another man showing me attention—no matter what almost happened at the finish line.

"Bathroom!" Unfolding my cane, I shoot up from my chair.

"Do you want—"

"Nope. Got it," I interrupt Kayla and move at a brisk pace toward the bathrooms inside the café.

Angry heat boils inside me. He doesn't get to do this. He doesn't get to almost kiss me, ignore me, and then be a petulant manchild when someone else shows me attention.

With each step, my resolve burns away any hesitation. This isn't a trope. This is my heart. I want Garrett. It's terrifying, but I'm not going to keep doing this. I won't wait, and I won't play this hot and cold game anymore. I'm cannonballing into the deep end. I may sink to the bottom, but I know I can swim my way back up. I've done it before. I just hope I don't have to again.

"Jensen," Garrett rasps as I enter the small alcove where the unisex bathrooms lie.

"Don't Jensen me." I jab a finger into his chest. "You don't get to do this. You don't almost kiss me, pull away, barely look at me, and then act like a spoiled child who's angry that someone else is looking at their favorite toy. I'm not a toy."

He leans in, his mouth inches from mine. "I never said you were."

"You're acting like it." I purse my lips.

"How am I supposed to act when minutes after we almost kiss, your brother shows up with flowers from another man? A man who clearly wants more, and whom you're still speaking to? The same man I watched you pine over for months. Only to have another man flirt with you not twenty minutes later."

I toss my hand in the air. "You're jealous?"

"Of course, I am." He moves closer, causing me to back into the wall. "I don't like literary fuckboys bringing you flowers because I want to be the only man bringing you flowers. I don't like other men—even my friends—telling you you're pretty because I want to be the only man that makes you blush like that."

"Garrett..." My breath stutters.

"I'm jealous of any man who looks at you. Who makes you smile. Makes you laugh." His hands come to my waist, holding me in place. "You are what I think about when I wake up and before I fall asleep..." He brushes his lips up my throat in a slow, sensual lick. "Not to mention you haunt my dreams."

"Garrett..." I whimper, my body melting against him.

"*Fuck*, all I want is to drag you into that bathroom, press you up against the wall, kiss you until the only air you breathe is me, and then plunge myself so fucking deep into you that I don't know where you begin and where I end. That there's no question." He skates his nose along my jawline, inhaling deep. "So sweet..."

"No question of what?" I moan with the bite of his fingers into my hips.

"That I'm yours."

The featherlight brush of his lips over mine causes a shudder to rip down my spine. My entire body thrums with need. My blood heats and skin burns for his touch. No man has ever made me hurt like this. The need for him is a deep ache. So is the fear that I may never have enough of him. Every minute with Garrett leaves me both satisfied and endlessly wanting.

I trail my hands up his torso, over his sculpted chest, along his throat, past his jawline, and cup his face. A quiet, pained groan escapes him with my slow march up his body, confirming I'm not alone in this. The knowledge that he aches for me as much as I do for him makes me drunkenly emboldened.

"Do it, then." Head tipped up, determination curls my lips. My words are a hopeful dare.

"Jensen…" He swallows thickly.

"Take me in there and make me yours."

"I…" Shaking his head, as if breaking a trance, he releases me and steps back.

"Garrett?" I croak.

He scrubs his hands over his face. "This isn't a good idea. We… I lost control… I'm sorry. I shouldn't… I'm sorry."

"You just said… Why?" My whisper is pained. Any quieter and he may hear my heart breaking. I knew this would happen. It's what held me back. I warned myself, but I still didn't listen. Here I am, again, wanting a man who, for whatever reason, doesn't want me back.

"I'm not good for you."

"That's bullshit." I narrow my eyes. "This isn't about not hurting me. It's about protecting yourself. I can't imagine what losing Val was like for you, but you don't get to do this. You don't get to use protecting me as an excuse for playing mind games with my heart, making me think you want me one moment and then you don't the next," I hiss.

"I'm not… It's not about *not* wanting you." His words are filled with sorrow.

As much as his pain slices into me, it's a mere prick to my own. This is a sad song I've heard before.

"And that's the problem. You want me, but you're too scared to do anything about it… Want me. Don't want me. Either way, it's the same ending." The ache surging in my chest causes my words to come out scratchy. "I've been here before, and I won't do it again."

"What are you saying?"

"I don't think you should be my guide anymore."

"Jensen—" he steps close. "No," he croaks.

"Yes." I inhale deep, my expression steely. "Otherwise, I may keep waiting for you to change your mind, and I won't do that again..." Tears prick in my eyes, their sting further blurring my vision.

"It doesn't need to be like this... I can still be your guide. We can still train together—"

"No, we can't..." I sniffle, trying to hold back my tears. The emotions boil over inside, resembling a pot left too long on the burner.

Though, isn't that what I've done? Catherine warned me at the start of this to be careful, but I still played with the fire of my feelings for Garrett. It's my fault that I got burned. I should have listened to my head, ignoring my heart, and stayed away.

"Jensen..." He scrubs his hands down his face. "I...I don't want to hurt you," he says, his voice gravelly.

"Too late." I swallow against the twinge in my throat. "I don't think we should train together anymore."

"No."

"Yes." I meet his stare and push as much icy determination into my own as I can. Even if this shreds the already tattered pieces of my heart, I know this is what's best.

"Jensen, don't do this," he says, his tone desperate.

"I've made my decision... I'm sorry." With a shuddered breath, I grip my cane and straighten my spine. "Now, I'm going to go into the bathroom to cry, wash my face, and then come back to our friends. We'll smile and pretend this didn't happen because I don't want to ruin this for them. Tomorrow, I'll find someone new to train with."

"No."

"It's for the best." I push away from the wall and move to the bathroom door.

"Jensen...please," he says softly, gripping my elbow and halting my steps.

"Turnip," I whisper.

It's too much. My resolve is already crumbling with internal protests not to do this. That I'm strong enough to have him as just a friend. But I'm not. The idea of only crumbs of Garrett twinges dully inside me.

There will always be a part of me that will want this man. I know that deep in my bones. This isn't a sappy love song where he'll realize we belong together by the last note. He may be the man I've been waiting for, but I won't wait anymore. Not for someone. Only *with* someone.

"Turnip." He releases me.

With a deep breath, I open the bathroom door and step in. "Goodbye, Garrett."

19

MILE NINETEEN
JUST KISSING

"I can stay," Catherine offers, running her fingers through my hair, as I snuggle against her on my sofa.

When I opened the door post my ugly bathroom cry at Bread, I found her standing in the small alcove. She knew something was up the moment Garrett returned to the table, in a rush to leave. Telling Anker a lie about me having "lady issues," we grabbed comfort pastries from the bakery and took a raincheck on breakfast. Considering he's a doctor, Anker gets unreasonably squeamish about my period, so he asked few questions.

Since then, she, Kayla, and I've been debriefing over pastries and many, many cups of tea. Both my friends reassured me that I did the right thing. As much as I realize this isn't like with Chase, it doesn't hurt any less. With Chase, he didn't want a woman like me—not as a girlfriend. With Garrett, he wants me, but won't let himself have me.

Whether it's his grief or guilt about being with someone else, it doesn't matter. At the end of the day, he doesn't want me enough to try. To work through the scary things together. I have my own things to deal with, but I'm willing to do that with him. If he's not willing to do it with me, then there's no future for us.

"No. You two have plans." I sit up.

Despite my friends' plan to drive to San Diego this afternoon, they've postponed to stay with me. I'm grateful, but they've done enough. Kayla is speaking at the National Jane Austen Society's conference as their breakfast keynote tomorrow morning. With several literary big-wigs speaking at the conference, including one of Catherine's favorite romance authors, a writer known for Austen retellings, she's Kayla's plus one.

"We can always leave early tomorrow," Kayla offers.

"You need a good night's sleep, so you can shine tomorrow." I scoop up the empty plate and shuffle to the kitchen.

"Please, literary Barbie always shines." Catherine laughs.

"If only I had a Malibu Dream House." Kayla sighs. "But she's right. I could give this talk in my sleep. I don't say this lightly, but you're more important than Austen."

I mock-gasp. "What would the National Jane Austen Society say if they knew their keynote speaker uttered such blasphemy?"

"I'll blame it on my friendship with a Brontë scholar," she sasses, grabbing our empty mugs from the coffee table.

"We Brontë scholars are the bad girls of the literary world, so that tracks," Catherine quips. "Jensen, are you sure you're okay?"

"No…" I heave a breath. "But I will be."

Right now, it's hard to feel okay about any of this. It's hard to see past the pain right now, but deep down I know I did the right thing.

Just like my friends have said, this needed to be in the open. I may have lost Garrett forever, but I'll pick up those pieces in the morning. If there's one thing I'm learning, it's that I can do hard things. I can train for a marathon. I can ask a man I care about for what I want, and stay true to that when he says no.

"San Diego isn't that far, and if I need you, we have these things called phones." I hold up my mobile, currently supplying the music we are listening to, and shake it. "I'm going to take a long, hot shower and lose myself in an audiobook."

"Perhaps one with female rage," Catherine suggests.

"Or a gory horror." Kayla wiggles beside me at the kitchen sink. "I have many suggestions."

Once my friends leave, I do just that. I take such a long shower that I worry I'm breaking some sort of California drought-related ordinance. After, I tug on pajamas. Braiding my wet hair, I stare at the hoodie at the end of my bed. It's Garret's, which I haven't returned. It's also my go-to hoodie most nights. I want to put it on to live in the delusion that his arms are wrapped around me and not just the soft fabric.

"Pathetic," I mutter, scooping it up and tossing it into my closet.

Slipping on a different hoodie, I take Catherine's suggestion and listen to a thriller with a gothic vibe. The sudden banshee-like scream of wind causes me to jump. Between that and the debris battering against my balcony's glass door, I'm almost transported into the book's spooky setting. It's a sharp contrast from this morning's sunshine.

The power goes out, plunging my apartment into darkness. "Crap."

I move to the balcony door, open it, and poke my head out. Outside is also blanketed in black. The lights that normally shine into the building's small courtyard are dark. Grabbing my phone, I turn off the audiobook to check the power company's website.

Losing power with my limited vision is an interesting experience. In so many ways, I'm better prepared than most to navigate in the dark. My apartment is set up so I can non-visually find and do most things. Still, I'm at a disadvantage if I leave my apartment or need to use some of the devices I rely on.

Locating my flashlight, I go through my internal power outage checklist. I turn on several battery-operated candles, placing them around the apartment for light. Next, I double-check that my door is locked, including the deadbolt. Then, I text Anker that the power is out, but I'm okay.

Anker: Here too. Want me to come over?

Me: Nope. I'm going to listen to my audiobook and go to bed.

Anker: By audiobook, do you mean your erotic audios?

Me: Yes.

Anker: I did that to myself.

The grimace that—no doubt—covers his face causes me to snicker. It will never not be fun to mess with him.

Saying goodbye, I crawl into bed. I nix the scary book for the latest F.M. Iversen audio to lose myself in a Prohibition Era romance between a high-society darling and a bootlegger. Their angst to lovers' story reminds me of Garrett and me. Only we didn't quite get to lovers.

I rub my chest, hoping to soothe the ache that comes with thinking of Garrett. Is he at the hospital right now? As much as I know his excuse for leaving early was bullshit, I wouldn't put it past him to go there to check in, especially with the power outage. The hospital has generators, so it's likely unimpacted, but both he and Anker talk about increased admissions during outages. I can picture Garrett, with that always-constant frown on his face, as the steady captain in the midst of all the chaos at the hospital. The thought pricks sadness as much as it comforts.

Sighing, I undo my now dry hair from its braid, allowing the wavy tendrils to hang loose. I plop against my pillow, trying to lose myself in Alicia and Tom's story, rather than my thoughts of Garrett and mine. At least, Alicia and Tom have a happy ending.

"Battery Low," my phone's robotic voice announces.

"Great," I grumble, sitting up in bed.

Between using my phone to play music earlier and its nonstop audiobook use, its battery is dying. I need to be better about charging it. The power company's website estimates it will be on in the next two hours. It's almost eleven, so I know Anker is already asleep. He's never been a night owl, so I opt to turn off my phone to conserve energy and go to sleep.

With the power out, I'm on high alert with every sound. The creepy howl of the wind doesn't help. This is why I seldom do scary movies or books. Every bit of debris that slaps against my balcony makes me think of the book's scythe-wielding killer.

The sound of loud banging at my door makes me bolt upright in bed. "Fuck!"

Heart racing, I grab my phone to turn it on again in case I need to call for help. There's no way I'm opening that door. Even if Kayla's suggested book didn't have me on edge, I never open the door to someone I don't know.

"Jensen! Are you there?" More banging echoes. "It's Garrett!"

Brow pinched, I jump out of bed. "Garrett?"

"Thank god." The relief in his voice is muffled.

I undo the deadbolt and the lock on the knob. "What are you doing here?" I ask, opening the door.

He rushes in. "The power is out."

"I know." I close the door and motion at him. "How did you get in?"

"I snuck in through the garage," he pants.

"You broke in... *Again*?"

"You weren't answering your phone," he grits out.

Dim candlelight outlines his form, but the rest of him is

shadowed in darkness. Even if I can't see him, not clearly, his energy paints the picture of a man in distress. Spine straight, chest heaving, and hands on his hips, he stares at me. My body ignites with the intensity of the gaze sweeping over my figure in assessment.

"Why do you never answer your fucking phone?" he barks, exasperated.

Indignation blazes within me. "It's off—"

"Why?"

"It was about to die. I turned it off to conserve the battery, so I could use it if there was an emergency," I hiss, holding it up.

"You should have called me." He prowls close. "I would have come. I—"

"We're not together."

"That doesn't matter. You still should have called," he shouts.

"Don't you dare yell at me, Garrett Marlowe." I poke his chest. "And don't pull this overprotective, possessive alpha male *bullshit* on me. You're not my boyfriend. You made it clear you don't want that job, so I'm not yours to worry about."

"I never said I didn't want the job," he leans close, his breath against my lips sends heat crisscrossing within me.

"You said—"

"That this isn't a good idea—" He motions between us. "That I don't want to hurt you. I never said I don't want the job. That I don't want you. All I do is *want* you. Every fucking minute of the day. From the moment you blathered on about whatever Chicago trivia you'd googled at Anker's birthday five years ago, I've wanted you."

I can't breathe. The punch of his confession steals my ability to say or do anything besides stare at him. I know Garrett wants me, but the fact that he's always wanted me sends my world off kilter.

The last five years flash through my mind's eye like a picture book. Each memory tells the story of a man pushing away the one thing he wants, and the girl too stupid to see what's been in front of her this entire time.

"It fucking hurts how much I want you," he says, his voice hoarse. "I'm no good for you, and I know that, but I want you anyway... Every day I fight it."

"Stop fighting it, then."

Tension crackles across the scant inches between us like a coming storm. Like a charge, daring him to take what he wants—what we both want.

"I'm done," he says.

"With me?"

"With fighting this." Gripping my hips, he pulls me flush against him, my cell phone tumbling to the floor.

His mouth meets mine in a hard kiss. The sheer bruising force of it ripples waves of pleasure through me. Each press drinks up everything I give, and right now, I want to give this man everything. The years of growing desire for him. My here and now with its swirls of emotions about and for him. Above all, my future wrapped up tight in the hope that this may be our first kiss and not our only one.

My fingers curl into his T-shirt, anchoring me to him—to this moment. I'm terrified if I let go, he'll float away.

"Garrett." Head tipped back, I moan as his teeth scrape down my neck before he sucks at the base of my throat.

"You taste so sweet," he groans with pleasure.

"Thank...you..." I breathe.

"Only you would thank a man for a compliment at a moment like this." His chuckle is dark.

"What can I say, I have manners." I slide my hands beneath his T-shirt, delighting in the clench of his muscles as I trace the cut ridges of his stomach.

It's a momentary respite from the emotional and sexually charged headiness enveloping us. This feels like us. The playful banter. The comfortability. It's a glimpse of what this all could be like if we unshackled the chains keeping us in the friends-only box. We could be friends, and so much more.

"Are we doing this? Like *really* doing this?" I bite my lip, my gaze drops to where my hands skim along the top of his jeans. "Or is this just tonight?"

He places his thumb on my chin, guiding my gaze to him. "It could never be just one night with you."

The corners of my mouth lift in a small smile. "Then, we're doing this... Like a real couple?"

"Yes." His deep timbre is laced with pain.

"Don't sound so excited." A furrow dips my brow.

"I am, but I'm also scared. I won't pretend I'm not." The pads of his fingers skate over my jawline and soothe against my cheeks. "I don't know what will happen, but what I do know is that being terrified with you is far better than any sense of safety without you. Walking away from you today is a mistake I don't want to make ever again."

"Is that why you're here? Is that why you were calling?"

"No." He combs his fingers into my hair. "I was at the hospital checking on things when the outage happened. All I could think about is you. I texted, and you didn't respond. When my calls went to voicemail, I panicked and headed straight here. I could have called Anker, but I couldn't think straight. All I could think about was getting to you."

"I'm sorry," I say softly.

He kisses the center of my forehead. "You didn't do anything wrong. This is my issue... Even if I didn't technically have the job, I always think about you. Your happiness. Your wants. Your safety."

"I'm safe." I press into him, hoping that settles the worry radiating from him.

He lets out a shaky breath. "Losing Val broke me, and my pieces are barely back together, and I'm scared they'll break—that I'll break—if I open my heart to someone again. It's why I pulled away… But you gave me no choice." He places my hand on his chest. "You're already burrowed so deep here."

"You're not broken," I murmur.

"I want you. I want to be with you. But I also know that I have issues that might get in the way of us, and I don't want them—for me—to hurt you."

"You want me?"

"Yes."

"And you want to be with me?"

"Yes." He presses my hand tighter against him.

"Then we'll figure the rest out together." I trail my other hand up to his cheek, cradling it. "I have issues, too. We just need to talk about this with each other. To do what we do on the track—communicate, support, and guide one another."

He captures my lips in a slow kiss. This one tender and grateful. It doesn't bruise like the first but the message is still intense. It's reminiscent of blooms opening to the sun, the petals outstretched in greeting. He's not hiding. He's not running. He's here with me.

"Garrett," I breathe between our deepening kisses. "My bed is just over there."

He lifts me into his arms, my legs wrapping around him. "Just kissing."

"But… Why?" I wrinkle my nose.

"Because I want to do this right. You deserve to have our first time be special, not a frenzied fuck after an emotional talk." Earnestness is audible in his low murmur.

The tingle low in my belly signs off on the idea of a frenzied fuck with this man. Though, I'd imagine my body is game for just about anything with him. His thoughtfulness thrums desire through me. At every turn, this man thinks about my needs first. Even some I've not yet thought of.

"I don't want special." I nuzzle my nose against his. "I just want you."

He huffs a laugh. "Thanks."

"That didn't come out right," I laughingly whine. "You know what I mean."

"I do." He carries me to the bed, placing me down. Kicking off his shoes, he crawls in and settles between my legs. "Still, I want special for you." He caresses my cheeks.

"Fine." I mock pout. "Please place my glasses on the bedstand. If we're going to just kiss, I want nothing in the way."

Chuckling, he takes my glasses and places them on the bedside table. Like two teenagers, we kiss between laughter. This may be my favorite thing about Garrett. We can move seamlessly from emotional conversations to just having fun. The comfort that ensconces me in his presence is addictive.

Our sweet kisses turn hungry. His strong hands slide up my thighs, gripping and squeezing the flesh. I move against him. A pleasure-filled hiss falls out of me with the rasp of his growing erection against my center. The barrier of denim and my cotton sleep shorts tease and fan the fire crackling within me.

"Just kissing…" he murmurs as I drag his T-shirt over his head.

"Yep." I run my hands over his pecs, tweaking his nipples.

"Jensen." He utters my name like a warning.

I bat my eyes. "Sorry. Just kissing." I move my mouth to him, kissing his chest. His fingers bite into my thighs as I playfully nip his nipples.

He raises up, sitting on his heels and dragging me onto his lap. "Someone likes to test boundaries."

"You know what to say if I push too much." I trail my finger up his chest.

"I do," he rasps.

"Good."

With a sultry expression, I pull my hoodie and then my tank top over my head. Tossing them to the end of the bed, I brush my hair behind my ears, allowing him to see me in the candle's incandescence.

"Look at you…" He runs his fingers through my loose tendrils. "You're fucking gorgeous."

"You're biased." I bite back my grin. "You're my…"

Oh god, was I about to call him boyfriend? Wait, is he my boyfriend?

"I'm yours." He caresses my face. "And that doesn't make what I say less true. This heart-shaped mouth. Those bright hazel eyes. These fucking dimples." He leans in, pressing a kiss to each cheek. "Your rosy complexion." He trails his mouth down. "These tits…"

"Tits?" I giggle. "Guess it is all about boobs with some men." My laughter morphs into a needy moan as he sucks a taut peak into his mouth.

Molten lava flows through my bloodstream. I've never felt so sexy or desired. It's indulgent the way he feasts on me as if I'm expensive champagne that he plans to savor every drop of.

"Oh god!" My head tips back with his delicious bite into the hard bud, followed by soothing kisses.

"You remember what to say if it's too much?" He moves to my other breast.

"Yes… God!" I cry as his teeth sink into me.

"You like it a little rough… Don't you, baby?"

"Yes!" My back bows with his hardening sucks. "How do you know?"

"Your books."

I rub my center against his hardness, searching for relief. "What about them?"

"I pay attention to which stories are your favorites." His fingers grip the globes of my ass, moving me against him. "And I've read them… A few times."

"You read my favorite books to learn what I like?"

"As much as I've fought this, I still wanted to know your

desires. What it would be like with you… Even if it was just a fantasy." He nips at me.

"And does this live up to the fantasy?"

"Fuck the fantasy… All there is, is this." He kisses a trail between my breasts.

The combination of rough tenderness spools tension tighter. He's not holding back with me. His mouth tests and plays, finding the right rhythm. The throb between my legs begs for release.

"Please…" I rake my fingers into his hair.

"Too much, baby?"

My skin sizzles with the sinful way *baby* falls from his lips. He's playing with me like a cat with a very needy mouse. The way I writhe against him telegraphs how very *not* too much this is.

"Make me yours. Ensure there's no question," I repeat his words from earlier like a breathless dare.

"Fuuuuuck." He presses his forehead to mine.

Two can play this game. "Too much? You know what to say, baby," I coo, mischief curling my lips with his pained groan.

He slides me off his lap. Before I can whimper my protest, his mouth is on me. His heavy body presses me into the bed. Like a ravenous animal, he devours. It's messy. It's rough. It's almost everything I want from this man. For him to be undone by his need for me, mirroring my own desire for him.

"Garrett…please fuck me…please." Raking my fingers into his hair, I grind against him in hopes of finding my own relief. The ache pulsing at my center threatens to consume me.

"Not yet, baby…but I will take care of you. I promise." His fingers slide beneath my sleep shorts and stroke over the tuft of hair along my pussy. "Fuck… Are you not wearing panties?" His question is tight, as if in pain.

"Correct." I nip at his lips.

"Just kissing… Just kissing…" It's almost a mantra accompanying his mouth's march down my body. Spreading my legs, he presses his mouth to my center through the barrier of my shorts. "You're so wet already."

"Gar—rett," I whine with his tongue's tease of my clit through the fabric.

It's the most decadent torture. His mouth on me, but not quite. My body begs for release, while praying it never comes. The sensation of his mouth on me, even through my sleep shorts, sets me on fire. I may die from this, and what a way to go.

"You're so close, aren't you?" His voice is wicked.

"Yes," I whine.

"Maybe…" He grips my waistband. "I could tip you over the edge."

"Yes!" Relief fills me as he drags my shorts down.

"Spread your legs wide for me."

I do as he says. Legs wide, his stare is focused on my pussy. Cool air kisses against my sensitive core. I've never been this exposed with someone. With Chase, most of our clothes remained on, even during sex. It was the frenzied fuck that Garrett didn't want. It wasn't this—indulgent, reverent, and wanton.

"Look at you…" He kisses me. "You're so sexy, baby. Cheeks flushed. Eyes glossy with need. Cunt dripping for me."

"Oh…" I make a mewling sound.

With a throaty growl, he dips his head between my legs. My entire body seizes with pleasure from his unhurried lick along my seam. His slow pace coils that pressure so tight that I may break into a million pieces.

Chest heaving, I grip the comforter for any sense of purchase. Like a feral creature, he squeezes me tighter, lifting my hips and sucking at my clit like it's the last scrap of food he'll ever have.

I may burn alive from the fire combusting inside me. Every muscle is taut. Promised release trembles my limbs.

"Fuck!" Climax slams through me.

"That's my girl." He soothes his fingers along my thighs.

Still shaking, he pulls me into his arms, pressing me against his sweat-coated chest. His hands trace up and down my spine. Waves of contentment waft off him. Boneless and sated, I nuzzle into him.

"I think I like *just kissing* with you." Tipping my head up to him, I swear I can see the smug expression that I imagine rests on his face. Licking my lips, I dance my fingers down the dusting of hair leading from his belly button to the top of his jeans.

"Jensen." An arched brow is audible in how he says my name.

I answer him with a deep kiss, my essence still on his lips. "Just kissing, remember?" My tongue skates down his torso. "You know what to say"—I pop the button on his jeans—"if you want me to stop."

He remains quiet. My gaze locked on his head's outline in the dim light, I drag down his zipper. He lifts his hips, allowing me to pull his jeans and boxer briefs past his knees. Despite my recent orgasm, need heats my blood with this power. I'm drunk with the idea that this strong man is falling apart at my touch.

"Fuck," he moans. His thick shaft jerks under my fingers.

"Don't worry, baby. My hands are just to help guide me. I remember our rules." With a sultry grin, I press a chaste kiss to the tip. "I'll only use my mouth. Just kissing, remember."

I lick down the veiny shaft before I close my mouth over him. Inch by inch, I take him deeper—sucking and lathing my tongue around him. The experience awakens my other senses. His saltiness fills my taste buds. His moans sing in my ears. His steely hardness is silky in my mouth.

"Look at you. So sexy with your mouth wrapped around my cock." His fingers tangle into my hair.

"Mm-hmm," I hum, sucking him a little harder.

The sting of his fingers tugging my hair urges me on. Relaxing my throat, I take him as deep as I can.

"Christ… You need…to stop or I'm gonna… Oh god…"

His unraveling will be my undoing. I press my thighs together, desire winding tight at the power I have to cause this man to fall apart. The pressure spools tight as if it's his mouth on me, and not mine on his.

"I'm going…to come."

Releasing him, I look up. "It's okay…I want it," I pant.

"Fuck…you're perfect." He brushes the hair from my face.

With a sensual smile, I pump him once, twice before I take him in my mouth again. It doesn't take long before he breaks. His guttural "Fuck, baby," rings in my ears as I drink him up. Despite my body's pulse for release, satisfaction drips through me. This strong man lies panting and sated because of me. It's an elixir that makes me tipsy.

Scooping me up, he claims my mouth. Our shared tastes blend in a salty sweetness.

"Look at you." He runs his thumb over my lips. "All blissed out, but still needy." He trails his hands down my body. "Does my greedy girl want more?"

"Garrett." Desire licks up my spine with his slow caress between my legs. "What happened to…just kissing?"

He strokes languid circles against my clit. "I think you deserve an extra treat. Just a little taste to tide you over. I told you I was going to take care of you."

"Oh god." My back arches as he slips a finger inside me.

Slow and deliberate, he pushes deeper into me. Cradled in his arms, he fucks me with his finger while murmuring sweet words into my ears about how good I feel and how gorgeous I am. His tenderness ensconces me in the sensation of just being adored like the queen he teases that I am. His unhurried ministrations seem as much for me as for him. The pleasure coursing through me is mirrored in the energy wafting off him. This isn't just about getting me ready for him. This is about both our pleasure.

"You're so tight, baby," he murmurs, pushing a second finger inside me.

"Sorry." I wince just a bit, my body adjusting to him.

"Don't apologize for that." He presses a tender kiss to my temple. "It just means I get to take my time with you. Making you come over and over before sinking into you." He rubs my clit with his thumb. "We'll go slow but let me know if it's too much."

"It's good... I'm good..." I breathe, moving my hips against his working fingers.

"You're perfect." He takes my mouth in a deep kiss, our tongues meeting in a long embrace.

The gentle caresses and deepening thrusts guide me closer to the edge. With the crook of his fingers inside me, I fall. The waves of climax slam away my ability to do anything but cling to him.

"I've got you." He takes my mouth in a tender kiss. Its heat soothes the aftershocks of orgasm, bringing me back to reality. A reality with this man.

"And I've got you." I raise my hand to his cheek.

20

MILE TWENTY
MY SISTER AND YOU?

Garrett Marlowe is snuggling me. He's a snuggler. The rightness enveloping me at waking up in his arms makes each morning not snuggled up against him wrong.

"Good morning," he says, his sleep-drunk voice husky and low.

"Morning." I sigh, contentment dripping through me. "I like that you're a snuggler."

"It helps that you're snuggly." He kisses the top of my head.

"Do I have more nights of you cuddling me in our future?" I dance my fingertips over his chest.

"Yes." He grips my bare ass. "Especially when you wear this."

"I'm naked."

"Exactly." He presses tickling kisses against my neck, causing me to wiggle with giggles.

"Stop being cute."

"Ditto." He combs his fingers into my messy tendrils. "What are your plans for today?"

"It's Sunday, so a lazy morning before I have to meet my grumpy running partner for our afternoon training session."

"I take it last night means you're not done with him?" His mouth quirks.

"I don't think I'll ever be done with him."

"Good... Pretty sure the feeling is mutual." He nuzzles my nose with his.

"Hope you don't get too jealous of him." I bat my lashes. "He's rather sexy."

He pushes me onto my back, holding his muscular body over mine. "Interesting because I have a mouthy running partner, who's sinfully sexy. Hopefully, you don't get jealous of her."

"Mouthy?" I hum. "You didn't complain about my mouth last night." I wrap my legs around his waist, letting out a hissed breath as his hard cock brushes my center.

"I have a newfound appreciation for your mouth." He moves against me, cranking the switch on and lighting me up with desire.

"Garrett." I move against him, seeking more.

"Not yet." He takes my mouth in a hard kiss. "But I will take care of you."

Flipping onto his back, he hurls me on top of him. Hands tight on my waist, he drags me up his body.

"Garrett..." My breath catches as he deposits me above his face, my knees bookending his head. "Oh...I've never...Are you sure?"

It's not like he didn't feast on me last night, but sitting on his face seems more intimate than him just going down on me. Chase went down on me a few times, but that was about getting me ready for him. With Garrett, his every action is about my pleasure.

"Grab the headboard, Jensen." His low growl sends heat zinging through me.

"*Sooo* bossy." Giggling, I comply.

Hands curled around the smooth wood, my head falls back with his first teasing lick. The heat pooling low in my belly simmers to a boil. Each lick savors me like a tasty treat, drinking up my pleasure with his own.

With a throaty growl, he tugs me down fully on top of his face. His playful flicks morph into hard, languid sucks of my clit. It's primal and unbridled the way I writhe against him and how he gulps me up. He consumes me as if I'm the air he breathes. Delicious pressure spools tighter, causing my body to tremble for release.

"Fuck!" I shudder.

Legs like jelly, I lean against the headboard, trying to hold myself up. I don't last long before he scoops me into his arms. Chest heaving, I snuggle against him, trying to catch my breath as I circle back to reality.

"That…escalated…quickly." Panting, I press my sated smile to his.

"I've been waiting a long time to do that."

"What other things have you been waiting to do?" I nibble on my lower lip, my brain spinning with the many, many things I want to do with this man. Some likely illegal in several states.

He traces my smile. "I'd like to take you out on a date."

A date? I turn into a gooey mess at that. He could say anything, and I'd agree. But a date? After everything that's transpired since last night, you'd think I know this. Somehow, the idea of him taking me out didn't register until now.

"We're really doing this, aren't we?"

"Yes." He brushes his thumb over my lips. "I am sorry my actions cause you to doubt this."

Sitting up, I heave a breath. "I don't doubt this. I don't doubt you." I motion at him. "I'm not used to this. To the man I care for not just wanting me, but caring about me."

It so cliché and a little sad, but it's my truth. The combination of hurt from past relationships—both romantic and platonic—has left me just as guarded as Garrett. He pushes people away, while I reach for those who reinforce the idea that I'm not wanted. That I'm not loveable. But I am loveable…and wanted. At least, I'm starting to believe that, and not just because of this man, but the last few months of therapy combined with marathon training is strangely helping me heal.

"Like I said last night, I have issues. I'm working on them with Dr. Nor, and I may question things or need some reassurance from time to time as I'm getting stronger, but know that I don't doubt you or us. The way I feel this morning tells me that." I cradle his cheek.

"And how's that?" he murmurs.

"That I am exactly where I'm supposed to be," I say, meeting his stare.

The confession is brazen. I'm laying my truths in front of him. In the past, I wouldn't have said anything. For the entirety of my situationships with Chase and Miles, I never confessed my feelings—not until it was too late. For the first time in my life, bravery courses within me to do things. I'm pushing past the boundaries that I've kept in place for so long.

"Me too, pretty girl." He leans over, pressing a gentle kiss.

"So, when do you want to take me on this date?" My grin is large. "Also, what will we be doing because I need to plan my outfit. I have these red heels I haven't had a chance to wear yet."

"I do like the idea of you in red heels." He settles me back against him, folding me tight within his warm embrace.

"I thought you didn't like my heels," I tease.

"I worry about you spraining an ankle in some of them, but I do like the idea of you wearing them during *certain* activities."

"Why Dr. Marlowe, do you want to fuck me in my new red heels?" I mock-gasp.

"Pretty girl, I want to fuck you in just about anything." He kisses my cheek. "But first, I need to take you out on an actual date."

"Once you ask me out properly, we can plan this special date and then commence with the fucking." I tap my chin thoughtfully. "How's noon today work for you?"

Laughter vibrates in his chest. "We have our training session. But how about Friday? Since Saturday is our off day, it will let us have a later night together."

"Excellent." I frown just a bit. "Wait… That means we'll miss happy hour. Are we telling our friends, and my brother, why we're missing it?"

"I'm sure Kayla and Catherine already know about us, or at least the dancing around each other we've been doing." An arched brow is audible in his tone.

"Well, duh." I smirk. "They're almost up-to-date, minus the little bit about me sitting on your face—"

He rumbles with laughter, making my grin pop with smug satisfaction.

"I'll probably tell them during our daily latte run tomorrow. Unless…"

"No. I have no problem telling our friends and your brother. Though I'm sure he'll have something to say about this."

This will be the first actual relationship of mine that Anker knows about. He'd caught me with Everett, but that wasn't a relationship, and he only knew pieces. I never told him about Chase, outside of that I was seeing someone and then I wasn't, because he would have hunted him down and gone scorched earth. My brother is chill, unless it comes to the people he loves being hurt in any real way.

"I guess that's another thing we'll handle together," He squeezes me. "When you told me about Chase, you mentioned Anker not knowing about him. Did he know about any of the other men you've dated?"

"Ah…" I swallow thickly. "Define dating."

He tilts his head. "Boyfriends. Casual things. Sexual partners."

"Chase is the only man I've ever been with sexually. Other than you." I motion to him. "I've never had a boyfriend." Mortification blazes up my neck. "Oh god, this is so embarrassing. I'm twenty-nine and the longest relationship I've had is with my vibrator." Cringing, I cover my face with my hands.

"Hey…" He pulls my hands down. "Can I tell you something?"

Frowning, I point at him. "If it's that you're taking back the date invite because you realize I have no experience in this and will be bad at it, I'm calling no backsies."

"As much as I want to punch every man who's ever hurt, ignored, or overlooked you, I'm glad they're idiots because I get to be with you. I don't care about what experiences you've had before me, all I care about is making sure that, whatever happens from here on out, you're happy, cherished, and safe with me. Emphasis on the 'with me' part."

And just like that, I fall a little more for Garrett Marlowe. My entire body melts for this man.

I take his lips in a slow, appreciative kiss. "And I want to do the same. To try to keep your big heart safe. To ensure that frown of yours is always turned upside down—even if it's involuntarily." I lift my fingers to his mouth and trace its upward curve.

"My silly girl." He sighs, contentment radiating from him.

"The keyword in that sentence is *try*," I say, resting my palm over his heart, the steady thump, thump vibrating beneath my touch.

Safe or safety always seems to slip from Garrett's lips. I know it's always at the forefront of his thoughts. The worry that nips at him that he can't always keep the people he cares about from meeting harm, emotional or otherwise.

"I know," he says, his throat bobbing.

"Do you?" My words are slow and deliberate as if approaching a sleeping animal. "You panicked last night because you couldn't get a hold of me, and as much as I like that you worry about me, I don't like the idea of you in distress—"

"Perhaps answer your phone." His grumble is lighthearted. "And don't turn it off in a power outage."

I roll my eyes. "Just as I need a little reassurance occasionally, I know you do too. I promise to message you in the future before turning off my phone and to be better about answering it, but you also need to work on not spinning out with the idea that something has happened to me if I don't pick up."

"I know," he says quietly. "I don't want you to feel like you have to check in with me. That's not what I want. I just…"

"You worry when you can't get a hold of someone that the worst has happened." I stroke his cheek. "Because that's what happened with Val."

"Fifteen minutes," he says, his voice pained and scratchy as if emotions claw at his throat. "She'd said she should be home in fifteen minutes, and she'd text when she got there. The rideshare was side-swiped by a drunk driver down the street from the hospital. The chief of staff was leaving and rushed to the accident to offer help. Both Val and the driver were already dead."

"Oh, Garrett…" I press into him.

"When the chief of staff called, he just said for me to get down to the hospital. That there'd been an accident, but I knew she was dead. He spoke to me in that same soft tone he used with families when telling them their loved one had died. Until he called, I just thought Val didn't answer my text because she'd hopped in the shower or… I didn't worry, because I thought she was fine. But she wasn't. Now, every time I can't get a hold of someone, I can't breathe. All the worst scenarios play on repeat until I know they are safe."

A pain, echoing his, twinges in my own chest as I think of each time he's grumbled about me not answering my phone through the years. On the surface, what appeared as just grumpy Garrett was actually him reliving the worst fifteen minutes of his life.

"Is that why you hold people at a distance?"

"I've never been the life of the party like Anker or my siblings, but it just got easier to manage the anxiety about something happening if I didn't have to deal with people. Then you and Anker came along. Your brother will not let anyone ignore him, and you... I couldn't ignore you if I tried." He snorts. "And believe me, I tried."

"*You* certainly tried." I poke him.

"And failed." He kisses my temple. "You two were the first people I let in after Val died. I rarely talk to the friends I had back in Chicago. It's too hard. Besides my family, I've just had me to worry about."

"And Ditka."

"My mom's intervention." His groan is laced with laughter.

"You love him." My eyes widen. "Oh my, he's home alone."

"He's okay. There's an automatic feeder and plenty of water. And—" He reaches over me and grabs his phone off my bedstand "We can spy on him," he says, unlocking his phone. "He's currently asleep on the couch."

"So, Ditka was your mom's attempt to bring you out of your hard candy shell?" I cuddle into his nook.

"Yeah... She thought it was time for me to have someone other than myself to come home to." Contentment radiates from him as he swipes his thumb over the phone's screen.

"You're a good cat dad." I smile. "Is Ditka your first cat?"

"Yeah." He reaches over and returns the phone to the bedstand.

"Did Val and you have pets?"

"No."

I gnaw on the corner of my mouth. "What was Val like?"

"Only you." Head tipped back, a laughing groan slips out.

"You know what to say if it's too much." I offer a sassy expression.

Despite the heaviness in the air from this conversation, it's nice that we can tease one another. This may be one of my favorite parts about us. *We're an us!* Even when we've argued in the past, there was always an undercurrent of playfulness. No matter how angry I'd get with him or the bite of our words to one another, deep down inside, I never worried that it was too much.

"You two would have liked each other." He chuckles.

"We're we alike?"

"No...not really. Very different from one another. She was no-nonsense and driven. Always focused on the next item on her to-do list."

"*Yeah*, so my complete opposite." I crinkle my nose.

"You're not exactly *not* driven, Ms. Running a Marathon." He squeezes me. "Val and you are different, but there are similarities. You're both soft in the same ways. Kind. Loving. But, you're also hard in the same ways. You stand your ground. You both push when needed. Though, she was a little less dog with a bone than you."

"Woof," I mock-bark, causing him to laugh.

"You're both funny. Your humor is silly and quippy. Hers was dry. But you both always make me smile," he says, trailing his fingers up my bare arm.

My heart swells with how relaxed he is. Each fact about Val is another gift. It's not just him telling me about her but sharing himself with me. It's all the reasons he loved her. All the things that are important to him. We remain like that. Naked in my bed while he tells me about his wife.

This should be weird, but it wraps me up like a cozy blanket. We're comfortable enough to talk about this. For him to share both his pain and joy about Val. For me to know that his love for her doesn't diminish his feelings for me.

"She didn't!" I roar with laughter.

"She did." He wipes at the tears of laughter in his eyes.

"She dumped a tub of salsa on your racist aunt during a Fourth of July BBQ?"

"Val said my aunt didn't get to enjoy Mexican cuisine while disparaging its people."

"Oh my god, she's my new hero." I lean back against the headboard.

He joins me. "Thank you," he says, wrapping his arm around me and tucking me close.

"Thank you for sharing Val with me." I snuggle in deeper. "You're right, I would have totally liked her."

"Yeah." He kisses my forehead.

A loud *knock, knock* breaks into our little bubble.

He twists in the bed. "Are you expecting someone?"

"No," I say, my forehead scrunched. "Most people call or text before they come over."

"Because you're stellar at answering your phone."

"Ha...ha." I pinch him.

"Easy, crab hands." He playfully bats me away. "Not to mention your phone is still off, despite the power being back on."

"I was a little distracted." I flash him a wry expression.

"Jensen, are you home?" Anker's muffled voice calls through my door.

Anker, I mouth.

"I'm aware," Garrett whisper-hisses.

"We're naked and in my bed." I motion between us.

"Also aware." He slides out of bed.

"Jensen, I can hear you moving around in there. Should I use my key? Are you okay?"

"No! I mean yes, I'm okay. Don't use your key!" I shout, scrambling and almost tumbling out of bed.

"Careful," Garrett whispers, catching me and helping me to my feet.

"Did I catch you listening to one of your dirty audios, or something?" Anker's laugh is taunting.

"Ha!" My voice is high-pitched and insincere. "Hilarious." I point to Garrett's still very naked body and mouth, *Clothes, now*.

We may plan to tell Anker about us, but this isn't the ideal scenario. As much as I'd love to have Garrett hide in my bathroom until I get rid of my brother like something out of a bad sitcom, this is happening. If we're going to tell Anker about us, I'd prefer both of us not look like we've spent the last ten hours doing—well, exactly what we've been doing.

"What are you doing here, Anker?"

"Being the dutiful big brother and checking on my sister post-power outage. I also brought bagels and lattes. Should I use my key, or are you going to let me in?"

"No! I'm getting dressed. Just got out of bed." I rush to the closet, because I have no idea where my clothes from last night are.

"I know Garrett is in there," Anker says.

"What!" I spin, my panicked gaze bouncing between where Garrett stands beside my bed, tugging up his jeans, and the door.

"His SUV is parked in front of your building."

Shaking his head, Garrett clears his throat. "Morning, Anker."

"Morning, Garrett..." he pauses for a beat, "...Can I come in or—"

"Ah...give us a minute," I yell, yanking on a pair of sweatpants.

"Just as I thought," Anker says.

I shimmy my hoodie on and brush my hair out of my face.

"Glasses," Garrett says, handing me my glasses.

"Thanks." I put them on.

"Ready?"

I suck in a breath and nod. "Ready."

Garrett strides to the door, me in tow, and opens it.

Anker leans on the door jamb—no doubt a smirk playing in his features. "So, this is finally happening."

"Finally?" I arch an eyebrow.

"Don't play coy. Why do you think I teased you about having hate sex with Garrett?" Straightening, he juts his chin toward Garrett. "Not to mention, you couldn't see how Mopey over there looked at you, but I could."

"That's one." I hold up a finger. "Also, I never hated Garrett," I protest with a small pout.

"I'm aware." Anker laughs, pushing past us and moving to the small kitchen island to deposit the drinks carrier and bag of bagels. "So, how long?"

"Last night," Garrett says, closing the door.

"I knew something was up after the race." He walks over and hands me a to-go cup. "Red Velvet Cupcake latte."

I shouldn't be that shocked. Anker isn't aloof. He may play the loveable cad, but he's tapped into people. It's what makes him a good doctor.

"Garrett, there's an Americano on the counter for you."

Garrett tilts his head. "How'd you know to bring me a coffee?"

"I drove by earlier this morning on my way to yoga in the park and saw your SUV. Jensen may be taking her training seriously, but not seven a.m. serious—especially on a Sunday. I figured if I was going to surprise my sister with breakfast, I should bring something for her guest." He pats Garrett's shoulder. "I'm assuming you were here all night."

"Yeah."

"No wonder you didn't want me to come over," he says over his shoulder, looking at me.

"Garrett wasn't here then," I say.

"But he's here now?" Turning toward Garrett, he steps back.

"I am," Garrett says, looking between me and Anker. "To be clear, this isn't just a one-time thing. I care about Jensen and—"

"We're dating," I cut in. "Or rather, we're going to. Our first date is on Friday, so we won't be at happy hour." I gesture wildly with my free hand. "Whatever we are, we're… uh…"

"Together," Garrett says, his tone emphatic.

"Good thing I brought breakfast, then."

"What does that—"

Anker slams his fist into Garrett's stomach. With a groan, Garrett lurches over.

"Figured breakfast both celebrates your coupling and makes amends for that." Anker shrugs.

"Anker! What the actual fuck!" Placing my cup on the coffee table, I rush to Garrett.

Garrett holds up his hand. "It's all good. I expected it."

"Sorry, man, but I want to be crystal clear that while I am very much okay with this, if you hurt her, I have no problem making my displeasure known." He slaps Garrett's back.

"Maybe just use your words next time," I hiss.

"I blame our Viking heritage," he quips. "We cool, man?"

"We're cool," Garrett groans and straightens.

"Oh, baby, I'm sorry. Are you okay?" I place my hands on Garrett's cheeks.

"Baby? Aw, you two are adorable," Anker coos, walking to the counter. "Who wants bagels? Garrett, I got your favorite. Sorry, Jensen, they didn't have blueberry, so I got your second favorite."

"I think he's taking this well." I grin.
"Yeah…so well." Garrett coughs.

21

MILE TWENTY-ONE
DATE NIGHT

A large grin kicks across my face as I run my hands down my dress. The velvet-soft fabric molds over my curves and falls above my knees. Thanks to all the running, I rather enjoy showing off my toned legs via a shorter hem line. For the first time ever, I feel sexy. It's not about my toned legs, but the confidence that pulses within me.

Tonight is happening because I asked for what I wanted and stood my ground. I was willing to say goodbye, rather than continue to settle for scraps or what ifs.

"Hey, pretty girl," Garrett says, greeting me at my door, a grin audible in his voice. "You're stunning." He leans in and presses a peck to my cheek.

"Are you wearing a suit?" I reach out and run my fingers along the soft fabric. "And a tie?"

"It's a black suit with a red tie."

"A red tie… Like my shoes?" Lips puckered, I tug at his tie.

"Yes." His tone is playful.

My belly swoops. "Look at you, Mr. Fancy Pants."

"Well"—he leans close, his rich masculine scent filling my nostrils—"I had to make sure I was new red heels-worthy."

Encircling his neck, I tip my head up. "You're always red heels-worthy."

"I'd like to keep it that way." Banding his arms around my back, he tucks me against him.

"It's good to have goals."

He brushes his lips along my jawline, causing heat to tiptoe up my spine. "Oh, I have lots of goals when it comes to you, pretty girl."

"Yeah?" I coo with a bat of my lashes. "Care to share some of these goals?"

"In due time." He kisses below my ear, causing me to melt against him.

It's not just the sensation of this strong man's gentle kisses, but the promise underscoring his words. For a man who just wants more time with the people he cares about, this is huge. He may say he doesn't know what will happen—that there's no guarantee—but goals speak of hope. This is the first step on a marathon that I hope takes a lifetime to conclude.

"But, tonight's goal is to take you out on our first date." He steps back but places his hands on my hips.

"And then fuck me in my red heels?" I shimmy my hips.

"Fuck!" Head tipped back, a deep belly laugh roars out of him, solidifying one of my many, many goals for this man.

Belly-deep laugh. Check.

This is by far the best date I've ever been on, and we've only ordered our drinks. Granted, I haven't had a lot of dates, but it's top tier. There isn't any awkward swirl inside me as if I'm saying or doing the wrong thing. I don't have to worry about explaining things to Garrett about my vision or any assistance I may need. The last five years of friendship assures me he knows.

Not only did he share with me where we'd be going, so I could look up the menu ahead of time, but he requested a table beneath one of the small chandeliers scattered around the dining room, near the bathroom, so I could easily navigate. Upon arrival, he spent a few minutes orienting me to the restaurant's layout and table's setting. His description not only helps me understand where things are but painted the image in my head of the dining room filled with round tables draped in white linen cloths—a flickering candle in the center of each one—and lush red leather chairs.

"How on earth did Catherine find a hockey jersey for Ditka?" Garrett holds up his phone and shakes his head.

Since Anker volunteered to watch Ditka for tonight, the ladies brought happy hour to his place. Our friends are currently making fancy cocktails, eating Thai, and watching tonight's LA Bobcats game.

"You know you love it." I grin.

"Your diet sodas in wine glasses," the server chuckles as he sets our glasses on the table.

My smile tugs up just a little more at Garrett's small, huffed laugh that almost says, "Only you." Since we're at a steakhouse along the shoreline, I thought the glasses added to the fancy-pants nature, so I requested our drinks be brought in them.

"Do we know what we want?" the server asks.

"Jensen?"

"The peppercorn-glazed sirloin—medium well—with the white cheddar mac and cheese and the broccolini." I lean back against the cushy leather chair.

"Broccolini?" Garrett clears his throat.

"Someone is a bad influence." I smirk.

"I'll have the same."

I lift one eyebrow. "Mac and cheese?"

"Someone's a bad influence." A wink plays in his low timbre.

Best date ever! How is it that I'm even having fun ordering food with this man?

"Anything else?" the server says.

"No, thank you."

"Very good. It will be out shortly," the server says before striding away.

"Your drink is at ten o'clock," Garrett says. "My mother will be aghast that I'm drinking soda out of a wineglass."

"I like that you do that," I murmur, my heart swelling.

He tilts his head. "Do what?"

"Tell me where my drink is and act like it's nothing." Placing my hand on the table as an anchor, I trail up until I grasp the glass's stem. "Most people don't think of it, or they make a big deal. You always remember but never make me feel bad about it."

He makes a low growly noise in his throat. "I don't like that anyone would make you feel bad for that."

I shrug. "Some people do."

"Also, I shouldn't be thanked for that. It's the minimum."

"For a lot of people, it seems like it's above and beyond." Sighing, I tap my fingers against the glass. "It's why I don't always ask, because I don't want to give them a reason to go away."

It's the quiet part that I rarely say out loud, except with Dr. Nor. I've shared a little with Catherine and Kayla, but I never talk about this with my family. It took them too long to see—pun intended—beyond my disability, that it feels like this would set us back.

"Most people suck," he says gruffly.

"You're not most people."

"I used to be." He sighs. "When my brother lost his leg, most of the family babied him—including me. It drove him nuts. Then, one day, he just let us have it. Here my brother was, navigating this new reality, and I never realized that we were the bigger issue to him than his leg. We kept getting in the way of him just living his life, because we were so focused on what he'd lost."

"My parents and Anker were the same after my Stargardt's diagnosis. They held on a little too tight."

"I know Anker is protective of you, but he doesn't seem to be like that now."

"He's not. Not really. Neither are my parents. They simmered before I went away to college." I take a sip of my drink and place it back down at ten o'clock. "Guess I should send your brother a 'thank you' card for breaking you in for me when it comes to proper inter-abled relationships."

"He'll love that." He chuckles. "But don't praise me for doing what should just be expected, and if I don't, please don't ever hesitate to ask for what you want with me. Call me out if I don't do what you need or if I pull some ableist bullshit."

"Agreed." A light bubbly sensation fizzes inside me. "While you may not want to be praised for it, I'm still grateful. Often, I'm stuck—for lack of better words—training people. It's made me hesitant to really put myself out there in so many areas of my life. Even with work. It's just nice not to have to do that with you."

He clears his throat. "Even with work?"

"As I'm pushing my personal boundaries, I'm starting to think about my professional ones. I worry I'm not pushing myself professionally. It's safe for me. My boss is disabled. I work with disabled students. Outside of interactions with non-disabled faculty, it's my comfort zone. Not to mention, I interned there in grad school, so I knew what I was getting into when I applied."

"But you love your job." He reaches across the table and takes my hand, offering a gentle squeeze.

With marathon training, the stronger my muscles get and the greater endurance I have to go further, it's opening up my eyes to other ways in which I can grow. Over the last few months, I've made huge strides in relationships... Like forming a friendship with Kayla. I've also pushed past my fear of rejection to ask for the things I want. It makes me wonder how else I've boxed myself in, and what possibilities are out there if I break down those barriers, too.

"I do..." Nibbling on my lip, I nod. "I really do, but I also don't know if it's where I want to be. At least for my entire career."

"What other things are you interested in doing?"

I wrinkle my nose. "I'm not sure. At least, not entirely, yet. I like working with students and the program development portion of my job. Although I don't get to do as much of that as I'd like. I'd like to find something that allows me to do a little bit more of both."

"Expanding on the work you're doing with the disabled students organization?"

My mouth lifts. "Yeah."

"Is there something like that out there?"

"Not at Pemberly. Not exactly." I tap my red-tipped fingernails against the table's surface. "There are student services, but the program is more general. And the school is definitely lacking in resources for disabled students."

While I worry that working within disability services doesn't push me beyond my comfort area, I don't want to leave my community. Even at a progressive university like Pemberly, disabled students are an afterthought.

"I'll do some online research to see what professional options are out there. I'm not talking about changing careers in the next year, but I want to look at what the possibilities are in my future." I sip my soda.

"Maybe we do Buffalo for the half-marathon."

"What?" I cock one eyebrow.

He rubs his nape. "I know we talked about San Fran, but

registration for Buffalo doesn't close until next week, and it would give you a chance to spend time with Bryce. He and his husband, Marshall, run a non-profit which offers social activities and adaptive athletics for disabled people."

"You want me to spend time with your brother?" My smile gets just a little bigger.

"For research." He picks up his soda. "He was in the same position. He wanted to offer more resources to some of the patients he's worked with as a PT, so Marshall and he cooked up an adaptive basketball league that then led to bowling nights, ski trips, and a bunch of other activities. Instead of waiting, he created what he wanted."

My heart swells. It's not just about picking Bryce's brain to help me figure out how I can expand my role in my current position, but Garrett's openness to invite me further into his life. His family is important to him. The fact that he wants us to travel to Buffalo reinforces how important I am to him. While I should run for the hills...a man is proposing a trip to visit his brother on our first date...Garrett and I aren't the typical couple. The last five years have merely served as a preamble to tonight.

"Thank you for always supporting me." Leaning in, I lift our joined hands and place an appreciative kiss on his knuckles.

"Again, don't thank me for doing what should be expected."

"Just because it's expected, doesn't mean I can't be appreciative for it," I say, a sweet defiance rings in my tone.

It's something my dad always says. Even if we expect someone to do something, we should still appreciate it because not everyone meets our expectations, and when someone does, we should cherish that. The coziness of Garrett's thoughtfulness leaves me feeling cherished. I want him to feel the same.

"You know the campus coffee shop is closed, right?" I tease as we park at the university.

While I knew all the details about dinner, the only thing Garrett shared about the post-dinner activity was that it would be someplace I'm very familiar with. My gears spun with so many scenarios. None of which landed on me coming back to campus on a Friday night.

Hands clasped, we walk through the quad. It's not proper human guide, but I use my cane and hold his hand anyway. I deserve to hold hands with my handsome date as we stroll in the cool night air, just like everyone else. The murmured conversations of students moseying between buildings hums around us.

He leads me to the egg-shaped theater building at the campus center, where a main stage and several smaller theaters are. I've attended a few performances here over the years—mostly to listen to some of the chamber music ensembles the university is known for.

"What are we seeing?" I press into him as we stand in line to get into the theater.

"The string quartet is doing a special *Bridgerton*-themed performance with music from the show."

"What?" Excitement vibrates through me. "How? I thought the tickets were sold out?"

When I'd seen the listing on the university's events calendar, I squealed obnoxiously at my desk. By the time the tickets were available for staff, they were sold out. Students and faculty always get first dibs on tickets.

"I have some connections." Playfulness dances in his timbre.

"Connections? I know you guest lecture at the medical

school, but am I dating a Pemberley big wig?" I shimmy my hips.

"Not a big wig." He chuckles. "Just a grateful dean of the medical school who had tickets that he agreed to swap me for." He places his palm on the small of my back, guiding me down the line.

"What did you swap him for? Kidney? Firstborn?"

"Weirdly, your brother has dibs on my kidney." He takes out his phone to show the attendant our tickets.

"How?" I guffaw.

"He won it in a poker game two years ago. But he only plans to collect if he needs it," he says, ushering us into the theater.

"Who has dibs on your firstborn?" I bite the inside of my cheek in immediate regret for that question.

He coughs. "Still up for grabs."

"Do you *want* a firstborn?" Bypassing any good sense, I lean into my true nature and just ask.

Kids are something I know I want. Even if we may not be there now—or ever—it's best to put this on the table. I'm sure I'm breaking all kinds of first-date etiquette here. In fairness, I have sat on this man's face, so traditional dating rules may not apply here.

"I did." He places my hand on a railing. "Human guide, or…"

"Human guide." I take his elbow, letting him lead us up the stairs to our seats. "You did, but you don't anymore?"

"I don't know…" His shoulders shrug. "Val and I talked about it, but after she… I just stopped thinking about wanting things beyond just time."

Worrying my lip, I nod, as if he could see me from behind him. "I want a firstborn, and maybe a secondborn. Though they don't have to be borne by me. Adoption. Foster parenting. However they get here, I'd like to be a mom. I'm open.

It's early for this type of conversation, but I want to be honest about what I hope for my future."

Looks like I'm pushing through all the little barriers I've put in place. In three months, I've gone from being unable to tell Miles I wanted to date to telling Garrett I want kids on our first date. This is not the Jensen I've always been, and it's somehow the right Jensen.

As much as I am falling for this man, I'm falling for myself even more. My needs and wants are important, and I won't stuff them inside out of fear they will scare someone away—not anymore.

He stops at the top of the stairs and twists to face me. "I'm open."

"Open to thinking about it or open to..."

"Having them with the right person," he murmurs.

"Okay." With a gentle squeeze of his bicep, my mouth lifts into a small smile.

It's too early to know if we are the *right* people for each other. We still have so many more chapters to write in the unfolding story of us, but the flutter in my chest has hope.

"Though, if I don't get a chance to be a mom, I'm okay with being the best damn aunt to Anker's future children. Especially now that I know he's got a kidney on reserve," I tease.

"I should let you know that in that same poker game, Anker forfeited naming rights of his first child to me."

"Oh god." I laugh. "So, what did the dean get out of you?"

"For the dean, I just had to agree to sit on their medical school interview panel."

"Hope this is worth several weeks of interviewing Type A overachievers." I crinkle my nose, remembering how much Garrett complained about doing resident interviews each spring.

"This—likely not. Here's our seats." He places my hand on the seat. "You—always."

"Smooth!" I place my other hand on my forehead and mock-swoon, causing him to laugh.

We're at the top of the rows of seats encircling the small stage. It's not a large theater—hence the reason for tickets selling out quickly—but the acoustics are fantastic. They tend to do instrumental concerts or Shakespearean shows done in the traditional style. The intimate setting makes it my favorite theater on campus. Each show somehow feels like a private spectacle just for you.

My only complaint about this theater is how cold it is. It's making me rethink my sexy little black dress and pull tighter on my jacket.

"Cold?" he asks, running the back of his palm over my bare knees.

"A little…" I lean into him. "Just means you get to snuggle me close during the show."

"That was always the plan, but also…" He shifts forward, slides his jacket off, and drapes it over my bare legs.

"Won't you be cold?" I wave at my lap.

"I think I'll survive the sixty-five-degree, climate-controlled room."

I roll my eyes. "Ha."

My mock laugh is demolished by the flutter in my chest accompanying the way he secures the jacket around me as if he's tucking me in at night. Even if he teases me about what a wimp I am anytime the temperature drops below seventy, it's clear that my comfort is his priority.

"Thank you." I snuggle into his side, his muscular arm folding around me and keeping me close.

Chamber music may not be Garrett's thing, but you'd never know it. Contentment wafts from him. His muscles are relaxed as he holds me close. As the quartet flows into more romantic songs, his hand strokes up and down my side, and he periodically kisses the top of my head.

Definitely best date ever! Eyes closed, happiness sighs

through me. The romantic melody twining around me nestles me into both the reality of being with Garrett and little fantasies of future dates. All the things I want to do with him. Dancing. Splashing in the waves at the beach. Kissing. *So much more kissing.*

The first notes of "Give me Everything" play, causing heat to zing up my spine with the memory of the steamy carriage scene from the show. Even with the show's robotic audio description, my cheeks flushed with what happened when I watched that episode. I may have watched it a few times.

As the music waltzes around the room, my breath shallows imagining Garrett and I replacing Penelope and Colin in that carriage. Instead of a carriage bumping along the streets of Mayfair, it's Garrett's SUV parked in the campus lot. His capable hands skating up my bare thighs. His mouth sucking at the base of my throat. His fingers skimming along the lacy trim of my panties, before sliding beneath the satin fabric.

"Soon," he murmurs in my ear, his husky voice slinks through me, igniting my nerve-endings into tiny bonfires.

"What?" My whisper is breathless.

"You think I don't know what you're thinking of with this rosy complexion?" He trails his finger over my cheek, past my chin, and down my neck. "You don't think I watched that carriage scene after you mentioned it?"

Pressing his smirking mouth against my cheek in a chaste kiss, he slips his hand beneath the jacket and rests it on my knee. With a featherlight touch, he makes lazy circles against my bare skin. Heat simmers beneath each swipe of his fingers.

"Garrett," I almost whimper.

"Shh." He nuzzles into my hair. "Eyes forward. You don't want to get us in trouble, do you?"

With a stuttered breath, I comply. My gaze fixes on the fuzzy outlines of the four musicians on stage. The stage lighting assures I see only them, and not the seats full of fellow concert-goers made up of students, faculty, and other staff. Even if I could see them, I don't think I'd care. Something about being with Garrett makes me brave, or maybe my bravery lets me lose myself in the desires and emotions bubbling over inside me about this man.

Whatever it is, all I know is that the only thing I'm thinking about is this man's finger tracing patterns up my leg. From my knee to my dress's hem, he dances his fingertips against my skin. I bite back the little moan that threatens to escape. Each slow stroke fans the flames—its heat crisscrossing within me.

"For years, you'd show up to happy hour in these tight little pencil skirts," he whispers, his hot breath kissing against the shell of my ear. "I'd sit across from you pretending I didn't want to slip my hands below those skirts." He slides his finger beneath my hem, skating the digit up my inner thigh. "Pretend I didn't want to yank it up, and pull these aside—" he traces the lacy barrier between panties and bare skin, causing my breath to shallow"—and bury myself in this tight, little pussy."

"Oh…" I try to stifle my little whine.

"Just as I thought." He traces a slow circle over the front of my underwear, already damp with need. "You're so fucking ready for me, aren't you, pretty girl?"

"My office…isn't that far," I breathe.

It might not be the "special" experience he said he wanted for our first time, but the need inside me is boiling over. All I want is to feel him driving into me, sending both of us into oblivion.

"Patience," he says, slipping his hand from beneath the jacket and resting it on top of my knee, making the fabric less blanket-like and more unwanted barrier.

"What?" I huff a breathy squeak. "Is this reciprocal torture for those pencil skirts?"

A smirk is evident in his silence. He's toying with me. Whether it's a playful payback for the five long years he'd wanted me, or to edge me in preparation for later, it doesn't matter. Tension spools in my muscles from unresolved need, making it hard to remember what relief feels like.

Asshole, I mouth, shooting him a frustrated but playful expression. Thighs pressed tight, I sit up straight and keep my eyes locked on the stage.

"Don't worry, pretty girl, I'm going to fuck that pout off of you later." He leans in, his low murmur rumbles through me.

I press my thighs even tighter, praying I'll make it that long. At this point, one more low murmur in his deep bass and I'll come.

Two can play this game. Wickedness licks through me. I lean close and purr, "As long as you don't mind my red lipstick on your cock."

"Fuck," he breathes, his fingers curl tight around the armrest.

"That's the plan—" I brush my lips below his earlobe. "First you get to fuck my mouth, then my tight, little pussy." I pat his cheek before settling back into my seat. "Now, be a good boy and watch the concert. We don't want to get in trouble."

The shift of his large body in the seat beside me is my victory lap. He's as wound up as I am. Despite the ache between my legs, teasing him is delicious. It's always been my favorite drug, and—let's face it—I'm addicted.

"Ready?" he says, shooting up in his chair, the moment the performance ends.

"Is someone in a hurry to get home?" I coo, taking his arm as we move along the row.

He guides us down the stairs. "Just thought we could take a nice *long* stroll through campus before we head out."

"We certainly *are not*." I poke at his back as we descend the stairs.

"Oh, did you have something else in mind?" he muses

ruefully, spinning to face me as we reach the bottom. "Perhaps, we can go for dessert?"

Head tipped up, I flash a sultry smile. "The only dessert I'm interested in is at my apartment, and I would like multiple helpings."

"Multiple?" He folds his arms around me. "Someone is starving."

"Famished."

"I wouldn't want you to waste away. Perhaps, something to tide you over until I can properly serve you dessert?" He bends, taking my mouth in a deep kiss.

My entire body jellies with each slow press. This taste only taunts of the promise of what's coming.

"Again, my office is just down the way."

He laughs. "Our first time will not be on a desk."

"There's always up against the file cabinet." I wiggle against him, making him rumble with laughter.

"Guess the romantic sabbatical is truly over," Miles drawls from behind us.

Mouth drawn into a firm line, I pivot towards his venom-laced voice. In the midst of the emptying theater, I easily spot Miles at the edge of the stage, the house lights shining down on him. Arms crossed, he stands there. The intensity of his glare carves at me like a knife's point.

"Miles. What are you doing here?" A furrow dips my brow.

"Here for the performance, though I didn't expect this one." He motions at us. "I thought the scene at the race was obnoxious, but your antics here..." he makes a tutting noise. "Quite the show you put on for a woman who *is not* dating."

I don't know how to respond. We weren't together. I made no promises. That doesn't quell the swirl of guilt in my gut. I rebuffed his advances because I said I wasn't dating anyone, and that was true...then. But this is now. Even if Garrett wasn't in the picture, Miles isn't who I want.

"I'd like to say, I'm surprised, but it explains why that one never liked me." He sneers as he points at Garrett.

"His name is Garrett, not *that* one." I glare.

"For the record, even if I didn't have feelings for Jensen, I was never going to like you," Garrett says, looping his arm around my middle and pressing me against his firm chest.

"You may not have, but she did." He saunters closer, his energy reading predatory, as if we're field mice for him to scoop up in his clutches.

I've never seen this side of Miles. He's charming and flirty, but never aggressive. There's an undercurrent of menace wafting off him.

"How does that feel? Knowing that she liked me. That while you pined for her like a lovesick hero from a clichéd Victorian romance, she daydreamed about me." He stops in front of us, a serpentine grin playing in his stance. "She probably went to bed at night wishing I was tangled in the sheets with her."

"You're her past, I'm her now." Garrett places a kiss on my neck. It both claims and reassures.

Miles huffs an incredulous laugh. "We'll see how long it lasts."

Fuck him! Anger roars through me. I want to slap him. But I don't know what the future holds for us. This may not last, but it may become the love I've always wanted.

I narrow my eyes. "We'll find out."

"You'll have to excuse me if I'm skeptical of your fickle heart," he scoffs. "One minute you're chasing me, then you're taking a break from relationships, and now you're with *him*."

"I'm not fickle." My jaw clenches.

He makes a mock cooing noise. "Dear Jensen, I don't think you know your head or your heart. The last few months demonstrate that. You've changed. Maybe you need to find a new therapist. That one you've been working with clearly isn't worth the copay."

"Asshole." Garrett lets go of me and starts towards Miles.

"No." I place my hand on his shoulder, stopping his movement. "Miles is right. I am different." I look toward the smug literary fuckboy. "There was a time when I liked you. It was a simpler time when I thought you were all I deserved." My mouth ticks up into a sardonic grin. "But now I know my value. I deserve the best, and you, Miles Calloway, are nobody's best, especially mine."

"First, the race. Now this. You're not what I believed you were. I thought you were sweet. Guess I was mistaken," he spits out the insult as if he has the power to hurt me.

Be sweet. Don't be too much trouble. Those little internal commands were my go-to for so long in hopes that I'd be liked. That a man like Miles would want me. But if I have to play at something, that's acting. I don't want theatre. I want real.

"But I am sweet," I say, my stare fierce. "What you don't realize is that sweet doesn't mean I'll wait around until someone decides they want me."

"That's not—"

"It is." I release a humorless laugh. "You fed me some gaslighting bullshit about me never saying anything. You knew what I wanted. Everyone knew. I'm not subtle."

"She's not. It's one of my favorite things about her," Garrett says, his tone impressed.

"Thanks, baby." Preening, I look over my shoulder at him, before turning back to Miles. "I'm not here to fluff your ego, and that's what you're mad about." I motion between us. "This isn't you being sad about me being with Garrett, it's about your bruised male ego. You don't have me around to make you feel wanted anymore."

"You really aren't who I thought you were," he mutters.

"I'm so much more." I make my spine tall and flash a large grin. "Now, if you don't mind, I'm on a date. Ready?" I hold out my hand to Garrett.

"Of course." Garrett takes it, and we turn to walk away.

"Goodbye, Miles," I say, moving toward the door.

"Miles…" Garrett stops me with a hand on my arm and looks behind his shoulder. "Jensen doesn't need me to speak for her, but if you ever talk to her like that again, remember I'm a doctor. I know all the ways someone can get hurt and how to fix them, so it can be done again."

"Are you threatening me?" he says, aghast.

"I don't make threats."

"Caveman," he mutters.

"Perhaps." And with that, Garrett drops my hand and hoists me over his shoulder. "But this caveman got the girl. Have the day you deserve, asshole."

"Bye, Miles." Laughing, I wave as Garrett carries me out of the theater.

The laughter and shocked gasps around us telegraph that the small crowd outside the theater is both bewildered and enjoying this spectacle. I should be mortified. This is my workplace, after all. As a blind person, I don't blend in, so most students, faculty, and staff—even if they don't know me directly—are aware of my existence. But I rather enjoy this.

"Is your possessive male point made, or are you carrying me all the way back to the SUV?" I tease as he carries me through the quad to the hoots and laughter of passing pedestrians.

"It's partly to make a point to Professor Dillweed, and mostly because we'll get to the car faster if I carry you since you're in heels."

"Eager to get me alone?" A wicked grin kicks across my face.

"Yes," he squeezes my ass, making me squeak. "That was about the sexiest goddamn thing watching you school literary fuckboy."

I sigh with contentment. "It really was, wasn't it?"

"I'm glad you know your worth, and I endeavor to be the man worthy enough to call you…"

"Yours," I say softly.

His nod brushes against my hip. He may not be ready to say it, but I know that I'm his, and he's mine. I don't need the words. It may be too soon. I may be swept up with this, but this is my truth. It may be all wrong, but since when have Garrett and I done any of this right? The only right I care about is how it feels with him.

22

MILE TWENTY-TWO
READY?

This is torture! Arms wrapped around my middle, Garrett kisses along my neck as I attempt to unlock my front door. My entire body is coiled so tight that I may split apart if I don't get release. The sensation of his hands slipping beneath my jacket and the press of his rigid length against my backside reiterates his own desperation.

"You're very distracting." Head lolled back, I moan as he drags his hands up my front, palming my breasts over my clothing.

His low hum is wicked against my neck. "If you think that's distracting—" He pulls my jacket down to my elbows, glides his hands to my dress's zipper, and with slow, taunting movements, drags it halfway down. "How's this for a distraction?" Kissing between my shoulder blades, he unclasps my bra and then slides his hands into my dress.

"Oh god." I bite back my little whimper when he tweaks my nipples.

"How's the door coming?"

"If you'd behave, I could concentrate." I rub my backside against his hardness. His sudden hiss causes my mouth to curl into a devilish smile.

The last hour—between the show and our trip back to my apartment—has been filled with us torturing each other. It's delicious, and has me riddled with frustration.

"Got it," I rasp, with the click of the door unlocking.

"Thank god," he groans, lifting me into his arms the moment I open the door and carrying me in.

"You really are a little bit of an alpha, aren't you?" I sass.

"Oh, pretty girl, I may be the one carrying you, but never forget you're the one with all the power here." He kicks my door shut and carries me fully into my apartment before depositing me in front of my sofa.

He's being playful, but I don't want power over him, or for him to have power over me. Even though I know we both do. We can hurt. We can care for.

"I think we both have the power here." I cradle his cheek.

"Are you ready for this?" He combs his fingers into my hair.

After all we've already done, it might seem silly to be nervous. Even if every single cell within me ignites for this man's touch, this is more than that. This solidifies what's been happening between us. Each moment together over the last five years has led us here. It's like running. The build is the longest part, but when you get there... it's glorious.

Nodding, I place my folded cane below the coffee table. "Yes..." I slip my jacket off and hang it on the sofa's arm. "You?"

"No," he breathes.

"We don't have to."

"No." He swipes his hands down my cheek in gentle strokes. "In so many ways, I'm not ready for you, but I want this. I want you. It's been a long time since I wanted someone this much."

"Me too," I murmur.

Though that is a lie. I can't remember ever wanting

someone in this way. It hurts and soothes in a way that is both comfort and torment.

"I've been with other women since Val died," he says softly.

"I know." I swallow down the worry that I may not live up to the other women he's been with.

It's not a secret. Anker has mentioned that Garrett has had a few *understandings*, but never a relationship beyond that.

"This isn't that." He brushes his thumb along my jawline. "I need you to understand that. This isn't just two people scratching an itch or me dipping my toe into something. This is more."

"I know."

And I really do know. This isn't false bluster. Even if I worry I may not live up to the experiences he's had with other women, I want this as much as he does.

Reaching out, I place my hand on his chest. My palm flexes with each beat of his heart. "You remember what to say if something is too much?"

"Turnip." His heart gallops. "And you remember what to say, too?" Taking my hips, he pulls me close.

"Turnip," I say saucily.

"Good." He drags my zipper down the rest of the way and steps away from me, allowing the dress to slide down my body. "Undress but, baby, keep the shoes on."

With the lick of my lips, I step out of the dress. Spinning my back to him, I slide my bra off and toss it on top of my dress. Blowing a kiss over my shoulder at him, I wiggle out of my panties. Dropping them atop the growing heap, I brush my hair behind my ears as I turn. It's not the first time that he's seen me like this, but the scorch of his gaze over my skin makes it feel as if I'm an undiscovered country for him to explore.

The wildfire erupting inside me from the desire radiating from this man surges my confidence. My past insecurities are silent. I've never felt so sexy or powerful with a man. Not power over him, but power in myself.

"Look at you, pretty girl."

"You like what you see?" I ask, my voice husky. "Do you like this?" I trace my fingertip over my mouth in the shape of an O.

"Yes."

I drag my hands down my neck, over my collarbone, and palm my breasts. "How about these?" A soft whine escapes with each roll and pinch of my taut peaks.

"Yes."

"And—" Sauntering to the sofa, I sit, and spread my legs wide. "What about this?" I slide my finger down my pussy's slick center.

"I fucking like it all."

Need twists deep in my core. All I want is for him to plunge inside me and end this throbbing ache. It doesn't need to be slow and sensual. I just want him to take me hard, fast, and deep.

"Yeah?" I press languid circles against my clit and let out a soft moan. "Show me how much you like it all."

He prowls close. "But I'm enjoying this."

"Wouldn't you enjoy it more if this were you?" I slide a finger inside myself.

Placing his arms on either side of me, he hovers over me. "But it is. Those may be your fingers, but I know it's me you're pretending is pumping into that sweet little cunt."

My belly clenches. I release an unintelligible whimper that somehow combines the words god, fuck, and oh.

"You like that? You like when I talk dirty to you?" he says, his mouth scant inches from my ear. "When you listen to your erotic audios, do they sound like me?"

"Yes."

"Just as I thought." He takes my earlobe between his teeth

and bites gently. "And it's me that you think about when you listen to them? When you touch yourself?"

"Yes," I whine, pushing a second finger inside of me.

"Some men would be jealous of that." He skates his nose down my neck. "But those audios just whetted your appetite for me, didn't they?"

"Yes."

"It's my cock you want inside you."

"Yes," I pant, pressure curling tight at my center.

"Then be a good girl and fuck yourself with your fingers like it is me," he growls.

I've never lost myself like this. The fantasy and reality twine together in a visceral experience. My body wound tight from both his words and my touch. It's as if he's the one deep inside me instead of hovering over me, his arms caging me in and the heat of his stare locked on me tipping me closer.

"Skin all pink. Eyes glossy. Brow sweat-kissed. You're so close, aren't you?"

"So close…" I cry, the crank turning tighter.

"Crook your fingers inside your cunt, pretty girl." His low bass rumbles through me.

And with that, I break. The orgasm slams into me with the force of a freight train. My body shudders around my shaking fingers.

"That's my girl." He drinks up my moans in a deep kiss. "Let me have a taste." He guides my fingers into his mouth.

The satiation that dripped along my veins is gone. Needs spools tight as he sucks my fingers clean.

"Not enough." He lowers to his knees in front of me, hooking my legs over his shoulders. "More," he growls before burying his face at my center.

He's greedy for me—consuming me in indulgent licks and sucks. As much as he takes, he gives. I am both wanton and fulfilled with the way he drinks me up.

"Oh!" I fall back against the couch, release crashing through me.

Kissing my forehead, he scoops me up and carries me to the bed.

Sated, I relax against him. This man can say depraved things and coax out the brazen side of me, a side I've only explored in my fantasies, but still wrap me in tenderness with how he holds me. With him, I don't have to be just one thing, and neither does he.

Once he deposits me on the bed, I slip my glasses off while he begins to undress. He places several condom packets on the bedstand beside my glasses. Grinning, I touch each packet, counting out loud.

"Eight condoms… Someone has plans."

He grabs a packet and opens it. "So many plans."

"Wait—" I skate my hands up his muscular thighs and grip his shaft, "—I thought the plan was for you to fuck my mouth and then my pussy."

"Fuuuuck." He places his hand on my cheek. "If you put your mouth on me, I'm going to lose it."

"Isn't that the point?" I purr.

"Yes, but the next time I come, I want to do it in your cunt."

Rising to my knees, I encircle his neck. "Technically, it will be in a condom inside my cunt," I say saucily.

"Ha!" He huffs a laugh. "How do you want me to fuck you, funny girl?"

"Pretty girl." I poke him. "I've not had a lot of experience and…"

Reminiscent of a determined mosquito, old insecurities buzz awake. This isn't one of my spicy audiobooks or erotic audios. Sex. Relationships. I'm so unpracticed. He may be navigating a relationship with me after losing a great love, but I've never even experienced the flimsy, fleeting kind of love.

"I don't want to disappoint you." My admission is quiet.

"Hey…" He presses a gentle kiss. "You are already a dream I didn't let myself have, but somehow still got lucky enough to have."

"I'm so new at all this," I confess, emotion thick in my throat.

He strokes against my cheek. "Me too, but we can learn to walk together."

"But you've done this."

"Not with you."

Those words hang between us. He's been with other women. He was married. He had this entire life before me. But that was then, and this is now. It's just like what he'd said tonight to Miles; that was his past, I'm his now.

"We don't have to—"

"I want to," I say.

"Jensen, we—"

"Garrett, *I* want to." Even if I worry that I'll make a mess of this, every bit of me still wants to run this race.

"We'll go slow. Listen to your body and do what feels good. Use your words to tell me what you like, and don't. You say turnip and we stop. Got it?"

"Yes."

"Good… I promise, I'll take care of you, but we'll stop when you say."

"I know you will." I look up at him, my heart so full that the emotion filling it drips along my veins.

With one last kiss, he steps back and rolls on the condom. Then, he slides onto the bed and sits up against the headboard.

"Come here, pretty girl," he whispers.

I crawl to him. Taking my waist, he guides me to straddle him.

"This way you can control how much you want to take." He eases me down onto him.

I hiss with the burn as my body stretches to make room for him. I know how big he is, but it didn't hit me until now. The fullness may twinge dully, but pleasure courses in tandem with the slight pain.

Placing my hands atop his on my hips, I rock in a slow rhythm. A delicious pressure replaces the twinge with each rock. Back bowing, I take him deeper. Each inch sparks my nerve endings awake, causing pleasure to pulse within me.

"You're doing so good." He moves under me.

"Thanks… I want—need—more," I moan, grinding against him.

"How's this?" He arches his hips, plunging into me.

"God!" I cry, my nails digging into his shoulders.

Chest heaving, he holds me in place. "You okay?" He runs his hands down my naked body.

"Better than okay." I wiggle just a bit, electricity zings with the feel of him filling me.

"Good." He drags his palms down my folded legs. Tapping my shoes, amusement plays in his expression. "I do like your new red shoes."

"Me too." I brush my nose against his.

In lazy caresses, he strokes his hands along my sides. Neither of us moves. It's the closest I've ever felt to another human. We're not rushing to the end. We're reveling in this connection. In how good this feels to be tethered to one another—not just with our bodies.

Despite the full sensation, my body hums for more. To have every inch of me experience every inch of him. I pull up just a bit and then slam back down on him, causing both of us to cry, "Fuck."

"You like that?" I murmur and repeat the action.

"Yes," he moans.

Our gentle pace becomes harder and faster. My blood almost sings with each note he hits inside me. Any lingering anxiety about not knowing what I'm doing is washed away.

Not just in how good this feels, but thanks to the pleasure his moans assure me he is experiencing. The quickening thrust of his hips up into me. His fingers biting into me.

"Baby… I'm going…" he rasps.

"O-kay."

"Are you…close?" He curls his hands around my ass, urging me on.

"Almost." I slip my finger between my legs and massage my clit, tipping myself over the edge.

He shudders. "Fuck, Jensen."

Falling against him, his arms wrap tightly around me. We just hold each other through our mutual climax. The aftershocks rippling through us. The gasping breaths. The tumbling back to reality. A reality where *that* just happened, and it's going to happen again.

23

MILE TWENTY-THREE
THE CLIFF

How am I already six months into marathon training? Sugar cakes! I've dated Garrett for almost three months.

Just like running, time marches at its own pace. It's that time when the initial ache of the start dissolves into the actual run, and I'm in it. The last six months have left me soaring. Friends. Marathon training. Garrett. It's all coming together.

Well, almost everything. I received an email that my department's grant application for the access technology center wasn't selected. The note came with the standard language about this not reflecting the merit of the application, but the limited resources available. They encourage us to apply again next year. Yadda, yadda.

It's frustrating because the university has denied this requested budget item each of the last three years, so I thought the grant might be an alternative funding resource.

I'll apply again next year, while I look for additional funding resources. As Garrett teases, I am like a dog with a bone, and I plan to find a way to make the access technology center a reality. As well as a few other ideas. This includes spending time with Bryce when we fly to Buffalo for the half-marathon to learn about some of the revenue resources he's tapped into for Boundless, his and his husband's nonprofit.

Thanks to my own experience and the work I do with students, I have a list of resources and programs needed to supplement the current lack of social and recreational activities for disabled students. It's not just the accessibility needs that aren't always addressed, but the lack of a culture that embraces and supports them—supports us. Ableist comments from others. People staring. Inaccessibility. It all leads to isolation.

"And isolation is something you know all too well," Dr. Nor says, handing me a cup of tea.

"It is." I take the cup and scoot back on the worn couch.

It's my weekly session with Dr. Nor before I sneak off for a romantic weekend with Garrett. After my appointment, we'll head to Palm Springs for the next three days—returning early Sunday afternoon so Garrett can make his virtual dinner date with his family.

"Rather, isolation *was* something I *knew* all too well." My mouth flexes into a contented smile.

The quiet loneliness that accompanied me for so long is a recently departed frenemy. It's not with me—not like it used to be—but the memory still lingers as if a ghost was just waiting to jump around the corner to shout boo!

I curl my fingers around the porcelain cup, letting the heat soothe my angst. "I was the only disabled kid at my high school. Being the only one, people often pointed out all the ways I didn't fit. Even my parents and Anker for a bit." I sigh. "I was somehow too much and not enough all at the same time. Same thing in college, and that has continued until now."

It seems indulgent to linger on the loneliness that once ached, given all I have now. Still, the memory of that pain twinges inside me like a dull, healing wound. But it's there, nonetheless, reminding me of its existence.

"What makes you no longer feel that loneliness?" she asks.

My family. The girl gang I have with Catherine and Kayla. Garrett. Each is important, but they're not the sum. At the root of my loneliness was a desire to be accepted by others—that I would fit. While I have people I fit with, they're not the puzzle piece that snapped into place, making me whole.

"It's me." Sitting up straight, I tilt my head to meet what I'm sure is her assessing gaze. "My loneliness was due in part to my hesitation to put myself truly out there. I've been burned in the past, and I blamed myself at some level. I didn't trust myself to make good choices about people."

"It's easy to pick the wrong people when they reinforce what we believe to be true about ourselves," she says in her soft, but matter-of-fact tone.

"Yeah." I swallow thickly.

It's something we've talked about often in our sessions. It's not just me picking the wrong people, but that I chose those who reinforced what I believed in myself; I'm not loveable. I'm too much. This doesn't absolve anyone who hurt me, but it opens my eyes, so I don't repeat old habits.

"I'm still a work in progress, but the woman who made those choices—who believed that—feels like someone I used to know, not who I am now."

"What makes you trust yourself now?" she asks.

"Everything started to shift the night Miles ditched me. It wasn't just him ditching me, but the moment I asked Garrett who Jenny Wren was. Deep down, I always knew Miles didn't want me, but I didn't admit it to myself. I just waited, hoping this time would be different. And it wasn't." I look into my teacup, the liquid contrasting with the white porcelain, allowing me to see the creamy brown color. "I know who Miles was, but I chose him. Just like with Chase."

At that time, I'd been blind to those things. Chase never invited me over to his dorm. He always came to me, saying it was because I had a single. The few times we went out on what I thought were actual dates had been in different cities away from campus. With my new clarity, I realize he'd always been hiding me.

"I was deliberately blind to who they were, believing it was all I deserved. Though, at the time, I thought each time would be different. That if I were the right kind of girl, they'd want me. I've never quite fit... Over the last few months, I've realized I didn't fit because I was trying to mold myself into what everyone else told me I should be."

With each lap of this new course that I run, I am becoming more me than I've ever allowed myself to be. Training has unlocked something in me, allowing it to run free and untethered from the things that have long kept me at the margins of my own life.

"I waited for someone else to rescue me. To make me happy, but I'm my own hero, and as long as I trust myself, I'll never be lonely." Warmth—whether from the tea I'm drinking or my realization—spreads through me.

"Self-reliance is important. We carry the keys to our own happiness, but we often can't unlock that door completely alone," she points out. "Let the relationship with yourself set the tone for others, not replace them."

I scrunch my nose. "That's cryptic. What does that mean?"

"Balance." She raises her hands as if saying "ta-da" causing me to snort. "The loneliness you've experienced speaks to the imbalance in your relationships—with yourself and others. Be your own hero but also let other people rescue you from time to time."

"How do I do that?"

"Practice. Lots and lots of practice. Just like marathon training." She waves at me. "It helps that you have good people in your life to do that with. To lean on when you need them and to pull back when you don't. Above all, be open and honest about your feelings and desires. Being the full Jensen."

The Full Jensen. For so long the idea of being unapologetically me in whatever setting I existed in terrified me. As Garrett's deep laugh hums around me while I sing a totally made-up song with the lyrics "Yum, yum in my tum, tum" to a baby giraffe I'm feeding at the Living Desert, I love being the Full Jensen.

It's not just that this man seems to adore every part of me, even the parts that frustrate him at times, but it's how I feel. I am unapologetically me, and I may be falling just as hard for me as I am for Garrett.

"Am I your girlfriend?" I blurt.

"Ah…excuse me?" the giraffe attendant coughs.

"I believe that was directed to me," Garrett says, his mouth likely ticked up into a half-smile.

Of late, I've noticed his normal firm line is replaced by half-smiles. It's been confirmed by our friends, and I take full credit for it.

"Sorry"—I wince—"I'm sure you're lovely, but I may or may not be taken."

"She's taken," Garrett says, his deep bass playfully gruff.

"Does that mean you're my boyfriend?" With a sassy wiggle, I pivot to where Garrett stands behind me taking a video of me feeding the giraffe.

"What do you want?" Chuckling, he pushes his phone into his pocket before stepping closer and handing me my cane.

Head tipped up, I bat my lashes. "I'm just confirming that you're my boyfriend."

He takes my hand, guiding us away from the giraffe feeding station. "I am, indeed, your boyfriend, which is why I know you're angling for something. I'm assuming it's either a stuffed giraffe from the souvenir shop or a latte from one of the food stands."

I am very much aware that Garrett Marlowe is my boyfriend. At least, officially as of a month ago. It didn't come with the fireworks of a big romantic proclamation, but it was perfect.

We'd stopped at the campus coffeeshop before he took me home, and the barista commented, "You and your girlfriend are so cute together."

To which Garrett said, "She is pretty cute, isn't she?"

"You didn't correct them," I say, as we slide down the counter to wait for our drinks.

"About?"

"The girlfriend thing." I gesture to him.

"I didn't," he says simply.

I arch one eyebrow. "So are we saying that is how you define me...as your girlfriend."

"If you want to be, pretty girl." He grabs my hips and pulls me close.

"I do."

"Good." He kisses my forehead.

"Does that make you my boyfriend?" I press into him.

"I'm whatever you want me to be," he murmurs, resting his chin on my head and banding his arms around me.

At twenty-nine, I have my first real boyfriend—whatever *real boyfriend* means. Without putting too much pressure on this relationship, I hope it's not an actual first and just an only situation.

"Why do we have to embrace a world of binaries—either or?" I bump my hip against Him. "Why not a world of ands? A latte *and* a giraffe."

"After the hike."

"Boo!" With a mock pout, I turn down the dirt path leading toward a series of trails within the park. "But it's *so* warm!"

Southern California may be known for its sunny weather, but May is gray. It makes it ideal for Palm Springs getaways before it gets so hot that you could fry an egg on the sidewalk. It's still warmer than Seal Beach, especially if you're going to do a five-mile desert hike.

"You love the heat," he teases.

"In blankets and beverages, not while exercising," I groan.

"It's not that warm. It will only be eighty-six today, and it's barely eight-thirty. You'll be fine. Five miles is nothing. We'll be done well before noon."

He's right, of course. With the half-marathon at the end of the month, we've been doing a combo of ten miles of a jog/power walk twice a week to work our way up to 13.1, so this is more than doable. Not to mention I'm in the best physical shape of my life between my solo treadmill runs and conditioning exercises the rest of the week.

Since we're on a mini getaway, we're giving ourselves the weekend off from training, but still built in some exercise between sightseeing, meals, and claiming each other on just about every surface at the condo Garrett borrowed for the weekend from a fellow doctor at the hospital. I have a moderate level of guilt for our antics, but not enough to not jump Garrett as soon as we're back.

Yesterday we took the Palm Springs Aerial Tramway and did a low-intensity hike on one of the trails at the top followed by lunch at a café at the overlook before a night in where we cooked dinner together and played Uno with my braille cards. Today is a more rigorous desert trail at the zoo. On top of the animals and other attractions, the Living Desert offers a few hiking trails within the park to simulate the full desert experience.

"It says it's this way," Garrett mutters as we stop.

"What's wrong?" Tilting my head, I tap my cane against the rocks stacked up on the path.

We're only a mile into the hike and it's been easy. The

trail is flat, outside of loose stones and pebbles, with a defined edge, allowing me to mostly use my cane and Garrett's verbal directions to navigate. Between visually scanning and my cane, I deduce that there's a rock pile made up of large misshapen stones and small rocks in the middle of the trail.

I scrunch my nose. "Are we supposed to climb it?"

"According to the map, it's this way." He looks around. "There's no sign saying it's closed, and there are people down the trail, so I think the rocks are part of it."

"Just part of the experience." I make jazz hands, causing him to snort.

"Maybe we just do the one-mile trail that led us here? We could do a few laps, and then head back to get your latte and giraffe."

"Embracing a world without binaries?" I wink.

"More like a world with you smiling like that?" With a soft kiss, he takes my hand. "Come on, let's just do a few laps."

"But you wanted to do this…" I tug him to a stop.

Even if I whine a bit about this hike, it does sound cool. According to the website, the trail offers lovely desert landscape views and vegetation. It's like a mini escape in the middle of the park, simulating what it might be like to do some of the trails in nearby Joshua Tree. Plus, Garrett geeked out just a bit while planning this. It's cute to see his excitement, even if it's more understated than mine about getting to feed baby giraffes. I don't want him to miss out because of me.

"It's not a big deal." He shrugs. "We can just—"

"No, we should do it." Head shaking, I wrinkle my face. "It's just a few rocks"—I tap my cane on top to gauge the height—"it's doable. What's the trail's intensity level ranking, again?"

"It's low to moderate for beginners."

"Which we can handle?" I don't intend it to sound like a question, but it does anyway.

"We can." He brushes his palm against my bare arm.

It's not needed, but his confirmation is reassuring, nonetheless. Even if I know his hesitation is a mixture of his default mode about my safety and comfort, I'm happy to hear the certainty in his voice in my ability to handle this.

"Especially if you give me a piggyback ride over these rocks." I flash a saucy expression.

"I'm tempted." He rubs his nape. "But I'm concerned I'll not have my bearings with the rocks and accidentally drop you."

"Anker would be pissed if you killed me on a hike."

He loops his arm around my waist. "I would also be very pissed about that."

I tip my head back and coo, "Because you'd be *so* sad without me."

"Yeah… Also, I'd prefer not to be featured on a *Dateline* special. *Man goes hiking with girlfriend, and returns without her…*"

I elbow his ribs. "Jerk."

He laughs. "Let's do human guide over the rocks."

"Good idea." I fold my cane and slip it into his backpack with our two bottles of water.

Just like running, the cane isn't ideal for something like this. There isn't a clear barrier to trail along the path to keep you on it. After we climb down from the rocks, the trail is a mixture of loose pebbles, stones, and rocks. It's more intense than I expected with the many obstacles and steady inclines between short plateaus. Something like this doesn't just test my physical endurance and strength, but my emotional bandwidth.

With this hike—just like marathon training—I went into it thinking about how I'd physically do this. If the last six months have taught me anything, it's that this is a mental game. I need to stay tapped into not just my surroundings and body, but Garrett's to navigate the path safely. Unexpected drop-offs, ruts, rogue branches, and whatever I just heard rustle in the distance all keep me on edge.

They keep him on edge as well. It's the same when we run. We trust each other and work together, but there's always a level of hypervigilance for both of us. I feel the way his muscles tighten, and his posture stiffens at different portions of the hike. Unlike with the rope, where we just have verbal communication and tugs connecting us when we run, human guide allows me to take in everything his body telegraphs. The same is likely true for him with my death grip as we traverse several large, uneven rocks with our upward climb.

Even if the hike is more challenging than I expected, it's exhilarating. Besides some tame beach paths, I've never done real hiking. Yesterday's hike wasn't this intense, which is strange because according to the map, they're both the same intensity level.

Accomplishment surges within me as the fitness tracker on my wrist pings with another mile completed. We're four miles into this hike, and I'm doing this. I kind of feel like a badass.

"Narrow path," he calls out, sliding his hand fully behind his back.

I trail my hand down to his wrist and position myself behind him. "Can you see the zoo from here?"

He slows to a stop. "Strangely no. If I didn't know we were at the zoo, I'd think we were in the middle of nowhere."

"Maybe it's a portal like the Bermuda Triangle... The Palm Springs Triangle." I laugh. "Describe the view. Like what do you see?"

"Lots of rocks."

"You should be a poet," I deadpan.

"I read books, not write them. I'll leave that to Catherine.

There's a reason I went into medicine," he says with a playful lilt. "The rocks have this sandy gray color like the beach on a cloudy day. There are no trees. A small mountain range or hills—not sure which—are in the distance. The sky is a pale blue that makes me think of that dress you wore when I picked you up from brunch with the girls last week."

"Thank you." I lean in, pressing my lips against his shoulder—his body relaxes with my kiss.

The long, narrow stretch starts to decline. We stay tucked close until it flattens at the bottom, allowing us to go back to a person and a half formation. My skin hums with the sunshine's hot breath against it. It may only be in the seventies, but the cloudless sky and treeless terrain offer no shade. Our only reprieve is the soft breeze whispering through the mini hill or mountain range—like Garrett, I'm not entirely sure what this is. What I do know is there is a mixture of steady and sharp inclines and declines along this path.

"Shouldn't we be done?" I ask, my brow creased.

It's been at least fifteen minutes since my fitness tracker pinged with the five-mile mark. I imagined the end would be soon, but it doesn't appear to be coming, or at least Garrett hasn't said anything.

"Yeah…" He stops, his body twisting left and right as if looking for any sign of the trail's end. "Let me check the map."

While Garrett reviews the map, I drink some of our water. It's strange how an almost six-mile hike can feel more rigorous than our ten-mile jog/power walks.

"Shit," Garrett mutters.

"What?"

"I misread the map. We're on the wrong trail."

My lips purse. "Which trail are we on?"

"The ten mile one."

"Ten miles!"

Somehow, I'm ten again and finding out there's no Easter

Bunny, which was weirdly more tragic than the *No Santa* revelation. It shouldn't be a big deal to find out there's about four miles left in this hike, but every muscle aches with the fever of a whiny child.

Shaking his head, he looks back at the map in his hands. "Shit… I'm sorry. I don't know how I fucked this up."

"Hey—" I step into him, wrapping my arms around his waist. "You didn't fuck anything up."

"This isn't what we planned," he murmurs, folding his arms around me, the map still clutched in his hand.

Head pressed against his chest, I can't miss the heavy thud of his heart. "It's okay, we can adjust our plans."

"This trail is harder."

I tip my head up. "Yeah… And we're over halfway through. We've got this."

"Yeah, but there's a steep uphill climb and a path along a cliffside before it declines back and meets up with the start." Releasing me, he steps back and studies the map again. Maybe we should turn back—"

"Absolutely not! I repeat—we're over halfway through." My laugh-filled protest is resolute. "I didn't come all this way to turn around. Even if the path forward may be harder, there's not a piece of me that wants to turn around."

"The intensity level is higher than the trail we thought we were on." He gestures to the trail.

"We can do this."

"It might be too difficult…"

For me are the words he's not saying. Each time he looks between the map and me, his concern slaps into me. He worries about my ability to traverse the rest of this. He doesn't need to say it, I know it. Certainty swirls in my gut like an acrid stew.

"*I* can do this." I stand tall, hoping something in my posture communicates to him that I'm able do this.

It's not that much further. We climbed over rocks, boulders, and up steep inclines already without me dragging us down. True, he's probably slower with me, but we're doing this. I'm doing this. Garrett and I need to trust in each other's abilities to know ourselves. Whether on the track, on a hike, or in other parts of our relationship.

"Are you sure?"

"Yes." I nod.

I try not to fixate on his lack of acknowledgment of my declaration that I can do this. He's just checking in. I need to settle into that, and not in the hiss inside me that he thinks I can't keep up.

"Okay, pretty girl." He reaches out and strokes my cheek. "Let's do this."

"Okay." I force a grin, hoping it hides the complicated feelings knotting inside me.

Putting the map and water back into his bag, we move down the path. A series of up and down mini hills leads to a steep incline. My calves burn with each step. Despite my internal mantra quoting Dori from *Finding Nemo*, the ache radiating along my limbs begs for me to just drop.

"Almost to the top?" I ask, my breath ragged.

"Yeah," he pants.

Thank god! From what Garrett explained—now that we know which trail we're actually on—this is the last upward climb. Once we're to the top, the trail tucks itself up against the hillside or mountain—I still have no clue what these formations are—before a steady decline to a flatter trail until the path's end. That and the ping on my fitness app calling out eight miles tugs me along.

He stops. "Fuck."

"What's wrong?" Head tilted, I wrinkle my brow.

"The trail…"

"What's wrong with the trail?" I say, my already thudding pulse ticking up. *Please, gentle hiking gods, don't make me have to go back!*

"It's a cliff and narrower than I thought."

"We knew that."

"Not like this. The trail is about three to four feet wide. There's no edge on the right side. It's just a drop-off to the bottom."

"How deep?" I poke my head around him, trying to see.

Depth perception isn't in my wheelhouse. Big and small drop-offs appear the same to me—if at all.

"About fifteen or twenty feet," he says.

I feel to our left, my hand coming into contact with dirt and rock. "Does whatever this is run all the way down on our left side?"

"Yeah."

"Single file. We go slow." I squeeze his bicep.

We're so close. The last thing I want to do—besides plummet to my death—is go back. It's not just about tripling what was only supposed to be a five-mile hike, but it's embarrassing. *We had to turn around because Jensen couldn't do it.* Even if he never says those exact words, it's implied. If it wasn't for me, he'd just keep going. Hikes like this aren't new to him.

"Jensen—"

I squeeze his arm. "We've got this. We'll stay tucked up against the wall and go slow. Even if this is more *cliffy* than we thought, people do this every day."

He lets out a loud sigh. "Fine… We go slow. Remain quiet, so we can stay focused. Hug the left," he says, his steady voice laced with a hard edge.

"Yes, sir!" Nodding, I position myself single file behind him, my hand wrapped tight on his wrist.

"If you feel like you're going to fall, fall left."

"Hopefully I don't need that advice," I say cheekily, attempting to smooth the tension crackling between us.

"Jensen."

"Sorry…" I clamp my mouth shut.

The stiff posture. The gruff timbre. The hard edge in his cadence. Anxiety drifts from Garrett.

Of course this is nerve-racking. We're on the side of a cliff with a fifteen to twenty-foot drop to a rocky floor that, if it doesn't kill us, would do so much damage. If I didn't make a joke, the emotions twisting inside me with the force of a hurricane may cause me to cry.

Slowly, we slide down the narrow path. The unexpected smoothness in the terrain settles the anxiety buzzing beneath my skin. Unlike the rest of the trail, there aren't as many ruts or rocks to deal with. Besides the death drop about two feet to my right, this is the easiest portion of the trail thus far. It's surprisingly peaceful. Sunshine mixes with the gentle breeze, caressing my skin. Outside of our footsteps and breaths, it's quiet. There's something lovely and serene up here.

"What does it look like?" I ask, twisting my head to the right to try to take in the view—but the glare stings my eyes, causing me to close them.

"It's…ah… Jensen, I need to focus," he says, his tenor curt.

Fine, I mouth, but immediately cringe at myself.

He's not being unreasonable. I'm being bratty, and I know it. Garrett will not relax until this is over. It's who he is. If he didn't need to worry about me, he could relax. If I could see, he wouldn't need to do any of this. He wouldn't need to describe the view, because I could see it. He could just walk without me dragging him down.

"Don't," I mutter in a self-chide.

There's no reason for me to submerge myself in those waters right now. Just like Garrett, I should focus on the task at hand—not being a disruption, so he can guide us safely down the path.

"What's that?"

"Nothing… Sorry…" I take another step, my ankle coming into contact with a rogue rock, causing me to lurch forward. "Oh!"

Before I register what's happening, my body is slammed against a small rock to the left. Garrett's body presses me tight against the cliff's side.

"Are you okay?" he says, his breath coming in heavy gulps. With his chest pressed against mine, keeping me secure against the cliffside, I feel every breath.

"I'm okay, I'm okay…" Blinking, I pant. "There was a rock. I tripped."

I'm not sure how that happened. The path had been so clean. What had been there, Garrett verbally indicated or telegraphed in his steps. I'm not sure how we missed it.

Because of you, a voice hisses inside me.

"Sit." He guides me to rest against a flat stone jutting out from the cliffside. "Are you sure you're okay?"

"Yes… You?"

"I'm not physically hurt, but I'm not fine," he grumbles. "That was too close—"

"I'm sorry. I'm not sure how this happened. I'm sorry." I chew on the corner of my mouth, guilt swirling inside me.

"It happened because I was distracted and missed the rock." He releases a snarled breath. "I told you to stay quiet, so I could focus."

"I know, I'm—"

"But still you talked. Damn it, Jensen, one wrong move and you could have—"

"I'm sorry," I say, swallowing against the hard lump in my throat.

Quiet. That's all he asked for. I know that. I pushed us to do this, because I thought we—*I*—could do this. All he asked was for me to be quiet, so he could guide us safely to the end, and I couldn't do that.

The one thing within my power, and I couldn't fucking do it. I can't read the map. I can't guide us. I can't watch out for rocks. All I can do is be led or be a liability.

"I need to focus on keeping us safe, not chatting." He straightens, his body casting a shadow over me.

"I know. I'm sorry," I repeat, my voice is a small tremor compared to the roar of emotions inside me. "I should have listened. We should have gone back like you suggested."

He crouches beside me. "We can still turn around if this is too much for you."

"It's not me this is too much for." Blinking back the sting of tears, I avert my gaze.

This isn't the typical alertness he has when we run. Yes, he's focused on my safety when we run together, but it isn't like this. There, we're a team, and I don't feel like a team right now. I feel like dead weight that he's tethered to.

"Baby." He tucks his fingers beneath my chin and gently lifts. "I'm sorry. I shouldn't have snapped at you—"

"No," I sniffle, shaking my head. "Please don't apologize. You're right. You need to focus on guiding us. I need to listen… This shouldn't be on you, and I'm sorry for that."

"That's not your fault—"

"But it is." I swipe at my eyes.

Stupid fucking tears! Just another thing I can't control.

"With other women, you don't have to do this. You don't have to worry about them tripping on a rock and falling off a cliff."

"That could happen to anyone. Look at Anker and the corgis."

"It's not the same. That was a freak accident. You don't have to guide Anker. You can just walk. Just like you could walk with other women."

"I don't want other women," he hisses.

"It would be easier if I could…" I don't let myself finish that sentence. Just forming that single word stabs pain within me.

As much as I've accepted this is how it is, there are times I wish I could see like everyone else. I don't always feel this way, but there are moments. Like now, as I sit back pressed against a cliffside, where I wish I were different.

He cradles my face. "And if you could, I'd find something else to worry about. This has nothing to do with that."

"It's okay if it does." I motion to myself. "I'm a lot to deal with at times."

"You are. You never stop with the questions. You make up these ridiculous songs. Despite packing an overnight bag, you steal my hoodies to wear at my place, which you never return. These things drive me nuts, but they don't change how I feel about you. In fact, they make me like you more. Even if I sometimes get frustrated with you, it's never because of your vision, and I'm sorry I made you think for one minute that it was."

"No…" I shake my head. "Please don't apologize. You didn't do anything wrong. I'm… It's just how it is. I'm not so naïve to think that it doesn't impact things—"

He silences me with a gentle kiss. "Listen to me, pretty girl, I do wish your vision was intact, and not because it would make my life easier, but yours. I want you to be able to see this view, not have it described poorly by your unpoetic boyfriend. I want you to see how I look when you walk into the room, so that you never fucking question how little interest I have in any woman but you."

Every part of me wants to melt into this. Garrett won't just tell me what he thinks will make me feel good. I know this. He's not like all the people who have placated me with dismissive comments that "It's just a joke" or "You're taking this too seriously," only to walk away.

"Like I said, I'll worry about everything when it comes to anything that could make you not smile…" He releases a stuttered breath. "Anything that could take you away from me."

"There are things that may, and will, do that."

He makes a throaty, growly noise. "Don't remind me."

"Sorry." I cup his cheek. "But it's true… And there will be times my vision loss is part of those things. Like today."

"It's not—"

"Not for you… For me," I cut in. "Today, you worried about our safety, and while I thought about that too, my internal monologue was dominated by old insecurities. I just kept thinking how easy this would be for you if I were different."

"I don't want a different Jensen, I want you." He claims my mouth. Like he wants to imprint himself on me, as if marking me so that there's no uncertainty.

"I know," I say breathlessly.

"Do you?"

"I *really* do."

There's no question in my heart about how much he wants me. Even if I worry that I'm too much or not enough, I know he wants me as I am. The Full Jensen with all her many pieces, even the misshapen ones I try to hide from everyone else.

"I don't always feel this way. Today just tested my limits. None of this"—I wave around us—"I could do without you. Just like with the marathon."

"I'm just your guide. *You're* still the one running the marathon, scaling the side of a mountain."

"Is this a mountain?" I say, my eyebrows kissing.

"I'm not sure." A soft chuckle falls out of him. "What I am sure of is that even if you have help, it doesn't change that you're doing this."

"And I know. Well, most of the time…" I slosh a hard breath. "But there are times I just get caught up in those old feelings that if I wasn't somebody people had to worry about, that I'd just be one of them. Just a friend. Just a colleague. Just a…"

"Girlfriend."

"Yeah." I offer a watery smile. "And I know with Anker, the girls, and you, I am just those things."

"You're so much more," he murmurs.

I am. Sometimes—like today—I need to remind myself of that. I need to remember that I'm not defined by what I can or can't do by the people that truly care for me. That includes me.

I squeeze his shoulder. "Today, I forgot. I got in my head and let those old demons play havoc. I want to be that confident woman who is able to just exist as is."

"I get it." He swipes his hand up and down my arm, the touch settling my fraying nerves. "Your demons got the best of you, and so did mine. The entire time, all I could think about was keeping you safe. When you tripped, it reminded me how helpless I am in that. That I can't ensure you never face danger. Literary fuckboys. Cracks in the sidewalk. Rogue rocks. I can't prevent them."

"But you caught me."

"I hope I always will." He shifts and sits beside me on the stone. "I am sorry I snapped at you," he says softly, folding his arm around me.

"And I'm sorry I pushed us past both our limits, and that I talked." I lean into him.

"I don't want you to be sorry about that." He sighs. "This is a moment where your shit and my shit tussled. Only you're actually doing something about your shit. I think it's time I talk to someone. I don't want my fear of something happening to you to cause me to lash out, or lose you."

"In fairness, chatting while scaling a cliffside isn't the best choice." I press tighter into him. "I don't want you to go see a therapist for me."

"It's for me. I want to breathe again. I want to just sit here with my girlfriend, taking in this view, and not panic that something could happen."

"Okay." I lift my head. "Do you want us to move?"

"Not yet." He guides me back against him and presses a kiss to my temple. "What I want right now is stronger than that fear."

My tension drains in the warmth of his body. It's probably not the best place to sit, but we do. Tucked up against the cliffside, we just settle into this moment with each other.

His throat's clearing breaks the silence. "It's cloudless, making it easy to see the birds. They glide through the air like a hot knife through butter."

"A hot knife through butter?" I bite back my smile.

"Your boyfriend isn't poetic, remember?"

"Yeah…" I nuzzle into him, "…but you're mine."

"That I am." He kisses the top of my head. "Sit a little longer, or finish?"

"I want to finish." I lift my head.

"Okay." He stands and takes my hand to help me up.

This time, the anxiety-ridden quiet is replaced by companionable silence. His muscles are still tight as we move down the path, but the tension between us isn't there. It's just Garrett's standard mode of wanting to keep me safe.

Just as I know my insecurities prickle beneath my skin like a threatening thundercloud, so do his. It's how we deal with them that matters. Difficulties will come; neither of us can prevent them. The way we take shelter in one another gives me hope that together we can weather any storm.

24

MILE TWENTY-FOUR
WITHOUT YOU

With a deep inhale, I close my eyes and immerse myself in the scene. The cacophony of cheering voices and noise makers—with their thunks, chimes, and whistles—singing around me. Downtown Buffalo hums with pre-race activity. The cool air, a hint of moisture in it from the rain forecasted for later today, whispers against my skin.

As much as an electric charge zings through me, my stomach knots. I'm about to run my first half-marathon. In so many ways, the build to get here has taken so long. Anker, Sonora, and the other runners in the group talk about this. Each sharing that as they trained for their first marathon, the build to the middle took the longest, but the rest happened in the blink of an eye. Before I know it, it will be marathon race day.

This is also my last race with Garrett. After today, I start training with Anker, whose ankle is healed, allowing him to get back to his daily runs. It's bittersweet. It means we're on the last leg of this journey which will—hopefully—see Anker and me cross the finish line together.

"How are you doing?" Garrett loops his arms around my middle and tucks me against him.

"Anxious. Excited"—I scrunch my nose—"I think I have to pee."

He chuckles. "Those are the nerves, but maybe we hit the bathroom before we start. Remember, we can take breaks if you need them during the race."

Throughout the course, stations are set up where people provide water, or for quick bathroom breaks. Downtown Buffalo is transformed for today's half-marathon. We flew in earlier in the week to give me a chance to check out some of the work Bryce does with Boundless, his nonprofit, and to do some sightseeing.

He and his husband, Marshall, have played our tour guides over the last few days. For the first "meet the family" interaction, it's going well. Granted, this isn't our first meeting, but it's in a different capacity. Our previous interactions were brief, and then, I was just Anker's sister. Now, I'm Garrett's girlfriend.

Buffalo is also a new city for Kayla to explore. She, Catherine, and Anker flew in with us to sightsee before today's race. The ladies, Bryce, and Anker are positioned at the finish line to livestream our crossing to my parents.

It's strange to think about how loneliness used to twinge inside me. As I've become more balanced in my relationship with myself, recognizing those old fears for what they are—lies—I'm able to better appreciate the people in my life. I still feel lucky to have them, but now recognize that I deserve their love just as I am.

Their love and support envelop me as tightly as Garrett's hand as we stroll toward the starting line. This race is triple the size of the fun run races we've entered. The race's roar makes the cheering at the 10Ks sound like a kitten's purr. Despite incorporating loud rock music blaring in my earbuds during my solo treadmill runs—a strategy recommended by several blind runners in the group to mentally prepare for this volume—my nerves twitch. The sensation is akin to being submerged in the deep end while someone shouts down to you from the surface. You're aware that someone's speaking, but it's more like a feeling prickling beneath your skin, rather than actually hearing anything.

It's only temporary is the mantra I tell myself as Garrett and I transition from our initial power walk into a slow jog during the first several minutes of our run. Where there are loud pockets sprinkled along the 10K courses we've already run, this is more consistent. Spectators appear to be camped out along the first mile of the course.

Their presence causes me to pull tight on the rope, keeping myself snug with Garrett. Tucked up against the far right of the course, the spectators with their hoots and clanging cowbells seem like they're right next to me. It makes me stiffen and tighten my grip. Even if I know they're there, my hackles still rise. It's like being on the cliffside with Garrett again, only instead of tumbling to my death, it's people I worry about. How is that scarier?

Just people, I mouth. Yes, people are scary. They can hurt you in all the ways. Haven't I experienced so many of those ways already? I've been mocked, used, discarded, and ignored by people.

I've also been cared for, befriended, guided, and just loved by people. With any human interaction there's the threat that a few steps to the right, you fall, and a few steps to the left you're safe and supported. Just like with that cliffside, it's about balance—trusting myself, and the people around me.

I loosen the slack just a bit.

Garrett tugs twice, causing my mouth to lift in a smile. Those two tugs telegraph his "You got this." My two tugs back reply my response: We got this.

"Rockstar!" Anker hoots, lifting me into a swinging hug as Garrett and I cross the finish line into a small park full of spectators and runners milling about.

I did it! Somehow, this is even better than completing the two 10Ks. I'm not sure why I am shocked. For the last few weeks, Garrett and I've consistently jogged/power walked 13.1 miles once a week. Other runners talk about this. It never gets old. Each race is like a new mountain climbed.

"Easy! If you break her, I'll kick your ass," Garrett laughingly grumbles.

"Your boyfriend is so protective," Anker teases, placing me back on my feet.

"That he...eep—" The breath wooshes out of me as both Kayla and Catherine slam into me, squealing as they hug me tight.

"Seriously, be careful with her. I'd like her undamaged for later."

"Is someone jealous we're not fussing over them?" Anker makes a mock-cooing sound.

The sound of a slapping hand and Garrett's grumbled, "Stop it," paint the picture of my brother pinching my boyfriend's cheeks.

"Don't worry, daddy, we won't break her," Catherine teases, hugging me tighter.

"She'll be fine for whatever sexy hotel shenanigans you have planned for later," Kayla quips.

"Gross..." Anker makes a gagging noise.

"Kayla, we've discussed this, no mentioning of Garrett and my sex life in front of Anker." Laughter curls my lips as I shake my head.

"I'm just happy to hear Garrett has some sort of sex life again." A male voice, which I recognize as Bryce's, breaks into our little group.

He and Garrett's tenors are both deep and a little rumbly. However, Bryce's is boosted with this hint of mischief. On the outside, Bryce and Garrett appear so similar. Each is well over six feet with broad shoulders and Viking-like builds—something my Danish father appreciates about my boyfriend. Each has chestnut hair and green eyes. While Garrett has an almost always present five o'clock shadow, a neat beard accentuates Bryce's strong jawline. Kayla described the Marlowe brothers in great detail while fanning herself and sighing, "That gene pool is a deep well of sexy."

"Nice job, you two." Bryce embraces me and then his brother. "And also, don't be mad at me. You know how she is."

"How who is?" Garrett pulls back, confusion likely furrowing his brow.

"Oh my god!" a random woman, whose voice I don't recognize, squeals before barreling into Garrett.

"Lara," he says, the breath seeming to whoosh out of him.

Lara? I incline my head. I'm assuming the Lara currently tackle-hugging my boyfriend is his younger sister.

"He just ran a half-marathon, let him breathe." Bryce's chide is warm.

"What are you doing here?" Garrett's tone teeters between bemused and exasperated, causing me to lift one eyebrow.

She slaps his arm. "Like I'd miss a chance to meet my big brother's new girlfriend."

"You've met Jensen before." He shakes his head.

"Not when she was your *girlfriend*." She places her hands on her hips. "You're lucky this weekend clashed with mom's library fundraiser, or else she'd be here too. Can't believe you kept this from the family!"

He kept this—me—from his family? Queasiness sloshes in my stomach.

"Technically not the whole family." A smirk is evident in Bryce's cheeky comment.

"Don't remind me." She wags a finger at her older brother. "Your collusion in his hiding Jensen from us is only forgiven because of your inability to keep a secret for long, ensuring you let it slip at last week's family dinner."

Garrett puffs out a short breath. "We had enough to focus on without making this a whole Marlowe family interrogation of my girlfriend."

"He said *my girlfriend*." Lara mock swoons. "Is our dear brother smitten?" She elbows Bryce.

"Yes." Garrett loops his arm around my shoulder and presses a soft kiss to my temple.

"Stop! Adorable!" She clutches her chest.

"Did you fly from Boston just to harass my girlfriend?"

"He said it again. Girlfriend!" she squeals. "Yes… Also, why are you hiding her from us?"

"More like saving her from your obnoxiousness."

"Whatever." She flicks her wrist. "She's going to love me. Probably already does. Hi, Jensen. I'm so happy to see you again." Lara envelops me in a tight squeeze. Just like her older brothers, she's tall—at least six feet—but with a curvier figure and long dark hair.

"Hi, I'm Jensen." I cringe. "I mean, yeah, I'm Jensen. But… ah…you already know that…" A staccato-like laugh huffs out of me as I step back. "I mean, hi. It's nice to see you again."

"You're adorable." She grasps my hands. "No wonder Garri is gone for you."

"Garri?" I blink.

"It's what I call Garrett."

"Excellent!" Anker claps his hands together, a mischievous expression audible in his playful lilt.

"You're not calling me Garri."

"Dr. Garri has such a ring to it. Don't you agree?" Anker bumps my shoulder.

I wrinkle my nose. "Not sure how I feel about dating a Garri."

"Could sound fancy if said in the right accent." Catherine clears her throat. "Garri," she purrs in a French accent.

"Test it out in the heat of passion. See how it rolls off the tongue, while he's using his," Kayla says saucily, causing Anker to groan.

"Oh! I love your friends," Lara gushes.

"On that note…" Garrett places his hands on my shoulders. "Jensen and I need to stretch and grab our post-run snacks to replenish at the runner's tent. We'll meet you all in the vendor area."

"Fine, run off with her, but it's only a matter of time before I get all the details about you two, and share with her my many, many embarrassing Garri facts." She releases me and places her hands on her hips in a sassy pose. "Did you know Garri and his friends would LARP at the park near our house as teenagers?" she says.

"Best day of my life!" Anker chortles.

"LARP?" Kayla tilts her head.

"Live action role playing. It's where people dress up as *Lord of the Rings*-like characters and battle with foam swords," Catherine explains.

"It's far more complex than that," Garrett mutters.

"You'll have to explain the complexity of LARPing on our walk to the runners' tent." I lean back against Garrett and tip my head up, a teasing grin twitching at my lips. "It may take me time to come to terms with your dorky backstory."

"Always lovely to have you around, Lara," he groans.

"Sorry, not sorry," she singsongs.

Taking my cane from Anker, I slip my hand into Garrett's to head to the runner's tent. There we stretch and then grab peanut butter banana smoothies and some almonds to help replenish ourselves after the race. So much of running is about what you put into your body, rather than how you use it. It's all fuel—what and when you eat. Just like with therapy and so many other things in my life, it's about the right nourishment to do the things you need to do.

"I'm not hiding you from my family," he says gruffly as he hands me a smoothie bottle.

"I know… I mean, I've spent the last four days with your brother and his husband. Also, it's clear from what Bryce and Lara have said that you talk about me." I flash a large grin, hoping to smooth down whatever worry nips at him.

"What Lara said about me making excuses for them to not meet you… I don't want you to think that's because of you."

"I know." I rake my top teeth over my lip. "For like a hot second, I worried, but those are my own insecurities. As much as I hate that they flared awake for a moment, I'm glad I recognized it quickly enough to rewrite the story in my head. Guess that's progress… But I know that's not what's happening here."

"I do want them to meet you," he murmurs.

"They've technically met me."

"But not as my girlfriend."

"When you're ready." I press into him, his arms banding around me and keeping me tucked against his chest. "Family integration is a huge step. I get it. It makes it real—"

He squeezes me tight. "This is real."

"I know… Perhaps, real is a poor word choice." I tip my head up to him. "What I'm saying is this doesn't change the way… I know you feel about me. You're my first actual boyfriend, and I'm the first woman you've been in a relationship with since Val. We're in uncharted waters, here."

He rests his chin atop my head. "I'm glad to be in these waters with you."

"Ditto, Garri."

"I'm going to kill Lara," he laughingly grumbles.

The initial post-race euphoria waves are now still, leaving me stiff and tired. Despite the endurance and strength I've built with months of training, muscles I wasn't aware existed ache. While the stretching exercises and healthy snacks help replenish us, I still have no desire to move from the hotel room bed where I lay sprawled in my towel post-shower.

Tonight, we're staying in with room service, while our friends hit the town with Bryce, Marshall, and Lara. After our recovery run in the morning, we'll meet everyone at Bryce and Marshall's for a celebratory brunch before catching our flight back home. Much like the stretching and nutrient-rich foods, the recovery run helps the body heal after the wear and tear caused by long-distance running. So much of running is about the build to the race and the way you deal with its aftermath to come back again.

"Hey," Garrett murmurs, kneading his fingers into my calves.

"Mm-hm…" Eyes closed, I let out a low moan.

"Undo the towel and lie on your stomach." With gentle pressure, he moves his fingers down my legs to my ankles.

"For butt stuff? I don't think I have the energy."

"No!" Laughter belts out of him. "Massage."

"Much better idea." Untucking the towel from around me, I then flop onto my stomach with the grace of a drunken toddler.

"Bryce gave me some CBD oil that will help with muscle aches and inflammation," he says, reaching over to the nightstand.

"I love your brother," I hum as Garrett swipes his hands down my back. Even though my muscles are tight despite his featherlight pressure, I know this temporary twinge will offer relief.

"Pretty sure the feeling is mutual." He chuckles, kneading his fingers into my hips. "Bryce mentioned he's connecting you with a contact at the MVP Foundation."

"Yeah," I hum. The tightness in my body loosens with each press.

Over the last few days, Bryce and Marshall have helped me figure out alternative pathways to get some of the things I want to do. While the position I want doesn't exist at Pemberly, they've shown me how I can just make it. My current role may focus on the academic needs, but I can expand it to work on my many, many ideas to offer more for disabled students.

Bryce did the same thing. He was constrained by what he could offer through the PT clinic where he works, and what was available in the community. He started small, but through donations, relationships with different foundations, and lots of grants, he's built something.

"I've never considered reaching out to them in the past, because their focus has been on disabled kids' recreation and athletic activities, but Bryce knows the couple who started the foundation and says they may be open to sponsoring an adaptive athletic center at the university." I scrunch my nose. "Well, at least a few pieces of equipment."

"One mile at a time." He increases the pressure.

"Yeah…"

Change is a marathon. Even if it may appear as if it happened in the blink of an eye, there is a build to get there. The difference is I'm not waiting for it to happen. Even if I never get there, I'm running towards that finish line.

"Ooh," I groan.

"Too much."

"Yes, but don't stop." I relax into the ache. Each press of his fingers unspools the tension in my muscles just a little more.

"This helping?"

"Yes." A smile slinks across my face. "If I don't pass out from how good this feels, I'll return the favor."

"Having you spread out naked on a bed is a return favor."

"Perv," I coo. "Though having a boyfriend with a massage kink does come in handy, especially when you're engaged in marathon training."

"Anytime." He moves down my hips towards the back of my thighs. "I'll be at the ready after your training sessions with Anker."

"Yeah…" I breathe. A dull ache clusters in my throat.

Tomorrow's run with Garrett may not be the last time we run together, but it will be our last training session. Next Sunday I'll be running with Anker.

"What's wrong, pretty girl?" His firm touches turn softer as he moves his hands up my spine in slow caresses.

"I don't want to do this without you." I swallow the lump gathering in my throat.

It's silly to get emotional about this. The whole reason I started training is to help my brother. Garrett was only ever supposed to be a stand-in.

"Hey…" He lies down beside me. "I'm still here. You still have me."

"I know." Shifting, I roll onto my side to face him. "This started because of Anker, but it's become about me and you. I can't imagine crossing that finish line without you."

He soothes his right hand down my side. "Today will not be the last race we run. That's a promise."

Those words surge warmth within me. Promises speak to something more than hope. They speak of plans—of expectations. Even if there isn't a guarantee, he still makes that promise.

"And if you want me to run a marathon with you, I will. I would do anything for you." He leans in and brushes his lips against mine. "But is this about wanting to run the race with me, or being scared to do it with someone else?"

"I…" I swallow thickly. "I made such a mess of it the first time with Anker. It took me so long to get here; what if I go back? What if I fail him? Myself?"

"Are you more worried about failing Anker or yourself?"

Somewhere between my brother's accident and now, this became about me. Maybe it had already been about me, and I had just used Anker as an excuse. Mere hours before I volunteered to do this, I faced yet another disappointment. Not just by Miles, but by myself. The last seven months have been about me taking charge of my own heart. I'm not the woman who waits for things anymore. I'm not the woman who allows herself to be someone's backup plan, especially her own.

"Myself," I murmur. "I don't want to fail myself. I want to do whatever ensures I cross that finish line."

"And what is that?"

25

MILE TWENTY-FIVE
THE FOUR-LETTER WORD

Pemberley is hauntingly beautiful in the early morning. The not-yet-burned-off marine layer paints the mix of early and mid-Twentieth-century brick buildings on campus with an eerie romantic hue, like the setting of a paranormal romance.

If I weren't so grumbly about the early morning training session, I'd revel in the campus's beauty. Thanks to the heat wave strangling the area, our training is relegated to early morning or evening to avoid the oppressive afternoon temperatures. It's well before eight a.m. on what should be my lazy Sunday morning.

"I'm getting two lattes today. One after this, and then a second one tonight." I yawn as Garrett and I stride toward the soccer field's track.

It's been a while since we've trained here. In the early days, we focused on getting comfortable with each other with the track's known safety. Over the last several months, we've primarily hit different parks for a change of scene.

"*Someone* insisted on an early start." His eyeroll is audible.

"What can I say, I'm a morning person?" Anker's warm chuckle greets us as we reach the field.

It's our first training session with Anker. Despite my hesitation after the half-marathon, I am continuing the course I had charted for myself. Part of this journey is about trusting my own decisions. This started as a plan to help my brother and me. The trust and feelings I have for Garrett doesn't change that. Neither does the fear nipping inside me that I may fail. As much as I need to learn to trust Anker as my guide runner as I do Garrett, I need to do the same in myself.

"Perhaps my least favorite quality of yours." My grumble is tease-filled.

"With so many remarkable qualities, I'd expect a few would fall out of the top ten ranking."

"Modesty not being one of them." Garrett shakes his head. "Shit, the rope. It's in the SUV. I'll be right back." With a quick kiss, Garrett jogs away.

Anker drapes his arm around my shoulder. "Are you sure you still want to do this?"

"Of course. I've come all this way." I jut my chin towards him.

"Yeah, but with someone else… If you want to run with Garrett, I'd understand. You two are a good team. One that I'm pretty sure will go the distance."

"It's too soon for talk like that."

"Sure." His mouth slants into a lopsided grin.

"Plus, I made a promise to do this with you."

Any hesitation I have is washed away with that truth. It's not just about promising Anker, but myself. I told myself at the start of this, I'd run the marathon with my brother. Even if this is no longer just about him, he's part of it. I chose to do this despite the residual lingering failure from our past. Somehow, I saw through the fogginess of past failures to have hope that this time would be different. In those moments, I believed in myself before I knew I could actually do it. I want to honor the Jensen I used to be, who believed enough in herself to take this chance.

"Promises can be broken, especially if they don't serve us anymore. I wouldn't be hurt. I just want you to do what's best for you," he says.

"And I am." I lean into him. "Garrett and I may be a team, but so are we."

"That we are." He kisses my temple.

"Not to mention, I'm your insurance policy to ensure the Larsen love magic finds you."

"And if it doesn't, I'll settle into my role as your incorrigible bachelor brother whom you're obligated to have over for family meals." He bumps his hip against me. "After all, you're with the future Mr. Jensen Larsen."

"Again, it's too soon for that talk."

"Keep telling yourself that," he says wryly.

"Also, I'm not thirty yet."

"Garrett and you didn't get together until this year. The *year* you turn thirty. The *year* you're running a marathon… It's the Larsen lore." He makes jazz hands.

I furrow my brow. "The Larsen lore is about meeting your one."

"*Finding* your one." He clears his throat. "Remember Uncle Christian and Pedro met in high school but didn't find each other again until they were in the same running group training for the Boston Marathon."

That thought resembles placing a hand close to a candle. Its flame licks against your palm, sending heat tingling along your nerves. But if you get too close, you could get burned, or worse, you could snuff it out. The idea of an endless marathon with Garrett surges joy and terror inside me, because I want that. I want that so much that it scares me.

"I think you two didn't *find* your way to each other until this year for a reason."

My brother may see fate's invisible hand in this, but I just see the natural procession of time. Just like running, relationships need to build. Muscles need to gain strength and endurance. Hearts need to have the will. It all needs to come together.

"I didn't find Garrett. I think I've found myself," I say, leaning into my brother. "Garrett is just the bonus."

"I got the rope," Garrett says, jogging back to us.

"Ready for this?" Anker asks.

"Are you?" I hum, my smirk likely matching the one kicked across my brother's face.

"Guess we'll find out."

Indeed.

While Garrett settles on the grass with a thermos of coffee and a medical romance novel Catherine talked him into, Anker and I hit the track. The first few minutes are focused on teaching him Garrett and my rope-based language. Two quick tugs equal agreement. One short tug means slow down—something we perfected after Garrett's tumble a few months back. Three quick tugs to go faster. Between the volume of noise at the races, and needing to focus on breathing as we run, conversations aren't always doable, so these commands, combined with our quick verbal callouts, do the trick.

With a nod, Anker takes the other end of the rope. Just like the first time with Garrett, we're walking this first lap as a warm-up to get used to each other.

Anker's more relaxed than I thought he'd be. His muscles are loose, and he doesn't pull back on the rope as I give us just a bit of slack. That is, until we increase to a slow jog in the middle of our second lap. Anker pulls just a little tighter, shortening our slack. Garrett only ever does this if we're surrounded by other runners and we need to go single file, but he always calls out *Madeline*, which is my term for getting into that formation like the character from my favorite childhood book. Right now, that's not what's happening.

"It's just us here," I say, giving the rope more slack.

"I just…" He puffs a breath then offers two quick tugs.

My mouth lifts into a large grin. While this is just the start, it reassures me that I'm making the right decision.

"My treat." I grin, slipping my credit card from the back pocket of my yoga pants.

Since the campus's coffee shop is closed on Sundays, the three of us are at a spot in downtown for a post-training treat. By our fifth lap, Anker finally settled into our system. He still pulled back a bit when I loosened the slack, but not as much. It will take time for us to build the guide/runner relationship that Garrett and I have, but I know we'll get there.

"In that case, I'm getting a scone with my coffee." Anker rubs his hands together.

"Good call." I tap my finger to my chin. "They do have the best scones here."

"Like either of you was going to enter a coffee shop without purchasing a pastry." Garrett chuckles.

"Says the man who's ordering a black coffee sweetened by the tears of the emergency room doctors whom he frightens when they don't follow admission protocol." Anker elbows Garrett.

"He's just a big old grumpy ogre with a heart of gold." I rise up to my tiptoes and squish Garrett's cheeks.

He bats my hands away. "You two tag-teaming me is a new level of obnoxious."

"He is kind of Shrek-like." Anker laughs.

"Which makes you Donkey, since you're the best friend," I coo.

"He *is* an ass." Garrett laughs.

"But what an ass." Anker wiggles his butt, causing the pair of elderly women behind us to giggle like teenage girls.

"Ladies." He turns and offers a bow before twisting back to us.

"Enough flirting, Casanova. Why don't you grab us a table while I help Jensen carry our order?" Garrett shakes his head.

"Thank you." I tuck myself against Garrett while we wait at the end of the counter for our order.

"It's a lot to carry." He folds his arm around me.

"Not this." I pat his chest. "For agreeing to let Anker replace you as my guide."

Even if I know this was always the plan, guilt still rattles inside me. Not only are Garrett and I a strong team, but he's dedicated so much time and energy to our training. The schedule and meal plan he developed before we started. His patience and support on and off the track.

"It's gotta be hard to have done all this work for me only to sit you on the bench before the big game."

"It's very sexy when you use sports metaphors." He brushes his mouth against my temple—his lips curved into a smile. "He may run this race with you, but I plan to run many, many others."

I snuggle into him. "Perhaps, London in the spring?"

Just as running this race is part of the plan, so is my new friend returning home. Next month, Kayla leaves Pemberly, but it won't be a goodbye. In such a short time, she, Catherine, and I have become like sisters. Catherine jokes were the sassy modern-day version of the Brontës. Only my literary prowess is in reading books, not writing them like my two besties. As hard as it will be to not see Kayla for our almost daily latte runs and weekly adventures, she'll not really be gone. I took a chance on this friendship, and just like with running with Anker, I am glad I listened to myself.

"Sounds like a plan, pretty girl." He brushes the back of his hand against my cheek. "Maybe before London, the first marathon we could run together is dinner with my family."

I tip my head up. "Like… Meet your parents?"

"Technically, you've met them."

"Not as your girlfriend." I shift foot-to-foot. "Are we talking about going to Chicago?"

"Yeah…" His laugh is breathy. "Maybe we start with the weekly virtual dinner. Specifically, today's virtual dinner."

This isn't just a meal with Ellie and Jason Marlowe, but an integration…me into Garrett's life as his *girlfriend*. Like Garrett said in Buffalo; this is real—even if we've not fully assimilated into each other's lives. Still, this is a huge step.

Since the night at the bus stop, all those months ago, both Garrett and I have begun navigating unfamiliar terrains. Each of us is pushing through the borders we had erected to protect ourselves from heartbreak. Between training and the therapy that we're both now going to, we're redrawing our boundaries. But we still need to walk before we run.

"If this is because of what Lara said in Buffalo, I told you it's not a big deal. When you're ready—"

"Nope."

"It's okay, Garrett."

He silences me with a kiss. "Just as I need to trust you when you push, pull, or need slack when we run, you need to trust that I know how to do that with this." He places my hand on his heart.

"I do." I flatten my palm on his sternum, enjoying the way my hand settles against his heart's gentle thump. The rhythmic beat is like a siren's song; coaxing out the truth about the way I feel about this man. "I love you, Garrett."

Those four words slip freely from my lips. They've lived there quietly for months, waiting for their chance to come out. Whether it's dinner with his family, or this new spirit of pushing the boundaries of relationships, I'm emboldened to say them.

"Jensen…"

"Don't..." I shake my head, but my gaze remains fixed on him.

This isn't just the first time I've told someone I loved them, but he's the only person I've loved like this. In the past, I would have been devastated to say those words and not hear them returned.

"Please, don't say it back. Not until you're ready. In fact, it's the last thing I want you to tell me right now. I just wanted—needed—to say it. I have no expectations. Just an 'I love you.' That's it."

"That's it?" A smirk plays in his timbre.

"Yep."

"Just casually dropping something as important as I love you at the coffee shop?"

"Yup." I flick my wrist in a dismissive *this isn't a big deal, but it's totally a big deal* gesture.

He makes a humming noise in his throat. "Since I can't tell you, guess I just need to do this." He captures my mouth in a deep kiss.

Like a song's crescendo, my entire body sings with each press. Somehow, he drinks up each crumb of those words from my lips, while giving me one undisputable truth. The words may be unspoken, but Garrett Marlowe is in love with me.

"You're in public. Show some decorum!" Anker laughingly shouts from the table he'd grabbed for us.

"Hush or I'll give your scone to Jensen," Garrett snarks, twisting toward my brother.

"Are you choosing a woman over your best friend?"

"Not *a* woman, but the woman *I* love."

"Excellent!" Anker guffaws.

Garrett twists back to me. "You said I couldn't tell you. You said nothing about me telling anyone else."

I encircle his nape with my arms. "Just a casual declaration of love in a coffee shop."

"Yep." He leans close, allowing me to take in his lopsided grin.

I press my smile against his, allowing our mouths to say all the things.

"The Larsen lore strikes again." Anker chuckles.

26

MILE TWENTY-SIX
BIRTHDAY PRESENT

My muscles hum with relief as the hot water licks against my body. The post-workout shower may be my favorite part of training. I glide the African Net Sponge along my legs, reveling in how toned they've gotten. Ten months ago, I joked with Garrett about how training and his meal plan would reshape my body, and it did—to an extent. I'm stronger with more muscle definition, but retain my soft curves and still slightly squishy belly. I love my body's strength and what it can do.

It's wild to think that I'm two weeks away from running an entire marathon. In the last three months, Anker and I have built a solid training routine. We train together three times a week with solo conditioning sessions on the other days, except Sundays. Since Anker is a morning person, and I want my lazy Sundays with Garrett, we swapped. I train with him Saturday mornings, go home to shower, and then head out for some lady bonding with Catherine. Each week, we have lunch, dialing in Kayla, who's back in Oxford, for a virtual check-in, before we head out for whatever activity Catherine has planned.

The only thing I know about this week's adventure is to

dress for tea. It makes me think, we're going to McKenna's Tea Cottage. It's one of my favorite places to go to on special occasions.

I slip on the large pink hat that matches the 1950's-inspired sundress that flatters my figure. With a spritz of perfume, I head to meet Catherine.

"Look at you rocking Barbie's dream tea party getup!" Catherine coos as I meet her in front of my building.

"Thank you." I offer a curtsy. "And I'm sure you're in something equally fancy."

"That I am." She touches the brim of her purple hat. "I'm even rocking Grandma O'Brien's pearls."

I tilt my head. "Okay, what's happening, woman?"

This is all a little fancy for a typical Saturday. It makes me suspect she has something up her sleeve.

"Patience, my dear Jensen." Playfulness hums in her sassy lilt.

Arms looped, we mosey down the street. My apartment is a short walk from downtown. The cool ocean breeze mixes with the sun's warmth, making it the perfect fall day stroll with my bestie. Plus, our outfits are too cute not to be on parade.

Hoots and cheers of "Happy birthday!" greet us as we walk into the cottage's outdoor courtyard.

"What! What did you do?" Laughing, I twist to face Catherine.

"Not me." She points to Garrett, who stands at the center of the cluster of people—my people. "Your man."

Garrett strides up. The sunshine allows me to take in how the pale gray suit he wears molds over his muscular frame.

"Happy birthday, pretty girl." He kisses my cheek.

"It's not until Wednesday." I laugh, which is my new coping mechanism for when the emotions overflow inside me.

My tears still come, but I'm getting better at redirecting

them with the work I'm doing with Dr. Nor. As she says, tears are just the body's natural safety valve to ensure things don't become too much.

It appears my boyfriend has booked the entire teahouse for the afternoon to celebrate my thirtieth birthday. Everyone is here. Even Kayla dialed in. My parents drove down from Solvang. They and Garrett's parents, Ellie and Jason, are swapping embarrassing stories about us over tea sandwiches. I can't believe they and Bryce, Lara, and Marshall all flew in.

Garrett even invited Andrew and his husband, who are trying to play matchmaker with Anker and Lara. Though, neither of them appears interested in the other beyond friends. It's for the best. Anker is still hung up on Sonora. Not to mention, as Catherine teases, this friend group has enough clichéd romantic trope pairings with Garrett and me.

"I can't believe you did all this," I whisper to Garrett.

"I'd do anything for you." He bands his arms around me. "I hope you know that."

"I do." I tip my head up to him, my heart about to burst with how much I love this man.

"Come with me." He takes my hand and guides us into the cottage. "I have something for you."

"Is it a quickie in the bathroom?" I wiggle my hips.

"Not when your father, who brags about being descended from Vikings, is ten feet away." He laughs.

"Not to mention my uncles and Aunt Margot, and she's a black belt."

Once in the cottage, he places a giftbox in my hand. I run my fingers on the smooth paper and the silky ribbon binding it.

"You didn't need to get me a present. This is already so much," I say, but open the gift anyway.

I pull out a scarf, a hat, and a pair of gloves. The fabric is buttery soft against my skin.

"Are these cashmere?"

"And they are pink." He grins. "Thought they'd keep you warm when we look at Christmas lights this year."

Plans. So many plans. For a man who only wanted time with the people he loves, Garrett has laid out more and more plans for us. A cooking class we signed up for next week. The joint Halloween costume of us as lion tamers and Ditka as our fierce feline. A trip to London in the spring for the marathon and to visit Kayla. With each big and small plan, I know that Garrett's own healing journey is progressing to the next mile marker.

"Chicago in December is no joke, so I'll want to ensure you're warm."

"Chicago?" Head tilted, my face wrinkles.

"I thought we could spend Christmas there."

I want to ask if he was sure, but bite back that question. Garrett knows when to push, pull back, and stop. Just as I do.

He folds his arms around me. "Anker has agreed to cover at the hospital and watch Ditka, so I thought we could take advantage of your two weeks off. A week with my family, and then I'll fly us off to some place warm that involves you wearing very few clothes."

"Okay," I murmur.

It's such a poor response for all that this means. This isn't just spending the holidays with his family but being with him for his first holiday season in Chicago since losing Val. Garrett's biweekly therapy sessions have helped him develop coping strategies to deal with his grief. This is a big step for us as a couple, but an even larger one for him.

"We'll even spend a few nights at the Palmer House, so I can take you to the home of the original brownie."

"Really?" I wiggle against him. "Best birthday ever!"

He brushes my nose with his. "Just wait until next year, pretty girl."

27

THE FINISH LINE

With one last hamstring stretch, I let out a steadying breath. Straightening, I unwind the rope and hand it to Anker. It's strange to think how this day both took forever to come and came in the blink of an eye. I'm at the start line of a marathon. *I'm about to run a fricking marathon!*

While we prepare to start, our people wait at the finish line. Catherine, Garrett, and our parents are there. Garrett's parents and siblings came as well. I told them they didn't have to, but just like Kayla, they are here. The way I cried when she appeared with Catherine at happy hour three nights ago to surprise me, saying, "Like I'd miss it."

The thump, thump of my heart as I reflect on the love waiting for me at the finish line quiets the roar of rock music, cheering, and PA announcements swirling around me. It may be just Anker and me in the sea of thousands of other runners readying to crisscross the streets of Seal Beach, but we're enveloped by an entire team of people that love us.

You just wanted to be loved. Garrett's words from months ago echo inside me.

"And I am," I whisper to myself. A soft smile kicks across my face.

"What?" Anker turns towards me.

"Nothing." I bat at the air.

"Are you Anker?" A male voice breaks into our little pre-race bubble.

"Yes?" Anker tilts his head. "Sonora," he says, his breath catching.

"Yeah." Her entire essence radiates a beaming smile. "Sorry to be a creeper. I showed Elliot your picture, so he could spot you and Jensen for me to wish you good luck. This is my cousin, Elliot."

"Hi," Elliot, says.

"Hi. I'm Jensen." I wave.

"Oh my god! Can we hug?" she asks.

"Totally." I reach out and fold my arms around her.

As much as I know Sonora is real, it's still strange to wrap my arms around her. She's tall, at least six feet, with an athletic frame. And she smells like sweet jasmine.

"I didn't know you were going to be here," Anker says.

"Yeah…" She shifts. "Kind of a last minute decision. I'm not running, but I wanted to find you both to wish you luck."

"I thought you were in Portland for a wedding with Micah."

"Micah," Elliot groans.

I arch an eyebrow. *Someone is not a fan of his cousin's boyfriend.*

She lets out a nervous laugh. "We broke up… At the wedding."

"I'm sorry." I try to hide how not sorry I actually am.

My brother may tease that he's destined to be the loveable single cad to Garrett and my coupling, but I suspect his feelings for Sonora are deep. Even their failed in-person meetcute at the New York City marathon, followed by her relationship with Micah, hasn't dulled his feelings. Since meeting Sonora on that online blind runners' group over a year ago, he hasn't dated anyone.

"I am so sorry, Sonora." Anker reaches over and squeezes her shoulder.

"How'd you end up here?" A smirk tips my mouth.

"After the breakup, I called Elliot. He works for the airline and got me a flight with a detour in Los Angeles. He lives in Long Beach. He's here volunteering with the MVP Foundation and dragged me along to cheer you on."

"How long is your detour in town for?"

"Until tomorrow," she says.

The laser-like focus of Anker's attention on Sonora is palpable. The air around us crackles with the charge between them. Part of me wants to tap Anker out, so he can run off with Sonora to take up as much time as he can while she's here, but I know he won't do that. Not to mention, we have a marathon to run to ensure the promise of the thing between them becomes something real.

"Let me take you out," Anker blurts.

"What?" Sonora guffaws. "You're about to run a marathon."

"After."

"I—"

"Runners, two-minute warning," the announcer booms from somewhere in the distance.

"We should head out to let you all get ready," Elliot says.

Anker reaches for Sonora's hand. "May I take you out tonight?"

Brushing her long, dark hair behind her ears, she shifts foot-to-foot. "Meet me at the MVP booth after?"

"Yeah." Anker grins, releasing Sonora's hand as she and Elliot begin to walk away.

"The Larsen lore strikes again." Tossing my hands up, I wiggle and dance beside my brother.

"Looks like someone is a Larsen lore convert."

"I'm a Sonora and you sitting in the tree, K-I-S-S-I-N-G, convert," I sing.

"Stop," he laughingly groans. "Let's focus on the 26.2 miles we need to run."

"Just name your firstborn after me."

"Talk to your boyfriend. He won naming rights in a poker game." He hands me one end of our tether.

"Oh god, I forgot… And you have dibs on his kidney." I shake my head. "Seriously, what kind of poker are you playing?"

With the airhorn's shrill whine, we take off in a power walk. We'll remain in the back of the running cluster to keep us safe as we work toward securing a spot hugging the right side of the course.

Chaotic. Loud. Too many people. It's everything I thought it would be and so much more. Once we break from the initial cluster of runners and find our spot hugging the right side of the track, we transition from a power walk to a steady jog. My muscles burn and twitch awake before settling into the run. A euphoric sensation drips along my veins.

We don't run 26.2 miles each time we train, but we have done a few practice marathon sessions. This is so different. One, this one really counts. Two, despite this being in the city where I live, the twists and turns of the course zigzagging through Seal Beach's streets are more disorienting than I anticipated. It's like looking through a smudged-up pair of glasses. Some shapes are familiar, while others are distorted. Three, the kinetic energy that ripples through the race pulses anxiety along my veins.

Our strategy is to toggle between power walking and slow jogs. Some miles flash by like the snap of fingers. Others drag on and on—like, now. The once delicious runner's high is replaced by this overwhelming urge to drop. My muscles scream to just stop. Each slap of my foot against the pavement pulses a dull ache down my legs.

"Uncle," I whine, tugging on the rope for him to slow.

"O—kay," he pants, slowing to a power walk.

Other runners call out, "On your left," as they breeze past us.

Hands on my waist, I gulp up air. We just passed the fifteen-mile marker, meaning there are 11.2 more to go. We're over halfway, which should buoy me, but it taunts. Pain radiates through every inch of me. All I want is to lay down on and claim the pavement as my new permanent home because once I stop moving, I won't be able to get back up again.

But you can't, a quiet voice somewhere inside me says. As distant as the finish line feels, it's also so close. Not close enough to reach out and touch, but within my grasp. All I have to do is just keep running. Just keep going for what I want.

"It's your call." He sucks in a deep breath. "But I know you've got this."

We could stop. There are points along the course for runners to do just that. But I realize I don't want to. Even if my body protests, my heart isn't listening.

Whether I run, walk, or am carried piggyback, all that matters is that I finish. My mouth ticks up, thinking of Garrett's encouragement during our first 10K. Months later, I'm 11.2 miles away from the finish line of my first marathon. Even if I never run another one, I'll have this.

I grin. "Onward."

"We got this." He tugs twice.

We power walk for a few miles before we ramp back into a slow jog. We teeter between power walking and jogging as we make our way through the course. The entire way, Anker and I cheer each other on. When he wants to stop, I nudge him, and vice versa.

"Twenty-six!" he shouts.

The roar from the gathered crowd almost drowns him out. I can't believe we're .2 miles away. I blink rapidly as if waking from a dream. How is this happening? How did I go from teasing Anker about the Larsen lore to this? I don't know if I'm a devout believer, like my brother, but I am no longer a skeptic.

Six years ago, Garrett and I met, but didn't find each other until the night before Anker was supposed to leave to run a marathon the year he turned thirty. As much as I want to believe we were on a trajectory to one another, I wonder if the first five years of our relationship were fate's way of giving us the time and space we needed on our healing journeys.

The day after a marathon, you do a recovery run. It nourishes and aids in your muscles recovery after the exertion, wear, and tear of running 26.2 miles. In so many ways, my relationship with Garrett is reminiscent of that, soothing the ache of what we've both been through.

Though maybe the Larsen lore isn't just about finding the love of your life, but also yourself. My uncles and father have shared that was the time in their life when the fogginess of their future cleared. They didn't just meet their partners, but started on their own personal journeys of happiness. My dad with the bakery. Uncle Christian became a teacher. Uncle Anders opened a bookshop.

The last ten months may have led me to Garrett, but more importantly, they have led me to myself. I'm stronger. I'm able to push past the boundaries I set for myself. I know what I want, and I'm not scared to let myself have it.

"Finish line!" Anker calls out.

I answer with three quick tugs of the rope, indicating to speed up. I will not walk across this finish line. Slack loosened, I steady my breath as much as possible and pick up my pace. My running shoes slap against the pavement. The cheers, hoots, and noise makers are a delicious song ringing in my ears.

"Endgame!" Anker's shout is breathless.

"Yes!" I cry out, tears tumbling from my eyes. I don't hold them back. They blend with the sweat coating my face.

"We did it!" Anker wraps his arms around me.

Breathless laughter. Tears. Obscenities. It all belts out of us.

"We did it!" I sob. "I did it."

Even if Anker was with me every step of the way, this is my victory. For so long, I held myself back from the things I wanted. No more. With the trust in the people who love me, including myself, I can cross any finish line.

"So proud of us." Anker kisses my forehead. "Here comes your man. I'm going to go stretch and then find Sonora."

"You mean…my future sister-in-law…" I huff breathlessly.

"Smartass." He balls up the rope and places it in my hands before walking away.

"Baby!" Garrett jogs over and lifts me into his arms. "Look at you, pretty girl. You did it."

"I did." I sniffle and wrap my arms around his neck.

"I love you so much." Garrett presses his lips to my forehead.

"Just think how much you're going to love me after we run London's marathon?" I say breathlessly.

"Pretty girl, I plan to fall a little bit more in love with you after each race we run."

"Good plan." I press my smirk against his.

The End.

A SNEAK PEEK OF IN THE HELLOW AND IN THEGOODBYE

Can distance bring breaking hearts back together? For Colm and Evie, they hope that the miles between him in Costa Rica and she in California can help them find each other again. Colm and Evie never made sense. She's a pumpkin spice latte. He's a large black coffee. But for the last five years they've been utterly in love. That is until a tragic night a year ago. Now Evie's big smile no longer reaches her eyes and far too often the seat beside her is empty.

When Colm leaves to teach in Costa Rica for sixty days the distance magnifies the growing emotional gap between them. They must choose to say goodbye or fight for each other. Colm proposes an experiment to long distance date in order to find each other again. Will the miles help them erase the space between them? Or are second chances only found in the romance novels…and not in real life?

IN THE HELLO AND
IN THE GOODBYE
CHAPTER ONE

In The Hello - Colm
The First Hello - Five Years Ago

Could this coffee line move any slower? Colm clenched and unclenched his fists as a young brunette ahead of him cooed about all things pumpkin. It was only August twenty-seventh and the heat of summer still gripped, but Jitter Bean Coffeehouse was already peddling autumn.

"I love a pumpkin chai!" she gushed to the older man that stood between them in the line.

The old man chuckled his agreement.

I am in the lesser-known tenth circle of Dante's Inferno.

"OMG! I love my pumpkin lip gloss. I stock up every fall," she giggled. Her pink dress hugged hips that were positively pulsating with joy, and the happy wiggle called his attention to her apple-shaped bottom.

Does her body always vibrate when she's happy? God, he needed coffee.

The coffee was vital not just because it was 6:48 a.m. on the last Tuesday before returning to The Land of Bad Excuses for Forgotten Homework, but because in two hours he'd be giving a talk to future special education teachers at his alma mater. Jonathan, his freshman roommate-turned best friend-turned associate college professor, roped him into it. Far too often, Jonathan talked him into things with his "hey buddys" over one too many cold beers.

Despite his chosen profession requiring him to speak to classrooms full of junior high students who only gave him half their attention, he hated getting up in front of people. You could call it his kryptonite, although he was more Clark Kent than Superman. On the outside he would appear cool as a cucumber, but inside was a tornado of anxiety. Tight chest, throat dry, his words elusive. A nervous jitter would vibrate through him the entire time. Still, he did it.

"Good morning. How are you?" The brunette's greeting to the barista oozed cheer, pulling Colm away from his musings to study her as if drawing the map of a newly discovered continent. Her thick dark hair hung loose against a paper white blazer. The fitted skirt of her dress stopped just below the back of her delicate knees. The fabric caressed each curve of her body creating a silhouette that was sexy, yet sweet.

Colm forced his eyes to the rows of mugs, tumblers, and bags of coffee for sale. No matter how the fabric luxuriated over her shape, staring was impolite. Besides, this woman was annoying, verbally fluttering between the barista and the old man chattering about seasonal treats while people waited.

Less chit-chat and more ordering, please.

"Hello. What would you like?" The brunette had spun to face him. Her big smile sucker-punched him with its brightness and stole his breath. Her eyes sparkled with anticipation of his response.

"What?" *Why was she asking? Also, do smiles come that big?* It was the type of smile that erupted like a volcano, happiness flooding all over like joyful lava.

Her dainty fingers fiddled with a gold butterfly necklace that dangled inches below her collarbone. When Jonathan asked if he was a tits or ass man, he'd normally choose ass. But in that moment, collarbones clinched the title of the sexiest part of a woman. There was an urge to press his lips against this little chatterbox's collarbone and make her purr.

Colm blinked away the thought. It wasn't like him to objectify a woman. Even if she had a smile that paralyzed him with its brilliance.

"To drink. What would you like? My treat." She bit her lower lip, eclipsing that big smile.

He wanted to untuck that lip and free that smile. *Keep your hands to yourself...* He shrugged, shoving his hands into the pockets of his grey slacks.

"Isn't she a sweetheart?" The old man turned with admiring eyes. "Evie here is buying our drinks since we've been waiting so long."

That big smile had a name. *Evie.* The corners of his lips tugged up as he stared at her Mediterranean blue eyes.

"They have the best pumpkin chai. That's what Stanley and I are getting. You can join our pumpkin patch..." she paused with a nervous giggle, "...or do your own thing."

Evie batted her eyelashes, peering up at him. At six foot five he towered over her. The top of her head, covered in shiny hair that his fingers itched to touch, would rest snug below his chin.

Dude, stop being creepy and order a goddamn drink!

"Large coffee...black," he said clearing his throat.

"Perfect." That big smile blasted him, causing an unfamiliar flip in his stomach.

In all the dates and two girlfriends he'd had since he was seventeen, nobody had ever made his stomach rumble like a herd of stampeding rhinos. That was something that only happened in the romance novels that Jonathan read, convinced they contained secrets to wooing the ladies. It did not occur in real life, but it was happening to him right now.

Spinning on her pointy pink heels, Evie ordered their drinks.

Evie. Each syllable of her name hummed like the notes of a new favorite song. Colm had never met an Evie. The name wasn't as rare as his own, but unique enough to not be common. Just like her smile.

While he splashed cream and two sugar packets into his coffee, his gaze flicked back to her. There was a desire to retreat, yet also a desire to remain.

He'd said thank you when she ordered their drinks, but nothing more. Mom had raised him right. Respectful, though he lacked the smoothness Jonathan had to chat up a pretty girl. He was Clark Kent, after all.

Hesitation lurked as he glanced at Evie, who still waited at the end of the counter for her drink. The alluring melody of her voice tangoed around him. He wanted to talk to her. He wanted to ask her to join him.

She's sunshine. You're a storm cloud. With a self-defeated shrug, he pivoted from where Evie waited for her drink.

In the sea of early morning patrons munching on stale pastries and drinking fancy coffees over laptops and cellphones, he located an isolated table tucked in the corner. He tried to focus on his breathing and ignore the distracting soundtrack of hushed chatter, chairs being pulled out, and the hissing espresso machine. The outside world often drained him. He drank up the solitude with his coffee while reviewing his notes for his talk.

"Hello." A honey sweet voice pierced his concentration.

Evie stood in front of his two-person table, an unabashed grin on her pretty face. Her delicate fingers clenched her coffee cup. *Evie* danced around the cup in fat cursive letters. Writing wasn't prone to dance, but damn if her name didn't appear to be doing just that.

"Hello." It was a statement punctuated with questioning.

"This place is as busy as the cantina from *Star Wars*." She gestured around at the full tables and clusters of waiting customers. "Except way fewer bounty hunters. At least, I think. There *are* a few sketchy looking folks in here."

Colm nodded, not getting the reference. "I've never seen *Star Wars*."

"I thought the sci-fi fairytale was a rite of passage for all millennials?"

"My mom never let me watch anything that she deemed killy."

"Killy?"

"Violent."

Evie tipped her head to the right and scrunched her face. "I wouldn't say it's *that* killy."

He smiled at her use of his mom's word, "killy." As if she was learning his native tongue. Learning him.

"Well, there was something about shooting wombats that mom found objectionable," he explained.

She nodded. "Makes sense. Animal cruelty shouldn't be tolerated. Come to think of it there are some other red flags with those movies. Like the weird incest angle when you find out Princess Leia is Luke's sister."

Quiet settled over them as they stared at each other. Was it seconds? Or hours? He wasn't sure.

"So…" There was another bite of that pink bottom lip and an anxious tug of her necklace. "Feel free to say no, but would you mind if I sat with you?"

Colm blinked at the empty seat across from him. When was the last time a stranger asked to sit with him? Especially such a pretty one. There were people on the bus or at the movies that asked if a seat was taken, but never to sit *with* you. Sitting with someone implied sharing a space versus just existing in it.

Evie's face pinched. "Sorry. I know it's weird for a stranger to ask to sit. But at least I'm not offering to show you my puppy in my windowless van," she laughed with a slight wince. "I'll go. Have a good day." She turned to leave.

"Wait...sit." The words slipped out like a plea. Maybe they were. There was something about this little chatterbox that made him want her to stay.

"Are you sure?" she asked, looking skeptical. "I don't want to intrude. Although I kind of already did. My bad. I had a plan to kill time here and all these people are putting a wrench in that. Drives me nuts when a plan doesn't go...well, *as planned*," she giggled.

Something in her uncertain giggle and the fact that she was a planner like him endeared her to him. "Sit." He motioned to the seat with a soft smile. At least he hoped it was soft.

Don't be creepy. Don't be creepy.

"Thanks. I'm Evie Johnson." She held her hand out.

"Colm Gallagher."

His hand enveloped hers. It was warm from holding her drink, but something told him that her hands would always be warm. Her smooth hand fit snug in his big rough one as if her hand was always meant to be in his.

There was that stomach flip again. Ridiculous! Thirty-year-old men weren't supposed to react like a teenage girl seeing BTS, but then, he never fit the mold. Why should this be different?

"Colm? Like Colm Feore?"

"Who?"

"He's an actor. Been in a bunch of stuff, but not like a household name. Not like Chris Evans. Oh, golly *The Nanny Diaries* is one of my favs!" Her face contorted. "Sorry. I'm sputtering about Chris Evans when you asked about Colm Feore. Stay on topic Evie," she simpered. "Colm Feore was in the *Chronicles of Riddick*. Truly terrible movie, but my mom has a thing for Vin Diesel, so I've seen all his movies—thrice.

My mom even has a Chihuahua named Diesel. Dreadful dog. He bites."

"Vin Diesel?" Listening to her rapid speech was like riding a tilt-a-whirl at the carnival. Your equilibrium was off kilter, but your heart sped with happy excitement. He did not want to get off this ride.

"Yeah. Mom loves sexy bald men. Vin Diesel and Bruce Willis are her fantasy men. Although neither are sexy to me."

"What's sexy to you?"

Pink rouged her cheeks. "Chris Hemsworth."

"Thor?" There was a knowing arch of his right brow. How often had Jonathan told him that he looked like a clean-cut version of the God of Thunder?

Evie's blush deepened. "Back to Bruce Willis. We watch *Die Hard* every Christmas."

"Oh," Colm said, cringing inside at his less than smooth response.

"Do you have a movie you watch each Christmas? Oh wait, do you not celebrate Christmas? That might have been insensitive of me to ask." There was a lip-biting frown on her face. "Although you can still watch Christmas movies even if you don't celebrate. My friend Leo's boyfriend Martin is Jewish but lives for the Hallmark Christmas movies. If it has a princess from a made-up Eastern European country where they speak with British accents falling in love with a Christmas tree farm owner, he's there." Evie's face twisted in self-reproach. "Sorry. I'm babbling again. Not even giving you a chance to answer."

"*It's a Wonderful Life*," he offered.

How strange that the sputtering ways that he'd found grating in line now seemed delightful. Evie's entire face lit up as she talked, and her voice was like an orchestra of inflections.

"Oh. That's a good one."

A cheeky grin covered his face. "Yup."

"That face. Colm Gallagher, are you *not* a fan of the story of George Bailey's redemption?" There was a glint of playful accusation in her eyes.

"The guy makes poor financial decisions and we're supposed to applaud that," Colm guffawed.

Mom would get so annoyed when he'd snark back at George Bailey, "Yeah, why did you have all those kids?" during their annual Christmas Eve viewing of the film. Colm related more to Mr. Potter and never understood why the only member of Bedford Falls with a sound business plan was vilified. Mom would grumble, but they'd watch the movie each year with peppermint hot chocolate and caramel popcorn. It was tradition. And he never broke from an established plan. That is, until today. Evie wasn't on his plan for today.

"Can I admit something to you?" Evie bent close. Her vanilla-lavender aroma wrapped around him like a hug.

Inhaling deep, he smiled. "Sure."

She wagged a warning finger. "You can't tell anyone or I'll…well I'll think of something terrible. Like buy you decaf and say it's regular the next time we have coffee."

"Diabolical." Colm liked the sound of a next time slipping from her heart-shaped mouth.

"I'm an evil genius." She winked. "When that little girl at the end says 'Daddy, Teacher says when a bell rings, an angel gets its wings' I find her voice as painful as a root canal. Like it's supposed to be cutesy, but it totally ruins the moment for me."

"I feel the same way about Tiny Tim in every version of *A Christmas Carol*."

Evie tapped her cup against his in a toast to them both being terrible humans.

"Colm. I like your name. How did you get it?" she asked, her fingernails skating across the smooth surface of the table.

Evie's fingers were delicate and long with a pale pink

sparkle polish. There was no ring. Again, his stomach did something men's bellies shouldn't do.

"I was named for my grandfather," Colm said, trying to figure out a not-obvious way to display that there wasn't now, nor had there ever been, a ring on his finger.

"Oh, good old Pop-Pop Colm." That big smile danced with mirth. "That's sweet that she named you after him."

"There's no Pop-Pop Colm, but a Grandfather Bill. My Grandfather was from Northern Ireland. Mom wanted an Irish name in honor of him but didn't want to be so on the nose by naming me after him. I don't know." He shrugged, sipping his coffee.

"I like that. It's *super* clever and *totally* original of your mom."

Most people would snark about how that didn't make sense. Nobody ever got his mom's reasoning behind his name, but Evie did. There was no sarcasm in her words, just an earnest admiration. To Evie, his mom was ingenious, not fanciful.

Something about those blue eyes told him that she could understand him, though there was no logical explanation for why he thought so. That made him uncomfortable. Decisions were made with research, facts, and lists, not with the gut. Especially when the gut was somersaulting like a backup dancer.

"I bet it must have been hard to find those pens with your name on them in gift shops as a kid. I could never find Evie, but sometimes I could find Evelyn. Evelyn is my birthname, but I go by Evie. I'm named after a character from a book my mom read in high school. Fun fact, she doesn't remember the name of the book or the plot, but still named me after that character."

"Huh," he said.

Really? Huh? So smooth, man.

Colm never wanted to be smooth as bad as he did right

now. To have all the swagger of Jonathan, who could chat up women at the bar like a modern-day Casanova. To be able to flow between topics, easing into a comfortable current of conversation.

As she spoke, he continued to nod and give one-word answers or grunts. More grunts than were appropriate for a non-neanderthal. He should have just said his name was "Ugg" with his monosyllabic answers.

Evie talked about her job as a hospital social worker. Colm nodded.

She asked what he did. He said "teach," and sipped his coffee. When she asked what he taught, he said "kids." They both cringed and she changed topics.

Evie talked about moving from Kansas City to Long Beach three years ago. Colm said, "Oh."

When she asked if he grew up in Long Beach, he said, "Nope" and didn't elaborate.

Evie talked about wanting to get a corgi. Colm wasn't sure what sound he made, but it was either a huff or a "Ha" in response.

I have no game. He sighed, closing his eyes.

"So, you're a coffee guy," she said, her smile collapsing in mortification. "I'm being awkward. Of course, you're a coffee guy. You ordered coffee. Sorry. I get nervous meeting new people. Look at me chattering away like a train with no brakes. Sorry...I'm clearly annoying you."

Whatever had fluttered in his stomach earlier now gave him a swift kick, telling him to reassure her and bring back that smile. God, he wanted to drink up that smile.

Drink up? You sound like an Ed Sheeran lyric.

This little whirlwind of cheerfulness shouldn't be darkened by his cloudiness. Even if his cloudiness was a mere trick of the mirrors of how people saw him.

"You're not talking too much," Colm assured. His eyes met hers, hoping to soothe her uncertainty.

"Phew." She wiped her brow with goofy theatrics. "Can I get you to sign an affidavit to that for my friend Leo? He'll never believe that someone said I didn't talk too much."

"Gladly." There was a playfulness to Colm's tone that he hadn't heard in a very long time. Dare he call it flirtatious?

"I was worried when you weren't talking that I was mowing you over with my blathering. I know I can do that at times. Like I only have one speed when I talk." Concern sobered her sweet features to serious as she spoke, "It's okay to tell me if I am. People tell me I talk too much all the time."

The idea of anyone making Evie feel bad for talking sparked a desire to get a list of their names and rage through the city like Liam Neeson seeking revenge on her behalf. Of course, he lacked Liam Neeson's particular skillset. The only skill he had would be quiet intimidation and pop quizzes.

Everyone would get a pop quiz!

While he wanted to protect Evie from sadness dulling her effervescence, this was another thing they shared. Neither quite fit the expectations of others. One too much. One not enough.

"People say I talk too little," he offered.

"So, it's not me?"

"No, it's me," he sighed, looking down. There was no *Colm* scribbled in ink dancing on his cup. Just another way he didn't fit in.

"Then it's us." Evie reached across the table, her warm hand resting on his in solidarity.

"Ok." He placed his other hand atop, blanketing hers. "Then it's us."

Book Two in this series, Our Nows And Our Thens will be coming Spring of 2026. You don't need to read In The Hello and In The Goodbye before it comes out, but if you want to, buy the book here

ACKNOWLEDGMENTS

Just like Jensen finds her people in this story, I've found mine through the years. I wouldn't be able to do any of this without my people, especially my husband Liam. Baby, I love you, but I want to take time to give flowers to everything that has made this book possible!

Thank you to my AMAZING editor Gemma Brocato, who puts the smile on each of my stories.

A huge thank you to the blind/guide runners that let me ask a million questions to help guide me in offering a realistic experience of training for and running a marathon as a blind person. To answer each of your question, I will NOT run a marathon but will cheer you all on from the sidelines.

Thank you to Earthly Charms and @Croquith for the beautiful cover art/design.

A HUGE thank you to my team of alpha and beta readers that helped me in crafting this story. Meghan, Alicia, Katie, Autumn, and Angela, I appreciate you so much!

Thank you to Threads! If someone hadn't tagged me in a random post where someone said they wanted to read a book about a blind runner/guide pair, this story may not have clawed its way out of me.

Above all, I want to thank you, my dear reader. My books would be nothing without you. Thank you for sharing your precious time with my story. I hope it fills you up reading it as it did for me to write it.

ALSO BY MELISSA WHITNEY

Available wherever you get e-book, paperback, and audiobooks

All books are available in e-book, paperback, and audio. You can get books at Amazon.com: Melissa Whitney: books, biography, latest update or by requesting at your local library or indie bookstore. Signed copies can be purchased through Heartbound Book Shop: Where Every Page is a Love Story.

The Home Series

Finding Home - Book One

Coming Home - Book Two

Making Home - Book Three

Hello/Goodbye Series

In the Hello and in the Goodbye – Book One

Out Now and Then – Book Two (Coming Summer 2026)

Stand Alone Titles

Happy Ever Afterlife

Book Boyfriends

At First Smile

ABOUT THE AUTHOR

Melissa Whitney, who hails from Western New York, is a contemporary romance author. As a legally blind woman much of Melissa's work focuses on the exploration of disability, mental health, and trauma through a heartfelt, sexy, and comedic lens.

Melissa's debut novel *In the Hello and in the Goodbye* released in April 2024, with a warm reception from readers for its thoughtful autism and mental health portrayal. Since then, she's released *Finding Home*, a Jane Austen inspired small town romance, *At First Smile*, an own voice hockey romance with blindness rep, and *Coming Home*, a *Little Women* inspired small town romance. Her work has been featured in several publications and on podcasts for its thoughtful, sensitive, and accurate representation of disability and mental health.

Ms. Whitney lives in Southern California with her husband and their rescue pugs Cookie and Milo. When not crafting her swoony stories, she's on the hunt for a pastry, brewing a cup of tea, and diving into her latest swoony romance.

To learn more about Melissa Whitney, you can visit www.melissawhitneywrites.com. Sign up for her newsletter to stay in the know with all things Melissa Whitney. Connect with her on social media (IG: @melissa_whitneyatuhor, Threads @melissa_whitneyauthor or Facebook: Melissa Whitney Author).

www.ingramcontent.com/pod-product-compliance
Lightning Source LLC
LaVergne TN
LVHW010308070526
838199LV00065B/5478